Sidonia the Sorceress

THE SUPPOSED DESTROYER OF THE WHOLE
REIGNING DUCAL HOUSE OF POMERANIA

Volume I of II

Sidonia the Sorceress

THE SUPPOSED DESTROYER OF THE WHOLE
REIGNING DUCAL HOUSE OF POMERANIA

Volume I of II

WILHELM MEINHOLD
Writing as Mary Schweidler

Translated from the German by
LADY WILDE

ÆGYPAN PRESS

Special thanks to Steve Schulze, Charles Franks, and the Online Distributed Proofreading Team (which can be found at http://www.pgdp.net).

Thanks also to the CWRU Preservation Department Digital Library.

A NOTE AS TO PROVENANCE

In 1841, a book was put forward, in German, as something by "Mary Schweidler" that Wilhelm Meinhold had found, fixed up, "edited," and presented to the world. A year or two into the hoax, Meinhold confessed that he'd committed a fraud. A few years later (in 1846), Lady Duff Gordon translated it into English; that book was published as *The Amber Witch.*

This note graced its opening pages of the original English edition: "The most interesting trial for witchcraft ever known. Printed from an imperfect manuscript by her father Abraham Schweidler, the pastor of Coserow, in the Island of Usedom."

Don't take that seriously.

This two-volume companion work never had that book's popularity — most likely because everyone was on to the lie by the time it came out — but it's well worth reading. It was published in English by Kelmscott Press in 1894.

Sidonia the Sorceress, Volume I of II
A publication of
ÆGYPAN PRESS

www.aegypan.com

DEDICATION OF THE GERMAN EDITION

To the Illustrious

Lady Lucy Duff Gordon,

THE

Young and Gifted Translator

OF

"The Amber Witch,"

This Work Is Respectfully Inscribed

Preface

Amongst all the trials for witchcraft with which we are acquainted, few have attained so great a celebrity as that of the Lady Canoness of Pomerania, Sidonia von Bork. She was accused of having by her sorceries caused sterility in many families, particularly in that of the ancient reigning house of Pomerania, and also of having destroyed the noblest scions of that house by an early and premature death. Notwithstanding the intercessions and entreaties of the Prince of Brandenburg and Saxony, and of the resident Pomeranian nobility, she was publicly executed for these crimes on the 19th of August 1620, on the public scaffold, at Stettin; the only favor granted being, that she was allowed to be beheaded first and then burned.

This terrible example caused such a panic of horror, that contemporary authors scarcely dare to mention her name, and, even then, merely by giving the initials. This forbearance arose partly from respect towards the ancient family of the Von Borks, who then, as now, were amongst the most illustrious and wealthy in the land, and also from the fear of offending the reigning ducal family, as the Sorceress, in her youth, had stood in a very near and tender relation to the young Duke Ernest Louis von Pommern-Wolgast.

These reasons will be sufficiently comprehensible to all who are familiar with the disgust and aversion in which the paramours of the evil one were held in that age, so that even upon the rack these subjects were scarcely touched upon.

The first public, judicial, yet disconnected account of Sidonia's trial, we find in the Pomeranian Library of Dähnert, fourth volume, article 7, July number of the year 1755.

Dähnert here acknowledges, page 241, that the numbers from 302 to 1080, containing the depositions of the witnesses, were not forthcoming up to his time, but that a priest in Pansin, near Stargard, by name Justus Sagebaum, pretended to have them in his hands, and accordingly, in the fifth volume of the above-named journal (article 4, of April 1756), some very important extracts appear from them.

The records, however, again disappeared for nearly a century, until Barthold announced, some short time since,* that he had at length discovered them in the Berlin Library; but he does not say which, for, according to Schwalenberg, who quotes Dähnert, there existed two or three different copies, namely, the *Protocollum Jodoci Neumarks,* the so-called *Acta Lothmanni,* and that of *Adami Moesters,* contradicting each other in the most important matters. Whether I have drawn the history of my Sidonia from one or other of the above-named sources, or from some entirely new, or, finally, from that alone which is longest known, I shall leave undecided.

Everyone who has heard of the animadversions which "The Amber Witch" excited, many asserting that it was only dressed-up history, though I repeatedly assured them it was simple fiction, will pardon me if I do not here distinctly declare whether Sidonia be history or fiction.

The truth of the material, as well as of the formal contents, can be tested by anyone by referring to the authorities I have named; and in connection with these, I must just remark, that in order to spare the reader any difficulties which might present themselves to eye and ear, in consequence of the old-fashioned mode of writing, I have modernized the orthography, and amended the grammar and structure of the phrases. And lastly, I trust that all just thinkers of every party will pardon me for having here and there introduced my supernatural views of Christianity. A man's principles, as put forward in his philosophical writings, are in general only read by his own party, and not by that of his adversaries. A Rationalist will fly from a book by a Supernaturalist as rapidly as this latter from one by a Friend of Light. But by introducing my views in the manner I have adopted, in place of publishing them in a distinct volume, I trust that all parties will be induced to peruse them, and that many will find, not only what is worthy their particular attention, but matter for deep and serious reflection.

I must now give an account of those portraits of Sidonia which are extant.

As far as I know, three of these (besides innumerable sketches) exist, one in Stettin, the other in the lower Pomeranian town Plathe, and a third at Stargard, near Regenwalde, in the castle of the Count von Bork. I am acquainted only with the last-named picture, and agree with many in thinking that it is the only original.

---

* "History of Rugen and Pomerania," vol. iv. p. 486.

Sidonia is here represented in the prime of mature beauty — a gold net is drawn over her almost golden yellow hair, and her neck, arms, and hands are profusely covered with jewels. Her bodice of bright purple is trimmed with costly fur, and the robe is of azure velvet. In her hand she carries a sort of pompadour of brown leather, of the most elegant form and finish. Her eyes and mouth are not pleasing, notwithstanding their great beauty — in the mouth, particularly, one can discover an expression of cold malignity.

The painting is beautifully executed, and is evidently of the school of Louis Kranach.

Immediately behind this form there is another looking over the shoulder of Sidonia, like a terrible specter (a highly poetical idea), for this specter is Sidonia herself painted as a Sorceress. It must have been added, after a lapse of many years, to the youthful portrait, which belongs, as I have said, to the school of Kranach, whereas the second figure portrays unmistakably the school of Rubens. It is a fearfully characteristic painting, and no imagination could conceive a contrast more shudderingly awful. The Sorceress is arrayed in her death garments — white with black stripes; and round her thin white locks is bound a narrow band of black velvet spotted with gold. In her hand is a kind of a work-basket, but of the simplest workmanship and form.

Of the other portraits I cannot speak from my own personal inspection; but to judge by the drawings taken from them to which I have had access, they appear to differ completely, not only in costume, but in the character of the countenance, from the one I have described, which there is no doubt must be the original, not only because it bears all the characteristics of that school of painting which approached nearest to the age in which Sidonia lived — namely, from 1540 to 1620 — but also by the fact that a sheet of paper bearing an inscription was found behind the painting, betraying evident marks of age in its blackened color, the form of the letters, and the expressions employed. The inscription is as follows: —

"This Sidonia von Bork was in her youth the most beautiful and the richest of the maidens of Pomerania. She inherited many estates from her parents, and thus was in her own right a possessor almost of a county. So her pride increased, and many noble gentlemen who sought her in marriage were rejected with disdain, as she considered that a count or prince alone could be worthy of her hand. For these reasons she attended the Duke's court frequently, in the hopes of winning over one of the seven young princes to her love. At length she was successful; Duke Ernest Louis von Wolgast, aged about twenty, and the handsomest youth in Pomerania, became her lover, and even promised her his hand in marriage. This promise he would faithfully have kept if the Stettin princes, who were displeased at the prospect of this unequal alliance, had not induced him to abandon Sidonia, by means of the portrait of the Princess Hedwig of Brunswick, the most beautiful princess in all Germany. Sidonia thereupon fell into such despair, that she resolved to renounce marriage forever, and bury the remainder of her life in the convent of Marienfliess, and thus she did. But the wrong done to her by the Stettin princes lay heavy upon her heart, and the desire for revenge increased with years; besides, in place of reading the Bible, her private hours were passed studying the *Amadis,* wherein she found many examples of how forsaken maidens have avenged themselves upon their false lovers by means of magic. So she at last yielded to the temptations of Satan, and after some years learned the secrets of witchcraft from an old woman. By means of this unholy knowledge, along with several other evil deeds, she so bewitched the whole princely race that the six young princes, who were each wedded to a young wife, remained childless; but no public notice was taken until Duke Francis succeeded to the duchy in 1618. He was a ruthless enemy to witches; all in the land were sought out with great diligence and burned, and as they unanimously named the Abbess of Marienfliess* upon the rack, she was brought to Stettin by command of the Duke, where she freely confessed all the evil wrought by her sorceries upon the princely race.

"The Duke promised her life and pardon if she would free the other princes from the ban; but her answer was that she had enclosed the spell in a padlock, and flung it into the sea, and having asked the devil if he could restore the padlock again to her, he replied, 'No; that was forbidden to him;' by which everyone can perceive that the destiny of God was in the matter.

"And so it was that, notwithstanding the intercession of all the neighboring courts, Sidonia was brought to the scaffold at Stettin, there beheaded, and afterwards burned.

"Before her death the Prince ordered her portrait to be painted, in her old age and prison garb, behind that which represented her in the prime of youth. After his death, Bogislaff XIV, the last Duke, gave this picture to my grandmother, whose husband had also been killed by the Sorceress. My father received it from her, and I from him, along with the story which is here written down.

"HENRY GUSTAVUS SCHWALENBERG"†

---

* Sidonia never attained this dignity, though Micraelius and others gave her the title.

† The style of this "Inscription" proves it to have been written in the beginning of the preceding century, but it is first noticed by Dähnert. I have had his version compared with the original in Stargord — through the kindness of a friend, who

Letter of Dr. Theodore Plönnies

TO BOGISLAFF THE FOURTEENTH, THE LAST DUKE OF POMERANIA

Most Eminent Prince and Gracious Lord, —

Serene Prince, your Highness gave me a commission in past years to travel through all Pomerania, and if I met with any persons who could give me certain "information" respecting the notorious and accursed witch Sidonia von Bork, to set down carefully all they stated, and bring

---

assures me that the transcription is perfectly correct, and yet can he be mistaken? for Horst (Magic Library, vol. ii. p. 246), gives the conclusion thus: "From whom my father received it, and I from him, along with the story precisely as given here by H. G. Schwalenberg." By this reading, which must have escaped my friend, a different sense is given to the passage; by the last reading it would appear that the "I" was a Bork, who had taken the tale from Schwalenberg's history of the Pomeranian Dukes, a work which exists only in manuscript, and to which I have had no access; but if we admit the first reading, then the writer must be a Schwalenberg. Even the "grandmother" will not clear up the matter, for Sidonia, when put to the torture, confessed, at the seventh question, that she had caused the death of Doctor Schwalenberg (he was counselor in Stettin then), and at the eleventh question, that her brother's son, Otto Bork, had died also by her means. Who then is this "I?" Even Sidonia's picture, we see, utters mysteries.

In my opinion the writer was Schwalenberg, and Horst seems to have taken his version from Paulis's "General History of Pomerania," vol. iv. p. 396, and not from the original of Dähnert.

For the picture at that early period was not in the possession of a Bork, but belonged to the Count von Mellin in Schillersdorf, as passages from many authors can testify. This is confirmed by another paper found along with that containing the tradition, but of much more modern appearance, which states that the picture was removed by successive inheritors, first from Schillersdorf to Stargord, from thence to Heinrichsberg (there are three towns in Pomerania of this name), and finally from Heinrichsberg, in the year 1834, was a second time removed to Stargord by the last inheritor.

This Schillersdorf lies between Gartz and Stettin on the Oder. — WILLIAM MEINHOLD

it afterwards into *connexum* for your Highness. It is well known that Duke Francis, of blessed memory, never would permit the accursed deeds of this woman to be made public, or her confession upon the rack, fearing to bring scandal upon the princely house. But your Serene Highness viewed the subject differently, and said that it was good for everyone, but especially princes, to look into the clear mirror of history, and behold there the faults and follies of their race. For this reason may no truth be omitted here.

To such princely commands I have proved myself obedient, collecting all information, whether good or evil, and concealing nothing. But the greater number who related these things to me could scarcely speak for tears, for wherever I traveled throughout Pomerania, as the faithful servant of your Highness, nothing was heard but lamentations from old and young, rich and poor, that this execrable Sorceress, out of Satanic wickedness, had destroyed this illustrious race, who had held their lands from no emperor, in feudal tenure, like other German princes, but in their own right, as absolute lords, since five hundred years, and though for twenty years it seemed to rest upon five goodly princes, yet by permission of the incomprehensible God, it has now melted away until your Highness stands the last of his race, and no prospect is before us that it will ever be restored, but with your Highness (God have mercy upon us!) will be utterly extinguished, and forever. "Woe to us, how have we sinned!" (Lament, v. 16).*

I pray therefore the all-merciful God, that He will remove me before your Highness from this vale of tears, that I may not behold the last hour of your Highness or of my poor fatherland. Rather than witness these things, I would a thousand times sooner lie quiet in my grave.

---

* Marginal note of Duke Bogislaff XIV — "In tuas manus commendo spiritum meum, quia tu me redemisti fide deus."

BOOK I

FROM THE RECEPTION OF SIDONIA AT THE DUCAL COURT OF WOLGAST UNTIL HER BANISHMENT THEREFROM

Chapter I

Of the education of Sidonia

*T*he illustrious and highborn prince and lord, Bogislaff, fourteenth Duke of Pomerania, Prince of Cassuben, Wenden, and Rugen, Count of Güzkow, Lord of the lands of Lauenburg and Butow, and my gracious feudal seigneur, having commanded me, Dr. Theodore Plönnies, formerly bailiff at the ducal court, to make search throughout all the land for information respecting the world-famed sorceress, Sidonia von Bork, and write down the same in a book, I set out for Stargard, accompanied by a servant, early one Friday after the *Visitationis Mariæ*, 1629; for, in my opinion, in order to form a just judgment respecting the character of anyone, it is necessary to make one's self acquainted with the circumstances of their early life; the future man lies enshrined in the child, and the peculiar development of each individual nature is the result entirely of education. Sidonia's history is a remarkable proof of this. I visited first, therefore, the scenes of her early years; but almost all who had known her were long since in their graves, seeing that ninety years had passed since the time of her birth. However, the old inn-keeper at Stargard, Zabel Wiese, himself very far advanced in years (whom I can recommend to all travelers – he lives in the Pelzerstrasse), told me that the old bachelor, Claude Uckermann of Dalow, an aged man of ninety-two years old, was the only person who could give me the information I desired, as in his youth he had been one of the many followers of Sidonia. His memory was certainly well nigh gone from age, still all that had happened in the early period of his life lay as fresh as the Lord's Prayer upon his tongue. Mine host also related some important circumstances to me myself, which shall appear in their proper place.

I accordingly proceeded to Dalow, a little town half a mile from Stargard, and visited Claude Uckermann. I found him seated by the chimney corner, his hair as white as snow. "What did I want? He was too old to receive strangers; I must go on to his son Wedig's house, and leave him in quiet," &c. &c. But when I said that I brought him a greeting from his Highness, his manner changed, and he pushed the seat over for me beside the fire, and began to chat first about the fine pine trees, from which he cut his firewood – they were so full of resin; and how his son, a year before, had found an iron pot in the turf moor under a tree, full of bracelets and earrings, which his little grand-daughter now wore.

When he had tired himself out, I communicated what his Highness had so nobly commanded to be done, and prayed him to relate all he knew and could remember of this detestable sorceress, Sidonia von Bork. He sighed deeply, and then went on talking for about two hours, giving me all his recollections just as they started to his memory. I have arranged what he then related, in proper order. It was to the following effect: –

Whenever his father, Philip Uckermann, attended the fair at Stramehl, a town belonging to the Bork family, he was in the habit of visiting Otto von Bork at his castle, who, being very rich, gave free quarters to all the young noblemen of the vicinity, so that from thirty to forty of them were generally assembled at his castle while the fair lasted; but after some time his father discontinued these visits, his conscience not permitting him further intercourse. The reason was this. Otto von Bork, during his residence in Poland, had joined the sect of the enthusiasts,* and had lost his faith there, as a young maiden might her honor. He made no secret of his new opinions, but openly at Martinmas fair, 1560, told the young nobles at dinner that Christ was but a man like other people, and ignorance alone had elevated Him to a God; which notion had been encouraged by the greed and avarice of the clergy. They should therefore not credit what the hypocritical priests chattered to them every

---

* Probably the sect afterwards named Socinians; for we find that Laelius Socinus taught in Poland, even before Melancthon's death (1560).

Sunday, but believe only what reason and their five senses told them was truth, and that, in fine, if he had his will, he would send every priest to the devil.

All the young nobles remained silent but Claude Zastrow, a feudal retainer of the Borks, who rose up (it was an evil moment to him) and made answer: "Most powerful feudal lord, were the holy apostles then filled with greed and covetousness, who were the first to proclaim that Christ was God, and who left all for His sake? Or the early Christians who, with one accord, sold their possessions, and gave the price to the poor?" Claude had before this displeased the knight, who now grew red with anger at the insolence of his vassal in thus answering him, and replied: "If they were not preachers for gain, they were at least stupid fellows." Hereupon a great murmur arose in the hall, but the aforesaid Zastrow is not silenced, and answered: "It is surprising, then, that the twelve stupid apostles performed more than twelve times twelve Greek or Roman philosophers. The knight might rage until he was black in the face, and strike the table. But he had better hold his tongue and use his understanding; though, after all, the intellect of a man who believed nothing but what he received through his five senses was not worth much; for the brute beasts were his equals, inasmuch as they received no evidence either but from the senses."

Then Otto sprang up raging, and asked him what he meant; to which the other answered: "Nothing more than to express his opinion that man differed from the brute, not through his understanding, but by his faith, for that animals had evidently understanding, but no trace of faith had ever yet been discovered in them."*

---

* This axiom is certainly opposed to modern ontology, which denies all ideas to the brute creation, and explains each proof of their intellectual activity by the unintelligible word "instinct." The ancients held very different opinions, particularly the new Platonists, one of whom (Porphyry, liber ii. *De abstinentia*) treats largely of the intellect and language of animals. Since Cartesius, however, who denied not only understanding, but even feeling, to animals, and represented them as mere animated machines (*De passionib. Pars i. Artic. iv. et de Methodo*, No. 5, page 29, &c.), these views upon the psychology of animals produced the most mischievous results; for they were carried out until if not feeling, at least intellect, was denied to all animals more or less; and modern philosophy at length arrived at denying intelligence even to God, in whom and by whom, as formerly, man no longer attains to consciousness, but it is by man and through man that God arrives to a conscious intelligent existence. Some philosophers of our time, indeed, are condescending enough to ascribe *Understanding* to animals and *Reason* to man as the generic difference between the two. But I cannot comprehend these new-fashioned distinctions; for it seems to me absurd to split into the two portions of reason and understanding one and the same spiritual power, according as the object on which it acts is higher or lower; just as if we adopted two names for the same hand that digs up the earth and directs

Otto's rage now knew no bounds, and he drew his dagger, roaring, "What! thou insolent knave, dost thou dare to compare thy feudal lord to a brute?" And before the other had time to draw his poignard to defend himself, or the guests could in any way interfere to prevent him, Otto stabbed him to the heart as he sat there by the table. (It was a blessed death, I think, to die for his Lord Christ.) And so he fell down upon the floor with contorted features, and hands and feet quivering with agony. Everyone was struck dumb with horror at such a death; but the knight laughed loudly, and cried, "Ha! thou base-born serf, I shall teach thee how to liken thy feudal lord to a brute," and striding over his quivering limbs, he spat upon his face.

Then the murmuring and whispering increased in the hall, and those nearest the door rushed out and sprang upon their horses; and finally all the guests, even old Uckermann, fled away, no one venturing to take up the quarrel with Otto Bork. After that, he fell into disrepute with the old nobility, for which he cared little, seeing that his riches and magnificence always secured him companions enough, who were willing to listen to his wisdom, and were consoled by his wine.

And when I, Dr. Theodore Plönnies, inquired from the old bachelor if his Serene Highness had not punished the noble for his shameful crime, he replied that his wealth and powerful influence protected him. At least it was whispered that justice had been blinded with gold; and the matter was probably related to the prince in quite a different manner from the truth; for I have heard that a few years after, his Highness even visited this godless knight at his castle in Stramehl.

As to Otto, no one observed any sign of repentance in him. On the contrary, he seemed to glory in his crime, and the neighboring nobles related that he frequently brought in his little daughter Sidonia, whom he adored for her beauty, to the assembled guests, magnificently attired; and when she was bowing to the company, he would say, "Who art thou, my little daughter?" Then she would cease the salutations which she had learned from her mother, and drawing herself up, proudly exclaim, "I

---

the telescope to heaven, or maintained that the latter was quite a different hand from the former. No. There is but one understanding for man and beasts, as but one common substance for their material forms. The more perfect the form, so much the more perfect is the intellect; and human and animal intellects are only dynamically different in human and animal bodies.

And even if, among animals of the more perfect form, understanding has been discovered, yet in man alone has been found the innate feeling of connection with the supernatural, or *Faith*. If this, as the generic sign of difference, be called *Reason*, I have nothing to object, except that the word generally conveys a different meaning. But *Faith* is, in fact, the pure Reason, and is found in all men, existing alike in the lowest superstitions as well as in the highest natures.

am a noble maiden, dowered with towns and castles!" Then he would ask, if the conversation turned upon his enemies — and half the nobles were so — "Sidonia, how does thy father treat his enemies?" Upon which the child would straighten her finger, and running at her father, strike it into his heart, saying, *"Thus* he treats them." At which Otto would laugh loudly, and tell her to show him how the knave looked when he was dying. Then Sidonia would fall down, twist her face, and writhe her little hands and feet in horrible contortions. Upon which Otto would lift her up, and kiss her upon the mouth. But it will be seen how the just God punished him for all this, and how the words of the Scriptures were fulfilled: "Err not, God is not mocked; for what a man soweth, that shall he also reap."

The parson of Stramehl, David Dilavius, related also to old Ucker-mann another fact, which, though it hardly seems credible, the bachelor reported thus to me: —

This Dilavius was a learned man whom Otto had selected as instruc-tor to his young daughter; "but only teach her," he said, "to read and write, and the first article of the Ten Commandments. The other Christian doctrines I can teach her myself; besides, I do not wish the child to learn so many dogmas."

Dilavius, who was a worthy, matter-of-fact, good, simple character, did as he was ordered, and gave himself no further trouble until he came to ask the child to recite the first article of the creed out of the catechism for him. There was nothing wrong in that; but when he came to the second article, he crossed himself, not because it concerned the Lord Christ, but her own father, Otto von Bork, and ran somewhat thus: —

"And I believe in my earthly father, Otto von Bork, a distinguished son of God, born of Anna von Kleist, who sitteth in his castle at Stramehl, from whence he will come to help his children and friends, but to slay his enemies and tread them in the dust."

The third article was much in the same style, but he had partly forgotten it, neither could he remember if Dilavius had called the father to any account for his profanity, or taught the daughter some better Christian doctrine. In fine, this was all the old bachelor could tell me of Sidonia's education. Yes — he remembered one anecdote more. Her father had asked her one day, when she was about ten or twelve years old, "What kind of a husband she would like?" and she replied, "One of equal birth." *Ille:** "Who is her equal in the whole of Pomerania?"

---

*   In dialogue the author makes use of the Latin pronouns, *Ille,* he; *Illa,* she, to denote the different characters taking part in it; and sometimes *Hic* and *Hæc,* for the same purposes. *Summa* he employs in the sense of "to sum up," or "in short."

Illa: "Only the Duke of Pomerania, or the Count von Ebersburg." *Ille:* "Right! therefore she must never marry any other but one of these."

It happened soon after, old Philip Uckermann, his father, riding one day through the fields near Stramehl, saw a country girl seated by the roadside, weeping bitterly. "Why do you weep?" he asked. "Has anyone injured you?" "Sidonia has injured me," she replied. "What could she have done? Come dry your tears, and tell me." Whereupon the little girl related that Sidonia, who was then about fourteen, had besought her to tell her what marriage was, because her father was always talking to her about it. The girl had told her to the best of her ability; but the young lady beat her, and said it was not so, that long Dorothy had told her quite differently about marriage, and there she went on tormenting her for several days; but upon this evening Sidonia, with long Dorothy, and some of the milkmaids of the neighborhood, had taken away one of the fine geese which the peasants had given her in payment of her labor. They picked it alive, all except the head and neck, then built up a large fire in a circle, and put the goose and a vessel of water in the center. So the fat dripped down from the poor creature alive, and was fried in a pan as it fell, just as the girls eat it on their bread for supper. And the goose, having no means of escape, still went on drinking the water as the fat dripped down, whilst they kept cooling its head and heart with a sponge dipped in cold water, fastened to a stick, until at last the goose fell down when quite roasted, though it still screamed, and then Sidonia and her companions cut it up for their amusement, living as it was, and ate it for their supper, in proof of which, the girl showed him the bones and the remains of the fire, and the drops of fat still lying on the grass.

Then she wept afresh, for Sidonia had promised to take away a goose every day, and destroy it as she had done the first. So my father consoled her by giving her a piece of gold, and said, "If she does so again, run by night and cloud, and come to Dalow by Stargard, where I will make thee keeper of my geese." But she never came to him, and he never heard more of the maiden and her geese.

So far old Uckermann related to me the first evening, promising to tell me of many more strange doings upon the following morning, which he would try to think over during the night.

Chapter II

Of the bear-hunt at Stramehl, and the strange things that befell there

The following morning, by seven o'clock, the old man summoned me to him, and on entering I found him seated at breakfast by the fire. He invited me to join him, and pushed a seat over for me with his crutch, for walking was now difficult to him. He was very friendly, and the eyes of the old man burned as clear as those of a white dove. He had slept little during the night, for Sidonia's form kept floating before his eyes, just as she had looked in the days when he paid court to her. Alas! he had once loved her deeply, like all the other young nobles who approached her, from the time she was of an age to marry. In her youth she had been beautiful; and old and young declared that for figure, eyes, bosom, walk, and enchanting smile, there never had been seen her equal in all Pomerania.

"Nothing shall be concealed from you," he said, "of all that concerns my foolish infatuation, that you and your children may learn how the all-wise God deals best with His servants when He uses the rod and denies that for which they clamor as silly children for a glittering knife." Here he folded his withered hands, murmured a short prayer, and proceeded with his story.

"You must know that I was once a proud and stately youth, upon whom a maiden's glance in no wise rested indifferently, trained in all knightly exercise, and only two years older than Sidonia. It happened in the September of 1566, that I was invited by Caspar Roden to see his eel-nets, as my father intended laying down some also at Krampehl* and along the coast. When we returned home weary enough in the evening, a letter arrived from Otto von Bork, inviting him the following day to a bear-hunt; as he intended, in honor of the nuptials of his eldest daughter Clara, to lay bears' heads and bears' paws before his guests, which even in Pomerania would have been a rarity, and desiring him to bring as many good huntsmen with him as he pleased. So I accom-

---

* A little river near Dalow.

panied Caspar Roden, who told me on the way that Count Otto had at first looked very high for his daughter Clara, and scorned many a good suitor, but that she was now getting rather old, and ready, like a ripe burr, to hang on the first that came by. Her bridegroom was Vidante von Meseritz, a feudal vassal of her father's, upon whom, ten years before, she would not have looked at from a window. Not that she was as proud as her young sister Sidonia. However, their mother was to blame for much of this; but she was dead now, poor lady, let her rest in peace.

So in good time we reached the castle of Stramehl, where thirty huntsmen were already assembled, all noblemen, and we joined them in the grand state hall, where the morning meal was laid out. Count Otto sat at the head of the table, like a prince of Pomerania, upon a throne whereon his family arms were both carved and embroidered. He wore a doublet of elk-skin, and a cap with a heron's plume upon his head. He did not rise as we entered, but called to us to be seated and join the feast, as the party must move off soon. Costly wines were sent round; and I observed that on each of the glasses the family arms were cut. They were also painted upon the window of the great hall, and along the walls, under the horns of all the different wild animals killed by Otto in the chase — bucks, deers, harts, roes, stags, and elks — which were arranged in fantastical groups.

After a little while his two daughters, Clara and Sidonia, entered. They wore green hunting-dresses, trimmed with beaver-skin, and each had a gold net thrown over her hair. They bowed, and bid the knights welcome. But we all remained breathless gazing upon Sidonia, as she lifted her beautiful eyes first on one, and then on another, inviting us to eat and drink; and she even filled a small wine-glass herself, and prayed us to pledge her. As for me, unfortunate youth, from the moment I beheld her I breathed no more through my lungs, but through my eyes alone, and, springing up, gave her health publicly. A storm of loud, animated, passionate voices soon responded to my words with loud vivas. The guests then rose, for the ladies were impatient for the hunt, and found the time hang heavily.

So we set off with all our implements and our dogs, and a hundred beaters went before us. It happened that my host, Caspar Roden, and I found an excellent sheltered position for a shot near a quarry, and we had not long been there (the beaters had not even yet begun their work) when I spied a large bear coming down to drink at a small stream not twenty paces from me. I fired; but she retired quickly behind an oak, and, growling fiercely, disappeared amongst the bushes. Not long after, I heard the cries of women almost close to us; and running as fast as possible in the direction from whence they came, I perceived an old bear trying to climb up to the platform where Clara and Sidonia stood. There was a ruined chapel here — which, in the time of papacy, had contained a holy image — and a scaffolding had been erected round it, adorned with wreaths of evergreen and flowers, from which the ladies could obtain an excellent view of the hunt, as it commanded a prospect of almost the entire wood, and even part of the sea. Attached to this scaffolding was a ladder, up which Bruin was anxiously trying to ascend, in order to visit the young ladies, who were now assailed by two dangers — the bear from below, and a swarm of bees above, for myriads of these insects were tormenting them, trying to settle upon their golden hair-nets; and the young ladies, screaming as if the last day had come, were vainly trying to beat them off with their girdles, or trample them under their feet. A huntsman who stood near fired, indeed, at Bruin, but without effect, and the bees assailing his hands and face at the same time, he took to flight and hid himself, groaning, in the quarry.

In the meantime I had reached the chapel, and Sidonia stretched forth her beautiful little hands, crying, along with her sister, "Help! help! He will eat us. Will you not kill him?" But the bear, as if already aware of my intention, began now to descend the ladder. However, I stepped before him, and as he descended, I ascended. Luckily for me, the interval between each step was very small, to accommodate the ladies' little feet, so that when Bruin tried to thrust his snout between them to get at me, he found it rather difficult work to make it pass. I had my dagger ready; and though the bees which he brought with him in his fur flew on my hands, I heeded them not, but watching my opportunity, plunged it deep into his side, so that he tumbled right down off the ladder; and though he raised himself up once and growled horribly, yet in a few seconds he lay dead before our eyes. How the ladies now tripped down the ladder, not two or three, but four or five steps at a time! and what thanks poured forth from their lips! I rushed first to Sidonia, who laid her little head upon my breast, while I endeavored to remove the bees which had got entangled in her hair-net. The other lady went to call the huntsman, who was hiding in the quarry, and we were left alone. Heavens! how my heart burned, more than my inflamed hands all stung by the bees, as she asked, how could she repay my service. I prayed her for one kiss, which she granted. She had escaped with but one sting from the bees, who could not manage to get through her long, thick, beautiful hair, and she advanced joyfully to meet her father and the hunting-train, who had heard the cries of the ladies. When Count Otto heard what had happened, and saw the dead bear, he thanked me heartily, praying me to attend his daughter Clara's wedding, which was to be celebrated next week at the castle, and to remain as his guest until then. There was nothing in the world I could have desired beyond this, and I gratefully accepted his offer. Alas! I suffered for it after, as the cat from poisoned dainties.

But to return to our hunt. No other bear was killed that day, but plenty of other game, as harts, stags, roes, boars — more than enough. And now we discovered what an old hunter had conjectured, that the dead bear was the father, who had been alarmed by the growls of his partner, at whom I had fired whilst he was endeavoring to carry off the honey from a nest of wild bees in a neighboring tree. For looking around us, we saw, at the distance of about twenty paces, a tall oak tree, about which clouds of bees were still flying, in which he had been following his occupation. No one dared to approach it, to bring away the honey-combs which still lay beneath, by reason of the bees, and, moreover, swarms of ants, by which they were covered. At length Otto Bork ordered the huntsman to sound the return; and after supper I obtained another little kiss from Sidonia, which burned so like fire through my veins that I could not sleep the whole night. I resolved to ask her hand in marriage from her father.

Stupid youth as I was, I then believed that she looked upon me with equal love; and although I knew all about the mode in which she had been brought up, and many other things beside, which have now slipped from my memory, yet I looked on them but as idle stories, and was fully persuaded that Sidonia was sister to the angels in beauty, goodness, and perfection. In a few days, however, I had reason to change my opinion.

Next day the two young ladies were in the kitchen, overseeing the cooking of the bear's head, and, as I passed by and looked in, they began to titter, which I took for a good omen, and asked, might I not be allowed to enter. They said, "Yes, I might come in, and help them to cleave the head." So I entered, and they both began to give me instructions, with much laughter and merry jesting. First, the bear's head had to be burned with hot irons; and when I said to Sidonia that thus she burned my heart, she nearly died of laughter. Then I cut some flesh off the mouth, broke the nose, and handed it all over to the maidens, who set it on the fire with water, wine, and vinegar. As I now played the part of kitchen-boy, they sent me to the castle garden for thyme, sage, and rosemary, which I brought, and begged them for a taste of the head; but they said it was not fit to eat yet — must be cooled in brine first; so in place of it I asked one little kiss from each of the maidens, which Sidonia granted, but her sister refused. However, I was not in the least displeased at her refusal, seeing it was only the little sister I cared for.

But judge of my rage and jealousy, that same day a cousin arrived at the castle, and I observed that Sidonia allowed him to kiss her every moment. She never even appeared to offer any resistance, but looked over at me languishingly every time to see what I would say. What could I say? I became pale with jealousy, but said nothing. At last I rushed from the hall, mute with despair, when I observed him finally draw her on his knee. I only heard the peal of laughter that followed my exit, and I was just near leaving the whole wedding-feast, and Stramehl forever, when Sidonia called after me from the castle gates to return. This so melted my heart, that the tears came into my eyes, thinking that now indeed I had a proof of her love. Then she took my hand, and said, "I ought not to be so unkind. That was her manner with all the young nobles. Why should she refuse a kiss when she was asked? Her little mouth would grow neither larger nor smaller for it." But I stood still and wept, and looked on the ground. "Why should I weep?" she asked. Her cousin Clas had a bride of his own already, and only took a little pastime with her, and so she must cure me now with another little kiss.

I was now again a happy man, thinking she loved me; and the heavens seemed so propitious, that I determined to ask her hand. But I had not sufficient courage as yet, and resolved to wait until after her sister's marriage, which was to take place next day. What preparations were made for this event it would be impossible adequately to describe. All the country round the castle seemed like a royal camp. Six hundred horses were led into the stables next day to be fed, for the Duke himself arrived with a princely retinue. Then came all the feudal vassals to offer homage for their fiefs to Lord Otto. But as the description is well worth hearing, I shall defer it for another chapter.

Chapter III

How Otto von Bork received the homage of his son-in-law, Vidante von Meseritz — And how the bride and bridegroom proceeded afterwards to the chapel — Item, what strange things happened at the wedding-feast

*N*ext morning the stir began in the castle before break of day, and by ten o'clock all the nobles, with their wives and daughters, had assembled in the great hall. Then the bride entered, wearing her myrtle wreath, and Sidonia followed, glittering with diamonds and other costly jewels. She wore a robe of crimson silk with a cape of ermine, falling from her shoulders, and looked so beautiful that I could have died for love, as she passed and greeted me with her graceful laugh. But Otto Bork, the lord of the castle, was sore displeased because his Serene Highness the Prince was late coming, and the company had been waiting an hour for his presence. A platform had been erected at the upper end of the hall covered with bearskin; on this was placed a throne, beneath a canopy of yellow velvet, and here Otto was seated dressed in a crimson doublet, and wearing a hat half red and half black, from which depended plumes of red and black feathers that hung down nearly to his beard, which was as venerable as a Jew's. Every instant he dispatched messengers to the tower to see if the prince were at hand, and as the time hung heavy, he began to discourse his guests. "See how this turner's apprentice* must have stopped on the road to carve a puppet. God keep us from such dukes!" For the prince passed all his leisure hours in turning and carving, particularly while traveling, and when the carriage came to bad ground, where the horses had to move slowly, he was delighted, and went on merrily with his work; but when the horses galloped, he grew ill-tempered and threw down his tools.

At length the warder announced from the tower that the duke's six carriages were in sight, and the knight spoke from his throne: "I shall remain here, as befits me, but Clara and Sidonia, go ye forth and receive his Highness; and when he has entered, the kinsman"† in full armor

---

* So this prince was called from his love of turning and carving dolls.

shall ride into the hall upon his warhorse, bearing the banner of his house in his hand, and all my retainers shall follow on horses, each bearing his banner also, and shall range themselves by the great window of the hall; and let the windows be open, that the wind may play through the banners and make the spectacle yet grander."

Then all rushed out to meet the Duke, and I, too, went, for truly the courtyard presented a gorgeous sight — all decorated as it was, and the pride and magnificence of Lord Otto were here fully displayed; for from the upper storey of the castle floated the banner of the Emperor, and just beneath it that of Lord Otto (two crowned wolves with golden collars on a field or for the shield), and the crest, a crowned red-deer springing. Beneath this banner, but much inferior to it in size and execution, waved that of the Dukes of Pomerania; and lowest of all, hung the banner of Otto's feudal vassals — but they themselves were not visible. Neither did the kinsman appear to receive and greet his Highness. Otto knew well, it seems, that he could defy the Duke (however, I think if my gracious Lord of Wolgast had been there, he would not have suffered such insults, but would have taken Otto's banner and flung it in the mud).* Be this as it may, Duke Barnim never appeared to notice anything except Otto's two daughters. He was a little man with a long grey beard, and as he stepped slowly out of the carriage held a little puppet by the arm, which he had been carving to represent Adam. It was intended for a present to the convent at Kobatz. His *superintendens generalis,* Fabianus Timæus (a dignified-looking personage), accompanied him in the carriage, for his Highness was going on the same day to attend the diet at Treptow, and only meant to pay a passing visit here. But Lord Otto concealed this fact, as it hurt his pride. The other carriages contained the equerries and pages of his Highness, and then followed the heavy wagons with the cooks, valets, and stewards.

When the Prince entered the state hall, Lord Otto rose from his throne and said: "Your Highness is welcome, and I trust will pardon me for not having gone forth with my greetings; but those of a couple of young damsels were probably more agreeable than the compliments of an old knight like myself, who besides, as your Grace perceives, is engaged here in the exercise of his duty. And now, I pray your Highness to take this seat at my right hand." Whereupon he pointed to a plain chair, not in the least raised from the ground, and altogether as common a seat as there was to be found in the hall; but his Highness sat down quietly (at which everyone wondered in silence) and took the little puppet in his

---

‡   This was the feudal term for the next relation of a deceased vassal, upon whom it
    devolved to do homage for the lands to the feudal lord.

*   Marginal note of Duke Bogislaff, "And so would I."

lap, only exclaiming in low German, "What the devil, Otto! you make more of yourself, man, than I do;" to which the knight replied, "Not more than is necessary."

"And now," continued the old man, "the ceremony of offering homage commenced, which is as fresh in my memory as if all had happened but yesterday, and so I shall describe it that you may know what were the usages of our fathers, for the customs of chivalry are, alas! fast passing away from amongst us.

When Otto Bork gave the sign with his hand, six trumpets sounded without, whereupon the doors of the hall were thrown wide open as far as they could go, and the kinsman Vidante von Meseritz entered on a black charger, and dressed in complete armor, but without his sword. He carried the banner of his house (a pale gules with two foxes running), and riding straight up to Lord Otto, lowered it before him. Otto then demanded, "Who art thou, and what is thy request?" to which he answered, "Mighty feudal Lord, I am kinsman of Dinnies von Meseritz, and pray you for the fief." "And who are these on horseback who follow thee?" "They are the feudal vassals of my Lord, even as my father was." And Otto said, "Ride up, my men, and do as your fathers have done." Then Frederick Ubeske rode up, lowered his banner (charged with a sun and peacock's tail) before the knight, then passed on up to the great windows of the hall, where he took his place and drew his sword, while the wind played through the folds of his standard.

Next came Walter von Locksted — lowered his banner (bearing a springing unicorn), rode up to the window, and drew his sword. After him, Claud Drosedow, waving his black eagle upon a white and red shield, rode up to the window and drew his sword; then Jacob Pretz, on his white charger, bearing two spears transverse through a fallen tree on his flag; and Dieterich Mallin, whose banner fell in folds over his hand, so that the device was not visible; and Lorenz Prechel, carrying a leopard gules upon a silver shield; and Jacob Knut, with a golden becker upon an azure field, and three plumes on the crest; and Tesmar von Kettler, whose spurs caught in the robe of a young maiden as he passed, and merry laughter resounded through the hall, many saying it was a good omen, which, indeed, was the truth, for that evening they were betrothed; and finally came Johann Zastrow, bearing two buffaloes' horns on his banner, and a green five-leaved bush, rode up to the window after the others, and drew his sword.

There stood the nine, like the muses at the nuptials of Peleus,* and the wind played through their banners. Then Lord Otto spoke —

---

* The nine muses were present at the marriage of Peleus and Thetis. — *See Pindar, pyth.* . 3, 160

"True, these are my leal vassals. And now, kinsman of Meseritz, dismount and pay homage, as did thy father, ere thou canst ride up and join them." So the young man dismounted, threw the reins of his horse to a squire, and ascended the platform. Then Otto, holding up a sword, spoke again —

"Behold, kinsman, this is the sword of thy father; touch it with me, and pronounce the feudal oath." Here all the vassals rode up from the window, and held their swords crosswise over the kinsman's head, while he spake thus —

"I, Vidante von Meseritz, declare, vow, and swear to the most powerful, noble, and brave Otto von Bork, lord of the lands and castles of Labes, Pansin, Stramehl, Regenwalde, and others, and my most powerful feudal lord, and to his lawful heirs, a right loyal fealty, to serve him with all duty and obedience, to warn him of all evil, and defend him from all injury, to the best of my ability and power."

Then he kissed the knight's hand, who girded his father's sword on him, and said —

"Thus I acknowledge thee for my vassal, as my father did thy father."

Then turning to his attendants he cried, "Bring hither the camp furniture." Hereupon the circle of spectators parted in two, and the pages led up, first, Vidante's horse, upon which he sprung; then others followed, bearing rich garments and his father's signet, and laid them down before him, saying, "Kinsman, the garments and the seal of thy father." A third and a fourth bore a large couch with a white coverlet, set it down before him, and said, "Kinsman, a couch for thee and thy wife." Then came a great crowd, bearing plates and dishes, and napkins, and table-covers, besides eleven tin cans, a fish-kettle, and a pair of iron pot-hooks; in short, a complete camp furniture; all of which they set down before the young man, and then disappeared.

During this entire time no one noticed his Highness the Duke, though he was indeed the feudal head of all. Even when the trumpets sounded again, and the vassals passed out in procession, they lowered their standards only before Otto, as if no princely personage were present. But I think this proud Lord Otto must have commanded them so to do, for such an omission or breach of respect was never before seen in Pomerania. Even his Highness seemed, at last, to feel displeasure, for he drew forth his knife, and began to cut away at the little wooden Adam, without taking further notice of the ceremony.

At length when the vassals had departed, and many of the guests also, who wished to follow them, had left the hall, the Duke looked up with his little glittering eyes, scratched the back of his head with the knife, and asked his Chancellor, Jacob Kleist, who had evidently been long raging with anger, "Jacob, what dost thou think of this *spectaculo?*" who replied, "Gracious lord, I esteem it a silly thing for an inferior to play the part of a prince, or for a prince to be compelled to play the part of an inferior." Such a speech offended Otto mightily, who drew himself up and retorted scornfully, "Particularly a poor inferior who, as you see, is obliged to draw the plow by turns with his serfs." Hereupon the Chancellor would have flung back the scorn, but his Highness motioned with the hand that he should keep silence, saying, "Remember, good Jacob, that we are here as guests; however, order the carriages, for I think it is time that we proceed on our journey."

When Otto heard this, he was confounded, and, descending from his throne, uttered so many flattering things, that his Highness at length was prevailed upon to remain (I would not have consented, to save my soul, had I been the Prince — no, not even if I had to pass the night with the bears and wolves in the forest before I could reach Treptow); so the good old Prince followed him into another hall, where breakfast was prepared, and all the lords and ladies stood there in glittering groups round the table, particularly admiring the bear's head, which seemed to please his Highness mightily also. Then each one drained a large goblet of wine, and even the ladies sipped from their little wine-glasses, to drink themselves into good spirits for the dance.

Otto now related all about the hunt, and presented me to his Grace, who gave me his hand to kiss, saying, "Well done, young man — I like this bravery. Were it not for you, in place of a wedding, and a bear's head in the dish, Lord Otto might have had a funeral and two human heads in a coffin." His Grace then pledged me in a silver becker of wine; and afterwards the bride and bridegroom, who had sat till then kissing and making love in a corner; but they now came forward and kissed the hand of the Duke with much respect. The bridegroom had on a crimson doublet, which became him well; but his father's jack-boots, which he wore according to custom, were much too wide, and shook about his legs. The bride was arrayed in a scarlet velvet robe, and bodice furred with ermine. Sidonia carried a little balsam flask, depending from a gold chain which she wore round her neck. (She soon needed the balsam, for that day she suffered a foretaste of the fate which was to be the punishment for her after evil deeds.) And now, as we set forward to the church, a group of noble maidens distributed wreaths to the guests; but the bride presented one to the Duke, and Sidonia (that her hand might have been withered) handed one to me, poor love-stricken youth.

It was the custom then, as now, in Pomerania, for all the bride-maidens, crowned with beautiful wreaths, to precede the bride and bridegroom to church. The crowd of lords, and ladies, and young knights pouring out of the castle gates, in order to see them, separated Sidonia from this group, and she was left alone weeping. Now the whole population of the little town were running from every street leading to the church; and it happened that a courser* of Otto Bork's came right against Sidonia with such violence, that, with a blow of his head, he knocked her down into the puddle (she was to lie there really in after-life). Her little balsam-flask was of no use here. She had to go back, dripping, to the castle, and appeared no more at her sister's nuptials, but consoled herself, however, by listening to the bellowing of the huntsman, whom they were beating black and blue by her orders beneath her window.

I would willingly have returned with her, but was ashamed so to do, and therefore followed the others to church. All the common people that crowded the streets were allowed to enter. Then the bridegroom and his party, of whom the Duke was chief, advanced up to the right of the altar, and the bride and her party, of which Fabianus Timæus was the most distinguished, arrayed themselves on the left.

I had now an opportunity of hearing the learned and excellent parson Dilavius myself; for he represented his patron (who was not present at the feast, but apologized for his absence by alleging that he must remain at the castle to look after the preparations) almost as an angel, and the young ladies, especially the bride, came in for even a larger share of his flattery; but he was so modest before these illustrious personages, that I observed, whenever he looked up from the book, he had one eye upon the Duke and another on Fabianus.

When we returned to the castle, Sidonia met the bridemaidens again with joyous smiles. She now wore a white silk robe, laced with gold, and dancing-slippers with white silk hose. The diamonds still remained on her head, neck, and arms. She looked beautiful thus; and I could not withdraw my eyes from her. We all now entered the bridechamber, as the custom is, and there stood an immense bridal couch, with coverlet and draperies as white as snow; and all the bridemaids and the guests threw their wreaths upon it. Then the Prince, taking the bridegroom by the hand, led him up to it, and repeated an old German rhyme concerning the duties of the holy state upon which he had entered.

When his Highness ceased, Fabianus took the bride by the hand, who blushed as red as a rose, and led her up in the same manner to the nuptial couch, where he uttered a long admonition on her duties to her husband, at which all wept, but particularly the bride-maidens. After this we proceeded to the state hall, where Otto was seated on his throne

---

* A man who courses greyhounds.

waiting to receive them, and when his children had kissed his hand the dancing commenced. Otto invited the Prince to sit near him, and all the young knights and maidens who intended to dance ranged themselves on costly carpets that were laid upon the floor all round by the walls. The trumpets and violins now struck up, and a band was stationed at each end of the hall, so that while the dancers were at the top one played, and when at the lower end the other.

I hastened to Sidonia, as she reclined upon the carpet, and bending low before her, said, "Beautiful maiden! will you not dance?"* Upon which she smilingly gave me her little hand, and I raised her up, and led her away.

I have said that I was a proficient in all knightly exercises, so that everyone approached to see us dance. When Sidonia was tired I led her back, and threw myself beside her on the carpet. But in a little while three other young nobles came and seated themselves around her, and began to jest, and toy, and pay court to her. One played with her left hand and her rings, another with the gold net of her hair, while I held her right hand and pressed it. She coquettishly repelled them all — sometimes with her feet, sometimes with her hands. And when Hans von Damitz extolled her hair, she gave him such a blow on the nose with her head that it began to bleed, and he was obliged to withdraw. Still one could see that all these blows, right and left, were not meant in earnest. This continued for some time until an Italian dance began, which she declined to join, and as I was left alone with her upon the carpet, "Now," thought I, "there can be no better time to decide my fate;" for she had pressed my hand frequently, both in the dance and since I had lain reclining beside her.

"Beautiful Sidonia!" I said, "you know not how you have wounded my heart. I can neither eat nor sleep since I beheld you, and those five little kisses which you gave me burn through my frame like arrows."

To which she answered, laughing, "It was your pastime, youth. It was your own wish to take those little kisses."

"Ah, yes!" I said, "it was my will; but give me more now and make me well."

"What!" she exclaimed, "you desire more kisses? Then will your pain become greater, if, as you say, with every kiss an arrow enters your heart, so at last they would cause your death."

"Ah, yes!" I answered, "unless you take pity on me, and promise to become my wife, they will indeed cause my death." As I said this, she sprang up, tore her hand away from me, and cried with mocking

---

* It will interest my fair readers to know that this was, word for word, the established form employed in those days for an invitation to dance.

laughter, "What does the knave mean? Ha! ha! the poor, miserable varlet!"

I remained some moments stupefied with rage, then sprung to my feet without another word, left the hall, took my steed from the stable, and turned my back on the castle forever. You may imagine how her ingratitude added to the bitterness of my feelings, when I considered that it was to me she owed her life. She afterwards offered herself to me for a wife, but she was then dishonored, and I spat out at her in disgust. I never beheld her again till she was carried past my door to the scaffold.

All this the old man related with many sighs; but his after-meeting with her shall be related more *in extenso* in its proper place. I shall now set down what further he communicated about the wedding-feast.

You may imagine, he said, that I was curious to know all that happened after I left the castle, and my friend, Bogislaff von Suckow of Pegelow, told me as follows.

After my departure, the young lords grew still more free and daring in their manner to Sidonia, so that when not dancing she had sufficient exercise in keeping them off with her hands and feet, until my friend Bogislaff attracted her whole attention by telling her that he had just returned from Wolgast, where the ducal widow was much comforted by the presence of her son, Prince Ernest Ludovick, whom she had not seen since he went to the university. He was the handsomest youth in all Pomerania, and played the lute so divinely that at court he was compared to the god Apollo.

Sidonia upon this fell into deep thought. In the meanwhile, it was evident that his Highness old Duke Barnim was greatly struck by her beauty, and wished to get near her upon the carpet; for his Grace was well known to be a great follower of the sex, and many stories are whispered about a harem of young girls he kept at St. Mary's — but these things are allowable in persons of his rank.

However, Fabianus Timæus, who sat by him, wished to prevent him approaching Sidonia, and made signs, and nudged him with his elbow; and finally they put their heads together and had a long argument.

At last the Prince started up, and stepping to Otto, asked him, Would he not dance? "Yes," he replied, "if your Grace will dance likewise." "Good," said the Prince, "that can be soon arranged," and therewith he solicited Sidonia's hand. At this Fabianus was so scandalized that he left the hall, and appeared no more until supper. After the dance, his Highness advanced to Otto, who was reseated on his throne, and said, "Why, Otto, you have a beautiful daughter in Sidonia. She must come to my court, and when she appears amongst the other ladies, I swear she will make a better fortune than by staying shut up here in your old castle."

On which Otto replied, sarcastically smiling, "Aye, my gracious Prince, she would be a dainty morsel for your Highness, no doubt; but there is no lack of noble visitors at my castle, I am proud to say." Jacob Kleist, the Chancellor, was now so humbled at the Duke's behavior that he, too, left the hall and followed Fabianus. Even the Duke changed color; but before he had time to speak, Sidonia sprang forward, and having heard the whole conversation, entreated her father to accept the Duke's offer, and allow her either to visit the court at Wolgast or at Old Stettin. What was she to do here? When the wedding-feast was over, no one would come to the castle but huntsmen and such like.

So Otto at last consented that she might visit Wolgast, but on no account the court at Stettin.

Then the young Sidonia began to coax and caress the old Duke, stroking his long beard, which reached to his girdle, with her little white hands, and prayed that he would place her with the princely Lady of Wolgast, for she longed to go there. People said that it was such a beautiful place, and the sea was not far off, which she had never been at in all her life. And so the Duke was pleased with her caresses, and promised that he would request his dear cousin, the ducal widow of Wolgast, to receive her as one of her maids of honor. Sidonia then further entreated that there might be no delay, and he answered that he would send a note to his cousin from the Diet at Treptow, by the Grand Chamberlain of Wolgast, Ulrich von Schwerin, and that she would not have to wait long. But she must go by Old Stettin, and stop at his palace for a while, and then he would bring her on himself to Wolgast, if he had time to spare.

While Sidonia clapped her hands and danced about for joy, Otto looked grave, and said, "But, gracious Lord, the nearest way to Wolgast is by Cammin. Sidonia must make a circuit if she goes by Old Stettin."

The conversation was now interrupted by the lackeys, who came to announce that dinner was served.

Otto requested the Duke to take a place beside him at table, and treated him with somewhat more distinction than he had done in the morning; but a hot dispute soon arose, and this was the cause. As Otto drank deep in the wine-cup, he grew more reckless and daring, and began to display his heretical doctrines as openly as he had hitherto exhibited his pomp and magnificence, so that everyone might learn that pride and ungodliness are twin brothers. May God keep us from both!

And one of the guests having said, in confirmation of some fact, "The Lord Jesus knows I speak the truth!" the godless knight laughed scornfully, exclaiming, "The Lord Jesus knows as little about the matter as my old grandfather, lying there in his vault, of our wedding-feast today."

There was a dead silence instantly, and the Prince, who had just lifted up some of the bear's paw to his lips, with mustard sauce and pastry all round it, dropped it again upon his plate, and opened his eyes as wide as they could go; then, hastily wiping his mouth with the salvet, exclaimed in low German, "What the devil, Otto! art thou a free-thinker?" who replied, "A true nobleman may, in all things, be a freethinker, and neither do all that a prince commands nor believe all that a pope teaches." To which the Duke answered, "What concerns me I pardon, for I do not believe that you will ever forget your duty to your Prince. The times are gone by when a noble would openly offer violence to his sovereign; but for what concerns the honor of our Lord Christ, I must leave you in the hands of Fabianus to receive proper chastisement."

Now Fabianus, seeing that all eyes were fixed on him, grew red and cleared his throat, and set himself in a position to argue the point with Lord Otto, beginning — "So you believe that Christ the Lord remained in the grave, and is not living and reigning for all eternity?"

Ille. — "Yes; that is my opinion."

Hic. — "What do you believe, then? or do you believe in anything?"

Ille. — "Yes; I believe firmly in an all-powerful and omniscient God."

Hic. — "How do you know He exists?"

Ille. — "Because my reason tells me so."

Hic. — "Your reason does not tell you so, good sir. It merely tells you that something supermundane exists, but cannot tell you whether it be one God or two Gods, or a hundred Gods, or of what nature are these Gods — whether spirits, or stars, or trees, or animals, or, in fine, any object you can name, for paganism has imagined a Deity in everything, which proves what I assert. You only believe in *one* God, because you sucked in the doctrine with your mother's milk."*

---

* The history of all philosophy shows that this is psychologically true. Even Lucian satirizes the philosophers of his age who see God or Gods in numbers, dogs, geese, trees, and other things. But monotheistic Christianity has preserved us for nearly 2000 years from these aberrations of philosophy. However, as the authority of Christianity declined, the pagan tendency again became visible; until at length, in the Hegelian school, we have fallen back helplessly into the same pantheism which we left 2000 years ago. In short, what Kant asserts is perfectly true: that the existence of God cannot be proved from reason. For the highest objects of all cognition — God, Freedom, and Immortality — can as little be evolved from the new philosophy as beauty from the disgusting process of decomposition. And yet more impossible is it to imagine that this feeble Hegelian pantheism should ever become the crown and summit of all human thought, and final resting-place for all human minds.

Ille. — "How did it happen, then, that Abraham arrived at the knowledge of the *one* God, and called on the name of the Lord?"

Hic. — "Do you compare yourself with Abraham? Have you ever studied Hebrew?"

Ille. — "A little. In my youth I read through the book of Genesis."

Hic. — "Good! then you know that the Hebrew word for *name* is *Shem?*"

Ille. — "Yes; I know that."

Hic. — "Then you know that from the time of Enos the *name** was preached (Genesis iv. 26), showing that the pure doctrine was known from the beginning. This doctrine was darkened and obscured by wise people like you, so that it was almost lost at the time of Abraham, who again preached the *name* of the Lord to unbelievers."

Ille. — "What did this primitive doctrine contain?"

Hic. — "Undoubtedly not only a testimony of the one living God of heaven and earth, but also clearly of Christ the Messiah, as He who was promised to our fallen parents in paradise (Genesis iii. 15)."

Ille. — "Can you prove that Abraham had the witness of Christ?"

Hic. — "Yes; from Christ's own words (John viii. 56): — 'Abraham, your father, rejoiced to see My day, and he saw it, and was glad.' Item: Moses and all the Prophets have witnessed of Him, of whom you say that He lies dead in the grave."

Ille. — "Oh, that is just what the priests say."

Hic. — "And Christ Himself, Luke xxvi. 25 and 27. Do you not see, young man, that you mock the Prince of Life, whom God, that cannot lie, promised before the world began — Titus i. 2 — aye, even more than you mocked your temporal Prince this day? Poor sinner, what does it help you to believe in one God?"

Reason, whether from an indwelling instinct, or from an innate causality-law, may assert that something supermundane exists, but can know nothing more and nothing further. So we see the absurdity of chattering in our journals and periodicals of the progress of reason. The advance has been only *formal,* not *essential.* The formal advance has been in printing, railroads, and such like, in which direction we may easily suppose progression will yet further continue. But there has been no essential advance whatever. We know as little now of our own being, of the being of God, or even of that of the smallest infusoria, as in the days of Thales and Anaximander. In short, when life begins, begins also our feebleness; "Therefore," says Paul, "we walk by faith, not by sight." Yet these would-be philosophers of our day will only walk by sight, not by faith, although they cannot see into anything — not even into themselves.

* In order to understand the argument, the reader must remember that the *name* here is taken in the sense of the Greek logos, and is considered as referring especially to Christ.

"Even the devils believe and tremble," added Jacob Kleist the Chancellor. "No, there is no other name given under heaven by which you can be saved; and will you be more wise than Abraham, and the Prophets, and the Apostles, and all holy Christian Churches up to this day? Shame on you, and remember what St. Paul says: 'Thinking themselves wise, they became fools.' And in 1st Cor. xv. 17: 'If Christ be not risen, than is your faith vain, and our preaching also vain. Ye are yet in your sins, and they who sleep in Christ are lost.'"*

So Otto was silenced and coughed, for he had nothing to answer, and all the guests laughed; but, fortunately, just then the offering-plate was handed round, and the Duke laid down two ducats, at which Otto smiled scornfully, and flung in seven rix-dollars, but laughed outright when Fabianus put down only four groschen.

This seemed to affront his Highness, for he whispered to his Chancellor to order the carriages, and rose up from table with his attendants. Then, offering his hand to Otto, said, "Take care, Otto, or the devil will have you one day in hell, like the rich man in Scripture." To which Otto replied, bowing low, "Gracious Lord, I hope at least to meet good company there. Farewell, and pardon me for not attending you to the castle gates, but I may not leave my guests."

Then all the nobles rose up, and the young knights accompanied his Highness, as did also Sidonia, who now further entreated his Grace to remove her from her father's castle, since he saw himself how lightly God's Word was held there. Fabianus was infinitely pleased to hear her speak in this manner, and promised to use all his influence towards having her removed from this Egypt.

Here ended all that old Uckermann could relate of Sidonia's youth; so I determined to ride on to Stramehl, and learn there further particulars if possible.

Accordingly, next day I took leave of the good old man, praying God to give him a peaceful death, and arrived at Stramehl with my servant. Here, however, I could obtain no information; for even the Bork family pretended to know nothing, just as if they never had heard of Sidonia (they were ashamed, I think, to acknowledge her), and the townspeople who had known her were all dead. The girl, indeed, was still living whose

---

* This proof of Christ's divinity from the Old Testament was considered of the highest importance in the time of the Apostles; but Schleiermacher, in his strange system, which may be called a mystic Rationalism, endeavors to shake the authority of the Old Testament in a most unpardonable and incomprehensible manner. This appears to me as if a man were to tear down a building from the sure foundation on which it had rested for 1000 years, and imagine it could rest in true stability only on the mere breath of his words.

goose Sidonia had killed, but she was now an old woman in second childhood, and fancied that I was myself Sidonia, who had come to take away another goose from her. So I rode on to Freienwald, where I heard much that shall appear in its proper place; then to Old Stettin; and, after waiting three days for a fair wind, set sail for Wolgast, expecting to obtain much information there.

Chapter IV

How Sidonia came to the court at Wolgast, and of what further happened to her there

*I*n Wolgast I met with many persons whose fathers had known Sidonia, and what they related to me concerning her I have summed up into connection for your Highness as follows.

When Duke Barnim reached the Diet at Treptow, he immediately made known Sidonia's request to the Grand Chamberlain of Wolgast, Ulrich von Schwerin, who was also guardian to the five young princes. But he grumbled, and said — "The ducal widow had maids of honor enough to dam up the river with if she chose; and he wished for no more pet doves to be brought to court, particularly not Sidonia; for he knew her father was ambitious, and longed to be called 'your Grace.'"

Even Fabianus could not prevail in Sidonia's favor. So the Duke and he returned home to Stettin; but scarcely had they arrived there, when a letter came from the ducal widow of Wolgast, saying, that on no account would she receive Sidonia at her court. The Duke might therefore keep her at his own if he chose.

So the Duke took no further trouble. But Sidonia was not so easily satisfied; and taking the matter in her own hands she left her father's castle without waiting his permission, and set off for Stettin.

On arriving, she prayed the Duke to bring her to Wolgast without delay, as she knew there was an honorable, noble lady there who would watch over her, as indeed she felt would be necessary at a court. And Fabianus supported her petition; for he was much edified with her expressed desire to crucify the flesh, with the affections and lusts.

Ah! could he have known her!

So the kind-hearted Duke embarked with her immediately, without telling anyone; and having a fair wind, sailed up directly to the little water-gate, and anchored close beneath the Castle of Wolgast.

Here they landed; the Duke having Sidonia under one arm, and a little wooden puppet under the other. It was an Eve, for whom Sidonia had served as the model; and truly she was an Eve in sin, and brought as much evil upon the land of Pomerania as our first mother upon the whole world. Sidonia was enveloped in a black mantle, and wore a hood lined with fur covering her face. The Duke also had on a large wrapping cloak, and a cap of yellow leather upon his head.

So they entered the private gate, and on through the first and second courts of the castle, without her Grace hearing a word of their arrival. And they proceeded on through the gallery, until they reached the private apartments of the princess, from whence resounded a psalm which her Grace was singing with her ladies while they spun, and which psalm was played by a little musical box placed within the Duchess's own spinning-wheel. Duke Barnim had made it himself for her Grace, and it was right pleasant to hear.

After listening some time, the Duke knocked, and a maid of honor opened the door. When they entered, her Grace was so confounded that she dropped her thread and exclaimed, "Dear uncle! is this maiden, then, Sidonia?" examining her from head to foot while she spoke. The Duke excused himself by saying that he had promised her father to bring her here; but her Grace cut short his apologies with "Dear uncle, Dr. Martin Luther told me on my wedding-day that he never allowed himself to be interrupted at his prayers, because it betokened the presence of something evil. And you have now broken in on our devotions; therefore sit down with the maiden and join our psalm, if you know it." Then her Grace took up the reel again, and having set the clock-work going with her foot, struck up the psalm once more, in a clear, loud voice, joined by all her ladies. But Sidonia sat still, and kept her eyes upon the ground.

When they had ended, her Grace, having first crossed herself, advanced to Sidonia, and said, "Since you arrived at my court, you may remain; but take care that you never lift your eyes upon the young men. Such wantons are hateful to my sight; for, as the Scripture says, 'A fair woman without discretion is like a circlet of gold upon a swine's head.'"

Sidonia changed color at this; but the Duke, who held quite a different opinion about such women, entreated her Grace not to be always so gloomy and melancholy — that it was time now for her to forget her late spouse, and think of gayer subjects. To which she answered, "Dear uncle, I cannot forget my Philip, particularly as my fate was foreshadowed at my bridal by a most ominous occurrence."

Now, the Duke had heard this story of the bridal a hundred times; yet to please her he asked, "And what was it, dear cousin?"

"Listen," she replied. "When Dr. Martin Luther exchanged our rings, mine fell from his hand to the ground; at which he was evidently troubled, and taking it up, he blew on it; then turning round, exclaimed — 'Away with thee, Satan! away with thee, Satan! Meddle not in this matter!' And so my dear lord was taken from me in his forty-fifth year, and I was left a desolate widow." Here she sobbed and put her kerchief to her eyes.

"But, cousin," said the Duke, "remember you have a great blessing from God in your five fine sons. And that reminds me — where are they all now?"

This restored her Grace, and she began to discourse of her children, telling how handsome was the young Prince Ernest, and that he and the little Casimir were only with her now.

Here Sidonia, as the other ladies remarked, moved restlessly on her chair, and her eyes flashed like torches, so that it was evident some plan had struck her, for she was strengthening day by day in wickedness.

"Aye, cousin," cried the Duke, "it is no wonder a handsome mother should have handsome sons. And now what think you of giving us a jolly wedding? It is time for you to think of a second husband, methinks, after having wept ten years for your Philip. The best doctor, they say, for a young widow, is a handsome lover. What think you of myself, for instance?" And he pulled off his leather cap, and put his white head and beard up close to her Grace.

Now, though her Grace could not help laughing at his position and words, yet she grew as sour as vinegar again immediately; for all the ladies tittered, and, as to Sidonia, she laughed outright.

"Fie! uncle," said her Grace, "a truce to such folly; do you not know what St. Paul says — 'Let the widows abide even as I'?"

"Aye, true, dear cousin; but, then, does he not say, too, 'I will that the younger widows marry'?"

"Ah, but, dear uncle, I am no longer young."

"Why, you are as young and active as a girl; and I engage, cousin, if any stranger came in here to look for the widow, he would find it difficult to make her out amongst the young maidens; don't you think so, Sidonia?"

"Ah, yes," she replied; "I never imagined her Grace was so young. She is as blooming as a rose."

This appeared to please the Princess, for she smiled slightly and then sighed; but gave his Grace a smart slap when he attempted to seize her hand and kiss it, saying — "Now, uncle, I told you to leave off this foolery."

At this moment the band outside struck up Duke Bogislaff's march — the same that was played before him in Jerusalem when he ascended the Via Dolorosa up to Golgotha; for it was the custom here to play this march half-an-hour before dinner, in order to gather all the household, knights, squires, pages, and even grooms and peasants, to the castle, where they all received entertainment. And ten rooms were laid with dinner, and all stood open, so that anyone might enter under the permission of the Court Marshal. All this I must notice here, because Sidonia afterwards caused much scandal by these means. The music now rejoiced her greatly, and she began to move her little feet, not in a pilgrim, but in a waltz measure, and to beat time with them, as one could easily perceive by the motion underneath her mantle.

The Grand Chamberlain, Ulrich von Schwerin, now entered, and having looked at Sidonia with much surprise, advanced to kiss the hand of the Duke and bid him welcome to Wolgast. Then, turning to her Grace, he inquired if the twelve pages should wait at table to do honor to the Duke of Stettin. But the Duke forbade them, saying he wished to dine in private for this day with the Duchess and her two sons; the Grand Chamberlain, too, he hoped would be present, and Sidonia might have a seat at the ducal table, as she was of noble blood; besides, he had taken her likeness as Eve, and the first of women ought to sit at the first table. Hereupon the Duke drew forth the puppet, and called to Ulrich — "Here! you have seen my Adam in Treptow; what think you now of Eve? Look, dear cousin, is she not the image of Sidonia?"

At this speech both looked very grave. Ulrich said nothing; but her Grace replied, "You will make the girl vain, dear uncle." And Ulrich added, "Yes, and the image has such an expression, that if the real Eve looked so, I think she would have left her husband in the lurch and run with the devil himself to the devil."

While the last verse of the march was playing — "To Zion comes Pomerania's Prince" — they proceeded to dinner — the Duke and the Princes leading, while from every door along the corridor the young knights and pages peeped out to get a sight of Sidonia, who, having

thrown off her mantle, swept by them in a robe of crimson velvet laced
with gold.

When they entered the dining-hall, Prince Ernest was leaning against
one of the pillars wearing a black Spanish mantle, fastened with chains
of gold. He stepped forward to greet the Duke, and inquire after his
health.

The Duke was well pleased to see him, and tapped him on the cheek,
exclaiming —

"By my faith, cousin, I have not heard too much of you. What a fine
youth you have grown up since you left the university."

But how Sidonia's eyes sparkled when (for his misfortune) she found
herself seated next him at table. The Duchess now called upon Sidonia
to say the "gratias;" but she blundered and stammered, which many
imputed to modesty, so that Prince Ernest had to repeat it in her stead.
This seemed to give him courage; for when the others began to talk
around the table, he ventured to bid her welcome to his mother's court.

When they rose from table, Sidonia was again commanded to say
grace; but being unable, the Prince came to her relief and repeated the
words for her. And now the evil spirit without doubt put it into the
Duke's head, who had drunk rather freely, to say to her Grace —

"Dear cousin, I have introduced the Italian fashion at my court,
which is, that every knight kisses the lady next him on rising from dinner
— let us do the same here." And herewith he first kissed her Grace and
then Sidonia. Ulrich von Schwerin looked grave at this and shook his
head, particularly when the Duke encouraged Prince Ernest to follow
his example; but the poor youth looked quite ashamed, and cast down
his eyes. However, when he raised them again Sidonia's were fixed on
him, and she murmured, "Will you not learn?" with such a glance
accompanying the words, that he could no longer resist to touch her
lips. So there was great laughing in the hall; and the Duke then, taking
his puppet under one arm and Sidonia under the other, descended with
her to the castle gardens, complaining that he never got a good laugh
in this gloomy house, let him do what he would.

And the next day he departed, though the Prince sent his equerry to
know would his Grace desire to hunt that day; or, if he preferred fishing,
there were some excellent carp within the domain. But the Duke replied,
that he would neither ride nor fish, but sail away at ten of the clock, if
the wind were favorable.

So many feared that his Grace was annoyed; and therefore the Duchess and Prince Ernest, along with the Grand Chamberlain, attended him
to the gate; and even to please him, Sidonia was allowed to accompany
them. The Pomeranian standard also was hoisted to do him honor, and

finally he bade the illustrious widow farewell, recommending Sidonia to her care. But the fair maiden herself he took in his arms, she weeping and sobbing, and admonished her to be careful and discreet; and so, with a fair wind, set sail from Wolgast, and never once looked back.

Chapter V

Sidonia knows nothing of God's Word, but seeks to learn it from the young Prince of Wolgast

Next day, Sunday, her Grace was unable to attend divine service in the church, having caught cold by neglecting to put on her mantle when she accompanied the Duke down to the water-gate. However, though her Grace could not leave her chamber, yet she heard the sermon of the preacher all the same; for an ear-tube descended from her apartment down on the top of the pulpit, by which means every word reached her, and a maid of honor always remained in attendance to find out the lessons of the day, and the other portions of the divine service, for her Grace, who thus could follow the clergyman word for word. Sidonia was the one selected for the office on this day.

But, gracious Heavens! when the Duchess said, Find me out the prophet Isaiah, Sidonia looked in the New Testament; and when she said, Open the Gospel of St. John, Sidonia looked in the Old Testament. At first her Grace did not perceive her blunders; but when she became aware of them, she started up, and tearing the Bible out of her hands, exclaimed, "What! are you a heathen? Yesterday you could not repeat a simple grace that every child knows by heart, and today you do not know the difference between the Old and New Testaments. For shame! Alas! what an ill weed I have introduced into my house."

So the cunning wench began to weep, and said, her father had never allowed her to learn Christianity, though she wished to do so ardently, but always made a mock of it, and for this reason she had sought a refuge with her Grace, where she hoped to become a truly pious and believing Christian. The Duchess was quite softened by her tears, and promised that Dr. Dionysius Gerschovius should examine her in the catechism, and see what she knew. He was a learned man from Daber*, and her Grace's chaplain. The very idea of the doctor frightened Sidonia so much, that her teeth chattered, and she entreated her Grace, while she kissed her hand, to allow her at least a fortnight for preparation and study before the doctor came.

The Duchess promised this, and said, that Clara von Dewitz, another of her maidens, would be an excellent person to assist her in her studies, as she came from Daber also, and was familiar with the views and doctrines held by Dr. Gerschovius. This Clara we shall hear more of in our history. She was a year older than Sidonia, intelligent, courageous, and faithful, with a quiet, amiable disposition, and of most pious and Christian demeanor. She wore a high, stiff ruff, out of which peeped forth her head scarcely visible, and a long robe, like a stole, sweeping behind her. She was privately betrothed to her Grace's Master of the Horse, Marcus Bork by name, a cousin of Sidonia's; for, as her Grace discouraged all kinds of gallantry or love-making at her court, they were obliged to keep the matter secret, so that no one, not even her Grace, suspected anything of the engagement.

This was the person appointed to instruct Sidonia in Christianity; and every day the fair pupil visited Clara in her room for an hour. But, alas! theology was sadly interrupted by Sidonia's folly and levity, for she chattered away on all subjects: first about Prince Ernest — was he affianced to anyone? was he in love? had Clara herself a lover? and if that old proser, meaning the Duchess, looked always as sour? did she never allow a feast or a dance? and then she would toss the catechism under the bed, or tear it and trample on it, muttering, with much ill-temper, that she was too old to be learning catechisms like a child.

Poor Clara tried to reason with her mildly, and said — "Her Grace was very particular on these points. The maids of honor were obliged to assemble weekly once in the church and once in her Grace's own room, to be examined by Dr. Gerschovius, not only in the Lutheran Catechism, which they all knew well, but also in that written by his brother, Dr. Timothy Gerschovius of Old Stettin; so Sidonia had better first learn the *Catechismum Lutheri,* and afterwards the *Catechismum Gerschovii.*" At last Sidonia grew so weary of catechisms that she determined to run away from court.

But Satan had more for her to do; so he put a little syrup into the wormwood draft, and thus it was. One day passing along the corridor

---

* A small town in Lower Pomerania

from Clara's room, it so happened that Prince Ernest opened his door, just as she came up to it, to let out the smoke, and then began to walk up and down, playing softly on his lute. Sidonia stood still for a few minutes with her eyes thrown up in ecstasy, and then passed on; but the Prince stepped to the door, and asked her did she play.

"Alas! no," she answered. "Her father had forbidden her to learn the lute, though music was her passion, and her heart seemed almost breaking with joy when she listened to it. If his Highness would but play one little air over again for her."

"Yes, if you will enter, but not while you are standing there at my door."

"Ah, do not ask me to enter, that would not be seemly; but I will sit down here on this beer-barrel in the corridor and listen; besides, music is improved by distance."

And she looked so tenderly at the young Prince that his heart burned within him, and he stepped out into the corridor to play; but the sound reaching the ears of her Grace, she looked out, and Sidonia jumped up from the beer-barrel and fled away to her own room.

When Sunday came again, all the maids of honor were assembled, as usual, in her Grace's apartment, to be examined in the catechism; and probably the Duchess had lamented much to the doctor over Sidonia's levity and ignorance, for he kept a narrow watch on her the whole day. At four of the clock Dr. Gerschovius entered in his gown and bands, looking very solemn; for it was a saying of his "that the devil invented laughter; and that it were better for a man to be a weeping Heraclitus than a laughing Democritus." After he had kissed the hand of her Grace, he said they had better now begin with the Commandments; and, turning to Sidonia, asked her, "What is forbidden by the seventh commandment?"

Now Sidonia, who had only learned the Lutheran Catechism, did not understand the question in this form out of the Gerschovian Catechism, and remained silent.

"What!" said the doctor, "not know my brother's catechism! You must get one directly from the court bookseller — the Catechism of Doctor Timothy Gerschovius — and have it learned by next Sunday." Then turning to Clara, he repeated the question, and she, having answered, received great praise.

Now it happened that just at this time the ducal horse were led up to the horse-pond to water, and all the young pages and knights were gathered in a group under the window of her Grace's apartment, laughing and jesting merrily. So Sidonia looked out at them, which the doctor no sooner perceived than he slapped her on the hand with the catechism, exclaiming, "What! have you not heard just now that all sinful desires are forbidden by the seventh commandment, and yet you look forth upon the young men from the window? Tell me what are sinful desires?"

But the proud girl grew red with indignation, and cried, "Do you dare to strike me?" Then, turning to her Grace, she said, "Madam, that sour old priest has struck me on the fingers. I will not suffer this. My father shall hear of it."

Hereupon her Grace, and even the doctor, tried to appease her, but in vain, and she ran crying from the apartment. In the corridor she met the old treasurer, Jacob Zitsewitz, who hated the doctor and all his rigid doctrines. So she complained of the treatment which she had received, and pressed his hand and stroked his beard, saying, would he permit a castle and land dowered maiden to be scolded and insulted by an old parson because she looked out at a window? That was worse than in the days of Popery. Now Zitsewitz, who had a little wine in his head, on hearing this, ran in great wrath to the apartment of her Grace, where soon a great uproar was heard.

For the treasurer, in the heat of his remonstrance with the priest, struck a little table violently which stood near him, and overthrew it. On this had lain the superb escritoire of her Highness, made of Venetian glass, in which the ducal arms were painted; and also the magnificent album of her deceased lord, Duke Philip. The escritoire was broken, the ink poured forth upon the album, from thence ran down to the costly Persian carpet, a present from her brother, the Prince of Saxony, and finally stained the velvet robe of her Highness herself, who started up screaming, so that the old chamberlain rushed in to know what had happened, and then he fell into a rage both with the priest and the treasurer. At length her Grace was comforted by hearing that a chemist in Grypswald could restore the book, and mend the glass again as good as new; still she wept, and exclaimed, "Alas! who could have thought it? all this was foreshadowed to her by Dr. Martinus dropping her ring."

Here the treasurer, to conciliate her Grace, pretended that he never had heard the story of the betrothal, and asked, "What does your Grace mean?" Whereupon drying her eyes she answered, "O Master Jacob, you will hear a strange story" — and here she went over each particular, though every child in the street had it by heart. So this took away her grief, and everyone got to rights again, for that day. But worse was soon to befall.

I have said that half-an-hour before dinner the band played to summon all within the castle and the retainers to their respective messes, as the custom then was; so that the long corridor was soon filled with a crowd of all conditions — pages, knights, squires, grooms, maids, and huntsmen, all hurrying to the apartments where their several tables were laid. Sidonia, being aware of this, upon the first roll of the drum skipped out into the corridor, dancing up and down the whole length of it to the music, so that the players declared they had never seen so beautiful a dancer, at which her heart beat with joy; and as the crowd came up, they stopped to admire her grace and beauty. Then she would pause and say a few pleasing words to each, to a huntsman, if he were passing — "Ah, I think no deer in the world could escape you, my fine young peasant;" or if a knight, she would praise the color of his doublet and the tie of his garter; or if a laundress, she would commend the whiteness of her linen, which she had never seen equaled; and as to the old cook and butler, she enchanted them by asking, had his Grace of Stettin ever seen them, for assuredly, if he had, he would have taken their fine heads as models for Abraham and Noah. Then she flung largess amongst them to drink the health of the Duchess. Only when a young noble passed, she grew timid and durst not venture to address him, but said, loud enough for him to hear, "Oh, how handsome! Do you know his name?" Or, "It is easy to see that he is a born nobleman" — and such like hypocritical flatteries.

The Princess never knew a word of all this, for, according to etiquette, she was the last to seat herself at table. So Sidonia's doings were not discovered until too late, for by that time she had won over the whole court, great and small, to her interests.

Amongst the cavaliers who passed one day were two fine young men, Wedig von Schwetzkow, and Johann Appelmann, son of the burgomaster at Stargard. They were both handsome; but Johann was a dissolute, wild profligate, and Wedig was not troubled with too much sense. Still he had not fallen into the evil courses which made the other so notorious. "Who is that handsome youth?" asked Sidonia as Johann passed; and when they told her, "Ah, a gentleman!" she exclaimed, "who is of far higher value in my eyes than a nobleman."

Summa: they both fell in love with her on the instant; but all the young squires were the same more or less, except her cousin Marcus Bork, seeing that he was already betrothed. Likewise after dinner, in place of going direct to the ladies' apartments, she would take a circuitous route, so as to go by the quarter where the men dined, and as she passed their doors, which they left open on purpose, what rejoicing there was, and such running and squeezing just to get a glimpse of her — the little putting their heads under the arms of the tall, and there they began to laugh and chat; but neither the Duchess nor the old chamberlain knew anything of this, for they were in a different wing of the castle, and besides, always took a sleep after dinner.

However, old Zitsewitz, when he heard the clamor, knew well it was Sidonia, and would jump up from the marshal's table, though the old marshal shook his head, and run to the gallery to have a chat with her himself, and she laughed and coquetted with him, so that the old knight would run after her and take her in his arms, asking her where she would wish to go. Then she sometimes said, to the castle garden to feed the pet stag, for she had never seen so pretty a thing in all her life; and she would fetch crumbs of bread with her to feed it. So he must needs go with her, and Sidonia ran down the steps with him that led from the young men's quarter to the castle court, while they all rose up to look after her, and laugh at the old fool of a treasurer. But in a short time they followed too, running up and down the steps in crowds, to see Sidonia feeding the stag and caressing it, and sometimes trying to ride on it, while old Zitsewitz held the horns.

Prince Ernest beheld all this from a window, and was ready to die with jealousy and mortification, for he felt that Sidonia was gay and friendly with everyone but him. Indeed, since the day of the lute-playing, he fancied she shunned him and treated him coldly. But as Sidonia had observed particularly, that whenever the young Prince passed her in the gallery he cast down his eyes and sighed, she took another way of managing him.

Chapter VI

How the young Prince prepared a petition to his mother, the Duchess, in favor of Sidonia — Item, of the strange doings of the Laplander with his magic drum

*T*he day preceding that on which Sidonia was to repeat the Catechism of Doctor Gerschovius (of which, by the way, she had not learned one word), the young Duke suddenly entered his mother's apartment, where she and her maidens were spinning, and asked her if she remembered anything about a Laplander with a drum, who had foretold some event to her and his father whilst they were at Penemunde some years before; for he had been arrested at Eldena, and was now in Wolgast.

"Alas!" said her Grace, "I perfectly remember the horrible sorcerer. One spring I was at the hunt with your father near Penemunde, when this wretch suddenly appeared driving two cows before him on a large ice-field. He pretended that while he was telling fortunes to the girls who milked the cows, a great storm arose, and drove him out into the wide sea, which was a terrible misfortune to him. But your father told him in Swedish, which language the knave knew, that it had been better to prophesy his own destiny. To which he replied, a man could as little foretell his own fate as see the back of his own head, which everyone can see but himself. However, if the Duke wished, he would tell him his fortune, and if it did not come out true, let all the world hold him as a liar for his life long.

"Alas! your father consented. Whereupon the knave began to dance and play upon his drum like one frenzied; so that it was evident to see the spirit was working within him. Then he fell down like one dead, and cried, 'Woe to thee when thy house is burning! Woe to thee when thy house is burning!'

"Therefore be warned, my son; have nothing to do with this fellow, for it so happened even as he said. On the 11th December '57, our castle was burned, and your poor father had a rib broken in consequence. Would that I had been the rib broken for him, so that he might still reign over the land; and this was the true cause of his untimely death. Therefore dismiss this sorcerer, for it is Satan himself speaks in him."

Here Sidonia grew quite pale, and dropped the thread, as if taken suddenly ill. Then she prayed the Duchess to excuse her, and permit her to retire to her own room.

The moment the Duchess gave permission, Sidonia glided out; but, in place of going to her chamber, she threw herself in a languid attitude upon a seat in the corridor, just where she knew Prince Ernest must pass, and leaned her head upon her hand. He soon came out of his mother's room, and seeing Sidonia, took her hand tenderly, asking, with visible emotion —

"Dear lady, what has happened?"

"Ah," she answered, "I am so weak that I cannot go on to my little apartment. I know not what ails me; but I am so afraid —"

"Afraid of what, dearest lady?"

"Of that sour old priest. He is to examine me tomorrow in the Catechism of Gerschovius, and I cannot learn a word of it, do what I will. I know Luther's Catechism quite well" (this was a falsehood, we know), "but that does not satisfy him, and if I cannot repeat it he will slap my hands or box my ears, and my lady the Duchess will be more angry than ever; but I am too old now to learn catechisms."

Then she trembled like an aspen-leaf, and fixed her eyes on him with such tenderness that he trembled likewise, and drawing her arm within his, supported her to her chamber. On the way she pressed his hand repeatedly; but with each pressure, as he afterwards confessed, a pang shot through his heart, which might have excited compassion from his worst enemy.

When they reached her chamber, she would not let him enter, but modestly put him back, saying, "Leave me — ah! leave me, gracious Prince. I must creep to my bed; and in the meantime let me entreat you to persuade the priest not to torment me tomorrow morning."

The Prince now left her, and forgetting all about the Lapland wizard whom he had left waiting in the courtyard, he rushed over the draw-bridge, up the main street behind St. Peter's, and into the house of Dr. Gerschovius.

The doctor was indignant at his petition.

"My young Prince," he said, "if ever a human being stood in need of God's Word, it is that young maiden." At last, however, upon the entreaties of Prince Ernest, he consented to defer her examination for four weeks, during which time she could fully perfect herself in the catechism of his learned brother.

He then prayed the Prince not to allow his eyes to be dazzled by this fair, sinful beauty, who would delude him as she had done all the other men in the castle, not excepting even that old sinner Zitsewitz.

When the Prince returned to the castle, he found a great crowd assembled round the Lapland wizard, all eagerly asking to have their fortunes told, and Sidonia was amongst them, as merry and lively as if nothing had ailed her. When the Prince expressed his surprise, she said, that finding herself much relieved by lying down, she had ventured into the fresh air, to recreate herself, and have her fortune told. Would not the Prince likewise wish to hear his?

So, forgetting all his mother's wise injunctions, he advanced with Sidonia to the wizard. The Lapland drum, which lay upon his knees, was a strange instrument; and by it we can see what arts Satan employs to strengthen his kingdom in all places and by all means. For the Laplanders are Christians, though they in some sort worship the devil, and therefore he imparts to them much of his own power. This drum which they use is made out of a piece of hollow wood, which must be either fir, pine, or birch, and which grows in such a particular place that it follows the course of the sun; that is, the pectines, fibræ, and lineæ in the annual rings of the wood must wind from right to left. Having hollowed out such a tree, they spread a skin over it, fastened down with little pegs; and on the center of the skin is painted the sun, surrounded by figures of men, beasts, birds, and fishes, along with Christ and the holy Apostles. All this is done with the rind of the elder tree, chewed first beneath their teeth. Upon the top of the drum there is an index in the shape of a triangle, from which hang a number of little rings and chains. When the wizard wishes to propitiate Satan and receive his power, he strikes the drum with a hammer made of the reindeer's horn, not so much to procure a sound as to set the index in motion with all its little chains, that it may move over the figures, and point to whatever gives the required answer. At the same time the magician murmurs conjurations, springs sometimes up from the ground, screams, laughs, dances, reels, becomes black in the face, foams, twists his eyes, and falls to the ground at last in an ecstasy, dragging the drum down upon his face.

Anyone may then put questions to him, and all will come to pass that he answers. All this was done by the wizard; but he desired strictly that when he fell upon the ground, no one should touch him with the foot, and secondly, that all flies and insects should be kept carefully from him. So after he had danced, and screamed, and twisted his face so horribly that half the women fainted, and foamed and raged until the demon seemed to have taken full possession of him, he fell down, and then everyone put questions to him, to which he responded; but the answers sometimes produced weeping, sometimes laughing, according as some gentle maiden heard that her lover was safe, or that he had been struck by the mast on shipboard and tumbled into the sea. And all came out true, as was afterwards proved.

Sidonia now invited the Prince to try his fortune; and so, forgetting the admonitions of the Duchess, he said, "What dost thou prophesy to me?"

"Beware of a woman, if you would live long and happily," was the answer.

"But of what woman?"

"I will not name her, for she is present."

Then the Prince turned pale and looked at Sidonia, who grew pale also, but made no answer, only laughed, and advancing asked, "What dost thou prophesy to me?" But immediately the wizard shrieked, "Away! away! I burn, I burn! thou makest me yet hotter than I am!"

Many thought these exclamations referred to Sidonia's beauty, particularly the young lords, who murmured, "Now everyone must acknowledge her beauty, when even this son of Satan feels his heart burning when she approaches." And Sidonia laughed merrily at their gallantries.

Just then the Grand Chamberlain came by, and having heard what had happened, he angrily dismissed the crowd, and sending for the executioner, ordered the cheating impostor to be whipped and branded, and then sent over the frontier.

The wizard, who had been lying quite stiff, now cried out (though he had never seen the Chamberlain before) — "Listen, Ulrich! I will prophesy something to thee: if it comes not to pass, then punish me; but if it does, then give me a boat and seven loaves, that I may sail away tomorrow to my own country."

Ulrich refused to hear his prophecy; but the wizard cried out — "Ulrich, this day thy wife Hedwig will die at Spantekow."

Ulrich grew pale, but only answered, "Thou liest! how can that be?" He replied, "Thy cousin Clas will visit her; she will descend to the cellar to fetch him some of the Italian wine for which you wrote, and which arrived yesterday; a step of the stairs will break as she is ascending; she will fall forward upon the flask, which will cut her throat through, and so she will die."

When he ceased, the alarmed Ulrich called loudly to the chief equerry, Appelmann, who just then came by — "Quick! saddle the best racer in the stables, and ride for life to Spantekow, for it may be as he has prophesied, and let us outwit the devil. Haste, haste, for the love of God, and I will never forget it to thee!"

So the equerry rode without stop or stay to Spantekow, and he found the cousin Clas in the house; but when he asked for the Lady Hedwig, they said, "She is in the cellar." So no misfortune had happened then; but as they waited and she appeared not, they descended to look for her, and lo! just as the wizard had prophesied, she had fallen upon the stairs while ascending, and there lay dead.

The mournful news was brought by sunset to Wolgast, and Ulrich, in his despair and grief, wished to burn the Laplander; but Prince Ernest hindered him, saying, "It is more knightly, Ulrich, to keep your word than to cool your vengeance." So the old man stood silent a long space, and then said, "Well, young man, if you abandon Sidonia, I will release the Laplander."

The Prince colored, and the Lord Chamberlain thought that he had discovered a secret; but as the prophecy of the wizard came again into Prince Ernest's mind, he said —

"Well, Ulrich, I will give up the maiden Sidonia. Here is my hand."

Accordingly, next morning the wizard was released from prison and given a boat, with seven loaves and a pitcher of water, that he might sail back to his own country. The wind, however, was due north, but the people who crossed the bridge to witness his departure were filled with fear when they saw him change the wind at his pleasure to suit himself; for he pulled out a string full of knots, and having swung it about, murmuring incantations, all the vanes on the towers creaked and whirled right about, all the windmills in the town stopped, all the vessels and boats that were going up the stream became quite still, and their sails flapped on the masts, for the wind had changed in a moment from north to south, and the north waves and the south waves clashed together.

As everyone stood wondering at this, the sailors and fishermen in particular, the wizard sprang into his boat and set forth with a fair wind, singing loudly, "Jooike Duara! Jooike Duara!"* and soon disappeared from sight, nor was he ever again seen in that country.

Chapter VII

*How Ulrich von Schwerin buries his spouse, and Doctor Gerschovius
comforts him out of God's Word*

*T*his affair with the Lapland wizard much troubled the Grand Chamberlain, and his faith suffered sore temptations. So he referred to Dr. Gerschovius, and asked him how the prophets of God differed from those of the devil. Whereupon the doctor recommended him to meditate on God's Word, wherein he would find a source of consolation and a solution of all doubts.

So the mourning Ulrich departed for his castle of Spantekow, trusting in the assistance of God. And her Grace, with all her court, resolved to attend the funeral also, to do him honor. They proceeded forth, therefore, dressed in black robes, their horses also caparisoned with black

---

* This is the beginning of a magic rhyme, chanted even by the distant Calmucks — namely, *Dschie jo eie jog.*

hangings, and the Duchess ordered a hundred wax lights for the ceremony. Sidonia alone declined attending, and gave out that she was sick
in bed. The truth, however, was, that as Duke Ernest was obliged to
remain at home to take the command of the castle, and affix his
signature to all papers, she wished to remain also.

The mourning cortège, therefore, had scarcely left the court, when
Sidonia rose and seated herself at the window, which she knew the young
Prince must pass along with his attendants on their way to the office of
the castle. Then taking up a lute, which she had purchased privately,
and practiced night and morning in place of learning the catechism,
she played a low, soft air, to attract their attention. So all the young
knights looked up; and when Prince Ernest arrived he looked up also,
and seeing Sidonia, exclaimed, with surprise, "Beautiful Sidonia, how
have you learned the lute?" At which she blushed and answered modestly, "Gracious Prince, I am only self-taught. No one here understands
the lute except your Highness."

"Does this employment, then, give you much pleasure?"

"Ah, yes! If I could only play it well; I would give half my life to learn
it properly. There is no such sweet enjoyment upon earth, I think, as
this."

"But you have been sick, lady, and the cold air will do you an injury."

"Yes, it is true I have been ill, but the air rather refreshes me; and
besides, I feel the melancholy of my solitude less here."

"Now farewell, dear lady; I must attend to the business of the castle."

This little word — "dear lady" — gave Sidonia such confidence, that
by the time she expected Prince Ernest to pass again on his return, she
was seated at the window awaiting him with her lute, to which she now
sang in a clear, sweet voice. But the Prince passed on as if he heard
nothing — never even once looked up, to Sidonia's great mortification.
However, the moment he reached his own apartment, he commenced
playing a melancholy air upon his lute, as if in response to hers. The
artful young maiden no sooner heard this than she opened her door.
The Prince at the same instant opened his to let out the smoke, and
their eyes met, when Sidonia uttered a feeble cry and fell fainting upon
the floor. The Prince, seeing this, flew to her, raised her up, and
trembling with emotion, carried her back to her room and laid her down
upon the bed. Now indeed it was well for him that he had given that
promise to Ulrich. When Sidonia after some time slowly opened her
eyes, the Prince asked tenderly what ailed her; and she said, "I must have
taken cold at the window, for I felt very ill, and went to the door to call
an attendant; but I must have fainted then, for I remember nothing
more." Alas! the poor Prince, he believed all this, and conjured her to

lie down until he called a maid, and sent for the physician if she desired it; but, no — she refused, and said it would pass off soon. (Ah, thou cunning maiden! it may well pass off when it never was on.)

However, she remained in bed until the next day, when the Princess and her train returned home from the funeral. Her Grace had assisted at the obsequies with all princely state, and even laid a crown of rosemary with her own hand upon the head of the corpse, and a little prayer-book beside it, open at that fine hymn "Pauli Sperati" (which also was sung over the grave). Then the husband laid a tin crucifix on the coffin, with the inscription from I John iii. 8 — "The Son of God was manifested that He might destroy the works of the devil." After which the coffin was lowered into the grave with many tears.

Some days after this, being Sunday, Doctor Gerschovius and the Grand Chamberlain were present at the ducal table. Ulrich indeed ate little, for he was filled with grief, only sipped a little broth, into which he had crumbled some reindeer cheese, not to appear ungracious; but when dinner was over, he raised his head, and asked Doctor Gerschovius to inform him now in what lay the difference between the prophets of God and those of the devil. The Duchess was charmed at the prospect of such a profitable discourse, and ordered a cushion and footstool to be placed for herself, that she might remain to hear it. Then she sent for the whole household — maidens, squires, and pages — that they too might be edified, and learn the true nature of the devil's gifts. The hall was soon as full, therefore, as if a sermon were about to be preached; and the doctor, seeing this, stroked his beard, and he begun as follows:*

---

* Perhaps some readers will hold the rationalist doctrine that no prophecy is possible or credible, and that no mortal can under any circumstances see into futurity; but how then can they account for the wonderful phenomena of animal magnetism, which are so well authenticated? Do they deny all the facts which have been elicited by the great advance made recently in natural and physiological philosophy? I need not here bring forward proofs from the ancients, showing their universal belief in the possibility of seeing into futurity, nor a cloud of witnesses from our modern philosophers, attesting the truth of the phenomena of somnambulism, but only observe that this very Academy of Paris, which in 1784 anathematized Mesmer as a quack, a cheat, and a charlatan or fool, and which in conjunction with all the academies of Europe (that of Berlin alone excepted) reviled his doctrines and insulted all who upheld them, as witches had been reviled in preceding centuries, and compelled Mesmer himself to fly for protection to Frankfort — this very academy, I say, on the 12th February 1826, rescinded all their condemnatory verdicts, and proclaimed that the wonderful phenomena of animal magnetism had been so well authenticated that doubt was no longer possible. This confession of faith was the more remarkable, because the members of the commission of inquiry had been carefully selected, on purpose, from physicians who were totally adverse to the doctrines of Mesmer.

strange and unknown depths of our own nature which magnetism has opened to us.

I am rejoiced to treat of this subject now, considering how lately that demon Lapp befooled ye all. And I shall give you many signs, whereby in future a prophet of God may be distinguished from a prophet of the devil. 1st, Satan's prophets are not conscious of what they utter; but God's prophets are always perfectly conscious, both of the inspiration they receive and the revelations they make known. For as the Laplander grew frenzied, and foamed at the mouth, so it has been with all false prophets from the beginning. Even the blind heathen called prophesying *mania*, or the wisdom of *madness*. The secret of producing this madness was known to them; sometimes it was by the use of roots or aromatic herbs, or by exhalations, as in the case of the Pythoness, whose incoherent utterances were written by the priests of Apollo, for when the fit was over, all remembrance of what she had prophesied vanished too. In the Bible we find all false prophets described as frenzied. In Isaiah xliv. 25 – "God maketh the diviners mad." In Ezekiel xiii. 3 – "Woe to the foolish prophets." Hosea ix. 7 – "The prophet is a fool, the spiritual man is mad." And Isaiah xxviii. 7 explains fully how this madness was produced.

Namely, by wine and the strong drink *Sekar*.* Further examples of this madness are given in the Bible, as Saul when under the influence

---

There are but two modes, I think, of explaining these extraordinary phenomena – either by supposing them effected by supernatural agency, as all seers and diviners from antiquity, through the Middle Ages down to our somnambulists, have pretended that they really stood in communication with spirit; or, by supposing that there is an innate latent divining element in our own natures, which only becomes evident and active under certain circumstances, and which is capable of revealing the *future* with more or less exactitude just as the mind can recall the *past*. For *past* and *future* are but different forms of our own subjective intuition of time, and because this internal intuition represents no figure, we seek to supply the defect by an analogy. For time exists *within* us, not *without* us; it is not something which subsists of itself, but it is the form only of our internal sense.

These two modes of explaining the phenomena present, I know, great difficulties; the latter especially. However, the pantheistical solution of the Hegelian school adopted by Kieser, Kluge, Wirth, Hoffman, pleases me still less. I even prefer that of Jung-Stilling and Kerner – but at all events one thing is certain, the *facts* are there; only ignorance, stupidity, and obstinacy can deny them. The *cause* is still a subject of speculation, doubt, and difficulty. It is only by a vast induction of facts, as in natural philosophy, that we can ever hope to arrive at the knowledge of a general law. The crown of all creation is *man*; therefore while we investigate so acutely all other creatures, let us not shrink back from the

* It is doubtful of what this drink was composed. Hieronymus and Aben Ezra imagine that it was of the nature of strong beer. Probably it resembled the potion with which the mystery-men amongst the savages of the present day produce this divining

of the evil spirit flung his spear at the innocent David; and the four hundred and fifty prophets of Baal, who leaped upon the altar, and screamed, and cut themselves with knives and lancets until the blood flowed; and the maiden with the spirit of divination, that met Paul in the streets of Philippi; with many others.

But all this is an abomination in the sight of God. For as the Lord came not to His prophet Elijah in the strong wind, nor in the earth-quake, nor in the fire, but in the still small voice, so does He evidence Himself in all His prophets; and we find no record in Scripture, either of their madness, or of their having forgotten the oracles they uttered, like the Pythoness and others inspired by Satan.* Further, you may observe that the false prophets can always prophesy when they choose, Satan is ever willing to come when they exorcise him; but the true prophets of God are but instruments in the hand of the Lord, and can only speak when He chooses the spirit to enter into them. So we find them saying invariably – "This is the word which came unto me," or "This is the word which the Lord spake unto me." For the Lord is too high and holy to come at the bidding of a creature, or obey the summons of his will. St. Peter confirms this, 2 Pet. i. 21, that no prophecy ever came at the will of man.

Again, the false prophets were persons of known infamous character, and in this differed from the prophets of God, who were always righteous men in word and deed. Diodorus informs us of the conduct of the Pythoness and the priests of Apollo, and also that all oracles were bought with gold, and the answer depended on the weight of the sack. As Ezekiel notices, xiii. 19; and Micah iii. 8. Further, the holy prophets suffered all manner of persecution for the sake of God, as Daniel, Elias, Micah, yet remained faithful, with but one exception, and were severely punished if they fell into crime, and the gift of prophecy taken from them; for God cannot dwell in a defiled temple, but Satan can dwell in no other.

Also, Satan's prophets speak only of temporal things, but God's people of spiritual things. The heathen oracles, for instance, never foretold any events but those concerning peace or war, or what men

---

frenzy. We find such in use throughout Tartary, Siberia, America, and Africa, as if the usage had descended to them from one common tradition. Witches, it is well known, made frequent use of potions, and as all somnambulists assert that the seat of the soul's greatest activity is in the stomach, it is not incredible what Van Helmont relates, that having once tasted the root *napellus,* his intellect all at once, accompanied by an unusual feeling of ecstasy, seemed to remove from his brain to his stomach.

* It is well known that somnambulists never remember upon their recovery what they have uttered during the crisis. Therefore phenomena of this class appear to belong, in some things, to that of the divining frenzy, though in others to quite a different category of the divining life.

desire in riches, health, or advancement — in short, temporal matters alone. Whereas God's people, in addition to temporal concerns, preached repentance and holiness to the Jewish people, and the coming of Christ's kingdom, in whom all nations should be blessed. For as the soul is superior to the body, so are God's prophets superior to those of the Prince of this world.

And in conclusion, observe that Satan's seers abounded with lies, as all heathen history testifies, or their oracles were capable of such different interpretations that they became a subject of mockery and contempt to the wise amongst the ancient philosophers. But be not surprised if they sometimes spoke truth, as the Lapland wizard has done, for the devil's power is superior to man's, and he can see events which, though close at hand, are yet hidden from us, as a father can foretell an approaching storm, though his little son cannot do so, and therefore looks upon his father's wisdom as supernatural.* But the devil has not the power to see into futurity, nor even the angels of God, only God Himself.

The prophets of God, on the contrary, are given power by Him to look through all time at a glance, as if it were but a moment; for a thousand years to Him are but as a watch of the night; and therefore they all from the beginning testified of the Saviour that was to come, and rejoiced in His day as if they really beheld Him, and all stood together as brothers in one place, and at the same time in His blessed presence. But what unanimity and feeling has ever been observed by the seers of Satan, when the contradictions amongst their oracles were notorious to everyone?

And as the eyes of all the holy prophets centered upon Christ, so the eyes of the greatest of all prophets penetrated the furthest depths of futurity. Not only His own life, sufferings, death, and resurrection were foretold by Him, but the end of the Jewish kingdom, the dispersion of their race, the rise of His Church from the grain of mustard-seed to the wide, world-spreading tree; and all has been fulfilled. Be assured, therefore, that this eternal glory, which He promised to those who trust in Him, will be fulfilled likewise when He comes to judge all nations. So, my worthy Lord Ulrich, cease to weep for your spouse who sleeps in Jesus, for a greater Prophet than the Lapland wizard has said, "I am the resurrection and the life, whosoever believeth in Me shall never die."†

---

* The somnambulists also can prophesy of those events which are near at hand, but never of the distant.

† In addition to the foregoing distinctions between the Satanic and the holy prophets, I may add the following — that almost all the diviners amongst the heathen were *women*. For instance, Cassandra, the Pythia in Delphi, Triton and Peristhæa in

Chapter VIII

How Sidonia rides upon the pet stag, and what evil consequences result therefrom

W hen the discourse had ended, her Grace retired to her apartment and Ulrich to his, for it was their custom, as I have said, to sleep after dinner. Doctor Gerschovius returned home, and the young Prince descended to the gardens with his lute. Now was a fine time for the young knights, for they had been sadly disturbed in their carouse by that godly prophesying of the doctor's, and they now returned to their own quarter to finish it, headed by the old treasurer Zitsewitz. Then a merry uproar of laughing, singing, and jesting commenced, and as the door lay wide open as usual, Sidonia heard all from her chamber; so stepping out gently with a piece of bread in her hand, she tripped along the corridor past their door. No sooner was she perceived than a loud storm of cheers greeted her, which she returned with smiles and bows, and then danced down the steps to the courtyard. Several rose up to pursue her, amongst whom Wedig and Appelmann were the most eager.

But they were too late, and saw nothing but the tail of her dress as she flew round the corner into the second court. Just then an old laundress, bringing linen to the castle for her Highness, passed by, and told the young men that the young lady had been feeding the tame stag

---

Dodona, the Sybils, the Velleda of Tacitus, the Mandragoras, and Druidesses, the witches of the Reformation age; and in fine, the modern somnambules are all women too. But throughout the whole Bible we find that the prophetic power was exclusively conferred upon *men*, with two exceptions — namely, Deborah, Judges iv. 4, and Hilda, 2 Chron. xxxiv. 22 — for there is no evidence that Miriam had a seer spirit; she was probably only God-inspired, though classed under the general term prophet. We find, indeed, that woe was proclaimed against the divining women who prophesy out of their own head, Ezekiel xiii. 17-23; so amongst the people of God the revelation of the future was confined to *men*, amongst the heathen to *women*, or if men are mentioned in these pagan rites, it is only as assistants and inferior agents, like animals, metals, roots, stones, and such like. See Cicero, *De Divinatione*, i. 18.

with bread, and then jumped on its back while she held the horns, and that the animal had immediately galloped off like lightning into the second court; so that the young knights and squires rushed instantly after her, fearing that some accident might happen, and presently they heard her scream twice. Appelmann was the first to reach the outer court, and there beheld poor Sidonia in a sad condition, for the stag had flung her off. Fortunately it was on a heap of soft clay, and there she lay in a dead faint.

Had the stag thrown her but a few steps further, against the manger for the knights' horses, she must have been killed. But Satan had not yet done with her, and therefore, no doubt, prepared this soft pillow for her head.

When Appelmann saw that she was quite insensible, he kneeled down and kissed first her little feet, then her white hands, and at last her lips, while she lay at the time as still as death, poor thing. Just then Wedig came up in a great passion; for the castellan's son, who was playing ball, had flung the ball right between his legs, out of tricks, as he was running by, and nearly threw him down, whereupon Wedig seized hold of the urchin by his thick hair to punish him, for all the young knights were laughing at his discomfiture; but the boy bit him in the hip, and then sprang into his father's house, and shut the door. How little do we know what will happen! It was this bite which caused Wedig's lamentable death a little after.

But if he was angry before, what was his rage now when he beheld the equerry, Appelmann, kissing the insensible maiden.

"How now, peasant," he cried, "what means this boldness? How dare this tailor's son treat a castle and land dowered maiden in such a way? Are noble ladies made for his kisses?" And he draws his poignard to rush upon Appelmann, who draws forth his in return, and now assuredly there would have been murder done, if Sidonia had not just then opened her eyes, and starting up in amazement prayed them for her sake to keep quiet. She had been quite insensible, and knew nothing at all of what had happened. The old treasurer, with the other young knights, came up now, and strove to make peace between the two rivals, holding them apart by force; but nothing could calm the jealous Wedig, who still cried, "Let me avenge Sidonia! — let me avenge Sidonia!" So that Prince Ernest, hearing the tumult in the garden, ran with his lute in his hand to see what had happened. When they told him, he grew as pale as a corpse that such an indignity should have been offered to Sidonia, and reprimanded his equerry severely, but prayed that all would keep quiet now, as otherwise the Duchess and the Lord Chamberlain would certainly be awakened out of their after-dinner sleep, and then what an afternoon they would all have. This calmed everyone, except the jealous Wedig, who, having drunk deeply, cried out still louder than before, "Let me go. I will give my life for the beautiful Sidonia. I will avenge the insolence of this peasant knave!"

When Sidonia observed all this, she felt quite certain that a terrible storm was brewing for all of them, and so she ran to shelter herself through the first open door that came in her way, and up into the second corridor; but further adventures awaited her here, for not being acquainted with this part of the castle, she ran direct into an old lumber-room, where she found, to her great surprise, a young man dressed in rusty armor, and wearing a helmet with a serpent crest upon his head. This was Hans von Marintzky, whose brain Sidonia had turned by reading the Amadis with him in the castle gardens, and as she had often sighed, and said that she, too, could have loved the serpent knight, the poor love-stricken Hans, taking this for a favorable sign, determined to disguise himself as described in the romance, and thus secure her love.

So when her beautiful face appeared at the door, Hans screamed for joy, like a young calf, and falling on one knee, exclaimed – "Adored Princess, your serpent knight is here to claim your love, and tender his hand to you in betrothal, for no other wife do I desire but thee; and if the Princess Rosaliana herself were here to offer me her love, I would strike her on the face."

Sidonia was rather thunderstruck, as one may suppose, and retreated a few steps, saying, "Stand up, dear youth; what ails you?"

"So I am dear to you," he cried, still kneeling; "I am then really dear to you, adored Princess? Ah! I hope to be yet dearer when I make you my spouse."

Sidonia had not foreseen this termination to their romance reading, but she suppressed her laughter, remembering how she had lost her lover Uckermann by showing scorn; so she drew herself up with dignity, and said, with as grave a face as a chief mourner –

"If you will not rise, sir knight, I must complain to her Highness; for I cannot be your spouse, seeing that I have resolved never to marry." (Ah! how willingly, how willingly you would have taken any husband half a year after.) "But if you will do me a service, brave knight, run instantly to the court, where Wedig and Appelmann are going to murder each other, and separate them, or my gracious lady and old Ulrich will awake, and then we shall all be punished."

The poor fool jumped up instantly, and exclaiming, "Death for my adored princess!" he sprung down the steps, though rather awkwardly, not being accustomed to the greaves; and rushing into the middle of the crowd, with his visor down, and the drawn sword in his hand, he began making passes at everyone that came in his way, crying, "Death for my adored princess! Long live the beautiful Sidonia! Knaves, have done with your brawling, or I shall lay you all dead at my feet."

At first everyone stuck up close by the wall when they saw the madman, to get out of reach of his sword, which he kept whirling about his head; but as soon as he was recognized by his voice, Wedig called out to him —

"Help, brother, help! Will you suffer that this peasant boor Appelmann should kiss the noble Sidonia as she lay there faint and insensible? Yet I saw him do this. So help me, relieve me, that I may brand this low-born knave for his daring."

"What? My adored princess!" exclaimed the serpent knight. "This valet, this groom, dared to kiss her? and I would think myself blessed but to touch her shoe-tie;" and he fell furiously upon Appelmann.

The uproar was now so great that it might have aroused the Duchess and Ulrich even from their last sleep, had they been in the castle.

But, fortunately, some time before the riot began, both had gone out by the little private gate, to attend afternoon service at St. Peter's Church, in the town. For the archdeacon was sick, and Doctor Gerschovius was obliged to take his place there. No one, therefore, was left in the castle to give orders or hold command; even the castellan had gone to hear service; and no one minded Prince Ernest, he was so young, besides being under tutelage; and as to old Zitsewitz, he was as bad as the worst of them himself.

The Prince threatened to have the castle bells rung if they were not quiet; and the uproar had indeed partially subsided just at the moment the serpent knight fell upon Appelmann. The Prince then ordered his equerry to leave the place instantly, under pain of his severe displeasure, for he saw that both had drunk rather deeply.

So Appelmann turned to depart as the Prince commanded, but Wedig, who had been relieved by Hans the serpent, sprung after him with his dagger, limping though, for the bite in his hip made him stiff. Appelmann darted through the little water-gate and over the bridge; the other pursued him; and Appelmann, seeing that he was foaming with rage, jumped over the rails into a boat. Wedig attempted to do the same, but being stiff from the bite, missed the boat, and came down plump into the water.

As he could not swim, the current carried him rapidly down the stream before the others had time to come up; but he was still conscious, and called to Hans, "Comrade, save me!" So Hans, forgetting his heavy cuirass, plunged in directly, and soon reached the drowning man. Wedig, however, in his death-struggles, seized hold of him with such force that they both instantly disappeared. Then everyone sprang to the boats to try and save them; but being Sunday, the boats were all moored, so that by the time they were unfastened it was too late, and the two unfortunate young men had sunk forever.

What calamities may be caused by the levity and self-will of a beautiful woman! From the time of Helen of Troy up to the present moment, the world has known this well; but, alas! this was but the beginning of that tragedy which Sidonia played in Pomerania, as that other wanton did in Phrygia.

Let us hear the conclusion, however. Prince Ernest, now being truly alarmed, dispatched a messenger to the church for her Highness; but as Doctor Gerschovius had not yet ended his exordium, her Grace would by no means be disturbed, and desired the messenger to go to Ulrich, who no sooner heard the tidings than he rushed down to the water-gate. There he found a great crowd assembled, all eagerly trying, with poles and hooks, to fish out the bodies of the two young men; and one fellow even had tied a piece of barley bread to a rope, and flung it into the water — as the superstition goes that it will follow a corpse in the stream, and point to where it lies. And the women and children were weeping and lamenting on the bridge; but the old knight pushed them all aside with his elbows, and cried — "Thousand devils! what are ye all at here?"

Everyone was silent, for the young men had agreed not to betray Sidonia. Then Ulrich asked the Prince, who replied, that Marintzky, having put on some old armor to frighten the others, as he believed, they pursued him in fun over the bridge, and he and another fell over into the water. This was all he knew of the matter, for he was playing on the lute in the garden when the tumult began.

"Thousand devils!" cries Ulrich; "I cannot turn my back a moment but there must be a riot amongst the young fellows. Listen! young lord — when it comes to your turn to rule land and people, I counsel you, send all the young fellows to the devil. Away with them! they are a vain and dissolute crew. Get up the bodies, if you can; but, for my part, I would care little if a few more were baptized in the same way. Speak! some of you: who commenced this tavern broil? Speak! I must have an answer."

This adjuration had its effect, for a man answered — "Sidonia made the young men mad, and so it all happened." It was her own cousin, Marcus Bork, who spoke, for which reason Sidonia never could endure him afterwards, and finally destroyed him, as shall be related in due time.

When Ulrich found that Sidonia was the cause of all, he raged with fury, and commanded them to tell him all. When Marcus had related the whole affair, he swore by the seven thousand devils that he would make her remember it, and that he would instantly go up to her chamber.

But Prince Ernest stepped before him, saying, "Lord Ulrich, I have made you a promise — you must now make one to me: it is to leave this maiden in peace; she is not to blame for what has happened." But Ulrich would not listen to him.

"Then I withdraw my promise," said the Prince. "Now act as you think proper."

"Thousand devils! she had better give up that game," exclaimed Ulrich. However, he consented to leave her undisturbed, and departed with vehement imprecations on her head, just as the Duchess returned from church, and was seen advancing towards the crowd.

Chapter IX

How Sidonia makes the young Prince break his word — Item, how Clara von Dewitz in vain tries to turn her from her evil ways

*I*t may be easily conjectured what a passion her Grace fell into when the whole story was made known to her, and how she stormed against Sidonia. At last she entered the castle; but Prince Ernest, rightly suspecting her object, slipped up to the corridor, and met her just as she had reached Sidonia's chamber. Here he took her hand, kissed it, and prayed her not to disgrace the young maiden, for that she was innocent of all the evil that had happened.

But she pushed him away, exclaiming — "Thou disobedient son, have I not heard of thy gallantries with this girl, whom Satan himself has sent into my royal house? Shame on thee! One of thy noble station to take the part of a murderess!"

"But you have judged harshly, my mother. I never made love to the maiden. Leave her in peace, and do not make matters worse, or all the young nobles will fight to the death for her."

"Aye, and thou, witless boy, the first of all. Oh, that my beloved spouse, Philippus Primus, could rise from his grave — what would he say to his lost son, who, like the prodigal in Scripture, loves strange women and keeps company with brawlers!" (Weeping.)

"Who has said that I am a lost son?"

"Doctor Gerschovius and Ulrich both say it."

"Then I shall run the priest through the body, and challenge the knight to mortal combat, unless they both retract their words."

"No! stay, my son," said the Duchess; "I must have mistaken what they said. Stay, I command you!"

"Never! Unless Sidonia be left in peace, such deeds will be done today that all Pomerania will ring with them for years."

In short, the end of the controversy was, that the Duchess at last promised to leave Sidonia unmolested; and then retired to her chamber much disturbed, where she was soon heard singing the 109th psalm, with a loud voice, accompanied by the little spindle clock.

Sidonia, who was hiding in her room, soon heard of all that had happened, through the Duchess's maid, whom she kept in pay; — indeed, all the servants were her sworn friends, in consequence of the liberal largess she gave them; and even the young lords and knights were more distractedly in love with her than ever after the occurrences of the day, for her cunning turned everything to profit.

So next morning, having heard that Prince Ernest was going to Eldena to receive the dues, she watched for him, probably through the keyhole, knowing he must pass her door. Accordingly, just as he went by, she opened it, and presented herself to his eyes dressed in unusual elegance and coquetry, and wearing a short robe which showed her pretty little sandals. The Prince, when he saw the short robe, and that she looked so beautiful, blushed, and passed on quickly, turning away his head, for he remembered the promise he had given to Ulrich, and was afraid to trust himself near her.

But Sidonia stepped before him, and flinging herself at his feet, began to weep, murmuring, "Gracious Prince and Lord, accept my gratitude, for you alone have saved me, a poor young maiden, from destruction."

"Stand up, dear lady, stand up."

"Never until my tears fall upon your feet." And then she kissed his yellow silk hose ardently, continuing, "What would have become of me, a helpless, forlorn orphan, without your protection?"

Here the young Prince could no longer restrain his emotions; if he had pledged his word to the whole world, even to the great God Himself, he must have broken it. So he raised her up and kissed her, which she did not resist; only sighed, "Ah! if anyone saw us now, we would both be lost." But this did not restrain him, and he kissed her again and again, and pressed her to his heart, when she trembled, and murmured scarcely audibly, "Oh! why do I love you so! Leave me, my lord, leave me; I am miserable enough."

"Do you then love me, Sidonia? Oh! let me hear you say it once more. You love me, enchanting Sidonia!"

"Alas!" she whispered, while her whole frame trembled, "what have I foolishly said? Oh! I am so unhappy."

"Sidonia! tell me once again you love me. I cannot credit my happiness, for you are even more gracious with the young nobles than with me, and often have you martyred my heart with jealousy."

"Yes; I am courteous to them all, for so my father taught me, and said it was safer for a maiden so to be — but —"

"But what? Speak on."

"Alas!" and here she covered her face with her hands; but Prince Ernest pressed her to his heart, and kissed her, asking her again if she really loved him; and she murmured a faint "yes;" then as if the shame of such a confession had killed her, she tore herself from his arms, and sprang into her chamber. So the young Prince pursued his way to Eldena, but took so little heed about the dues that Ulrich shook his head over the receipts for half a year after.

When mid-day came, and the band struck up for dinner, Sidonia was prepared for a similar scene with the young knights, and, as she passed along the corridor, she gave them her white hand to kiss, glittering with diamonds, thanking them all for not having betrayed her, and praying them to keep her still in their favor, whereat they were all wild with ecstasy; but old Zitsewitz, not content with her hand, entreated for a kiss on her sweet ruby lips, which she granted, to the rage and jealousy of all the others, while he exclaimed, "O Sidonia, thou canst turn even an old man into a fool!"

And his words came true; for in the evening a dispute arose as to which of them Sidonia liked best, seeing that she uttered the same sweet things to all; and to settle it, five of them, along with the old fool Zitsewitz, went to Sidonia's room, and each in turn asked her hand in marriage; but she gave them all the same answer — that she had no idea then of marriage, she was but a young, silly creature, and would not know her own mind for ten years to come.

One good resulted from Sidonia's ride upon the stag: her promenades were forbidden, and she was restricted henceforth entirely to the women's quarter of the castle. Her Grace and she had frequent altercations; but with Clara she kept upon good terms, as the maiden was of so excellent and mild a disposition.

This peace, however, was destined soon to be broken; for though her Grace was silent in the presence of Sidonia, yet she never ceased complaining in private to the maids of honor of this artful wench, who had dared to throw her eyes upon Prince Ernest. So at length they asked why her Highness did not dismiss the girl from her service.

"That must be done," she replied, "and without delay. For that purpose, indeed, I have written to Duke Barnim, and also to the father of the girl, at Stramehl, acquainting them with my intention."

Clara now gently remonstrated, saying that a little Christian instruction might yet do much for the poor young sinner, and that if she did not become good and virtuous under the care of her Grace, where else could she hope to have her changed?

"I have tried all Christian means," said her Grace, "but in vain. The ears of the wicked are closed to the Word of God."

"But let her Grace recollect that this poor sinner was endowed with extraordinary beauty, and therefore it was no fault of hers if the young men all grew deranged for love of her."

Here a violent tumult, and much scornful laughing, arose amongst the other maids of honor; and one Anna Lepels exclaimed — "I cannot imagine in what Sidonia's wonderful beauty consists. When she flatters the young men, and makes free with them as they are passing to dinner, what marvel if they all run after her? Any girl might have as many lovers if she chose to adopt such manners."

Clara made no reply, but turning to her Grace, said with her permission she would leave her spinning for a while, to visit Sidonia in her room, who perhaps would hearken to her advice, as she meant kindly to her.

"You may go," said her Grace; "but what do you mean to do? I tell you, advice is thrown away on her."

"Then I will threaten her with the Catechism of Doctor Gerschovius, which she must repeat on Sunday, for I know that she is greatly afraid of that and the clergyman."

"And you think you will frighten her into giving up running after the young men?"

"Oh yes, if I tell her that she will be publicly reprimanded unless she can say it perfectly."

So her Grace allowed her to depart, but with something of a weak faith.

Although Sidonia had absented herself from the spinning, on the pretext of learning the catechism quietly in her own room, yet, when Clara entered, no one was there except the maid, who sat upon the floor at her work. She knew nothing about the young lady; but as she heard a great deal of laughter and merriment in the court beneath, it was likely Sidonia was not far off. On stepping to the window, Clara indeed beheld Sidonia.

In the middle of the court was a large horse-pond built round with stones, to which the water was conducted by metal pipes communicating with the river Peene. In the middle of the pond was a small island, upon which a bear was kept chained. A plank was now thrown across the pond to the island; upon this Sidonia was standing feeding the bear with bread, which Appelmann, who stood beside her, first dipped into a can of syrup, and several of the young squires stood round them laughing and jesting.

The idle young pages were wont to take great delight in shooting at the bear with blunt arrows, and when it growled and snarled, then they would calm it again by throwing over bits of bread steeped in honey or syrup. So Sidonia, waiting to see the fun, had got upon the plank ready to give the bread just as the bear had got to the highest pitch of irritation, when he would suddenly change his growling into another sort of speech after his fashion. All this amused Sidonia mightily, and she laughed and clapped her hands with delight.

When the modest Clara beheld all this, and how Sidonia danced up and down on the plank, while the water splashed over her robe, she called to her — "Dear Lady Sidonia, come hither: I have somewhat to tell thee." But she answered tartly — "Dear Lady Clara, keep it then: I am too young to be told everything." And she danced up and down on the plank as before.

After many vain entreaties, Clara had at length to descend and seize the wild bird by the wing — I mean thereby the arm — and carry her off to the castle. The young men would have followed, but they were engaged to attend his Highness on a fishing excursion that afternoon, and were obliged to go and see after their nets and tackle. So the two maidens could walk up and down the corridor undisturbed; and Clara asked if she had yet learned the catechism.

Illa. — "No; I have no wish to learn it."

Hæc. — "But if the priest has to reprimand you publicly from the pulpit?"

Illa. — "I counsel him not to do it."

Hæc. — "Why, what would you do to him?"

Illa. — "He will find that out."

Hæc. — "Dear Sidonia, I wish you well; and therefore let me tell you that not only the priest, but our gracious lady, and all the noble maidens of the court, are sad and displeased that you should make so free with the young men, and entice them to follow you, as I have seen but too often myself. Do it not, dear Sidonia I mean well by you; — do it not. It will injure your reputation."

Illa. — "Ha! you are jealous now, you little pious housesparrow, that the young men do not run after you too. How can I help it?"

Hæc. — "Every maiden can help it; were she as beautiful as could be seen, she can help it. Leave off, Sidonia, or evil will come of it, particularly as her Grace has heard that you are seeking to entice our young lord the Prince. See, I tell you the pure truth, that it may turn you from your light courses. Tell me, what can you mean by it? — for when noble youths demand your hand in marriage, you reject them, and say you never mean to marry. Can you think that our gracious Prince, a son of Pomerania, will make thee his duchess — thou who art only a common nobleman's daughter?"

Illa. — "A common nobleman's daughter! — that is good from the peasant-girl. You are common enough and low enough, I warrant; but my blood is as old as that of the Dukes of Pomerania, and besides, I am a castle and land dowered maiden. But who are you? who are you? Your forefathers were hunted out of Mecklenburg, and only got footing here in Pomerania out of charity."

Hæc. — "Do not be angry, dear lady — you say true; yet I must add that my forebears were once Counts in Mecklenburg, and from their loyalty to the Dukes of Pomerania were given possessions here in Daber, where they have been lords of castles and lands for two hundred and fifty years. Yet I will confess that your race is nobler than mine; but, dear child, I make no boast of my ancestry, nor is it fitting for either of us to do so. The right royal Prince, who is given as an example and model to us all — who is Lord, not over castle and land, but of the heavens and the earth — the Saviour, Jesus Christ — He took no account of His arms or His ancestry, though the whole starry universe was His banner. He was as humble to the little child as to the learned doctors in the temple — to the chiefs among the people, as to the trembling sinner and the blind beggar Bartimæus. Let us take, then, this Prince for our example, and mind our life long what He says — 'Come unto Me, and learn of Me, for I am meek and lowly of heart.' Will you not learn of Him, dear lady? I will, if God give me grace."

And she extended her hand to Sidonia, who dashed it away, crying — "Stuff! nonsense! you have learned all this twaddle from the priest, who, I know, is nephew to the shoe-maker in Daber, and therefore hates anyone who is above him in rank."

Clara was about to reply mildly; but they happened now to be standing close to the public flight of steps, and a peasant-girl ran up when she saw them, and flung herself at Clara's feet, entreating the young lady to save her, for she had run away from Daber, where they were going to burn her as a witch. The pious Clara recoiled in horror, and desiring her to rise, said — "Art thou Anne Wolde, some time keeper of the swine to my father? How fares it with my dearest father and my mother?"

They were well when she ran away, but she had been wandering now for fourteen days on the road, living upon roots and wild berries, or what the herds gave her out of their knapsacks for charity.

Hæc. — "What crime wast thou suspected of, girl, to be condemned to so terrible a death?"

Illa. — "She had a lover named Albert, who followed her everywhere, but as she would not listen to him he hated her, and pretended that she had given him a love-drink."

Here Sidonia laughed aloud, and asked if she knew how to brew the love-drink?

Illa. — "Yes; she learned from her elder sister how to make it, but had never tried it with anyone, and was perfectly innocent of all they charged her with."

Here Clara shook her head, and wished to get rid of the witch-girl; for she thought, truly if Sidonia learns the brewing secret, she will poison and destroy the whole castleful, and we shall have the devil bodily with us in earnest. So she pushed away the girl, who still clung to her, weeping and lamenting. Hereupon Sidonia grew quite grave and pious all of a sudden, and said —

"See the hypocrite she is! She first sets before me the example of Christ, and then treats this poor sinner with nothing but cross thorns! Has not Christ said, 'Blessed are the merciful, for they shall obtain mercy'? But only see how this bigot can have Christ on her tongue, but not in her heart!"

The pious Clara grew quite ashamed at such talk, and raising up the wretch who had again fallen on her knees, said —

"Well, thou mayest remain; so get thee to my maid, and she will give thee food. I shall also write to my father for thy pardon, and meanwhile ask leave from her Grace to allow thee to remain here until it arrives;

but if thou art guilty, I cannot promise thee my protection any longer, and thou wilt be burned here, in place of at Daber."

So the witch-girl was content, and importuned them no further.

Chapter X

How Sidonia Wished to learn the mystery of love-potions, but is hindered by Clara and the young Prince

*W*hen Prince Ernest returned home after an absence of some days, Sidonia had changed her tactics, for now she never lifted up her eyes when they met, but passed on blushing and confused, and in place of speaking, as formerly, only sighed. This turned his head completely, and sent the blood so quickly through his veins that he found it a hard matter to conceal his feelings any longer. For this reason he determined to visit Sidonia in her own room as soon as he could hit upon a favorable opportunity, and bring her then a beautiful lute, inlaid with gold and silver, which he had purchased for her at Grypswald.

Now, it happened soon after, that her Grace and Clara went away one day into the town to purchase a jerkin for the little Prince Casimir, who accompanied them. Sidonia was immediately informed of their absence, and sought out Clara's maid without delay, put a piece of gold into her hand, and said —

"Send the strange girl from Daber to my room for a few minutes; she can perhaps give me some tidings of my dear father and family, for Daber is only a little way from Stramehl. But mind," she added, "keep this visit a secret, as well from her Grace as from your mistress Clara; otherwise we shall all be scolded."

So the maid very willingly complied, and brought the witch-girl directly to Sidonia's little apartment, and then ran to Clara's room to watch for the return of her Grace in time to give notice.

The witch-girl was quite confounded (as she afterwards confessed upon the rack) when Sidonia began —

"Thou knowest, Anne, that my entreaties alone obtained thee a shelter here, for I pitied thee from the first; and from what I hear, it is certain that her Grace means to deal no better with thee than thy judges at Daber, therefore my advice is — escape if thou canst."

Illa, weeping. — "Where can I go? I shall die of hunger, or they will arrest me again as an evil-minded witch, and carry me back to Daber."

"But do not tell them, stupid goose, that thou hast come from Daber."

Illa. — "But what could she say? Besides, she had no money, and so must be lost and ruined forever."

"Well, I shall give thee gold enough to get thee through all dangers. I give it, mind, out of pure Christian charity; but now tell me honestly — canst thou really make a love-drink?"

Illa. — "Yes; her sister had taught her."

"Is the drink of equal power for men and women?"

Illa. — "Yes; without doubt, it would make either mad with love."

"Has it ever an injurious effect upon them? does it take away their strength?"

Illa. — "Yes; they fall down like flies. Some lose their memory, others become blind or lame."

"Has she ever tried its effects upon anyone herself?"

Illa. — "But will the lady betray me?"

"Out, fool! When I have promised thee gold enough to insure thy escape! I betray thee!"

Illa. — "Then she will tell the lady the whole truth. She did give a love-drink to Albert, because he grew cross, and spent the nights away from her, and complained if she idled a little, so that her master beat her. Therefore she determined to punish him, and a rash came out over his whole body, so that he could neither sit nor lie for six weeks, and at night he had to be tied to a post with a hand-towel; but all this time his love for her grew so burning, that although he had previously hated and beaten her, yet now if she only brought him a drink of cold water, for which he was always screaming, he would kiss her hands and feet even though she spat in his face, and he would certainly have died if his relations had not found out an old woman who unbewitched him; whereupon his love came to an end, and he informed against her."

That must be a wonderful drink. Would the girl teach her how to brew it?

But just then our Lord God sent yet another warning to Sidonia, through His angel, to turn her from her villainy, for as the girl was going to answer, a knock was heard at the chamber-door. They both grew as white as chalk; but Sidonia bethought herself of a hiding place, and bid the other creep under the bed while she went to the door to see who knocked, and as she opened it, so there stood Prince Ernest bodily before her eyes, with the lute in his hand.

"Ah, gracious Prince, what brings you here? I pray your Highness, for the sake of God, to leave me. What would be said if anyone saw you here?"

"But who is to see us, my beautiful maiden? My gracious mother has gone out to drive; and now, just look at this lute that I have purchased for you in Grypswald. Will it please thee, sweet one?"

Illa. – "Alas, gracious Prince, of what use will it be to me, when I have no one to teach me how to play?"

"I will teach thee, oh, how willingly, but – thou knowest what I would say."

Illa. – "No, no, I dare not learn from your Highness. Now go, and do not make me more miserable."

"What makes thee miserable, enchanting Sidonia?"

Illa. – "Ah, if your Highness could know how this heart burns within me like a fire! What will become of me? Would that I were dead – oh, I am a miserable maiden! If your Highness were but a simple noble, then I might hope – but now. Woe is me! I must go! Yes, I must go!"

"Why must thou go, my own sweet darling? and why dost thou wish me to be only a simple noble? Canst thou not love a duke better than a noble?"

Illa. – "Gracious Prince, what is a poor count's daughter to your princely Highness? and would her Grace ever consent? Ah no, I must go – I must go!"

Here she sobbed so violently, and covered her eyes with her hands, that the young Duke could no longer restrain his feelings. He seized her passionately in his arms, and was kissing away the crocodile tears, when lo, another knock came to the door, and Sidonia grew paler even than the first time, for there was no place to hide the Prince in, as the witch-wench was already under the bed, and not even quite hidden, for some of her red petticoat was visible round the post, and one could easily see by the way it moved that some living body was in it, for the girl was trembling with the most horrible fear and fright. But the Prince was too absorbed in love either to notice all this or to mind the knock at the door.

Sidonia, however, knew well that it was over with them now, and she pushed away the young Prince, just as the door opened and Clara entered, who grew quite pale, and clasped her hands together when she saw the Duke and Sidonia together; then the tears fell fast from her eyes, and she could utter nothing but — "Ah, my gracious Prince — my poor innocent Prince — what has brought you here?" but neither of them spoke a word. "You are lost," exclaimed Clara; "the Duchess is coming up the corridor, and has just stopped to look at her pet cat and the kittens there by the page's room. Hasten, young Prince — hasten to meet her before she comes a step further."

So the young lord darted out of the chamber, and found his gracious mother still examining her kittens, whereupon he prayed her then to descend with him to the courtyard and look also at his fine hounds, to which she consented.

The moment Prince Ernest disappeared, Clara commenced upbraiding Sidonia for her evil ways, which could not be any longer denied — for had she not seen all with her own eyes? — and she now conjured her by the living God to turn away from the young Duke, and select some noble of her own rank as her husband. This could easily be done when so many loved her; but as to the Prince, as long as her Grace and Ulrich lived, or even one single branch of the princely house of Pomerania, this marriage would never be permitted, let the young lord do or say what he chose.

"Ah, thou pious old priest in petticoats," exclaimed Sidonia, "who told thee I wanted to marry the Prince? How can I help if he chooses to come in here and, though I weep and resist, takes me in his arms and kisses me? So leave off thy preaching, and tell me rather what brings thee spying to my room?"

Then Clara remembered what had really been her errand, although the love-scene had put everything else out of her head until now, and replied — "I was seeking the witch-girl from Daber, for when I went out with her Grace, I left her in charge of my maid; but as we returned home by the little garden gate, I slipped up to my room by the private stairs without anyone seeing me, and found my maid looking out of the window, but no girl was to be seen. When I asked what had become of her, the maid answered she knew not, the girl must have slipped away while her back was turned, so I came here to ask if you had seen the impudent hussy, for I fear if her wings are not clipped she will do harm to someone."

Here Sidonia grew quite indignant — what could she know of a vile witch-wench? Besides, she had not been ten minutes there in the room.

"But perchance the bird has found herself a nest somewhere," said Clara, looking towards the bed; "methinks, indeed, I see some of the feathers, for surely a red gown never trembled that way under a bed unless there was something living inside of it." When the witch-girl heard this her fright increased, so that, to make matters worse, she pulled her gown in under the bed, upon which Clara kneeled down, lifted the coverlet, and found the owl in its nest. Now she had to creep out weeping and howling, and promised to tell everything.

But Sidonia gave her a look which she understood well, and therefore when she stood up straight by the bed, begged piteously that the Lady Clara would not scold her for having tried to escape, because she herself had threatened her with being burned there as well as at Daber, so not knowing where to hide, and seeing the Lady Sidonia's door open, she crept in there and got under the bed, intending to wait till night came and then ask her aid in effecting her flight, for the Lady Sidonia was the only one in the castle who had shown her Christian compassion.

Hereat Sidonia rose up as if in great rage, and said, "Ha! thou impudent wench, how darest thou reckon on my protection!" and seizing her by the hand — in which, however, she pressed a piece of gold — pushed her violently out of the door.

Now Clara, thinking that this was the whole truth, fell weeping upon Sidonia's neck, and asked forgiveness for her suspicions. "There, that will do," said Sidonia, — "that will do, old preacher; only be more cautious in future. What! am I to poke under my bed to see if anyone is hiding there? You may go, for I suppose you have often hidden a lover there, your eyes turn to it so naturally."

As Clara grew red with shame, Sidonia drew the witch-girl again into the room, and giving her a box on the ear that made her teeth chatter — "Now, confess," said she, "what I said to the young lord without knowing that you were listening." So the poor girl answered weeping, "Nothing but what was good did you say to him, namely, that he should go away; and then you pushed him so violently when he attempted to kiss you, that he stumbled over against the bed."

"See, now, my pious preacher," said Sidonia, "this girl confirms exactly what I told you; so now go along with you, you hussy, or mayhap you will come off no better than she has done."

Hereupon Clara went away humbly with the witch-girl to her own room, and never uttered another word. Nevertheless the affair did not seem quite satisfactory to her yet. So she conferred with her betrothed, Marcus Bork, on the subject. For when he carried books for her Highness from the ducal library, it was his custom to scrape with his feet in a peculiar manner as he passed Clara's door; then she knew who it was, and opened it. And as her maid was present, they conversed together in the Italian tongue; for they were both learned, not only in God's Word, but in all other knowledge, so that people talk about them yet in Pomeranian land for these things.

Clara therefore told him the whole affair in Italian, before her maid and the witch-girl — of the visit of the young Prince, and how the girl was lying hid under the bed, and asked him was it not likely that Sidonia had brought her there to teach her how to brew the love-drink, with which she would then have bewitched the Prince and all the menfolk in the castle, and ought she not to warn her Grace of the danger.

But Marcus answered, that if the witch-girl had been at the castle weeks before, he might have supposed that Sidonia had received the secret of the love-potion from her, since every man, old and young, was mad for love of her — but now he must needs confess that Sidonia's eyes and deceiving mouth were magic sufficient; and that it was not likely she would bring a vile damsel to her room to teach her that which she knew already so perfectly. So he thought it better not to tell her Highness anything on the subject. Besides, if the wench were examined, who knows what she might tell of Sidonia and the young lord that would bring shame on the princely house of Wolgast, since she had been hid under the bed all the time, and perhaps only kept silence through fear. It were well therefore on every account not to let the matter get wind, and to shut up the wench safely in the witches' tower until the answer came from Daber. If she were pronounced really guilty, it would then be time enough to question her on the rack about the love-drink and the conversation between the young lord and Sidonia.

So this course was agreed on. It is, however, much to be regretted that Clara did not follow the promptings of her good angel, and tell all to her Grace and old Ulrich; for then much misfortune and scandal would have been spared to the whole Pomeranian land. But she followed her bride-groom's advice, and kept all secret. The witch-girl, however, was locked up that very day in the witches' tower, to guard against future evil.

Chapter XI

*How Sidonia repeated the catechism of Dr. Gerschovius, and how she
whipped the young Casimir, out of pure evil-mindedness*

The Sunday came at last when Sidonia was to be examined publicly
in the catechism of Dr. Gerschovius. Her Grace was filled with anxiety
to see how all would terminate, for everyone suspected (as indeed was
the case) that not one word of it would she be able to repeat. So the
church was crowded, and all the young men attended without exception,
knowing what was to go forward, and fearing for Sidonia, because this
Dr. Gerschovius was a stern, harsh man; but she herself seemed to care
little about the matter, for she entered her Grace's closet as usual (which
was right opposite the pulpit), and threw herself carelessly into a corner.
However, when the doctor entered the pulpit she became more grave,
and finally, when his discourse was drawing near to the close, she rose
up quietly and glided out of the closet, intending to descend to the
gardens. Her Grace did not perceive her movement, in consequence of
the hat with the heron's plume which she wore, for the feathers drooped
down at the side next Sidonia, and the other ladies were too much
alarmed to venture to draw her attention to the circumstance. But the
priest from the pulpit saw her well, and called out – "Maiden! maiden!
Whither go you? Remember ye have to repeat your catechism!"

Then Sidonia grew quite pale, for her Grace and all the congregation
fixed their eyes on her. So when she felt quite conscious that she was
looking pale, she said, "You see from my face that I am not well; but if
I get better, doubt not but that I shall return immediately." Here all the
maids of honor put up their kerchiefs to hide their laughter, and the
young nobles did the same.

So she went away; but they might wait long enough, I think, for her
to come back. In vain her Grace watched until the priest left the pulpit,
and then sent two of her ladies to look for the hypocrite; but they
returned declaring that she was nowhere to be seen.

Summa. — The whole service was ended, and her Grace looked as angry as the doctor; and when the organ had ceased, and the people were beginning to depart, she called out from her closet —

"Let everyone come this way, and accompany me to Sidonia's apartment. There I shall make her repeat the catechism before ye all. Messengers shall be dispatched in all directions until they find out her hiding place."

This pleased the doctor and Ulrich well. So they all proceeded to Sidonia's little room; for there she was, to their great surprise, seated upon a chair with a smelling-bottle in her hand. Whereupon her Grace demanded what ailed her, and why she had not stayed to repeat the catechism.

Illa. — "Ah! she was so weak, she would certainly have fainted, if she had not descended to the garden for a little fresh air. She was so distressed that her Grace had been troubled sending for her, of which she was not aware until now."

"Are you better now?" asked her Grace.

Illa. — "Rather better. The fresh air had done her good."

"Then," quoth her Grace, "you shall recite the catechism here for the doctor; for, in truth, Christianity is as necessary to you as water to a fish."

The doctor now cleared his throat to begin; but she stopped him pertly, saying —

"I do not choose to say my catechism here in my room, like a little child. Grown-up maidens are always heard in the church."

Howbeit, her Grace motioned to him not to heed her. So to his first question she replied rather snappishly, "You have your answer already."

No wonder the priest grew black with rage. But seeing a book lying open on a little table beside her bed, and thinking it was the catechism of Dr. Gerschovius which she had been studying, he stepped over to look. But judge his horror when he found that it was a volume of the *Amadis de Gaul,* and was lying open at the eighth chapter, where he read — "How the Prince Amadis de Gaul loved the Princess Rosaliana, and was beloved in return, and how they both attained to the accomplishment of their desires."

He dashed the book to the ground furiously, stamped upon it, and cried —

"So, thou wanton, this is thy Bible and thy catechism! Here thou learnest how to make young men mad! Who gave thee this infamous book? Speak! Who gave it to thee?"

So Sidonia looked up timidly, and said, weeping, "It was his Highness Duke Barnim who gave it to her, and told her it was a merry book, and good against low spirits."

Here the Duchess, who had lifted up her hand to give her a box on the ear, let it fall again with a deep sigh when she heard of the old Prince having given her such an infamous book, and lamented loudly, crying —

"Who will free me from this shameless wanton, who makes all the court mad? Truly says Scripture, 'A beautiful woman without discretion is like a circlet of gold upon a swine's head.' Ah! I know that now. But I trust my messengers will soon return whom I have dispatched to Stettin and Stramehl, and then I shall get rid of thee, thou wanton, for which God be thanked forevermore."

Then she turned to leave the room with old Ulrich, who only shook his head, but remained as mute as a fish. Doctor Gerschovius, however, stayed behind with Sidonia, in order to exhort her to virtue; but as she only wept and did not seem to hear him, he grew tired, and finally went his way, also with many sighs and uplifting of his hands.

A little after, as Sidonia was howling just out of pure ill-temper, for, in my opinion, nothing ailed her, the little Prince Casimir ran in to look for his mamma — she had gone to hear Sidonia her catechism, they told him.

"What did he want with his lady mamma?"

"His new jerkin hurt him, he wanted her to tie it another way for him; but is it really true, Sidonia, that you do not know your catechism? I can say it quite well. Just come now and hear me say it."

It is probable that her Grace and the doctor had devised this plan in order to shame Sidonia, by showing her how even a little child could repeat it; but she took it angrily, and, calling him over, said, "Yes; come — I will hear you your catechism." And as the little boy came up close beside her, she slung him across her knee, pulled down his hose, and — oh, shame! — whipped his Serene Highness upon his princely *podex*, that it would have melted the heart of a stone. How this shows her cruel and evil disposition — to revenge on the child what she had to bear from the mother. Fie on the maiden!

And here my gracious Prince will say — "O Theodore, this matter surely might have been passed over, since it brings a disrespect upon my princely house."

I answer — "Gracious Lord and Prince, my most humble services are due to your Grace, but truth must be still truth, however it may displease your Highness. Besides, by no other act could I have so well proved the infernal evil in this woman's nature; for if she could dare to lay her godless hand upon one of your illustrious race, then all her future acts are perfectly comprehensible.* When the malicious wretch let the boy go, he darted out of the room and ran down the whole corridor, screaming out that he would tell his mamma about Sidonia; but Zitsewitz met him, and having heard the story, the amorous old fool took him up in his arms, and promised him heaps of beautiful things if he would hold his tongue and not say a word more to anyone, and that he would give Sidonia a good whipping himself, in return for what she had done to him. So, in short, her Grace never heard of the insult until after Sidonia's departure from court."

Had her Highness been in her apartment, she must have heard the child scream; but it so happened that just then she was walking up and down the ducal gardens, whither she had gone to cool her anger.

Soon after a stately ship was seen sailing down the river from Penemunde,† which attracted all eyes in the castle, for on the deck stood a noble youth, with a heron's plume waving from his cap, and he held a tame sea-gull upon his hand, which from time to time flew off and dived into the water, bringing up all sorts of fish, great and small, in its beak, with which it immediately flew back to the handsome youth.

"Ah!" exclaimed Clara, "there must be the sons of our gracious Princess! for tomorrow is her birthday, and here comes the noble bishop, Johann Frederick of Camyn, and his brother, Duke Bogislaff XIII, to pay their respects to their gracious mother."

Her Grace, however, would scarcely credit that the handsome youth who was fishing after so elegant a manner was indeed her own beloved son; but Clara clapped her hands now, crying, "Look! your Grace — look! there is the flag hoisted!" And indeed there fluttered from the mast now the bishop's own arms. So the warder blew his horn, which was answered by the warder of St. Peter's in the town, and the bells in all the towers rang out, and the castellan ordered the cannon in the courtyard to be fired off.

Her Grace was now thoroughly convinced, and weeping for joy, ran down to the little water-gate, where old Ulrich already stood waiting to receive the princes. As the vessel approached, however, they discovered that the handsome youth was not the bishop, but Duke Bogislaff, who had been staying on a visit at his brother's court at Camyn, along with several high prelates. The bishop, Johann Frederick, did not accompany

---

* Note by Duke Bogislaff XIV — This is true, and therefore I consent to let it remain; and I remember that Prince Casimir told me long afterwards that the scene remained indelibly impressed on his memory. "For," he said, "the wild eyes and the terrible voice of the witch frightened me more even than her cruel hand; as if even there I detected the devil in her, though I was but a little boy at the time."

† A town in Pomerania.

him, for he was obliged to remain at home, in order to receive a visit from the Prince of Brandenburg.

When the Duke stepped on shore he embraced his weeping mother joyfully, and said he came to offer her his congratulations on her birthday, and that she must not weep but laugh, for there should be a dance in honor of it, and a right merry feast at the castle on the morrow.

Then he tumbled out on the bridge all the fish which the bird had caught; and her Grace wondered greatly, and stroked it as it sat upon the shoulder of the Prince. So he asked if the bird pleased her Grace, and when she answered "Yes," he said, "Then, dearest mother, let it be my birthday gift to you. I have trained it myself, and tried it here, as you see, upon the river. So any afternoon that you and your ladies choose to amuse yourselves with a sail, this bird will fish for you as long as you please, while you row down the river."

Ah, what a good son was this handsome young Duke! — and when I think that Sidonia murdered them all — all — even this noble Prince, my heart seems to break, and the pen falls from my fingers.*

But to continue. The Duchess embraced the fine young Prince, who still continued talking of the dance they must have next day. It was time now for his gracious mother to give up mourning for her deceased lord, he said.

But her Grace would not hear of a dance; and replied that she would continue to mourn for her dear lord all the rest of her life, to whom she had been wedded by Doctor Martinus. However, the Duke repeated his entreaties, and all the young nobles added theirs, and finally Prince Ernest besought her Grace not to deny them permission to have a festival on the morrow, as it was to honor her birthday. So she at last consented; but old Ulrich shook his head, and took her Grace aside to warn her of the scandal which would assuredly arise when the young nobles had drunk and grew excited by Sidonia. Hereupon her Grace made answer that she would take care Sidonia should cause no scandal — "As she has refused to learn her catechism, she must not appear at the feast. It will be a fitting punishment to keep her a prisoner for the whole day, and therefore I shall lock her up myself in her own room, and put the key in my pocket."

---

* Note by Duke Bogislaff XIV — Et quid mihi, misero filio? Domine in manus tuas commando spiritum meum, quia tu me redemisti fide Deus! (And what remains to me, wretched son? Lord, into Thy hands I commend my spirit, for Thou hast redeemed me, Thou God of truth.) — When one thinks that it was the general belief in that age that the whole ducal race had been destroyed and blasted by Sidonia's sorceries, it is impossible not to be affected by these melancholy yet resigned and Christian words of the last orphaned and childless representative of the ancient and illustrious house of Wolgast.

So Ulrich was well pleased, and all separated for the night with much contentment and hopes of enjoyment on the morrow.

Chapter XII

Of Appelmann's knavery — Item, how the birthday of her Highness was celebrated, and Sidonia managed to get to the dance, with the uproar caused thereby

*B*efore I proceed further, it will be necessary to state what happened a few days before concerning Prince Ernest's chief equerry, Johann Appelmann, otherwise many might doubt the facts I shall have to relate, though God knows I speak the pure truth.

One came to his lordship the Grand Chamberlain — he was a shoemaker of the town — and complained to him of Appelmann, who had been courting his daughter for a long while, and running after her until finally he had disgraced her in the eyes of the whole town, and brought shame and scandal into his house. So he prayed Lord Ulrich to make the shameless profligate take his daughter to wife, as he had fairly promised her marriage long ago.

Now Ulrich had long suspected the knave of bad doings, for many pearls and jewels had lately been missing from her Grace's shabrack and horse-trappings, and the groom, who always laid them on her Grace's white palfrey, knew nothing about them, though he was even put to the torture; but as Appelmann had all these things in his sole keeping, it was natural to think that he was not quite innocent. Besides, three hundred sacks of oats were missing on the new year, and no one knew what had become of them.

Therefore Ulrich sent for the cheating rogue, and upbraided him with his profligate courses, also telling him that he must wed the shoemaker's daughter immediately. But the cunning knave knew better, and swore by all the saints that he was innocent, and finally prevailed upon Prince

Ernest to intercede for him, so that Ulrich promised to give him a little longer grace, but then assuredly he would bring him to a strict account.

And Appelmann drove the Prince that same day to Grypswald, to find out more musicians for the castle band, as the march of Duke Bogislaff the Great was to be played by eighty drums and forty trumpets in the grand ducal hall, to honor the birthday of her Highness.

One can imagine what Sidonia felt when the Duchess announced that as she had refused to learn the catechism, and was neither obedient to God nor her Grace, she should remain a strict prisoner in her own room during the festival, as a signal punishment for her ungodly behavior. But her maid might bring her food of all that she chose from the feast.

Sidonia first prayed her Grace to forgive her for the love of God, and she would learn the whole catechism by heart. But as this had no effect, then she wept and lamented loudly, and at length fell down upon her knees before her Grace, who would, however, be neither moved nor persuaded; and when Sidonia threatened at last to leave her room, the Duchess went out, locked the door, and put the key in her pocket. The prisoner howled enough then, I warrant.

But what did she do now, the cunning minx? She gave her maid a piece of gold, and told her to go up and down the corridor, crying and wringing her hands, and when anyone asked what was the matter, to say, "That her beautiful young lady was dying of grief, because the Duchess had locked her up, like a little schoolgirl, in her own room, and all for not knowing the catechism of Dr. Gerschovius, which indeed was not taught in her part of the country, but another, which she had learned quite well in her childhood. And so for this, her poor young lady was not to be allowed to dance at the festival." The maid was to say all this in particular to Prince Ernest; or if he did not pass through the corridor, she was to stop weeping and groaning at his chamber-door, until he came out to ask what was the matter.

The maid followed the instructions right well, and in less than an hour every soul in the castle, down to the cooks and washerwomen, knew what had happened, and everywhere the Duchess went she was assailed by old and young, great and small, with petitions of pardon for Sidonia.

Her Grace, however, bid them all be silent, and threatened if they made such shameless requests to forbid the festival altogether. But when Prince Ernest likewise petitioned in her favor, she was angry, and said, "He ought to be ashamed of himself. It was now plain what a fool the girl had made of him. Her maternal heart would break, she knew it would — and this day would be one of sorrow in place of joy to her; all on account of this girl."

So the young Prince had to hold his peace for this time; but he sent a message, nevertheless, to Sidonia, telling her not to fret, for that he would take her out of her room and bring her to the dance, let what would happen.

Next morning, by break of day, the whole castle and town were alive with preparations for the festival. It was now seven years — that is, since the death of Duke Philip — since anyone had danced in the castle except the rats and mice, and even yet the splendor of this festival is talked of in Wolgast; and many of the old people yet living there remember it well, and gave me many curious particulars thereof, which I shall set down here, that it may be known how such affairs were conducted in old time at our ducal courts.

In the morning, by ten of the clock, the young princes, nobles, clergy, and the honorable counselors of the town, assembled in the grand ducal hall, built by Duke Philip after the great fire, and which extended up all through the three stories of the castle. At the upper end of the hall was the grand painted window, sixty feet high, on which was delineated the pilgrimage of Duke Bogislaff the Great to Jerusalem, all painted by Gerard Homer;* and round on the walls banners, and shields, and helmets, and cuirasses, while all along each side, four feet from the ground, there were painted on the walls figures of all the animals found in Pomerania: bears, wolves, elks, stags, deer, otters, &c., all exquisitely imitated.

When all the lords had assembled, the drums beat and trumpets sounded, whereupon the Pomeranian marshal flung open the great doors of the hall, which were wreathed with flowers from the outside, and the princely widow entered with great pomp, leading the little Casimir by the hand. She was arrayed in the Pomeranian costume — namely, a white silk under-robe, and over it a surcoat of azure velvet, brocaded with silver, and open in front. A long train of white velvet, embroidered in golden laurel wreaths, was supported by twelve pages dressed in black velvet cassocks with Spanish ruffs. Upon her head the Duchess wore a coif of scarlet velvet with small plumes, from which a white veil, spangled with silver stars, hung down to her feet. Round her neck she had a scarlet velvet band, twisted with a gold chain; and from it depended a balsam flask, in the form of a greyhound, which rested on her bosom.

---

* A Frieslander, and the most celebrated painter on glass of his time.

As her Serene Highness entered with fresh and blushing cheeks, all bowed low and kissed her hand, glittering with diamonds. Then each offered his congratulations as best he could.

Amongst them came Johann Neander, Archdeacon of St. Peter's, who was seeking preferment, considering that his present living was but a poor one; and so he presented her Grace with a printed *tractatum* dedicated to her Highness, in which the question was discussed whether the ten virgins mentioned in Matt. xxv. were of noble or citizen rank. But Doctor Gerschovius made a mock of him for this afterwards, before the whole table.*

Now, when all the congratulations were over, the Duchess asked Prince Ernest if the water-works in the courtyard had been completed,† and when he answered "Yes," "Then," quoth her Grace, "they shall run with Rostock beer today, if it took fifty tuns; for all my people, great and small, shall keep festival today; and I have ordered my court baker to give a loaf of bread and a good drink to everyone that cometh and asketh. And now, as it is fitting, let us present ourselves in the church."

So the bells rung, and the whole procession swept through the corridor and down the great stairs, with drums and trumpets going before. Then followed the marshal with his staff, and the Grand Chamberlain, Ulrich von Schwerin, wearing his beautiful hat (a present from her Highness), looped up with a diamond aigrette, and spangled with little golden stars. Then came the Duchess, supported on each side by the young princes, her sons; and the nobles, knights, pages, and others brought up the rear, according to their rank and dignity.

As they passed Sidonia's room, she began to beat the door and cry like a little spoiled child; but no one minded her, and the procession moved on to the courtyard, where the soldatesca fired a salute, not only from their muskets, but also from the great cannon called "the Old

---

* Over these exegetical disquisitions of a former age we smile, and with reason; but we, pedantic Germans, have carried our modern exegetical mania to such absurd lengths, that we are likely to become as much a laughingstock to our contemporaries, as well as to posterity, as this Johannes Neander. In fact, our exegetists are mostly pitiful schoolmasters — word-anatomists — and one could as little learn the true spirit of an old classic poet from our pedantic philologists, as the true sense of holy Scripture from our scholastic theologians. What with their grammar twistings, their various readings, their dubious punctuations, their mythical, and who knows what other meanings, their hair-splittings, and prosy vocable tiltings, we find at last that they are willing to teach us everything but that which really concerns us, and, like the Danaides, they let the water of life run through the sieve of their learning. We may apply to them truly that condemnation of our Lord's (Matt, xxiii. 24) — "Ye blind guides; ye strain at a gnat, and swallow a camel."

† The Prince took much interest in hydraulics, and built a beautiful and costly aqueduct for the town of Wolgast.

Aunt," which gave forth a deep joy-sigh. From all the castle windows hung banners and flags bearing the arms of Pomerania and Saxony, and the pavement was strewed with flowers.

As they passed Sidonia's window she opened it, and appeared magnificently attired, and glittering with pearls and diamonds, but also weeping bitterly. At this sight old Ulrich gnashed his teeth for rage, but all the young men, and Prince Ernest in particular, felt their hearts die in them for sorrow. So they passed on through the great north gate out on the castle wall, from whence the whole town and harbor were visible. Here the flags fluttered from the masts and waved from the towers, and the people clapped their hands and cried "Huzza!" (for in truth they had heard about the beer, to my thinking, before the Princess came out upon the walls). *Summa*: There was never seen such joy; and after having service in church, they all returned to the castle in the same order, and set themselves down to the banquet.

I got a list of the courses at the table of the Duchess from old Küssow, and I shall here set it down, that people may see how our fathers banqueted eighty years ago in Pomerania; but, God help us! in these imperial days there is little left for us to grind our teeth upon. So smell thereat, and you will still get a delicious savor from these good old times.

First Course. — 1. A soup; 2. An egg-soup, with saffron, peppercorns, and honey thereon; 3. Stewed mutton, with onions strewed thereon; 4. A roasted capon, with stewed plums.

Second Course. — 1. Ling, with oil and raisins; 2. Beef, baked in oil; 3. Eels, with pepper; 4. Dried fish, with Leipzig mustard.

Third Course. — 1. A salad, with eggs; 2. Jellies strewed with almond and onion seed; 3. Omelets, with honey and grapes; 4. Pastry, and many other things besides.

Fourth Course. — 1. A roast goose with red beet-root, olives, capers, and cucumbers; 2. Little birds fried in lard, with radishes; 3. Venison; 4. Wild boar, with the marrow served on toasted rolls. In conclusion, all manner of pastry, with fritters, cakes, and fancy confectionery of all kinds.

So her Grace selected something from each dish herself, and dispatched it to Sidonia by her maid; but the maiden would none of them, and sent all back with a message that she had no heart to gormandize and feast; but her Grace might send her some bread and water, which was alone fitting for a poor prisoner to receive.

The young men could bear this no longer, their patience was quite exhausted, and their courage rose as the wine-cups were emptied. So at length Prince Ernest whispered to his brother Bogislaus to put in a good word for Sidonia. He refused, however, and Prince Ernest was ashamed to name her himself; but some of the young pages who waited on her

Grace were bold enough to petition for her pardon, whereupon her Grace gave them a very sharp reproof.

After dinner the Duchess and Prince Bogislaus went up the stream in a pleasure-boat to try the tame sea-gull, and her Grace requested Lord Ulrich to accompany them. But he answered that he was more necessary to the castle that evening than a night-watch in a time of war, particularly if the young Prince was to have Rostock beer play from the fountains in place of water.

And soon his words came true, for when the Duchess had sailed away the young men began to drink in earnest, so that the wine ran over the threshold down the great steps, and the peasants and boors who were going back and forward with dried wood to the ducal kitchen, lay down flat on their faces, and licked up the wine from the steps (but the Almighty punished them for this, I think, for their children now are glad enough to sup up water with the geese).

Meanwhile many of the youths sprang up, swearing that they would free Sidonia; others fell down quite drunk, and knew nothing more of what happened. Then old Ulrich flew to the corridor, and marched up and down with his drawn dagger in his hand, and swore he would arrest them all if they did not keep quiet; that as to those who were lying dead drunk like beasts, he must treat them like other beasts — whereupon he sends to the castle fountain for buckets of cold water, and pours it over them. Ha! how they sprang up and raged when they felt it; but he only laughed and said — if they would not hold their peace he would treat them still worse; they ought to be ashamed of their filthiness and debauchery.*

But now to the uproar within was added one from without, for when the fountains began to play with Rostock beer, all the town ran thither, and drank like leeches, while they begged the serving-wenches to bring them loaves to eat with it. How the old shoemaker threw up his cap in the air, and shouted — "Long live her Grace! no better Princess was in the whole world — they hoped her Grace might live for many years and celebrate every birthday like this!" Then they would pray for her right heartily, and the women chattered and cackled, and the children screamed so that no one could hear a word that was saying, and Sidonia tried for a long time in vain to make them hear her. At last she waved a white kerchief from the window, when the noise ceased for a little, and she then began the old song, namely, "Would they release her?"

Now there were some brave fellows among them to whom she had given drink-money, or purchased goods from, and they now ran to fetch

---

* Almost all writers of that age speak of the excesses to which intoxication was carried in all the ducal courts, but particularly that of Pomerania.

a ladder and set it up against the wall; but old Ulrich got wind of this proceeding, and dispersed the mob forthwith, menacing Sidonia, before their faces, that if she but wagged a finger, and did not instantly retire from the window, and bear her well-merited punishment patiently, he would have her carried straightway through the guardroom, and locked up in the bastion tower. This threat succeeded, and she drew in her head. Meantime the Duchess returned from fishing, but when she beheld the crowd she entered through the little water-gate, and went up a winding stair to her own apartment, to attire herself for the dance.

The musicians now arrived from Grypswald, and all the knights and nobles were assembled except Zitsewitz, who lay sick, whether from love or jealousy I leave undecided; so the great affair at length began, and in the state hall the band struck up Duke Bogislaus' march, played, in fact, by eighty drums and forty-three trumpets, so that it was as mighty and powerful in sound as if the great trumpet itself had played it, and the plaster dropped off from the ceiling, and the picture of his Highness the Duke, in the north window, was so disturbed by the vibration, that it shook and clattered as if it were going to descend from the frame and dance with the guests in the hall, and not only the folk outside danced to the music, but down in the town, in the great marketplace, and beyond that, even in the horse-market, the giant march was heard, and everyone danced to it whether in or out of the house, and cheered and huzzaed. Now the Prince could no longer repress his feelings, for, besides that he had taken a good Pomeranian draft that day, and somewhat rebelled against his lady mother, he now flung the fourth command-ment to the winds (never had he done this before), and taking three companions with him, by name Dieterich von Krassow, Joachim von Budde, and Achim von Weyer, he proceeded with them to the chamber of Sidonia, and with great violence burst open the door. There she lay on the bed weeping, in a green velvet robe, laced with gold, and embroidered with other golden ornaments, and her head was crowned with pearls and diamonds, so that the young Prince exclaimed, "Dearest Sidonia, you look like a king's bride. See, I keep my word; come now, and we shall dance together in the hall."

Here he would willingly have kissed her, but was ashamed because the others were by, so he said, "Go ye now to the hall and see if the dance is still going on. I will follow with the maiden." Thereat the young men laughed, because they saw well that the Prince did not just then desire their company, and they all went away, except Joachim von Budde, the rogue, who crept behind the door, and peeped through the crevice.

Now, the young lord was no sooner left alone with Sidonia than he pressed her to his heart — "Did she love him? She must say yes once again." Whereupon she clasped his neck with her little hands, and with every kiss that he gave her she murmured, "Yes, yes, yes!" "Would she be his own dear wife?" "Ah, if she dared. She would have no other spouse, no, not even if the Emperor came himself with all the seven electors. But he must not make her more miserable than she was already. What could they do? he never would be allowed to marry her." "He would manage that." Then he pressed her again to his heart, with such ardor that the knave behind the door grew jealous, and springing up, called out — "If his Highness wishes for a dance he must come now."

When they both entered the hall, her Grace was treading a measure with old Ulrich, but he caught sight of them directly, and without making a single remark, resigned the hand of her Grace to Prince Bogislaus, and excused himself, saying that the noise of the music had made his head giddy, and that he must leave the hall for a little. He ran then along the corridor down to the courtyard, from thence to the guard, and commanded the officer with his troop, along with the executioner and six assistants, to be ready to rush into the hall with lighted matches, the moment he waved his hat with the white plumes from the window.

When he returns, the dance is over, and my gracious lady, suspecting nothing as yet, sits in a corner and fans herself. Then Ulrich takes Sidonia in one hand and Prince Ernest in the other, brings them up straight before her Highness, and asks if she had herself given permission for the Prince and Sidonia to dance together in the hall. Her Highness started from her chair when she beheld them, her cheeks glowing with anger, and exclaimed, "What does this mean? Have you dared to release Sidonia?"

Ille. — "Yes; for this noble maiden has been treated worse than a peasant-girl by my lady mother."

Illa. — "Oh, woe is me! this is my just punishment for having forgotten my Philip so soon, and even consenting to tread a measure in the hall." So she wept, and threw herself again upon the seat, covering her face with both hands.

Now old Ulrich began. "So, my young Prince, this is the way you keep the admonitions that your father, of blessed memory, gave you on his deathbed! Fie — shame on you! Did you not give your promise also to me, the old man before you? Sidonia shall return to her chamber, if my word has yet some power in Pomerania. Speak, gracious lady, give the order, and Sidonia shall be carried back to her room."

When Sidonia heard this, she laid her white hand, all covered with jewels, upon the old man's arm, and looked up at him with beseeching glances, and stroked his beard after her manner, crying, with tears of anguish, "Spare a poor young maiden! I will learn anything you tell me; I will repeat it all on Sunday. Only do not deal so hardly with me." But the little hands for once had no effect, nor the tears, nor the caresses; for Ulrich, throwing her off, gave her such a slap in the face that she uttered a loud cry and fell to the ground.

If a firebrand had fallen into a barrel of gunpowder, it could not have caused a greater explosion in the hall than that cry; for after a short pause, in which everyone stood silent as if thunderstruck, there arose from all the nobles, young and old, the terrible war-cry – "Jodute! Jodute!* to arms, to arms!" and the cry was re-echoed till the whole hall rung with it. Whoever had a dagger or a sword drew it, and they who had none ran to fetch one. But the Prince would at once have struck old Ulrich to the heart, if his brother Bogislaus had not sprung on him from behind and pinioned his arms. Then Joachim von Budde made a pass at the old knight, and wounded him in the hand. So Ulrich changed his hat from the right hand to the left, and still kept retreating till he could gain the window and give the promised sign to the guard, crying as he fought his way backward, step by step, "Come on now – come on, Ernest. Murder the old grey-headed man whom thy father called friend – murder him, as thou wilt murder thy mother this night."

Then reaching the window, he waved his hat until the sign was answered; then sprang forward again, seized Sidonia by the hand, crying, "Out, harlot!" Hereupon young Lord Ernest screamed still louder, "Jodute! Jodute! Down with the grey-headed villain! What! will not the nobles of Pomerania stand by their Prince? Down with the insolent grey-beard who has dared to call my princely bride a harlot!" And so he tore himself from his brother's grasp, and sprang upon the old man; but her Grace no sooner perceived his intention than she rushed between them, crying, "Hold! hold! hold! for the sake of God, hold! He is thy second father." And as the young Prince recoiled in horror, she seized Sidonia rapidly, and pushing her before Ulrich towards the door, cried, "Out with the accursed harlot!" But Joachim Budde, who had already wounded the Grand Chamberlain, now seizing a stick from one of the drummers, hit her Grace such a blow on the arm therewith that she had to let go her hold of Sidonia. When old Ulrich beheld this, he

---

* The learned have puzzled their heads a great deal over the etymology of this enigmatical word, which is identical in meaning with the terrible *"Zettergeschrei"* of the Reformation era. It is found in the Swedish, Gothic, and Low German dialects, and in the Italian *Goduta*. One of the best essays on the subject – which, however, leads to no result – the lover of antiquarian researches will find in Hakeus's "Pomeranian Provincial Papers," vol. v. p. 207.

screamed, "Treason! treason!" and rushed upon Budde. But all the young nobles, who were now fully armed, surrounded the old man, crying, "Down with him! down with him!" In vain he tried to reach a bench from whence he could defend himself against his assailants; in a few moments he was overpowered by numbers and fell upon the floor. Now, indeed, it was all over with him, if the soldatesca had not at that instant rushed into the hall with fierce shouts, and Master Hansen the executioner, in his long red cloak, with six assistants accompanying them.

"Help! help!" cried her Grace; "help for the Lord Chamberlain!"

So they sprang to the center of the hall where he was lying, dashed aside his assailants, and lifted up the old man from the floor with his hand all bleeding.

But Joachim Budde, who was seated on the very same bench which Ulrich had in vain tried to reach, began to mock the old knight. Whereupon Ulrich asked if it were he who had struck her Grace with the drumstick. "Aye," quoth he, laughing, "and would that she had got more of it for treating that darling, sweet, beautiful Sidonia no better than a kitchen wench. Where is the old hag now? I will teach her the catechism with my drumstick, I warrant you."

And he was going to rise, when Ulrich made a sign to the executioner, who instantly dropped his red cloak, under which he had hitherto concealed his long sword, and just as Joachim looked up to see what was going on, he whirled the sword round like a flash of lightning, and cut Budde's head clean off from the shoulders, so that not even a quill of his Spanish ruff was disturbed, and the blood spouted up like three horse-tails to the ceiling (for he drank so much that all the blood was in his head), and down tumbled his gay cap, with the heron's plume, to the ground, and his head along with it.

In an instant all was quietness; for though some of the ladies fainted, amongst whom was her Grace, and others rushed out of the hall, still there was such a silence that when the corpse fell down at length heavily upon the ground the clap of the hands and feet upon the floor was quite audible.

When Ulrich observed that his victory was complete, he waved his hat in the air, exclaiming, "The princely house of Pomerania is saved! and, as long as I live, its honor shall never be tarnished for the sake of a harlot! Remove Prince Ernest and Sidonia to separate prisons. Let the rest go their ways; — this devil's festival is at an end, and with my consent, there shall never be another in Wolgast."

Chapter XIII

How Sidonia is sent away to Stettin — Item, of the young lord's dangerous illness, and what happened in consequence

*N*ow the Grand Chamberlain was well aware that no good would result from having Sidonia brought to a public trial, because the whole court was on her side.

Therefore he called Marcus Bork, her cousin, to him in the night, and bid him take her and her luggage away next morning before break of day, and never stop or stay until they reached Duke Barnim's court at Stettin. The wind was halfway round now, and before nightfall they might reach Oderkruge. He would first just write a few lines to his Highness; and when Marcus had made all needful preparation, let him come here to his private apartment and receive the letter. He had selected him for the business because he was Sidonia's cousin, and also because he was the only young man at the castle whom the wanton had not ensnared in her toils.

But that night Ulrich had reason to know that Sidonia and her lovers were dangerous enemies; for just as he had returned to his little room, and seated himself down at the table, to write to his Grace of Stettin the whole business concerning Sidonia, the window was smashed, and a large stone came plump down upon the ink-bottle close beside him, and stained all the paper. As Ulrich went out to call the guard, Appelmann, the equerry, came running up to him, complaining that his lordship's beautiful horse was lying there in the stable groaning like a human creature, for that some wretches had cut its tail clean off.

Ille. — "Were any of the grooms in the stable lately? or had he seen anyone go by the window?"

Hic. — "No; it was impossible to see anyone, on account of the darkness; but he thought he had heard someone creeping along by the wall."

Ille. — "Let him come then, fetch a lantern, and summon all the grooms; he would give it to the knaves. Had he heard anything of her Highness recently?"

Hic. — "A maid told him that her Grace was better, and had retired to rest."

Ille. — "Thank God. Now they might go."

But as they proceeded along the corridor, which was now almost quite dark, the old knight suddenly received such a blow upon his hat that the beautiful aigrette was broken, and he himself thrown against the wall with such violence that he lay a quarter of an hour insensible; then he shook his grey head. What could that mean? Had Appelmann seen anyone?

Hic. — "Ah! no; but he thought he heard steps, as if of someone running away."

So they went on to the ducal stables, but nothing was to be seen or heard. The grooms knew nothing about the matter — the guard knew nothing. Then the old knight lamented over his beautiful horse, and told Appelmann to ride next morning, with Marcus Bork and Sidonia, to the Duke's castle at Stettin, and purchase the piebald mare for him from his Grace, about which they had been bargaining some time back; but he must keep all this secret, for the young nobles were to know nothing of the journey.

Ah, what fine fun this is for the cunning rogue. "If his lordship would only give him the purse, he would bring him back a far finer horse than that which some knaves had injured." Whereupon the old knight went down to reckon out the rose-nobles — but, lo! a stone comes whizzing past him close to his head, so that if it had touched him, methinks the old man would never have spoken a word more. In short, wherever he goes, or stops, or stands, stones and buffets are rained down upon him, so that he has to call the guard to accompany him back to his chamber; but he lays the saddle on the right horse at last, as you shall hear in another place.

After some hours everything became quiet in the castle, for the knaves were glad enough to sleep off their drunkenness. And so, early in the morning before dawn, while they were all snoring in their beds, Sidonia was carried off, scream as she would along the corridor, and even before the young knight's chamber; not a soul heard her. For she had not been brought to the prison tower, as at first commanded, but to her own little chamber, likewise the young lord to his; for the Grand Chamberlain thought afterwards this proceeding would not cause such scandal.

But there truly was great grief in the castle when they all rose, and the cry was heard that Sidonia was gone; and some of the murderous lords threatened to make the old man pay with his blood for it. *Item,* no sooner was it day than Dr. Gerschovius ran in, crying that some of the young profligates had broken all his windows the night before, and turned a goat into the rectory, with the catechism of his dear and learned brother tied round his neck.

Then old Ulrich's anger increased mightily, as might be imagined, and he brought the priest with him to the Duchess, who had got but little rest that night, and was busily turning her wheel with the little clock-work, and singing to it, in a loud, clear voice, that beautiful psalm (120th) — "In deep distress I oft have cried." She paused when they entered, and began to weep. "Was it not all prophesied? Why had she been persuaded to throw off her mourning, and slight the memory of her loved Philip? It was for this the wrath of God had come upon her house; for assuredly the Lord would avenge the innocent blood that had been shed."

Then Ulrich answered that, as her Grace knew, he had earnestly opposed this festival; but as to what regarded, the traitor whose head he had chopped off, he was ready to answer for that blood, not only to man but before God. For had not the coward struck his own sovereign lady the Princess with the drumstick? *Item,* was he not in the act of rising to repeat the blow, as the whole nobility are aware, only he lost his head by the way; and if this had not been done, all order and government must have ceased throughout the land, and the mice and the rats rule the cats, which was against the order of nature and contrary to God's will. But his gracious lady might take consolation, for Sidonia had been carried from the castle that morning by four of the clock, and, by God's grace, never should set foot in it again. But there was another *gravamen,* and that concerned the young nobles, who, no doubt, would become more daring after the events of last evening. Then he related what had happened to the priest. "*Item,* what did my gracious lady mean to do with those drunken libertines? If her Grace had kept up the huntings and the fishings, as in the days of good Duke Philip, mayhap the young men would have been less given to debauchery; but her Grace kept an idle house, and they had nothing to do but drink and brew mischief. If her Grace had no fitting employment for these young fellows, then he would pack them all off to the devil the very next morning, for they brought nothing but disrespect upon the princely house of Wolgast."

So her Grace rejoiced over Sidonia's departure, but could not consent to send away the young knights. Her beloved husband and lord, Philippus Primus, always kept a retinue of such young nobles, and all the princely courts did the same. What would her cousin of Brandenburg and Mecklenburg say, when they heard that she had no longer knights or pages at her court? She feared her princely name would be mentioned with disrespect.

So Ulrich replied, that at all events, this set of young boisterers must be sent off, as they had grown too wild and licentious to be endured any longer; and that he would select a new retinue for her Grace from the discreetest and most sober-minded young knights of the court. Marcus Bork, however, might remain; he was true, loyal, and brave — not a wine-bibber and profligate like the others.

So her Grace at last consented, seeing that no good would come of these young men now; on the contrary, they would be more daring and riotous than ever from rage, when they found that Sidonia had been sent away; and that business of the window-smashing and the goat demanded severe punishment. So let Ulrich look out for a new household; these gay libertines would be sent away.

While she was speaking, the door opened, and Prince Ernest entered the chamber, looking so pale and haggard, that her Grace clasped her hands together, and asked him, with terror, what had happened.

Ille. — "Did she ask what had happened, when all Pomerania rung with it? — when nobles were beheaded before her face as if they were nothing more than beggars' brats? — when the delicate and highborn Lady Sidonia, who had been entrusted to her care by Duke Barnim himself, was turned out of the castle in the middle of the night as if she were a street-girl, because, forsooth, she would not learn her catechism? The world would scarcely credit such scandalous acts, and yet they were all true. But tomorrow (if this weakness which had come over him allowed of it) he would set off for Stettin, also to Berlin and Schwerin, and tell the princes there, his cousins, what government they held in Wolgast. He would soon be twenty, and would then take matters into his own hands; and he would pray his guardian and dear uncle, Duke Barnim, to pronounce him at once of age; then the devil might take Ulrich and his government, but he would rule the castle his own way."

Her Grace. — "But what did he complain of? What ailed him? She must know this first, for he was looking as pale as a corpse."

Ille. — "Did she not know, then, what ailed him? Well, since he must tell her, it was anger-anger that made him so pale and weak."

Her Grace. — "Anger, was it? Anger, because the false wanton, Sidonia, had been removed by her orders from her princely castle? Ah! she knew now what the wanton had come there for; but would he kill his mother? She nearly sank upon the ground last night when he called the impudent wench his bride. But she forgave him; it must have been the wine he drank made him so forget himself; or was it possible that he spoke in earnest?"

Ille (sighing). – "The future will tell that." "Oh, woe is me! what must I live to hear? If thy father could look up from his grave, and see thee disgracing thy princely blood by a marriage with a bower maiden! –. thou traitorous, disobedient son, do not lie to me. I know from thy sighs what thy purpose is – for this thou art going to Stettin and Berlin."

The Prince is silent, and looks down upon the ground.

Her Grace. – "Oh, shame on thee! shame on thee for the sake of thy mother! shame on thee for the sake of this servant of God, thy second father, this old man here! What! a vile knave strike thy mother, before the face of all the court, and thou condemnest him because he avenged her! Truly thou art a fine, brave son, to let thy mother be struck before thy face, for the sake of a harlot. Canst thou deny it? I conjure thee by the living God, tell me is it thy true purpose to take this harlot to thy wife?"

Ille. – "He could give but one answer, the future would decide."

Her Grace (weeping). – "Oh, she was reserved for all misfortunes! Why did Doctor Martinus let her ring fall? All, all has followed from that! If he had chosen a good, humble, honest girl, she would say nothing; but this wanton, this light maiden, that ran after every carl and let them court her!"

Here the young Prince was seized with such violent convulsions that he fell upon the floor, and her Grace raised him up with loud lamentations. He was carried in a dead faint to his chamber, and the court physician, Doctor Pomius, instantly summoned. Doctor Pomius was a pompous little man (for my father knew him well), dry and smart in his words, and with a face like a pair of nutcrackers, for his front teeth were gone, so that his lips seemed dried on his gums, like the skin of a mummy. He was withal too self-conceited and boastful, and malicious, full of gossip and ill-nature, and running down everyone that did not believe that he (Doctor Pomius) was the only learned physician in the world. Following the celebrated rules laid down by Theophrastus Paracelsus, he cured everything with trash – and asses' dung was his infallible panacea for all complaints. This pharmacopoeia was certainly extremely simple, easily obtained, and universal in its application. If the dung succeeded, the doctor drew himself up, tossed his head, and exclaimed, "What Doctor Pomius orders always succeeds." But if the wretched patient slipped out of his hands into the other world, he shook his head and said, "There is an hour for every man to die; of course his had come – physicians cannot work miracles."

Pomius hated every other doctor in the town, and abused them so for their ignorance and stupidity, that finally her Grace believed that no one in the world knew anything but Doctor Pomius, and that a vast amount of profound knowledge was expressed, if he only put his finger to the end of his nose, as was his habit.

So, as I have said, she summoned him to attend the young lord; and after feeling his pulse and asking some questions respecting his general health, the doctor laid his finger, as usual, to his nose, and pronounced solemnly — "The young Prince must immediately take a dose of asses' dung stewed in wine, with a little of the *laudanum paracelsi* poured in afterwards — this will restore him certainly."

But it was all in vain; for the young Prince still continued day and night calling for Sidonia, and neither the Duchess nor Doctor Gerschovius could in any wise comfort him. This afflicted her Grace almost to the death; and by Ulrich's advice, she dispatched her second son, Duke Barnim the younger, and Dagobert von Schwerin, to the court of Brunswick, to solicit in her name the hand of the young Princess Sophia Hedwig, for her son Ernest Ludovicus. Now, in the whole kingdom, there was no more beautiful princess than Sophia of Brunswick; and her Grace was filled with hope that, by her means, the influence of the detestable Sidonia over the heart of the young lord would be destroyed forever.

In due time the ambassadors returned, with the most favorable answer. Father, mother, and daughter all gave consent; and the Duke of Brunswick also forwarded by their hands an exquisite miniature of his beautiful daughter for Prince Ernest.

This miniature her Grace now hung up beside his bed. Would he not look at the beautiful bride she had selected for him? Could there be a more lovely face in all the German empire? What was Sidonia beside her, but a rude country girl! — would he not give her up at last, this light wench? While, on the contrary, this illustrious princess was as virtuous as she was beautiful, and this the whole court of Brunswick could testify.

But the young lord would give no heed to her Grace, and spat out at the picture, and cried to take away the daub — into the fire with it — anywhere out of his sight. Unless his dear, his beautiful Sidonia came to tend him, he would die — he felt that he was dying.

So her Grace took counsel with old Ulrich, and Doctor Pomius, and the priest, what could be done now. The doctor mentioned that he must have been witch-struck. Then more doctors were sent for from the Grypswald, but all was in vain — no one knew what ailed him; and from day to day he grew worse.

Clara von Dewitz now bitterly reproached herself for having concealed her suspicions about the love-drink from her Grace — though indeed she did so by desire of her betrothed, Marcus Bork. But now, seeing that the young Prince lay absolutely at the point of death, she could no longer hold her peace, but throwing herself on her knees before her Grace, told her the whole story of the witch-girl whom she had sheltered in the castle, and of her fears that Sidonia had learned from her how to brew a love-philter, which she had afterwards given to the Prince.

Her Grace was sore displeased with Clara for having kept all this a secret, and said that she would have expected more wisdom and discretion from her, seeing that she had always counted her the most worthy amongst her maidens; then she summoned Ulrich, and laid the evil matter before him. He shook his head; believed that they had hit on the true cause now. Such a sickness had nothing natural about it — there must be magic and witchwork in it; but he would have the whole land searched for the girl, and make her give the young lord some potion that would take off the spell.

Now the witch-girl had been pardoned a few days before that, and sent back to Usdom, near Daber; but bailiffs were now sent in all directions to arrest her, and bring her again to Wolgast without delay.

So the wretched creature was discovered, before long, in Kruge, near Mahlzow, where she had hired herself as a spinner for the winter, and brought before Ulrich and her Grace. She was there admonished to tell the whole truth, but persisted in asseverating that Sidonia had never learned from her how to make a love-drink. Her statement, however, was not believed; and Master Hansen was summoned, to try and make her speak more. The affair, indeed, appeared so serious to Ulrich, that he himself stood by while she was undergoing the torture, and carried on the *protocollum,* calling out to Master Hansen occasionally not to spare his squeezes. But though the blood burst from her finger-ends, and her hip was put out of joint, so that she limped ever after, she confessed nothing more, nor did she alter the statement which she had first made.

Item, her Grace, and the priest, and all the bystanders exhorted her in vain to confess the truth (for her Grace was present at the torture). At last she cried out, "Yes, I know something that will cure him! Mercy! mercy! and I will tell it."

So they unbound her, and she was going straightway to make her witch-potion, but old Ulrich changed his mind. Who could know whether this devil's fiend was telling them the truth? May be she would kill the young lord in place of curing him. So they gave her another stretch upon the rack. But as she still held by all her assertions, they spared her any further torture.

But, in my opinion, the young lord must have obtained something from her, otherwise he could not have recovered all at once the moment that Sidonia was brought back, as I shall afterwards relate.

Sum total. — The young Prince screamed day and night for Sidonia, and told her Grace that he now felt he was dying, and requested, as his last prayer upon this earth, to be allowed to see her once more. The maiden was an angel of goodness; and if she could but close his dying eyes, he would die happy.

It can be easily imagined with what humor her Grace listened to such a request, for she hated Sidonia like Satan himself; but as nothing else could satisfy him, she promised to send for her, if Prince Ernest would solemnly swear, by the corpse of his father, that he would never wed her, but select some princess for his bride, as befitted his exalted rank — the Princess Hedwig, or some other — as soon as he had recovered sufficiently to be able to quit his bed. So he quickly stretched forth his thin, white hand from the bed, and promised his dearly beloved mother to do all she had asked, if she would only send horsemen instantly to Stettin, for the journey by water was insecure, and might be tedious if the wind were not favorable.

Hereupon a great murmur arose in the castle; and young Duke Bogislaus fell into such a rage that he took his way back again to Camyn, and his younger brother, Barnim, accompanied him. But the anger of the Grand Chamberlain no words can express. He told her Grace, in good round terms, that she would be the mock of the whole land. The messengers had only just returned who had carried away Sidonia from the castle under the greatest disgrace; and now, forsooth, they must ride back again to bring her back with all honor.

"Oh, it was all true, quite true; but then, if her dearest son Ernest were to die —"

Ille. — "Let him die. Better lose his life than his honor."

Hæc. — "He would not peril his honor, for he had sworn by the corpse of his father never to wed Sidonia."

Ille. — "Aye, he was quick enough in promising, but performing was a different thing. Did her Grace think that the passion of a man could be controlled by promises, as a tame horse by a bridle? Never, never. Passion was a wild horse, that no bit, or bridle, or curb could guide, and would assuredly carry his rider to the devil."

Her Grace. — "Still she could not give up her son to death; besides, he would repent and see his folly. Did not God's Word tell us how the prodigal son returned to his father, and would not her son return likewise?"

Ille. – "Aye, when he has kept swine. After that he may return, but not till then. The youngster was as great a fool about women as he had ever come across in his life."

Her Grace (weeping). – "He was too harsh on the young man. Had she not sent away the girl at his command; and now he would let her own child die before her eyes, without hope or consolation?"

Ille. – "But if her child is indeed dying, would she send for the devil to attend him in his last moments? Her Grace should be more consistent. If the young lord is dying, let him die; her Grace has other children, and God will know how to comfort her. Had he not been afflicted himself? and let her ask Dr. Gerschovius if the Lord had not spoken peace unto him."

Her Grace. – "Ah, true; but then neither of them are mothers. Her son is asking every moment if the messengers have departed, and what shall she answer him? She cannot lie, but must tell the whole bitter truth."

Ille. – "He saw the time had come at last for him to follow the young princes. He was of no use here any longer. Her Grace must give him permission to take his leave, for he would sail off that very day for his castle at Spantekow, and then she might do as she pleased respecting the young lord."

So her Grace besought him not to leave her in her sore trouble and perplexity. Her two sons had sailed away, and there was no one left to advise and comfort her.

But Ulrich was inflexible. "She must either allow her son quietly to leave this miserable life, or allow him to leave this miserable court service."

"Then let him go to Spantekow. Her son should be saved. She would answer before the throne of the Almighty for what she did. But would he not promise to return, if she stood in any great need or danger? for she felt that both were before her; still she must peril everything to save her child."

Ille. – "Yes, he would be ready on her slightest summons; and he doubted not but that Sidonia would soon give her trouble and sorrow enough. But he could not remain now, without breaking his knightly oath to Duke Philip, his deceased feudal seigneur of blessed memory, and standing before the court and the world as a fool."

So after many tears her Grace gave him his dismissal, and he rode that same day to Spantekow, promising to return if she were in need, and also to send her a new retinue and household immediately.

This last arrangement displeased Marcus Bork mightily, for he had many friends amongst the knights who were now to be dismissed, and so he, too, prayed her Grace for leave to resign his office and retire from court. He had long looked upon Clara von Dewitz with a holy Christian love, and, if her Grace permitted, he would now take her home as his dear loving wife.

Her Grace replied that she had long suspected this betrothal — particularly from the time that Clara told her of his advice respecting the concealment of the witch-girl's visit to Sidonia; and as he had acted wrongly in that business, he must now make amends by not deserting her in her greatest need. Her sons and old Ulrich had already left her; someone must remain in whom she could place confidence. It would be time enough afterwards to bring home his beloved wife Clara, and she would wish them God's blessing on their union.

Ille. — "True, he had been wrong in concealing that business with the witch-girl, but her Grace must pardon him. He never thought it would bring the young lord to his dying bed. Whatever her Grace now commanded he would yield obedience to."

"Then," said her Grace, "do you and Appelmann mount your horses instantly, ride to Stettin, and bring back Sidonia. For her dearly beloved son had sworn that he could not die easy unless he beheld Sidonia once more, and that she attended him in his last moments."

It may be easily imagined how the good knight endeavored to dissuade her Highness from this course, and even spoke to the young Prince himself, but in vain. That same day he and Appelmann were obliged to set off for Stettin, and on their arrival presented the following letter to old Duke Barnim: —

"MARIA, BY THE GRACE OF GOD, BORN DUCHESS OF SAXONY, &c.
"ILLUSTRIOUS PRINCE AND MY DEAR UNCLE, —

"It has not been concealed from your Highness how our clear son Ernest Ludovicus, since the departure of Sidonia, has fallen, by the permission of God, into such a state of bodily weakness that his life even stands in jeopardy.

"He has declared that nothing will restore him but to see Sidonia once more. We therefore entreat your Highness, after admonishing the aforesaid maiden severely upon her former light and unseemly behavior, to dismiss her with our messengers, that they may return and give peace and health to our dearly beloved son.

"If your Highness would enjoy a hunt or a fishing with a tame sea-gull, it would give us inexpressible pleasure.

"We commend you lovingly to God's holy keeping.

"Given from our Castle of Wolgast, this Friday, April 15, 1569.

"MARIA"

Chapter XIV

How Duke Barnim of Stettin and Otto Bork accompany Sidonia back to Wolgast

W hen his Highness of Stettin had finished the perusal of her Grace's letter, he laughed loudly, and exclaimed —

"This comes of all their piety and preachings. I knew well what this extravagant holiness would make of my dear cousin and old Ulrich. If people would persist in being so wonderfully religious, they would soon become as sour as an old cabbage head; and Sidonia declared, that, for her part, a hundred horses should not drag her back to Wolgast, where she had been lectured and insulted, and all because she would not learn her catechism like a little schoolgirl."

Nor would Otto Bork hear of her returning. (He was waiting at Stettin to conduct her back to Stramehl.) At last, however, he promised to consent, on condition that his Highness would grant him the dues on the Jena.

Now the Duke knew right well that Otto wanted to revenge himself upon the people of Stargard, with whom he was at enmity; but he pretended not to observe the cunning knight's motives, and merely replied —

"They must talk of the matter at Wolgast, for nothing could be decided upon without having the opinion of his cousin the Duchess."

So the knight taking this as a half-promise, and Sidonia having at last consented, they all set off on Friday with a good south wind in their favor, and by that same evening were landed by the little water-gate at Wolgast. His Highness was received with distinguished honors — the ten knights of her Grace's new household being in waiting to receive him as he stepped on shore.

So they proceeded to the castle, the Duke having Sidonia upon one arm, and a Cain under the other, which he had been carving during the passage, for the Eve had long since been finished. Otto followed; and all the people, when they beheld Sidonia, uttered loud cries of joy that the dear young lady had come back to them.

This increased her arrogance, so that when her Grace received her, and began a godly admonishment upon her past levities, and conjured her to lead a modest, devout life for the future, Sidonia replied indiscreetly — "She knew not what her Grace and her parson meant by a modest, devout life, except it were learning the catechism of Dr. Gerschovius; from such modesty and devoutness she begged to be excused, she was no little schoolgirl now — she thought her Grace had got rid of all her whims and caprices, by sending for her after having turned her out of the castle without any cause whatever — but it was all the old thing over again."

Her Grace colored up with anger at this bitter speech, but held her peace. Then Otto addressed her, and begged leave to ask her Grace what kind of order was held at her court, where a priest was allowed to slap the fingers of a noble young maiden, and a chamberlain to smite her on the face? Had he known that such were the usages at her court of Wolgast, the Lady Sidonia (such he delighted to call her, as though she were of princely race) never should have entered it, and he would now instantly take her back to Stramehl, if her Grace would not consent to give him up the dues on the Jena.

Now her Grace knew nothing about the dues, and therefore said, turning to the Duke — "Dear uncle, what does this arrogant knave mean? I do not comprehend his insolent speech." Hereupon Otto chafed with rage, that her Grace had named him with such contempt, and cried — "Then was your husband a knave, too! for my blood is as noble and nobler than your own, and I am lord of castles and lands. Come, my daughter; let us leave the robbers' den, or mayhap thy father will be struck even as thou wert."

Now her Grace knew not what to do, and she lamented loudly — more particularly because at this moment a message arrived from Prince Ernest, praying her for God's sake to bring Sidonia to him, as he understood that she had been in the castle now a full quarter of an hour. Then old Otto laughed loudly, took his daughter by the hand, and cried again, "Come — let us leave this robber hole. Come, Sidonia!"

This plunged her Grace into despair, and she exclaimed in anguish, "Will you not have pity on my dying child?" but Otto continued, "Come, Sidonia! come, Sidonia!" and he drew her by the hand.

Here Duke Barnim rose up and said, "Sir Knight, be not so obstinate. Remember it is a sorrowing mother who entreats you. Is it not true, Sidonia, you will remain here?"

Then the cunning hypocrite lifted her kerchief to her eyes, and replied, "If I did not know the catechism of Doctor Gerschovius, yet I know God's Word, and how the Saviour said, 'I was sick and ye visited Me,' and James also says, 'The prayer of faith shall save the sick.' No, I will not let this poor young lord die, if my visit and my prayer can help him."

"No, no," exclaimed Otto, "thou shall not remain, unless the dues of the Jena be given up to me." And as at this moment another page arrived from Prince Ernest, with a similar urgent request for Sidonia to come to him, her Grace replied quickly, "I promise all that you desire," without knowing what she was granting; so the knight said he was content, and let go his daughter's hand.

Now the good town of Stargard would have been ruined forever by this revengeful man, if his treacherous designs had not been defeated (as we shall see presently) by his own terrible death. He had long felt a bitter hatred to the people of Stargard, because at one time they had leagued with the Greifenbergers and the Duke of Pomerania to ravage his town of Stramehl, in order to avenge an insult he had offered to the old burgomaster, Jacob Appelmann, father of the chief equerry, Johann Appelmann. In return for this outrage, Otto determined, if possible, to get the control of the dues of the Jena into his own hands, and when the Stargardians brought their goods and provisions up the Jena, and from thence prepared to enter the river Haff, he would force them to pay such exorbitant duty upon everything, that the merchants and the people, in short, the whole town, would be ruined, for their whole subsistence and merchandise came by these two rivers, and all this was merely to gratify his revenge. But the just God graciously turned away the evil from the good town, and let it fall upon Otto's own head, as we shall relate in its proper place.

So, when the old knight had let go his daughter's hand, her Grace seized it, and went instantly with Sidonia to the chamber of the young lord, all the others following. And here a moving scene was witnessed, for as they entered, Prince Ernest extended his thin, pale hands towards Sidonia, exclaiming, "Sidonia, ah, dearest Sidonia, have you come at last to nursetend me?" then he took her little hand, kissed it, and bedewed it with his tears, still repeating, "Sidonia, dearest Sidonia, have you come to nursetend me?"

So the artful hypocrite began to weep, and said —. "Yes, my gracious Prince, I have come to you, although your priest struck me on the fingers, and your mother and old Ulrich called me a harlot, before all the court, and lastly, turned me out of the castle by night, as if I had been a swine-herd; but I have not the heart to let your Highness surfer, if my poor prayers and help can abate your sickness; therefore let them strike me, and call me a harlot again, if they wish."

This so melted the heart of my gracious Prince Ernest, that he cried out, "O Sidonia, angel of goodness, give me one kiss, but one little kiss upon my mouth, Sidonia! bend down to me — but one, one kiss!" Her Grace was dreadfully scandalized at such a speech, and said he ought to be ashamed of such words. Did he not remember what he had sworn by the corpse of his father at St. Peter's? But old Duke Barnim cried out, laughing — "Give him a kiss, Sidonia; that is the best plaster for his wounds; 'a kiss in honor brings no dishonor,' says the proverb."

However, Sidonia still hesitated, and bending down to the young man, said, "Wait, gracious Prince, until we are alone."

If the Duchess had been angry before, what was it to her rage now — "Alone! she would take good care they were never to be alone!"

Otto took no notice of this speech, probably because he saw that matters were progressing much to his liking between the Prince and his daughter; but Duke Barnim exclaimed, "How now, dearest cousin, are you going to spoil all by your prudery? You brought the girl here to cure him, and what other answer could she give? Bend thee down, Sidonia, and give him one little kiss upon the lips — I, the Prince, command thee; and see, thou needst not be ashamed, for I will set thee an example with his mother. Come, dear cousin, put off that sour face, and give me a good, hearty kiss; your son will get well the sooner for it:" but as he attempted to seize hold of her Grace, she cried out, and lifted up her hands to Heaven, lamenting in a loud voice — "Oh, evil and wicked world! may God release me from this wicked world, and lay me down this day beside my Philip in the grave!" Then weeping and wringing her hands, she left the chamber, while the old knight, and — God forgive him! — even Duke Barnim, looked after her, laughing.

"Come, Otto," said his Grace, "let us go too, and leave this pair alone; I must try and pacify my dear cousin." So they left the room, and on the way Otto opened his mind to the Duke about this love matter, and asked his Grace, would he consent to the union, if Prince Ernest, on his recovery, made honorable proposals for his daughter Sidonia.

But his Grace was right crafty, and merely answered — "Time enough to settle that, Otto, when he is recovered; but methinks you will have some trouble with his mother unless you are more civil to her; so if you desire her favor, bear yourself more humbly, I advise you, as befits a subject."

This the knight promised, and the conversation ceased, as they came up with the Duchess just then, who was waiting for them in the grand corridor. No sooner did she perceive that Sidonia was not with them than she cried out, "So my son is alone with the maiden!" and instantly dispatched three pages to watch them both.

Otto had now changed his tone, and instead of retorting, thanked her Grace for the praiseworthy and Christian care she took of his daughter. He did not believe this at first, but now he saw it with his own eyes. Alas, it was too true, the world was daily growing worse and worse, and the devil haunted us with his temptations, like our own flesh and blood. Then he sighed and kissed her hand, and prayed her Grace to pardon him his former bold language – but, in truth, he had felt displeased at first to see her Grace so harsh to Sidonia, when everyone else at the castle received her with rapture; but he saw now that she only meant kindly and motherly by the girl.

Then the Duke asked, her pardon for his little jest about the kissing. She knew well that he meant no harm; and also that it was not in his nature to endure any melancholy or lamentable faces around him.

So her Grace was reconciled to both, and when the Duke announced that he and the knight proposed visiting Barth* and Eldena, from whence they would return in a few days, to take their leave of her, she said that if her dearest son Ernest grew any better, she would have a grand *battue* in honor of his Highness Duke Barnim, upon their return.

Accordingly, after having amused themselves for a little fishing with the tame sea-gull, the Duke and Otto rode away, and her Grace went to the chamber of the young Prince, to keep watch there during the night. She would willingly have dismissed Sidonia, but he forbade her; and Sidonia herself declared that she would watch day and night by the bedside of the young lord. So she sat the whole night by his bed, holding his hand in hers, and told him about her journey, and how shamefully she had been smuggled away out of the castle by old Ulrich, because she would not learn the catechism; and of her anguish when the messengers arrived, and told of their young lord's illness. She was quite certain Ulrich must have given him something to cause it, as a punishment for having released her from prison, for if he could strike a maiden, it was not surprising that he would injure even his future reigning Prince to gratify his malice. It was well the old malignant creature was away now, as she was told, and if his Grace did right he would play him a trick in return, and set fire to his castle at Spantekow as soon as he was able to move.

Her Grace endured all this in silence, for her dear son's sake, though in truth her anger was terrible. The young lord, however, grew better rapidly, and the following day was even able to creep out of bed for a

---

* Barth, a little town; and Eldena was at that time a richly endowed convent near Greifswald.

couple of hours, to touch the lute. And he taught Sidonia all, and placed her little fingers himself on the strings, that she might learn the better. Then, for the first time, he called for something to eat, and after that fell into a profound sleep which lasted forty-eight hours. During this time he lay like one dead, and her Grace would have tried to awaken him, but the physician prevented her. At length, when he awoke, he cried out loudly, first for Sidonia, and then for some food.

At last, to the great joy of her Grace, he was able, on the fourth day, to walk in the castle garden, and arranged to attend the hunt with his dear uncle upon his return to Wolgast. The Duke, on his arrival, rejoiced greatly to find the young lord so well, and said with his usual gay manner, "Come here, Sidonia; I have been rather unwell on the journey: come here and give me a kiss too, to make me better!" and Sidonia complied. Whereupon her Grace looked unusually sour, but said nothing, for fear of disturbing the general joy. Indeed, the whole castle was in a state of jubilee, and her Grace promised that she and her ladies would attend the hunt on the following day.

About this time the castle was troubled by a strange apparition – no other than the specter of the serpent knight, who had been drowned some time previously. It was reported that every night the ghost entered the castle by the little water-gate, though it was kept barred and bolted, traversed the whole length of the corridor, and sunk down into the earth, just over the place where the ducal coaches and sleighs were kept.

Everyone fled in terror before the ghost, and scarcely a lansquenet could be found to keep the night watch. What this specter betokened shall be related further on in this little history, but at present I must give an account of the grand *battue* which took place according to her Grace's orders, and of what befell there.

Chapter XV

Of the grand battue, and what the young Duke and Sidonia resolved on there

The preparations for the hunt commenced early in the morning, and the knights and nobles assembled in the hall of fishes (so called because the walls were painted with representations of all the fishes that are indigenous to Pomerania). Here a superb breakfast was served, and pages presented water in finger-basins of silver to each of the princely personages. Then costly wines were handed round, and Duke Barnim, having filled to the brim a cup bearing the Pomeranian arms, rose up and said, "Give notice to the warder at St. Peter's." And immediately, as the great bell of the town rang out, and resounded through the castle and all over the town, his Grace gave the health of Prince Ernest, who pledged him in return. Afterwards they all descended to the courtyard, and his Grace entered the ducal mews himself, to select a horse for the day. Now these mews were of such wonderful beauty, that I must needs append a description of them here.

First there was a grand portico, and within a corridor with ranges of pillars on each side, round which were hung antlers and horns of all the animals of the chase. This led to the pond with the island in the center, where the bear was kept, as I have already described. When Duke Barnim and the old knight emerged from the portico to enter the stable, they were met by Johann Appelmann, the chief equerry, who spread before the feet of his Highness a scarlet horse-cloth, embroidered with the ducal arms, whereon he laid a brush and a riding-whip; and then demanded his *Trinkgeld.*

On entering, they observed numerous stalls filled with Pomeranian, Hungarian, Frisian, Danish, and Turkish horses — each race by itself, and each horse standing ready saddled and bridled since the morning. *Item,* all along the walls were ranged enormous brazen lions' heads, which conveyed water throughout the building, and cleansed the stables completely every day.

Otto wondered much at all this magnificence, and asked his Grace what could her Highness want with all these horses.

"They eat their oats in idleness, for the most part," replied the Duke. "No one uses them but the pages and knights of the household, who may select any for riding that pleases them; but her Highness would never diminish any of the state maintained by her deceased lord, Duke Philip. So there has been always, since that time, particular attention paid to the ducal stables at Wolgast."

Now the train began to move towards the hunt, in all about a hundred persons, and in front rode her Grace upon an ambling palfrey, dressed in a riding-habit of green velvet, and wearing a yellow hat with plumes. Her little Casimir rode by her side on a Swedish pony; then followed her ladies-in-waiting, amongst whom rode Sidonia, all likewise dressed in green velvet hunting-dresses, fastened with golden clasps; but in place of yellow, they wore scarlet hats, with gilded herons' plumes. Duke Barnim and Prince Ernest rode along with her Grace; and though none but those of princely blood were allowed to join this group, yet Otto strove to keep near them, as if he really belonged to the party, just as the sacristan strives to make the people think he is as good as the priest by keeping as close as he can to him while the procession moves along the streets.

After these came the marshal, the castellan, and then the treasurer, with the office-bearers, knights, and esquires of the household. Then the chief equerry, with the master of the hounds and the principal huntsmen. But the beaters, pages, lackeys, drummers, coursers, and runners had already gone on before a good way; and never had the Wolgastians beheld such a stately hunt as this since the death of good Duke Philip. So the whole town ran together, and followed the procession for a good space, up to the spot where blue tents were erected for her Grace and her ladies. The ground all round was strewed with flowers and evergreens, and before the tents palisades were erected, on which lay loaded rifles, ready to discharge at any of the game that came that way; and for two miles round the master of the hunt had laid down nets, which were all connected together at a point close to the princely tent.

When the beaters and their dogs had started the animals, he left the tent to reconnoiter, and if the sport promised to be plentiful, he ordered the drums to beat, in order to give her Highness notice. Then she took a rifle herself, and brought down several head, which was easily accomplished, when they passed upon each other as thick as sheep. Sidonia, who had often attended the hunts at Stramehl, was a most expert shot, and brought down ten roes and stags, whereon she had much jesting with the young lords, who had not been half so successful. And let no one imagine that there was danger to her Highness and her ladies in thus firing at the wild droves from her tent, for it was erected upon a scaffolding raised five feet from the ground, and surrounded by palisades, so that it was impossible the animals could ever reach it.

On that day, there were killed altogether one hundred and fifty stags, one hundred roes, five hundred hares, three hundred foxes, one hundred wild boars, seven wolves, five wildcats, and one bear, which was entangled in the net and then shot. And at last the right hearty pleasure of the day began.

For it was the custom at the ducal court for each huntsman, from the master of the hunt down, to receive a portion of the game; and her Grace took much pleasure now in seeing the mode in which the distribution was made. It was done in this wise: each man received the head of the animal, and as much of the neck as he could cover with the ears, by dragging them down with all his might.

So the huntsmen stood now toiling and sweating, each with one foot firmly planted against a stone and the other on the belly of the beast, dragging down the ears with all his force to the very furthest point they could go, when another huntsman, standing by, cut off the head at that point with his hunting-knife.

Then each man let his dog bite at the entrails of a stag, while they repeated old charms and verses over them, such as: —

"Diana, no better e'er track'd a wood;
 There's many a huntsman not half so good."

Or, in Low German: —

"Wasser, if ever the devil you see,
 Bite his leg for him, or he will bite me."

These old rhymes pleased the young Casimir mightily: if his lady mother would only lend him a ribbon, he would lead up little Blaffert his dog to them, and have a rhyme said over him. So her Grace consented, and broke off her sandal-tie to fasten in the little dog's collar, because in her hurry she could find no other string, and left the tent herself with the child to conduct him to the huntsmen.

Now the moment her Grace had taken her eyes off Sidonia, and that all the other ladies had left the tent to follow her and the little boy, who was laughing and playing with his dog, the young maiden, looking round to see that no one was observing her, slipped out and ran in amongst the bushes, and my lord, Prince Ernest, slipped after her. No one observed them, for all eyes were turned upon the princely child, who sprang to a huntsman and begged of him to say a rhyme or two over his little dog Blaffert. The carl rubbed his forehead, and at last gave out his psalm, as follows, in Low German: —

"Blaffert, Blaffert, thou art fat!
  If my lord would only feed
All his people like to that
  'Twould be well for Pommern's need."*

All the bystanders laughed heartily, and then the hounds were given their dinner according to the usage, which was this: — A number of oak and birch trees were felled, and over every two and two there was spread a tablecloth — that is, the warm skin of a deer or wild-boar; into this, as into a wooden trencher, was poured the warm blood of the wild animals, which the hounds lapped up, while forty huntsmen played a march with drums and trumpets, which was re-echoed from the neighboring wood, to the great delight of all the listeners. When the hounds had lapped up all the blood, they began to eat up the tablecloths likewise; but as these belonged to the huntsmen, a great fight took place between them and the dogs for the skins, which was right merry to behold, and greatly rejoiced the ducal party and all the people.

In the meantime, as I said, Sidonia had slipped into the wood, and the young lord after her. He soon found her resting under the shadow of a large nut tree, and the following conversation took place between them, as he afterwards many times related: —

"Alas, gracious Prince, why do you follow me? if your lady mother knew of this we should both suffer. My head ached after all that firing, and therefore I came hither to enjoy a little rest and quietness. Leave me, leave me, my gracious lord."

"No, no, he would not leave her until she told him whether she still loved him; for his lady mother watched him day and night, like the dragon that guarded the Pomeranian arms, and until this moment he had never seen her alone."

"But what could he now desire to say? Had he not sworn by the corpse of his father never to wed her?"

"Yes; in a moment of anguish he had sworn it, because he would have died if she had not been brought back to the castle."

"But still he must hold by his word to his lady mother, would he not?"

---

* Pomerania.

"Impossible! all impossible! He would sooner renounce land and people forever than his beautiful Sidonia. How he felt, for the first time, the truth of the holy words, 'Love is strong as death.'"* Then he throws his arms round her and kissed her, and asked, would she be his?

Here Sidonia covered her face with both hands, and sinking down upon the grass, murmured, "Yours alone, either you or death."

The Prince threw himself down beside her, and besought her not to weep. "He could not bear to see her tears; besides, there was good hope for them yet, for he had spoken to old Zitsewitz, who wished them both well, and who had given him some good advice."

Sidonia (quickly removing her hands). — "What was it?"

"To have a private marriage. Then the devil himself could not separate them, much less the old bigot Ulrich. There was a priest in the neighborhood, of the name of Neigialink. He lived in Crummyn,$FA town near Wolgast. with a nun whom he had carried off from her convent and married; therefore he would be able to sympathize with lovers, and would help them."

"But his Highness should remember his kingly state, and not bring misery on them both forever."

"He had considered all that, they should therefore keep this marriage private for a year; she could live at Stramehl during that period, and receive his visits without his mother knowing of the matter. At the end of that year he would be of age, and his own master."

Sidonia (embracing him). — "Ah, if he really loved her so, then the sooner the better to the church. But let him take care that evil-minded people would not separate them forever, and bring her to an early grave. Had the priest been informed that he would be required to wed them?"

"Not yet; but if he continued as strong as he felt today, he would ride over to Crummyn himself (for it was quite near to Wolgast) the moment Duke Barnim and her father quitted the castle."

"But how would she know the result of his visit? his mother watched her day and night. Could he send a page or a serving-maid to her? — though indeed there were none now he could trust, for Ulrich had dismissed all her good friends. And if he came himself to her room, evil might be spoken of it."

"He had arranged all that already. There was the bear, as she remembered, chained upon the little island in the horse-pond, just under her window. Now when he returned from Crummyn, he would go out by seven in the morning, before his lady mother began her spinning, and commence shooting arrows at the bear, by way of sport; then, as if by

---

* Song of Solomon viii. 6.

chance, he would let fly an arrow at her window and shiver the glass, but the arrow would contain a little note, detailing his visit to the priest at Crummyn, and the arrangement he had made for carrying her away secretly from the castle. She must take care, however, to move away her seat from the window, and place it in a corner, lest the arrow might strike herself."

But then a loud "Sidonia! Sidonia!" resounded through the wood, and immediately after, "Ernest! Ernest!"

So she sprang up, and cried, "Run, dearest Prince, run as fast as you are able, to the other side, where the huntsmen are gathering, and mix with them, so that her Grace may not perceive you." This he did, and began to talk to the huntsmen about their dogs and the sweep of the chase, and as her Grace continued calling "Ernest! Ernest!" he stepped slowly towards her out of the crowd, and asked what was her pleasure? So she suspected nothing, and grew quite calm again.

Duke Barnim now began to complain of hunger, and asked her Grace where she meant to serve them a collation, for he could never hold out until they reached Wolgast, and his friend Otto also was growing as ravenous as a wolf.

Her Grace answered, the collation was laid in the Cisan tower, close beside them, and as the weather was good, his Grace could amuse himself with the *tubum opticum,* which a Pomeranian noble had bought in Middelburg from one Johann Lippersein,* and presented to her. By the aid of this telescope he would see as far as his own town of Stettin. Neither the Duke nor Otto Bork believed it possible to see Stettin, at the distance of thirteen or fourteen miles, with any instrument. But her Grace, who had heard of Otto's godless infidelity, rebuked him gravely, saying, "You will soon be convinced, sir knight; so we often hold that to be impossible in spiritual matters, which becomes not only possible, but certain, when we look through the telescope which the Holy Spirit presents to us, weak and short-sighted mortals. God give to every infidel such a *tubum opticum!*" The Duke, fearing now that her Grace would continue her sermon indefinitely, interrupted her in his jesting way — "Listen, dear cousin! I will lay a wager with you. If I cannot see Stettin, as you promise, you shall give me a kiss; but if I see it and recognize it clearly, then I shall give you a kiss."

Her Grace was truly scandalized, as one may imagine, and replied angrily — "Good uncle! if you attempt to offer such indignities to me, the princely widow, I must pray your Grace to leave my court with all speed, and never to return!" This rebuke made everyone grave until they

---

* An optician, and the probable inventor of the telescope, which was first employed about the end of the sixteenth and the beginning of the seventeenth century.

reached the Cisan tower. This building lay only half a mile from the hunting-ground, and was situated on the summit of the Cisanberg, from whence its name. It was built of wood, and contained four stories, besides excellent stabling for horses. The apartments were light, airy, and elegant, so that her Grace frequently passed a portion of the summertime there. The upper story commanded a view of the whole adjacent country. At the foot of the hill ran the little river Cisa into the Peen, and many light, beautiful bridges were thrown over it at different points. The hill itself was finely wooded with pines and other trees, and the tower was made more light and airy than that which Duke Johann Frederick afterwards erected at Friedrichswald, and commanded a far finer prospect, seeing that the Cisanberg is the highest hill in Pomerania.

While the party proceeded to the tower, Sidonia rode along by her father, and to judge from her animation and gestures, she was, no doubt, communicating to him all that the young lord had promised, and her hopes, in consequence, that a very short period would elapse before he might salute her as Duchess of Pomerania.

When they reached the tower, all admired the view even from the lower window, for they could see the Peen, the Achterwasser, and eight or nine towns, besides the sea in the distance. I say nothing of Wolgast, which seemed to lie just beneath their feet, with its princely castle and cathedral perfectly distinct, and all its seats laid out like a map, where they could even distinguish the people walking. Then her Grace bade them ascend to the upper story, and look out for Stettin, but they sought for it in vain with their unassisted eyes; then her Grace placed the *tubum opticum* before the Duke, and no sooner had he looked through it than he cried out, "As I live, Otto, there is my strong tower of St. James's, and my ducal castle to the left, lying far behind the Finkenwald mountain." But the unbelieving Thomas laughed, and only answered, "My gracious Prince! do not let yourself be so easily imposed upon."

Hereupon the Duke made him look through the telescope himself; and no sooner had he applied his eye to the glass than he jumped back, rubbed his eyes, looked through a second time, and then exclaimed –

"Well, as true as my name is Otto Bork, I never could have believed this."

"Now, sir knight," said her Grace, "so it is with you as concerns spiritual things. How if you should one day find that to be true which your infidelity now presumptuously asserts to be false? Will not your repentance then be bitter? If you have found my words true – the words of a poor, weak, sinful woman, will you not much more find those of the holy Son of God? Yes, to your horror and dismay, you will find His words to be truth, of whom even His enemies testified that He never lied — Matt. xxii. 16. Tremble, sir knight, and bethink you that what often seems impossible to man is possible to God."

The bold knight was now completely silenced, and the good-natured Duke, seeing that he had not a word to say in reply, advanced to his rescue, and changed the conversation by saying —

"See, Otto, the wind seems so favorable just now, that I think we had better say 'Vale' to our gracious hostess in the morning, and return to Stettin."

Not a word did his Grace venture to say more about the wager of the kisses, for his dear cousin's demeanor restrained even his hilarity. Otto had nothing to object to the arrangement; and her Grace said, if they were not willing longer to abide at her widowed court, she would bid them both Godspeed upon their journey. "And you, sir knight, may take back your daughter Sidonia, for our dear son, as you may perceive, is now quite restored, and no longer needs her nursing. For the good deed she has wrought in curing him, I shall recompense her as befits me. But at my court the maiden can no longer abide."

The knight was at first so thunderstruck by these words that he could not speak; but at last drawing himself up proudly, he said, "Good; I shall take the Lady Sidonia back with me to my castle; but as touching the recompense, keep it for those who need it." Sidonia, however, remained quite silent, as did also the young lord.

But hear what happened. The festival lasted until late in the night, and then suddenly such a faintness and bodily weakness came over the young Prince Ernest that all the physicians had to be sent for; and they with one accord entreated her Grace, if she valued his life, not to send away Sidonia.

One can imagine what her Grace felt at this news. Nothing would persuade her to believe but that Sidonia had given him some witch-drink, such as the girl out of Daber had taught her to make.

No one could believe either that his Highness affected this sickness, in order to force his mother to keep Sidonia at the court; indeed, he afterwards strongly asseverated, and this at a time when he would have killed Sidonia with a look, if it had been possible, that this weakness came upon him suddenly like an ague, and that it could not have been caused by anything she had given him, for he had eaten nothing, except at the banquet at the Cisan tower.

In short, the young Prince became as bad as ever; but Sidonia never heeded him, only busied herself packing up her things, as if she really intended going away with Otto, and finally, as eight o'clock struck the next morning, she wrapped herself in her mantle and hood, and went with her father and Duke Barnim to take leave of her Grace. She looked as bitter and sour as a vinegar-cruet — nothing would tempt her to remain even for one day longer. What was her Grace to do? the young lord was dying, and had already dispatched two pages to her, entreating for one sight of Sidonia! She must give the artful hypocrite good words — but they were of no avail — Sidonia insisted on leaving the castle that instant with her father; then turning to Duke Barnim, she exclaimed with bitter tears, "Now, gracious Prince, you see yourself how I am treated here."

Neither would the cunning Otto permit his daughter to remain on any account, unless, indeed, her Grace gave him a written authority to receive the dues on the Jena. Such shameless knavery at last enraged the old Duke Barnim to such a degree that he cried out — "Listen, Otto, my illustrious cousin here has no more to do with the dues on the Jena than you have; they belong to me alone, and I can give no promise until I lay the question before my council and the diet of the Stettin dukedom: be content, therefore, to wait until then." One may easily guess what was the termination of the little drama got up by Otto and his fair daughter — namely, that Otto sailed away with the Duke, and that Sidonia remained at the court of Wolgast.

Chapter XVI

How the ghost continued to haunt the castle, and of its daring behavior —
Item, how the young lord regained his strength, and was able to visit
Crummyn, with what happened to him there.

So Sidonia was again seated by the couch of the young Prince, with her hand in his hand; but her Grace, as may well be imagined, was never very far off from them; and this annoyed Sidonia so much, that she did not scruple to treat the mourning mother and princely widow with the utmost contempt; at last disdaining even to answer the questions addressed to her by her Grace. All this the Duchess bore patiently for the sake of her dear son. But even Prince Ernest felt, at length, ashamed of such insolent scorn being displayed towards his mother, and said —

"What, Sidonia, will you not even answer my gracious mother?"

Hereupon the hypocrite sighed, and answered —

"Ah, my gracious Prince! I esteem it better to pray in silence beside your bed than to hold a loud chattering in your ears. Besides, when I am speaking to God I cannot, at the same time, answer your lady mother."

This pleased the young man, and he pressed her little hand, and kissed it. And very shortly after, his strength returned to him wonderfully, so that her Grace and Sidonia only watched by him one night. The next day he fell into a profound sleep, and awoke from it perfectly recovered.

In the meantime, the ghost became so daring and troublesome, that all the house stood in fear of it. Oftentimes it would be seen even in the clear morning light; and a maid, who had forgotten to make the bed of one of the grooms, and ran to the stables at night to finish her work, encountered the ghost there, and nearly died of fright. *Item,* Clara von Dewitz, one beautiful moonlight night, having gone out to take a turn up and down the corridor, because she could not sleep from the toothache, saw the apparition, just as day dawned, sinking down into the earth, not far from the chamber of Sidonia, to her great horror and astonishment. *Item,* her Grace, that very same night, having heard a noise in the corridor, opened her door, and there stood the ghost before her, leaning against a pillar. She was horror-struck, and clapped to her door hastily, but said nothing to the young Prince, for fear of alarming him.

He had recovered, as I have said, in a most wonderful manner, and though still looking pale and haggard, yet his love for the maiden would not permit him to defer his visit to Crummyn any longer; particularly as it lay only half a mile from the castle, but on the opposite bank of the river, near the island of Usdom.

Thereupon, on the fourth night, he descended to the little water-gate, having previously arranged with his chief equerry, Appelmann, to have a boat there in readiness for him, and also a good horse, to take across the ferry with them to the other side. So, at twelve o'clock, he and Appelmann embarked privately, with Johann Bruwer, the ferryman, and were safely landed at Mahlzow. Here he mounted his horse, and told the two others to await his return, and conceal themselves in the wood if anyone approached. Appelmann begged permission to accompany his Highness, which, however, was denied; the young Prince charging them strictly to hold themselves concealed till his return, and never reveal to human being where they had conducted him this evening, on pain of his severe anger and loss of favor forever; but if they held their secret close, he would recompense them at no distant time, in a manner even far beyond their hopes.

So his Highness rode off to Crummyn, where all was darkness, except, indeed, one small ray of light that glanced from the lower windows of the cloister — for it was standing at that time. He dismounted, tied his horse to a tree, and knocked at the window, through which he had a glimpse of an old woman, in nun's garments, who held a crucifix between her hands, and prayed.

"Who are you?" she demanded. "What can you want here at such an hour?"

"I am from Wolgast," he answered, "and must see the priest of Crummyn."

"There is no priest here now."

"But I have been told that a priest of the name of Neigialink lived here."

Illa. — "He was a Lutheran swaddler and no priest, otherwise he would not live in open sin with a nun."

"It is all the same to me; only come and show me the way."

Illa. — "Was he a heathen or a true Christian?"

His Highness could not make out what the old mother meant, but when he answered, "I am a Christian," she opened the door, and let him enter her cell. As she lifted up the lamp, however, she started back in terror at his young, pale, haggard face. Then, looking at his rich garments, she cried —

"This must be a son of good Duke Philip's, for never were two faces more alike."

The Prince never imagined that the old mother could betray him, and therefore answered, "Yes; and now lead me to the priest."

So the old mother began to lament over the downfall of the pure Christian doctrine, which his father, Duke Philip, had upheld so bravely. And if the young lord held the true faith (as she hoped by his saying he was a Christian), if so, then she would die happy, and the sooner the better — even if it were this night, for she was the last of all the sisterhood, all the other nuns having died of grief; and so she went on chattering.

Prince Ernest regretted that he had not time to discourse with her upon the true faith, but would she tell him where the priest was to be found.

Illa. — "She would take him to the parson, but he must first do her a service."

"Whatever she desired, so that it would not detain him."

Illa. – "It was on this night the vigil of the holy St. Bernard, their patron saint, was held; now, there was no one to light the altar candles for her, for her maid, who had grown old along with her, lay a-dying, and she was too old and weak herself to stretch up so high. And the idle Lutheran heretics of the town would mock, if they knew she worshipped God after the manner of her fathers. The old Lutheran swaddler, too, would not suffer it, if he knew she prayed in the church by nights. But she did not care for his anger, for she had a private key that let her in at all hours; and his Highness, the Prince, at her earnest prayers, had given her permission to pray in the church, at any time she pleased, from then till her death."

So the old mother wept so bitterly, and kissed his Highness's hand, entreating him with such sad lamentations to remain with her until she said a prayer, that he consented. And she said, if the heretic parson came there to scold her, which of a surety he would, knowing that she never omitted a vigil, he could talk to him in the church, without going to disturb him and his harlot nun at their own residence. Besides, the church was the safest place to discourse in, for no one would notice them, and he would be able to protect her from the parson's anger besides.

Here the old mother took up the church keys and a horn lantern, and led the young Prince through a narrow corridor up to the church door. Hardly, however, had she put the key in the lock, when the loud bark of a dog was heard inside, and they soon heard it scratching, and smelling, and growling at them close to the door.

"What can that dog be here for?" said his Highness in alarm.

"Alas!" answered the nun, "since the pure old religion was destroyed, profanity and covetousness have got the upper hand; so every church where even a single pious relic of the wealth of the good old times remains, must be guarded, as you see, by dogs.* And she had herself

---

* It is an undeniable fact, that the immorality of the people fearfully increased with the progress of the Reformation throughout Pomerania. An old chronicler, and a Protestant, thus testifies, 1542: – "And since this time (the Reformation) a great change has come over all things. In place of piety, we have profanity; in place of reverence, sacrilege and the plundering of God's churches; in place of alms-deeds, stinginess and selfishness; in place of feasts, greed and gluttony; in place of festivals, labor; in place of obedience and humility of children, obstinacy and self-opinion; in place of honor and veneration for the priesthood, contempt for the priest and the church ministers. So that one might justly assert that the preaching of the evangelism had made the people worse in place of better."

Another Protestant preacher, John Borkmann, asserts, 1560: – "As for sin, it overflows all places and all stations. It is growing stronger in all offices, in all trades, in all employments, in every station of life – what shall I say more? – in every

locked up her pretty dog Störteback* here, that no one might rob the altar of the golden candlesticks and the little jewels, at least as long as she lived."

So she desired Störteback to lie still, and then entered the church with the Prince, who lit the altar candles for her, and then looked round with wonder on the silver lamps, the golden pix and caps, and other vessels adorned with jewels, used by the Papists in their ceremonies.

The old mother, meanwhile, took off her white garment and black scapulary, and being thus naked almost to the waist, descended into a coffin, which was lying in a corner beside the altar. Here she groped till she brought up a crucifix, and a scourge of knotted cords. Then she kneeled down within the coffin, lashing herself with one hand till the blood flowed from her shoulders, and with the other holding up the crucifix, which she kissed from time to time, whilst she recited the hymn of the holy St. Bernard: —

"Salve caput cruentatum,
  Totum spinis coronatum,
  Conquassatum, vulneratum,
  Arundine verberatum
  Facie sputis illita."

When she had thus prayed, and scourged herself a while, she extended the crucifix with her bleeding arm to the Prince, and prayed him, for the sake of God, to have compassion on her, and so would the bleeding Saviour and all the saints have compassion upon him at the last day. And when his Highness asked her what he could do for her, she besought him to bring her a priest from Grypswald, who could break the Lord's body once more for her, and give her the last sacrament of extreme unction here in her coffin. Then would she never wish to leave it, but die of joy if this only was granted to her.

So the Prince promised to fulfill her wishes; whereupon she crouched down again in the coffin, and recommenced the scourging, while she repeated with loud sobs and groans the two last verses of the hymn. Scarcely had she ended when a small side-door opened, and the dog Störteback began to bark vociferously.

"What!" exclaimed a voice, "is that old damned Catholic witch at her mummeries, and burning my good wax candles all for nothing?"

---

individual" — and so on. I would therefore recommend the blind eulogists of the good old times to examine history for themselves, and not to place implicit belief either in the pragmatical representations of the old and new Lutherans."

* The name of a notorious northern pirate.

And, silencing the dog, a man stepped forward hastily, but, seeing the Prince, paused in astonishment. Whereupon the old mother raised herself up out of the coffin, and said, "Did I not tell your Grace that you would see the hardhearted heretic here? – that is the man you seek." So the Prince brought him into the choir, and told him that he was Prince Ernest Ludovicus, and came here to request that he would privately wed him on the following night, without knowledge of any human being, to his beloved and affianced bride, Sidonia von Bork.

The priest, however, did not care to mix himself up with such a business, seeing that he feared Ulrich mightily; but his Grace promised him a better living at the end of the year, if he would undertake to serve him now.

To which the priest answered – "Who knows if your Highness will be alive by the end of the year, for you look as pale as a corpse?"

"He never felt better in his life. He had been ill lately, but now was as sound as a fish. Would he not marry him?"

Hic. – "Certainly not; unless he received a handsome consideration. He had a wife and dear children; what would become of them if he incurred the displeasure of that stern Lord Chamberlain and of the princely widow?"

"But could he not bring his family to Stettin; for he and his young bride intended to fly there, and put themselves under the protection of his dear uncle, Duke Barnim?"

Hic. – "It was a dangerous business; still, if his Highness gave him a thousand gulden down, and a written promise, signed and sealed, that he would provide him with a better living before the year had expired, why, out of love for the young lord, he would consent to peril himself and his family; but his Highness must not think evil of him for demanding the thousand gulden paid down immediately, for how were his dear wife and children to be supported through the long year otherwise?"

His Highness, however, considered the sum too large, and said that his gracious mother had scarcely more a year for herself than a thousand gulden – she that was the Duchess of Pomerania.

However, they finally agreed upon four hundred gulden; for his Highness showed him that Doctor Luther himself had only four hundred gulden a year, and surely he would not require more than the great *reformator ecclesia.*

So everything was arranged at last, the priest promising to perform the ceremony on the third night from that; "For some time," he said, "would be necessary to collect people to assist them in their flight, and money must be distributed; but his Highness would, of course, repay all that he expended in his behalf, and further promise to give him and his family free quarters when they reached Stettin."

After the ceremony, they could reach the boat through the convent garden, and sail away to Warte.* Then he would have four or five peasants in waiting, with carriages ready, to escort them to East Clune, from whence they could take another boat and cross the Haff into Stettin; for, as they could not reckon on a fair wind with any certainty, it was better to perform the journey half by land and half by water; besides, the fishermen whom he intended to employ were not accustomed to sail up the Peen the whole way into the Haff, for their little fishing-smacks were too slight to stand a strong current.

Hereupon the Prince answered, that, since it was necessary, he would wait until the third night, when the priest should have everything in readiness, but meanwhile should confide the secret to no one. So he turned away, and comforted the old mother again with his promises as he passed out.

The next morning, having written all down for Sidonia, and concealed the note in an arrow, he went forth as he had arranged, and began to tease the bear by shooting arrows at him, till the beast roared and shook his chain. Then, perceiving that Sidonia had observed him from the window, he watched a favorable opportunity, and shot the arrow up, right through her window, so that the pane of glass rattled down upon the floor. In the billet therein concealed he explained the whole plan of escape; and asked her to inform him, in return, how she could manage to come to him on the third night. Would his dearest Sidonia put on the dress of a page? He could bring it to her little chamber himself the next night. She must write a little note in answer, and conceal it in the arrow as he had done, then throw it out of the window, and he would be on the watch to pick it up.

So Sidonia replied to him that she was content; but, as regarded the page's dress, he must leave it, about ten o'clock the next night, upon the beer-barrel in the corridor, but not attempt to bring it himself to her chamber. Concerning the manner in which she was to meet him on the third night, had he forgotten that the old castellan barred and bolted all that wing of the castle by eleven o'clock, so that she could never leave the corridor by the usual way; but there was a trapdoor near her little chamber which led down into the ducal stables, and this door no one ever thought of or minded — it was never bolted night or day, and was quite large enough for a man to creep through. Her dear Prince might wait for her, by that trapdoor, at eleven o'clock on the appointed night.

---

* A town near Usdom.

He could not mistake it, for the large basket lay close behind, in which her Grace kept her darling little kittens; from thence they could easily get into the outer courtyard, which was never locked, and, after that, go where they pleased. If he approved of this arrangement, let him shoot another arrow into her room; but, above all things, he was to keep at a distance from her during the day, that her Grace might not suspect anything.

Having thrown the arrow out of the window, and received another in answer from the Prince, which the artful hypocrite flung out as if in great anger, she ran to Clara's room, and complained bitterly how the young lord had broken her window, because, forsooth, he must be shooting arrows at the bear; and so she had to come into her room out of the cold air, until the glazier came to put in the glass. When Clara asked how she could be so angry with the young Prince — did she not love him any longer? — Sidonia replied, that truly she had grown very tired of him, for he did nothing but sigh and groan whenever he came near her, like an asthmatic old woman, and had grown as thin and dry as a baked plum. There was nothing very lovable about him now. Would to Heaven that he were quite well, and she would soon bid farewell to the castle and everyone in it; but the moment she spoke of going his sickness returned, so that she was obliged to remain, which was much against her inclination; and this she might tell Clara in confidence, because she had always been her truest friend.

Then she pretended to weep, and cursed her beauty, which had brought her nothing but unhappiness; thereupon the tender-hearted Clara began to comfort her, and kissed her; and the moment Sidonia left her to get the glass mended, Clara ran to her Grace to tell her the joyful tidings; but, alas! that very day the wickedness of the artful maiden was brought to light. For what happened in the afternoon? See, the nun of Crummyn steps out of a boat at the little water-gate, and places herself in a corner of the courtyard, where the people soon gather round in a crowd, to laugh at her white garments and black scapulary; and the boys begin to pelt the poor old mother with stones, and abuse her, calling her the old Papist witch; but by good fortune the castellan comes by, and commands the crowd to leave off tormenting her, and then asks her business.

Illa. — "She must speak instantly to her Grace the princely widow."

So the old man brings her to her Grace, with whom Clara was still conversing, and the old nun, after she had kneeled to the Duchess and kissed her hand, began to relate how her young lord, Prince Ernest, had been with her the night before, while she was keeping the *vigilia* of holy St. Bernard to the best of her ability, and had urgently demanded to see the Lutheran priest named Neigialink, and that when this same priest came into the church to scold her, as was his wont, he and the Prince had retired into the choir, and there held a long conversation which she did not comprehend. But the priest's mistress had told her the whole business this morning, under a promise of secrecy — namely, that the priest, her leman, had promised to wed Prince Ernest privately, on the third night from that, to a certain young damsel named Sidonia von Bork. That the Prince had given him a thousand gulden for his services, and a promise of a rich living when he succeeded to the government, so that in future she could live as grand as an abbess, and have what beautiful horses she chose from the ducal stables.

"And this," said the nun, "was told me by the priest's mistress; but as I have a true Pomeranian heart, although, indeed, the Prince has left the good old religion, I could not rest in peace until I stepped into a boat, weak and old as I am, and sailed off here direct to inform your Grace of the plot." She only asked one favor in return for her service. It was that her Grace would permit her to end the rest of her days peaceably in the cloister, and protect her from the harshness of the Lutheran priests and the fury of the mob, who fell on her like mad dogs here in the castle court, and would have torn her to pieces if the castellan had not come by and rescued her. But above all, she requested and prayed her Grace to permit a true priest to come to her from Grypswald, who could give her the holy Eucharist, and prepare her for death. But her Grace was struck dumb by astonishment and alarm, and Clara could not speak either, only wrung her hands in anguish. And her Grace continued to walk up and down the room weeping bitterly, until at last she sat down before her desk to indite a note to old Ulrich, praying for his presence without delay, and straightway dispatched the chief equerry, Appelmann, with it to Spantekow.

The old nun still continued crying, would not her Grace send her a priest? But her Grace refused; for in fact she was a stern upholder of the pure doctrine. Anything else the old mother demanded she might have, but with the abominations of Popery her Grace would have nothing to do. Still the old nun prayed and writhed at her feet, crying and groaning, "For the love of God, a priest! for the love of God, a priest!" but her Grace drew herself up stiff and stern, and let the old woman writhe there unheeded, until at length she motioned to Clara to have her removed to the courtyard, where the poor creature leaned up against the pump in bitter agony, and drew forth a crucifix from her bosom, kissed it, and looking up to heaven, cried, "Jesu! Jesu! art Thou come at last?" and then dropped down dead upon the pavement, which the crowd no sooner observed than they gathered round the corpse, screaming out,

"The devil has carried her off! See! the devil has carried off the old Papist witch!" Hearing the uproar, her Grace descended, as did also the young lord and Sidonia, who both appeared as if they knew nothing at all about the old nun. And her Grace commanded that the executioner should by no means drag away the body, as the people demanded, who were now rushing to the spot from all quarters of the town, but that it should be decently lifted into the boat and conveyed back again to Crummyn, there to be interred with the other members of the sisterhood at the cloister.

No word did she speak, either to her undutiful son or to Sidonia, about what she had heard; only when the latter asked her what the nun came there for, she answered coldly, "For a Popish priest." Hereupon the young Prince was filled with joy, concluding that nothing had been betrayed as yet. And it was natural the old nun should come with this request, seeing that she had made the same to him. Her Grace also strictly charged Clara to observe a profound silence upon all they had heard, until the old chamberlain arrived, and this she promised.

Chapter XVII

Of Ulrich's counsels — Item, how Clara von Dewitz came upon the track of the ghost

*A*t eleven o'clock that same night, the good and loyal Lord Ulrich arrived at the castle with Appelmann, from Spantekow, and just waited to change his traveling dress before he proceeded to the apartment of her Grace. He found her seated with Clara and another maiden, weeping bitterly. Dr. Gerschovius was also present. When the old man entered, her Grace's lamentations became yet louder — alas! how she was afflicted! Who could have believed that all this had come upon her because the devil, out of malice, had made Dr. Luther drop her wedding-ring at the bridal! And when the knight asked in alarm what had happened, she replied that tears prevented her speaking, but Dr. Gerschovius would tell him all.

So the doctor related the whole affair, from the declaration of the old nun to the hypocritical conduct of Sidonia towards Clara von Dewitz, upon which the old knight shook his head, and said, "Did I not counsel your Grace to let the young lord die, in God's name, for better is it to lose life than honor. Had he died then, so would the Almighty have raised him pure and perfect at the last day, but now he is growing daily in wickedness as a young wolf in ferocity."

Then her Grace made answer, the past could not now be recalled; and that she was ready to answer before God for what she had done through motherly love and tenderness. They must now advise her how to save her infatuated son from the snares of this wanton. Dr. Gerschovius, thereupon, gave it as his opinion that they should each be placed in strict confinement for the next fourteen days, during which time he would visit and admonish them twice a day, by which means he hoped soon to turn their hearts to God.

Here old Ulrich laughed outright, and asked the doctor, was he still bent upon teaching Sidonia her catechism? As to the young lord, no admonition would do him good now; he was thoroughly bewitched by the girl, and though he made a hundred promises to give her up, would never hold one of them. Alas! alas! that the son of good Duke Philip should be so degenerate.

But her Grace wept bitterly, and said, that never was there a more obedient, docile, and amiable child than her dear Ernest; skilled in all the fine arts, and gifted by nature with all that could ensure a mother's love. "But how does all this help him now?" cried Ulrich. "It is with a good heart as with a good ship, unless you guide it, it will run aground — stand by the helm, or the best ship will be lost. What had the country to expect from a Prince who would die, forsooth? unless his mistress sat by his bedside? Ah! if he could only have followed the funeral of the young lord, he would have given a hundred florins to the poor that very day!"

"It was not her son's fault — that base hypocrite had caused it all by some hell magic."

Ille. — "That was quite impossible; however, he would believe it to please her Grace."

"Then let him speak his opinion, if the counsel of Dr. Gerschovius did not please him."

Ille. — "His advice, then, was to keep quiet until the third night, then secretly place a guard round the castle and at the wing, and when the bridal party met, take them out prisoners, send my young lord to the tower, but disgrace Sidonia publicly, and send her off where she pleased – to the fiend, if she liked."

"Then they would have the same old scene over again; her son would fall sick, and Sidonia could not be brought back to cure him, if once she had been publicly disgraced before all the people. So matters would be worse than ever."

Hereupon old Ulrich fell into such a rage that he cursed and swore, that her Grace treated him no better than a fool, to bring him hither from Spantekow, and then refuse to take his advice. As to Sidonia, her Grace had already brought disgrace upon her princely house, by first turning her out, and then praying her to come back before three days had elapsed. All Pomerania talked of it, and old Otto Bork did not scruple to brag and boast everywhere, that her Grace had no peace or rest from her conscience until she had asked forgiveness from the Lady Sidonia (as the vain old knave called her) and entreated her to return. Now if she took the advice of Doctor Gerschovius, and first imprisoned and then turned away Sidonia, no one would believe in her story of the intended marriage, but look on her conduct as only a confirmation of all the hard treatment which her Grace was reported to have employed towards the girl; whereas if she only waited till the whole bridal party were ready to start, and then arrested Sidonia, her Grace was justified before the whole world, for what greater fault could be committed than thus to entrap the young Prince into a secret marriage, and run away with him by night from the castle? Let her Grace then send for the executioner, and let him give Sidonia a public whipping before all the people. No one would think the punishment too hard, for seducing a Prince of Pomerania into a marriage with her.

So the princely widow of Duke Philip will be justified before all the world; and when the young lord sees his bride so disgraced, he will assuredly be right willing to give her up; even if he fall sick, it is impossible that he could send for a maiden to sit by his bed who had been publicly whipped by the executioner. Those were stern measures, perhaps, but a branch of the old Pomeranian tree was decayed; it must be lopped, or the whole tree itself would soon fall.

When the Grand Chamberlain ceased speaking, her Grace considered the matter well, and finally pronounced that she would follow his advice, whereupon, as the night waxed late, she dismissed the party to their beds, retaining only Clara with her for a little longer.

But a strange thing happened as she, too, finally quitted her Grace, and proceeded along the corridor to her own little apartment – and here let everyone consider how the hand of God is in everything, and what great events He can bring forth from the slightest causes, as a great oak springs up from a little acorn.

For as the maiden walked along, her sandal became unfastened, and tripped her, so that she nearly fell upon her face, whereupon she paused, and placing her foot upon a beer-barrel that stood against the wall not far from Sidonia's chamber, began to fasten it, but lo! just at that moment the head of the ghost appeared rising through the trapdoor, and looked round, then, as if aware of her presence, drew back, and she heard a noise as if it had jumped down on the earth beneath. She was horribly frightened, and crept trembling to her bed; but then on reflecting over this apparition of the serpent knight, it came into her head that it could not be a ghost, since it came down on the ground with such a heavy jump; she prayed to God, therefore, to help her in discovering this matter, and as she could not sleep, rose before the first glimmer of daylight to examine this hole which lay so close to Sidonia's chamber, and there truly she discovered the trapdoor, and having opened, found that it lay right over a large coach in the ducal stables; thereupon she concluded that the ghost was no other than the Prince himself who thus visited Sidonia.

Then she remembered that the ghost had been particularly active while the young Prince lay sick on his bed watched by his mother; so to make the matter clearer she went the next evening into the stables, and observing the coach, which lay just beneath the hole, sprinkled fine ash-dust all round it. Then returning to her room, she waited until it grew quite dark, and as ten o'clock struck and all the doors of the corridor leading to the women's apartments were barred and bolted, she wrapped herself in a black mantle and stole out with a palpitating heart into the gallery. Remembering the large beer-barrel near Sidonia's room, she crouched down behind it, and from thence had a distinct view of the trapdoor, and also of Sidonia's chamber. There she waited for about an hour, when she perceived the young Prince coming, but not through the trapdoor. He knocked lightly at Sidonia's door, who opened it instantly, and they held a long whispering conversation together. He had brought her the page's dress, and there was nothing to be feared now, for he had examined the trap and found they could easily get out through it on the top of the coach, and from thence into the stables. After that the way was clear. Surely some good angel had put the idea into her head. Then he kissed her tenderly.

Illa. — "What did the old nun come for? Could she have betrayed them?"

Hic. — "Impossible. She did not know a syllable of their affairs, and had come to ask his lady mother to send her a Popish priest, as she had asked himself." Then he kissed her again, but she tore herself from his arms, threw the little bundle into the room, and shut the door in his face. Whereupon the young Prince went his way, sighing as if his heart would break.

Now Clara concluded, with reason, that the young lord was not the ghost, inasmuch as he did not creep through the trapdoor, nor did he wear helmet or cuirass, or any sort of disguise. But when she heard Sidonia talk with such knowledge of the trapdoor, she guessed there was some knavery in the matter, and though she sat the night there she was determined to watch. And behold! at twelve o'clock there was a great clattering heard below, and presently a helmet appeared rising through the hole, and then the entire figure of the ghost clambered up through it, and after cautiously looking round it, approached Sidonia's door, and knocked lightly. Immediately she opened it herself, admitted the ghost, and Clara heard her drawing the bolts of the door within.

The pious and chaste maiden felt ready to faint with shame; for it was now evident that Sidonia deceived the poor young Prince as well as everyone else, and that this ghost whom she admitted must be a favored lover. She resolved to watch until he came out. But it was about the dawn of morning before he again appeared, and took his hellish path down through the trapdoor, in the same way as he had risen. But to make all certain she took a brush, and before it was quite day, descended to the stables, where, indeed, she observed large, heavy footprints in the ashes all round the coach, quite unlike those which the delicate little feet of his Highness would have made. So she swept them all clean away to avoid exciting any suspicion, and crept back noiselessly to her little room. Then waiting till the morning was somewhat advanced, she dispatched her maid on some errand into the town, in order to get rid of her, and then watched anxiously for her bridegroom, Marcus Bork, who always passed her door going to his office; and hearing his step, she opened her door softly, and drew him in. Then she related fully all she had heard and seen on the past night.

The upright and virtuous young man clasped his hands together in horror and disgust, but could not resolve whether it were fitter to declare the whole matter to her Highness instantly or not. Clara, however, was of opinion that her Grace would derive great comfort from the information, because when the Prince found how Sidonia had betrayed him, he would give up the creature of his own accord. To which Marcus answered, that probably the Prince would not believe a word of the story, and then matters would be in a worse way than ever.

Illa. – "Was he afraid to disgrace Sidonia because she was his kins-woman? Was it the honor of his name he wished to shield by sparing her from infamy?"

Hic. – "No; she wronged him. If she were his sister, he would still do his duty towards her Grace. The honor of the whole Pomeranian house was periled here, and he would save it at any cost. But did his darling bride know who the ghost was?"

Illa. – "No; she had been thinking the whole night about him till her head ached, but in vain."

At this moment the Grand Chamberlain passed the room on his way to the Duchess, and they both went to the door, and entreated him to come in and give them his advice. How the old knight laughed for joy when he heard all; it was almost as good news to him as the death of the young lord would have been. But no; they must not breathe a syllable of it to her Highness. Wait for this night, and if the dear ghost appeared again, he would give him and his paramour something to think of to the end of their lives. Then he walked up and down Clara's little room, thinking over what should be done; and finally resolved to open the matter to the young Prince that night between ten and eleven o'clock, and show him what a creature he was going to make Duchess of Pomerania. After which they should all, Marcus included, go armed to the stables – for the Prince, no doubt, would be slow of belief – and there conceal themselves in the coach until the ghost arrived. If he came, as was almost certain, they would follow him to Sidonia's room, break it open, and discover them together. In order that witnesses might not be wanting, he would desire all the pages and household to be collected in his room at that hour; and the moment they were certain of having trapped the ghost, Marcus should slip out of the coach, and run to gather them all together in the grand corridor. To ensure all this being done, he would take the keys from the castellan himself that night, and keep them in his own possession. But, above all things, they were to keep still and quiet during the day; and now he would proceed to her Grace.

But Marcus Bork begged to ask him, if the ghost did not come that night, what was to be done? For the next was to be that of the marriage, and unless the Prince was convinced by his own eyes, nothing would make him credit the wickedness of his intended bride. Sidonia would swear by heaven and earth that the story was a malicious invention, and a plot to effect her utter destruction.

This view of the case puzzled the old knight not a little, and he rubbed his forehead and paced up and down the room, till suddenly an idea struck him, and he exclaimed – "I have it, Marcus! You are a brave youth, dear Marcus, and a loyal subject and servant to her Grace. Your conduct will bring as much honor upon the noble name of Bork as Sidonia's has brought disgrace. Therefore I will trust you. Listen, Marcus. If the ghost does not appear tonight, then you must ride the morrow morn to Crummyn. Bribe the priest with gold. Tell him that he must write instantly to the young Prince, saying, that the marriage must be delayed for eight days, for there was no boat to be had safe enough to carry him and his bride up the Haff, seeing that all the boats and their crews were engaged at the fisheries, and would not be back to Crummyn until the following Saturday. The young lord, therefore, must have patience. Should the priest hesitate, then Marcus must threaten him with the loss of his living, as the whole princely house should be made acquainted with his villainy. He will then consent. I know him well!

"If that is once arranged, then we shall seat ourselves every night in the coach until the ghost comes; and, methinks, he will not long delay, since hitherto he has managed his work with such security and success."

The discreet and virtuous Marcus promised to obey Ulrich in all things, and the Grand Chamberlain then went his way.

Chapter XVIII

How the horrible wickedness of Sidonia was made apparent; and how in consequence thereof she was banished with ignominy from the ducal court of Wolgast

*T*he night came at last. And the Grand Chamberlain collected, as he had said, all the officials and pages of the household together in his office at the treasury, and bid them wait there until he summoned them. No one was to leave the apartment under pain of his severe displeasure. *Item,* he had prayed her Grace not to retire to rest that night before twelve of the clock; and when she asked wherefore, he replied that she would have to take leave of a very remarkable visitor that night; upon which she desired to know more, but he said that his word was passed not to reveal more. So her Grace thought he meant himself, and promised to remain up.

As ten o'clock struck, the castellan locked, up, as was his wont, all that portion of the castle leading to the women's apartments. Whereupon Ulrich asked him for the keys, saying that he would keep them in his own charge. Then he prayed his Serene Highness Prince Ernest to accompany him to the lumber-room.

His Highness consented, and they both ascended in the dark. On entering, Ulrich drew forth a dark lantern from beneath his cloak, and made the light fall upon an old suit of armor. Then turning to the Prince — "Do you know this armor?" he said.

"Ah, yes; it was the armor of his dearly beloved father, Duke Philip."

Ille. — "Right. Did he then remember the admonitions which the wearer of this armor had uttered, upon his deathbed, to him and his brothers?"

"Oh yes, well he remembered them; but what did this long sermon denote?"

Ille. — "This he would soon know. Had he not given his right hand to the wearer of that armor, and pledged himself ever to set a good example before the people committed to his rule?"

Hic. — "He did not know what all this meant. Had he even set a bad example to his subjects?"

Ille. — "He was on the high-road to do it, when he had resolved to wed himself secretly to a maiden beneath his rank. (Here the young Prince became as pale as a corpse.) Let him deny, if he could, that he had sworn by his father's corpse, with his hand upon the coffin, to abandon Sidonia. He would not upbraid him with his broken promises to him, but would he bring his loving mother to her grave through shame and a broken heart? Would he make himself on a level with the lowest of the people, by wedding Sidonia the next night in the church at Crummyn?"

Hic. — "Had that accursed Catholic nun then betrayed him? Ah, he was surrounded by spies and traitors; but if he could not obtain Sidonia now, he would wed her the moment he was of age and succeeded to the government. If he could in no way have Sidonia, then he would never wed another woman, but remain single and a dead branch for his whole life long. Her blood was as noble as his own, and no devil should dare to part them."

Ille. — "But if he could prove, this very night, to the young lord, that Sidonia was not an honorable maiden, but a dishonored creature —"
Here the young Prince drew his dagger and rushed upon the old man,

with lips foaming with rage; but Ulrich sprang behind the armor of Duke Philip, and said calmly, "Ernest, if thou wouldst murder me who have been so leal and faithful a servant to thee and thine, then strike me dead here through the links of thy father's cuirass."

And as the young man drew back with a deep groan, he continued — "Hear me, before thou dost a deed which eternity will not be long enough to repent. I cannot be angry with thee, for I have been young myself, and would have stricken anyone to the earth who had called my own noble bride dishonored. Listen to me, then, and strike me afterwards, if thou wilt." Hereupon the old knight stepped out from behind the armor, which was fixed upon a wooden frame in the middle of the apartment, with the helmet surmounting it, and leaning against the shoulder-piece, he proceeded to relate all that Clara had seen and heard.

The young Prince turned first as red as scarlet, then pale as a corpse, and sunk down upon a pile of old armor, unable to utter anything but sighs and groans.

Ulrich then asked if he remembered the silly youth who had been drowned lately in consequence of Sidonia's folly; for it was his apparition in the armor he then wore which it was reported haunted the castle. And did he remember also how that armor (in which the poor young man's father also had been killed fighting against the Bohemians) had been taken off the corpse and hung up again in that lumber-room?

Hic. — "Of course he remembered all that; it had happened too lately for him to forget the circumstance."

Ille. — "Well, then, let him take the lantern himself, and see if the armor hung still upon the wall." So the young lord took the lantern with trembling hands, and advanced to the place; but no — there was no armor there now. Then he looked all round the room, but the armor with the serpent crest was nowhere to be seen. He dropped the lantern with a bitter execration. Hereupon the old knight continued — "You see, my gracious Prince, that the ghost must have flesh and blood, like you or me. The castellan tells me that when the ghost first began his pranks, the helmet and cuirass were still found every morning in their usual place here. But for eight days they have not been forthcoming; for the ghost, you see, is growing hardy and forgetting his usual precautions. However, the castellan had determined to watch him, and seize hold of him, for, as he rightly conjectured, a spirit could not carry away a heavy iron suit of armor on him; but his wife had dissuaded him from those measures up to the present time. Come now to the stables with me," continued Ulrich, "and let us conceal ourselves in the coach which I mentioned to you; Marcus Bork shall accompany us, and let us wait there until the ghost appears, and creeps through the trapdoor. After some time we shall follow him; and then this wicked cheat will be detected. But before we move, swear to me that you will await the issue peaceably and calmly in the coach; you must neither sigh nor groan, nor scarcely breathe. No matter what you hear or see, if you cannot control your fierce, jealous rage, all will be lost."

Then the young Prince gave him his hand, and promised to keep silence, though it should cost him his life, for no one could be more anxious to discover the truth or falsehood of this matter than he himself. So they both descended now to the courtyard, Ulrich concealing the lantern under his mantle; and they crouched along by the wall till they reached the horse-pond, where Marcus Bork stood awaiting them; then they glided on, one by one, into the stables, and concealed themselves within the coach.

It was well they did so without longer delay, for scarcely had they been seated when the ghost appeared. No doubt he had heard of the intended marriage, and wished to take advantage of his last opportunity. As the sound of his feet became audible approaching the coach, the Prince almost groaned audibly; but the stout old knight threw one arm powerfully round his body, and placed the hand of the other firmly over his mouth. The ghost now began to ascend the coach, and they heard him clambering up the hind wheel; he slipped down, however (a bad omen), and muttered a half-curse; then, to help himself up better, he seized hold of the sash of the window, and with it took a grip of Ulrich's beard, as he was leaning close to the side of the coach to watch his proceedings. Not a stir did the brave old knight make, but sat as still as marble, and even held his breath, lest the ghost might feel it warm upon his hand, and so discover their ambuscade.

At last he was up; and they heard him clattering over their heads, then creeping through the trapdoor into the corridor, and a little after, the sound of a door gently opening.

All efforts were in vain to keep the Prince quiet. He must follow him. He would rush through the trapdoor after him, though it cost him his life! But old Ulrich whispered in his ear, "Now I know that Prince Ernest has neither honor nor discretion, and Pomerania has little to hope from such a ruler." All in vain — he springs out of the coach, but the knight after him, who hastily gave Marcus Bork the keys of the castle, and bade him go fetch the household, down to the menials, here to the gallery. Marcus took them, and left the stables instantly. Then Ulrich seized the hand of Prince Ernest, who was already on the top of the coach, and asked him was it thus he would, leave an old man without anyone to assist him. Let him in first through the trapdoor, while the Prince held the lantern. To this he consented, and helped the old knight up, who, having reached the trapdoor, put his head through; but, alas! the portly stomach of the stout old knight would not follow. He stretched out his head, however, on every side, as far as it could go, and heard distinctly low whispering voices from Sidonia's little room; then a sound as of the tramp of many feet became audible in the courtyard, by which he knew that Marcus and the household were advancing rapidly.

But the young lord, who was waiting at the top of the coach, grew impatient, and pulled him back, endeavoring to creep through the hole himself. Praised be Heaven, however, this he failed to do from weakness; so he was obliged to follow the Grand Chamberlain, who whispered to him to come down, and they could reach the corridor through the usual entrance. Hereupon they both left the stables, and met Marcus in the courtyard with his company.

Then all ascended noiselessly to the gallery, and ranged themselves around Sidonia's door. Ulrich now told eight of the strongest carls present to step forward and lean their shoulders against the door, but make no stir until he gave a sign; then when he cried "Now!" they should burst it open with all their force.

As to the young Prince, he was trembling like an aspen leaf, and his weakness was so great that two young men had to support him. In short, as all present gradually stole closer and closer up to the door of Sidonia's room, the old knight drew forth his lantern, and signed to the men, who stood with their shoulders pressed against it; then when all was ready, he cried "Now!" and the door burst open with a loud crash. Every lock, and bar, and bolt shivered to atoms, and in rushed the whole party, Ulrich at their head, with his lantern lifted high up above them all.

Sidonia and her visitor were standing in the middle of the room. Ulrich first flashed the light upon the face of the man. Who would have believed it? — no other than Johann Appelmann! The knight hit him a heavy blow across the face, exclaiming, "What! thou common horse-jockey — thou low-born varlet — is it thus thou bringest disgrace upon a maiden of the noblest house in Pomerania? Ha, thou shalt be paid for this. Wait! Master Hansen shall give thee some of his gentle love-touches this night!"

But meanwhile the young Prince had entered, and beheld Sidonia, as she stood there trembling from shame, and endeavoring to cover her face with her long, beautiful golden hair that fell almost to her knees. "Sidonia!" he exclaimed, with a cry as bitter as if a dagger had passed through his heart — "Sidonia!" and fell insensible before her.

Now a great clamor arose amongst the crowd, for beside the couch lay the helmet and cuirass of the ghost; so everyone knew now who it was that had played this trick on them for so long, and kept the castle in such a state of terror.

Then they gathered round the poor young Prince, who lay there as stiff as a corpse, and lamented over him with loud lamentations, and some of them lifted him up to carry him out of the chamber; but the Grand Chamberlain sternly commanded them to lay him down again before his bride, whom he had arranged to wed privately at Crummyn on the following night. Then seizing Sidonia by the hand, and dashing back her long hair, he led her forward before all the people, and said with a loud voice, "See here the illustrious and highborn Lady Sidonia, of the holy Roman Empire, Duchess of Pomerania, Cassuben, and Wenden, Princess of Rügen, Countess of Gützkow, and our Serene and most Gracious Lady, how she honors the princely house of Pomerania by sharing her love with this stable groom, this tailor's son, this debauched profligate! Oh! I could grow mad when I think of this disgrace. Thou shameless one! have I not long ago given thee thy right name? But wait — the name shall be branded on thee this night, so that all the world may read it."

Just then her Grace entered with Clara, followed by all the other maids of honor; for, hearing the noise and tumult, they had hastened thither as they were, some half undressed, others with only a loose night-robe flung round them. And her Grace, seeing the young lord lying pale and insensible on the ground, wrung her hands and cried out, "Who has killed my son? who has murdered my darling child?"

Here stepped forward Ulrich, and said, "The young lord was not dead; but, if it so pleased God, was in a fair way now to regain both life and reason." Then he related all which had led to this discovery; and how they had that night been themselves the witnesses of Sidonia's wickedness with the false ghost. Now her Grace knew his secret, which he had not told until certain of success.

As he related all these things, her Grace turned upon Sidonia and spat on her; and the young lord, having recovered somewhat in consequence of the water they had thrown on him, cried out, "Sidonia! is it possible? No, Sidonia, it is not possible!"

The shameless hypocrite had now recovered her self-possession, and would have denied all knowledge of Appelmann, saying that he forced himself in when she chanced to open the door; but he, interrupting her, cried, "Does the girl dare to lay all the blame on me? Did you not press my hand there when you were lying after you fell from the stag? Did you not meet me afterwards in the lumber-room — that day of the hunt when Duke Barnim was here last?"

"No, no, no!" shrieked Sidonia. "It is a lie, an infamous lie!" But he answered, "Scream as you will, you cannot deny that this disguise of the ghost was your own invention to favor my visits to you. Did you not drop notes for me down on the coach, through the trapdoor, fixing the nights when I might come? and bethink you of last night, when you sent me a note by your maid, wrapped up in a little horse-cloth which I had lent you for your cat, with the prayer that I would not fail to be with you that night nor the next" — Oh, just Heaven! to think that it was upon that very night that Clara should break her shoestring, by which means the Almighty turned away ruin and disgrace from the ancient, illustrious, and princely house of Pomerania — all by a broken shoestring! For if the ghost had remained away but that one night, or Clara had not broken her shoestring, Sidonia would have been Duchess of Pomerania; but what doth the Scripture say? "Man's goings are of the Lord. What man understandeth his own way?" (Prov. xx. 24).

When Sidonia heard him tell all this, and how she had written notes of entreaty to him, she screamed aloud, and springing at him like a wildcat, buried her ten nails in his hair, shrieking, "Thou liest, traitor; it is false! it is false!"

Now Ulrich rushed forward, and seized her by her long hair to part them, but at that moment Master Hansen, the executioner, entered in his red cloak, with six assistants (for Ulrich had privately sent for him), and the Grand Chamberlain instantly let go his hold of Sidonia, saying, "You come in good time, Master Hansen; take away this wretched pair, lock them up in the bastion tower, and on the morn bring them to the horse-market by ten of the clock, and there scourge and brand them; then carry them both to the frontier out of our good State of Wolgast, and let them both go their ways from that, whither it may please them."

When Sidonia heard this, she let go her paramour and fell fainting upon the bed; but recovering herself in a little time, she exclaimed, "What is this you talk of? A noble maiden who is as innocent as the child in its cradle, to be scourged by the common executioner? Oh, is there no Christian heart here to take pity on a poor, helpless girl! Gracious young Prince, even if all the world hold me guilty, you cannot, no, you cannot; it is impossible!"

Hereupon the young lord began to tremble like an aspen leaf, and said in a broken voice, "Alas, Sidonia! you betrayed yourself: if you had not mentioned that trapdoor to me, I might still have believed you innocent (I, who thought some good angel had guided you to it!); now it is impossible; yet be comforted, the executioner shall never scourge you nor brand you — you are branded enough already." Then turning to the Grand Chamberlain he said, that with his consent a hangman should never lay his hands upon this nobly born maiden, whom he had once destined to be Duchess of Pomerania; but Appelmann, this base-born vassal, who had eaten of his bread and then betrayed him like a Judas, let him be flogged and branded as much as they pleased; no word of his should save the accursed seducer from punishment.

Notwithstanding this, old Ulrich was determined on having Sidonia scourged, and my gracious lady the Duchess must have her scourged too. "Let her dear son only think that if the all-merciful God had not interposed, he would have been utterly ruined and his princely house disgraced, by means of this girl. Nothing but evil had she brought with her since first she set foot in the castle: she had caused his sickness; item, the death of two young knights by drowning; item, the terrible execution of Joachim Budde, who was beheaded at the festival; and had she not, in addition, whipped her dear little Casimir, which unseemly act had only lately come to her knowledge? and had she not also made every man in the castle that approached her mad for love of her, all by her diabolical conduct? No — away with the wretch: she merits her chastise-ment a thousand and a thousand-fold!" And old Ulrich exclaimed likewise, "Away with the wretch and her paramour!"

Here the young lord made an effort to spring forward to save her, but fell fainting on the ground; and while the attendants were busy running for water to throw over him, Clara von Dewitz, turning away the executioner with her hand from Sidonia, fell down on her knees before her Grace, and besought her to spare at least the person of the poor, unfortunate maiden; did her Grace think that any punishment could exceed what she had already suffered? Let her own compassionate heart plead along with her words — and did not the Scripture say, "Vengeance is mine, saith the Lord."

Hereupon her Grace looked at old Ulrich without speaking; but he understood her glance, and made answer — "No; the hangman must do his duty towards the wretch!" when her Grace said mildly, "But for the sake of this dear, good young maiden, I think we might let her go, for, remember, if she had not opened out this villainy to us, the creature would have been my daughter-in-law, and my princely house disgraced forevermore."

Now Marcus Bork stepped forward, and added his prayers that the noble name he bore might not be disgraced in Sidonia. "He had ever been a faithful feudal vassal to her princely house, and had not even scrupled to bring the secret wicked deeds of his cousin before the light of day, though it was like a martyrdom of his own flesh and blood for conscience' sake."

Here old Ulrich burst forth in great haste — "Seven thousand devils! Let the wench be off, then. Not another night should she rest in the castle. Let her speak — where would she go to? where should they bring her to?"

And when Sidonia answered, sobbing, "To Stettin, to her gracious lord, Duke Barnim, who would take pity on her because of her innocence," Ulrich laughed outright in scorn. "I shall give the driver a letter to him, and another to thy father. Perhaps his Grace will show thee true pity, and drive thee with his horsewhip to Stramehl. But thou shalt journey in the same coach whereon thy leman clambered up to the trapdoor, and Master Hansen shall sit on the coach-box and drive thee himself. As to thy darling stablegroom here, the master must set his mark on him before he goes; but that can be done when the hangman returns from Stettin."

When Appelmann heard this, he fell at the feet of the Lord Chamberlain, imploring him to let him off too. "Had he not ridden to Spantekow, without stop or stay, at the peril of his life, to oblige Lord Ulrich that time the Lapland wizard made the evil prophecy; and though his illustrious lady died, yet that was from no fault of his, and his lordship had then promised not to forget him if he were but in need. So now he demanded, on the strength of his knightly word, that a horse should be given him from the ducal stables, and that he be permitted to go forth, free and scathless, to ride wherever it might please him. His sins were truly heavy upon him, and he would try and do better, with the help of God."

When the old knight heard him express himself in this godly sort (for the knave knew his man well), he was melted to compassion, and said, "Then go thy way, and God give thee grace to repent of thy manifold sins."

Her Grace had nothing to object; only to put a fixed barrier between the Prince and Sidonia, she added, "But send first for Dr. Gerschovius, that he may unite this shameless pair in marriage before they leave the castle, and then they can travel away together."

Hereupon Johann Appelmann exclaimed, "No, never! How could he hope for God's grace to amend him, living with a thing like that, tied to him for life, which God and man alike hold in abhorrence?" At this speech Sidonia screamed aloud, "Thou lying and accursed stable-groom, darest thou speak so of a castle and land dowered maiden?" and she flew at him, and would have torn his hair, but Marcus Bork seized hold of her round the waist, and dragged her with great effort into Clara's room.

Now the tears poured from the eyes of her Grace at such a disgraceful scene, and she turned to her son, who was slowly recovering — "Hast thou heard, Ernest, this groom – this servant of thine – refuses to take the girl to wife whom thou wast going to make Duchess of Pomerania? Woe! woe! what words for thy poor mother to hear; but it was all foreshadowed when Dr. Luther –" &c. &c.

In short, the end of the infamous story was, that Sidonia was carried off that very night in the identical coach we know of, and Master Hansen was sent with her, bearing letters to the Duke and Otto from the Grand Chamberlain, and one also to the burgomaster Appelmann in Stargard; and the executioner had strict orders to drive her himself the whole way to Stettin. As for Appelmann, he sprung upon a Friesland clipper, as the old chamberlain had permitted, and rode away that same night. But the young lord was so ill from grief and shame, that he was lifted to his bed, and all the *medici* of Grypswald and Wolgast were summoned to attend him.

And such was the end of Sidonia von Bork at the ducal court of Wolgast. But old Küssow told me that for a long while she was the whole talk of the court and town, many wondering, though they knew well her light behavior, that she should give herself up to perdition at last for a common groom, no better than a menial compared to her. But I find the old proverb is true for her as well as for another, "The apple falls close to the tree; as is the sheep, so is the lamb;" for had her father brought her up in the fear of God, in place of encouraging her in revenge, pride, and haughtiness, Sidonia might have been a good and honored wife for her life long. But the libertine example of her father so destroyed all natural instincts of modesty and maidenly reserve within her, that she fell an easy prey to the first temptation.

In short, my gracious Prince Bogislaus XIV, as well as all those who love and honor the illustrious house of Wolgast, will devoutly thank God for having turned away this disgrace in a manner so truly wonderful.

I have already spoken of the broken shoe-tie, but in addition, I must point out that if Sidonia had counseled her paramour to take the armor of Duke Philip, which hung in the same lumber-room, in place of that belonging to the serpent knight, that wickedness would never have come to light. For assuredly all in the castle would have believed that it was truly the ghost of the dead duke, who came to reproach his son for not holding the oath which he had sworn on his coffin, to abandon Sidonia. And consequently, respect and terror would have alike prevented any human soul in the castle from daring to follow it, and investigate its object. Therefore let us praise the name of the Lord who turned all things to good, and fulfilled, in Sidonia and her lover, the Scripture which saith, "Thinking themselves wise, they became fools" (Rom. i. 21).

BOOK II

FROM THE BANISHMENT OF SIDONIA FROM THE DUCAL COURT OF WOLGAST UP TO HER RECEPTION IN THE CONVENT OF MARIENFLIESS.

Chapter I

Of the quarrel between Otto Bork and the Stargardians, which caused him to demand the dues upon the Jena

MOST EMINENT AND ILLUSTRIOUS PRINCE! —

Your Grace must be informed, that much of what I have here set down, in this second book, was communicated to me by that same old Uckermann of Dalow of whom I have spoken already in my first volume.

Other important facts I have gleaned from the Diary of Magdalena von Petersdorfin, *Priorissa* of the convent of Marienfliess. She was an old and worthy matron, whom Sidonia, however, used to mock and insult, calling her the old cat, and suchlike names. But she revenged herself on the shameless wanton in no other way than by writing down what facts she could collect of her disgraceful life and courses, for the admonition and warning of the holy sisterhood.

This little book the pious nun left to her sister Sophia, who is still living in the convent at Marienfliess; and she, at my earnest entreaties, permitted me to peruse it.

Before, however, I continue the relation of Sidonia's adventures, I must state to your Grace what were the circumstances which induced Otto von Bork to demand so urgently the dues upon the Jena from their Highnesses of Stettin and Wolgast. In my opinion, it was for nothing else than to revenge himself upon the burgomaster of Stargard, Jacob Appelmann, father of the equerry. The quarrel happened years before, but Otto never forgot it, and only waited a fitting opportunity to take vengeance on him and the people of Stargard.

This Jacob Appelmann was entitled to receive a great portion of the Jena dues, which were principally paid to him in kind, particularly in foreign spices, which he afterwards sold to the Polish Jews, at the annual fair held in Stramehl.

It happened, upon one of these occasions, as Jacob, with two of his porters, appeared, as usual, carrying bags of spices, to sell to the Polish Jews, that Otto met him in the marketplace, and invited him to come up to his castle, for that many nobles were assembled there who would, no doubt, give him better prices for his goods than the Polish Jews, and added that the worthy burgomaster must drink his health with him that day.

Now, Jacob Appelmann was no despiser of good cheer or of broad gold pieces; so, unfortunately for himself, he accepted the invitation. But the knight had only lured him up to the castle to insult and mock him. For when he entered the hall, a loud roar of laughter greeted his appearance, and the half-drunk guests, who were swilling the wine as if they had tuns to fill, and not stomachs, swore that he must pledge each of them separately, in a lusty draft. So they handed him an enormous becker, cut with Otto's arms, bidding him drain it; but as the Herr Jacob hesitated, his host asked him, laughing, was he a Jesu disciple, that he refused to drink?

Hereupon the other answered, he was too old for a disciple, but he was not ashamed to call himself a servant of Jesus.

Then they all roared with laughter, and Otto spoke —

"My good lords and dear friends, ye know how that the Stargard knaves joined with the Pomeranian Duke to ravage my good town of Stramehl, so that it can be only called a village now. And it is also not unknown to you that my disgrace then passed into a proverb, so that people will still say, 'He fell upon me as the Stargardians upon Stramehl.' Let us, then, revenge ourselves today. If this Jesu's servant will not drink, then tear open his mouth, put a tun-dish therein, and pour down a good draft till the knave cries 'enough!' As to his spices, let us scatter them before the Polish Jews, as pease before swine, and it will be merry pastime to see how the beasts will lick them up. Thus will Stramehl retort upon Stargard, and the whole land will shout with laughter. For wherefore does this Stargard peddler come here to my fairs? Mayhap I shall visit his."

Peals of laughter and applause greeted Otto's speech; but Jacob, when he heard it, determined, if possible, to effect his escape; and watching his opportunity, for he was the only one there not drunk, sprang out of the hall, and down the flight of steps, and being young then, never drew breath till he reached the marketplace of Stramehl, and jumped into his own wagon.

In vain Otto screamed out to "stop him, stop him!" all his servants were at the fair, where, indeed, the people of the whole country round were gathered. Then the host and the guests sprang up themselves, to run after Jacob Appelmann, but many could not stand, and others tumbled down by the way. However, with a chorus of cries, curses, and threats, Otto and some others at last reached the wagon, and laid hold of it. Then they dragged out the bags of spices, and emptied them all down upon the street, crying —

"Come hither, ye Jews; which of you wants pepper? Who wants cloves?"

So all the Jews in the place ran together, and down they went on all-fours picking up the spices, while their long beards swept the pavement quite clean. Hey! how they pushed and screamed, and dealt blows about among themselves, till their noses bled, and the place looked as if gamecocks had been fighting there, whereat Otto and his roistering guests roared with laughter.

One of the bags they pulled out of the wagon contained cinnamon; but a huntsman of Otto Bork's, not knowing what it was, poured it down likewise into the street. Cinnamon was then so rare, that it sold for its weight in gold. So an old Jew, spying the precious morsel, cried out, "Praise be to God! Praise be to God!" and ran through Otto Bork's legs to get hold of a stick of it. This made the knight look down, and seeing the cinnamon, he straightway bid the huntsman gather it all up again quick, and carry it safely home to the castle.

But the old Jew would by no means let go his hold of the booty, and kept the sticks in one hand high above his head, while with the other he dealt heavy buffets upon the huntsman. An apprentice of Jacob Appelmann's beheld all this from the wagon, and knowing what a costly thing this cinnamon was, he made a long arm out of the wagon, and snapped away the sticks from the Jew. Upon this the huntsman sprang at the apprentice; but the latter, seizing a pair of pot-hooks, which his master had that day bought in the fair, dealt such a blow with them upon the head of the huntsman, that he fell down at once upon the ground quite dead.

Now everyone cried out "Murder! murder! Jodute! Jodute! Jodute!" and they tore the bags right and left from the wagon, Jews as well as Christians; but Otto commanded them to seize the apprentice also. So they dragged him out too. He was a fine young man of twenty-three, Louis Griepentroch by name. There was such an uproar, that the men who held the horses' heads were forced away. Whereupon the burgomaster resolved to seize this opportunity for escape; and without heeding the lamentations of the other apprentice, Zabel Griepentroch, who prayed him earnestly to stop and save his poor brother, desired the driver to lash the horses into a gallop, and never stop nor stay until the unlucky town was left far behind them.

Otto von Bork ordered instant pursuit, but in vain. The burgomaster could not be overtaken, and reached Wangerin in safety. There he put up at the inn, to give the panting horses breathing-time; and now the aforesaid Zabel besought him, with many tears, to write to Otto Bork on behalf of his poor brother, to which the burgomaster at last consented; for he loved these two youths, who were orphans and twins, and he had brought them up from their childhood, and treated them in all things like a true and loving godfather. So he wrote to Otto, "That if aught of ill happened to the young Louis Griepentroch, he (the burgomaster) would complain to his Grace of Stettin, for the youth had only done his duty in trying to save the property of his master from the hands of robbers." The good Jacob, however, admonished Zabel to make up his mind for the worst, for the knight was not a man whose heart could be melted, as he himself had experienced but too well that day.

But the sorrowing youth little heeded the admonitions, only seized the letter, and ran with it that same evening back to Stramehl. Here, however, no one would listen to him, no one heeded him; and when at last he got up to Otto and gave him the letter, the knight swore he would flay him alive if he did not instantly quit the town. Now the poor youth gnashed his teeth in rage and despair, and determined to be revenged on the knight.

Just then came by a great crowd leading his brother Louis to the gallows; and on his head they had stuck a high paper cap with the Stargard arms painted thereon, namely, a tower with two griffins (Sidonia, indeed, had painted it, and she was by, and clapping her hands with delight); and for the greater scandal to Stargard, they had tied two hares' tails to the back of the cap, with the inscription written in large letters above them – "So came the Stargardians to Stramehl!"

And Otto and his guests gathered round the gallows, and all the market-folk, with great uproar and laughter. *Summa,* when the poor carl saw all this, and that there was no hope for his heart's dear brother, neither could he even get near him just to say a last "good-night," he ran like mad to the castle, which was almost empty now, as everyone had gone to the marketplace; and there, on the hill, he turned round and saw how the hangman had shoved his dear Louis from the ladder, and the body was swinging lamentably to and fro between heaven and earth. So he seized a brand and set fire to the brew-house, from which a thick smoke and light flames soon rose high into the air. Now all the people rushed towards the castle, for they suspected well who had done the deed, particularly as they had observed a young fellow running, as if for life or death, in the opposite direction towards the open country. So they pursued him with wild shouts from every direction; right and left they hemmed him in, and cut off his escape to the wood. And Otto Bork sprang upon a fresh horse, and galloped along with them, roaring out, "Seize the rascal! – seize the vile incendiary! He who takes him shall have a tun of my best beer!" But others he dispatched to the castle to extinguish the flames.

Now the poor Zabel knew not what to do, for on every side his pursuers were gaining fast upon him, and he heard Otto's voice close behind crying, "There he runs! there he runs! Seize the gallows-bird, that he may swing with his brother this night. A tun of my best beer to the man who takes him! Seize the incendiary!" So the poor wretch, in his anguish, threw off his smock upon the grass and sprang into the lake, hoping to be able to swim to the other side and reach the wood.

"In after him!" roared Otto; and a fellow jumped in instantly, and seizing hold of Zabel by the hose, dragged him along with him; but they were soon both carried into deep water – Zabel, however, was the uppermost, and held the other down tight to stifle him. Another seeing this, plunged in to rescue his companion, and from the bank dived down underneath Zabel, intending to seize him round the body; but it so happened that the fishermen of Stramehl had laid their nets close to the place, and he plunged direct into the middle of the largest, and stuck there miserably; which when Zabel observed, he let the other go, who was now quite dead, and struck out boldly for the opposite bank. The fishermen sprang into their boats to pursue him, and the crowd ran round, hoping to cut off the pass before he could gain the bank; but he was a brave youth, and distanced them all, jumped on land before one of them could reach him, and plunged into the thick wood. Here it was vain to follow him, for night was coming on fast; so he pursued his path in safety, and returned to his master at Stramehl.

Otto von Bork, however, would not let the matter rest here, for he had sustained great loss by the burning of his brew-house (the other buildings were saved); therefore he wrote to the honorable council at Stargard — "That by the shameful and scandalous burning of his brew-house, he had lost two fine hounds named Stargard and Stramehl, which he had brought himself from Silesia; *item,* two old servants and a woman; *item,* in the lake, two other servants had been drowned; and all by the revenge of an apprentice, because he had justly caused his brother to be executed. Therefore this apprentice must be given up to him, that he might have him broken on the wheel, otherwise their vassals on the Jena should suffer in such a sort, that the Stargardians would long have reason to remember Otto Bork."

Now, some of the honorable councilors were of opinion that they should by no means give up the apprentice; first, because Otto had insulted the Stargard arms, and secondly, lest it might appear as if they feared he would fulfill his threats respecting the Jena.

But Jacob Appelmann, the burgomaster, who lay sick in his bed from the treatment he had received at Stramehl, entirely disapproved of this resolution; and when they came to him for his advice, proposed to give for answer to the knight that he should first indemnify him for the loss of his costly spices, which he valued at one thousand florins, and when this sum was paid down, they might treat of the matter concerning the apprentice.

The knight, however, mocked them for making such an absurd demand as compensation, and reiterated his threats, that if the young man were not delivered up to him, he would punish Stargard with a great punishment.

The council, however, were still determined not to yield; and as the burgomaster lay sick in his bed, they released the apprentice from prison; and replied to Otto, "That if he broke the public peace of his Imperial Majesty, let the consequences fall on his own head — there was still justice for them to be had in Pomerania."

When the burgomaster heard of this, he had himself carried in a litter, sick as he was, to the honorable council, and asked them, "Was this justice, to release an incendiary from prison? If they sought justice for themselves, let them deal it out to others. No one had lost more by the transaction than he: his income for the next two years was clean gone, and the care and anxiety he had undergone, besides, had reduced him to this state of bodily weakness which they observed. It was a heart-grief to him to give up the young man, for he had reared him from the baptism water, and he had been a faithful servant unto him up to this day. Could he save him, he would gladly give up his house and all he was worth, and go and take a lodging upon the wall; for this young man had once saved his life, by slaying a mad dog which had seized him by the tail of his coat; but it was not to be done. They must set an honorable example, as just and upright citizens and fearless magistrates, who hold that old saying in honor — '*Fiat justitia et pereat mundus*,' which means, 'Let justice be done, though life and fortune perish.' But the punishment of the wheel was, he confessed, altogether too severe for the poor youth; and therefore he counseled that they should hang him, as Otto had hung his brother."

This course the honorable society consented at last to adopt; but the knight had disgraced their arms, and they ought in return to disgrace his. They could get the court painter from Stettin at the public expense, and let him paint Otto Bork's arms on the back of the young man's hose.

Here the burgomaster again interfered — "Why should the honorable council attempt a stupid insult, because the knight had done so?" But he talked in vain; they were determined on this retaliation. At last (but after a great deal of trouble) he obtained a promise that they would have the arms painted before, upon his smock, and not behind, upon the hose, for that would be a sore disgrace to Otto, and bring his vengeance upon them. "Why should they do more to him than he had done unto them? The Scripture said, 'Eye for eye, tooth for tooth,' and not two eyes for an eye, two teeth for a tooth." Hereupon the honorable council pronounced sentence on the young man, and fixed the third day from that for his execution. But first the executioner must bring him up before the bed of the burgomaster, who thus spoke — "Ah, Zabel, wherefore didst thou not behave as I admonished thee in Wangerin?" And as the young man began to weep, he gave him his hand, and admonished him to be steadfast in the death-hour, asked his forgiveness for having condemned him, but it was his duty as a magistrate so to do — thanked him for having saved his life by slaying the mad dog; finally, bid him "Good-night," and then buried his face in the pillow.

So the hangman carried back the weeping youth to the council-hall, where the honorable councilors had the Bork arms fastened upon his smock, and out of further malice against Otto (for they knew the burgomaster, being sick in his bed, could not hinder them), they placed over them a large piece of pasteboard, on which was written, "So did the Stargardians with Stramehl." *Item*, they fastened to the two corners a pair of wolf's ears, because Bork, in the Wendig tongue, signifies wolf. This was to revenge themselves for the hares' tails.

Then the poor apprentice was carried to the gallows, amid loud laughter from the common people. And even the honorable councilors waxed merry at the sight; and as the hangman pushed him from the ladder, they cried out, "So will the Stargardians do to Stramehl!"

Now Otto heard tidings of all these doings, but he feared to complain to his Highness the Duke, because he himself had begun the quarrel, and they had only retorted as was fair. *Item,* he did not dare to stop the boats upon the Jena — for he knew that although Duke Barnim was usually of a soft and placable temper, yet when he was roused there was no more dangerous enemy. And if the Stargardians leagued with him, they might fall upon his town of Stramehl, as they had done once before.

Therefore he waited patiently for an opportunity of revenge, and held his peace until Sidonia acquainted him with the love of the young Prince Ernest. Then he resolved to demand the dues upon the Jena to be given up to him, and if his wicked desire had been gratified, I think the good citizens of Stargard might have taken to the beggar's staff for the rest of their days, for like all the old Hanseatic towns, their entire subsistence came to them by water, and all their wares and merchandise were carried up the Jena in boats to the town. These the knight would have rated so highly, if he had been made owner of the dues, that the town and people would have been utterly ruined.

It has been already stated that the Duke Barnim gave an ambiguous answer to Otto upon the subject; but the knight, after his visit to Wolgast, was so certain of seeing his daughter in a short time Duchess of Pomerania, that he already looked upon the Jena dues as his own, and proceeded to act as shall be related in the next chapter.

Chapter II

*How Otto von Bork demands the Jena dues from the Stargardians, and how the burgomaster Jacob Appelmann takes him prisoner, and locks him up in the Red Sea.**

As the aforesaid knight and my gracious lord, Duke Barnim, journeyed home from Wolgast, the former discoursed much on this matter of the Jena dues, but his Grace listened in silence, after his manner, and nicked away at his doll. (I think, however, that his Grace did not quite understand the matter of the Jena dues himself.)

Summa, while Otto was at Stettin, he received information that three vessels, laden with wine and spices, and all manner of merchandise, were on their way to Stargard. So he took this for a good sign, and went straight to the town and up to the burgomaster, Jacob Appelmann, would not sit down, however, but made himself as stiff as if his back would break, and asked whether he (Appelmann) was aware that the lands of the Bork family bordered close upon the Jena.

Ille. — "Yes, he knew it well."

Hic. — "Then he could not wonder if he now demanded dues from every vessel that went up to Stargard."

Ille. — "On the contrary, he would wonder greatly; since by an Act passed in the reign of Duke Barnim the First, A.D. 1243, the freedom of the Jena had been secured to them, and they had enjoyed it up to the present date."

Hic. — "Stuff! what was the use of bringing up these old Acts. His Grace of Stettin, as well as the Duchess of Wolgast, had now given them over to him."

Ille. — "Then let his lordship produce his charter; if he had got one, why not show it?"

Hic. — "No, he had not got the written order yet, but he would soon have it."

---

* A watchtower, built in the Moorish style, upon the town wall of Stargard, from which the adjacent streets take their name.

Ille. — "Well, until then they would abide by the old law."

Hic. — "By no means. This very day he would insist on being paid the dues."

Ille. — "That meant, that he purposed to break the peace of our lord the Emperor. Let him think well of it. It might cost him dear."

Hic. — "That was his care. The Stargardians should not a second time hang his arms on the gallows."

Ille. — "It was a simple act of retaliation; had he not read, 'An eye for an eye, a tooth for a tooth'?"

Hic. — "Nonsense! was that retaliation, when a set of low burgher carls took upon themselves to disgrace the lord of castles and lands; as well might one of his serfs, when he struck him, strike him in return; that would be retaliation too. Ha! ha! ha!"

Ille. — "What did his lordship mean? He was no village justice, nor were the burghers of this good town serfs or boors."

Hic. — "If he knew not now what he meant, he would soon learn; aye, and take off his hat so low to the Bork arms that it would touch the ground. Then, too, he might himself get a lesson in retaliation."

And herewith the knight strode firmly out of the room, without even saluting the burgomaster; but Jacob knew well how to deal with him, so he sent instantly for the keeper of the forest, who lived in the thick wood on the banks of the Jena, and told him to watch by night and day, and if he observed anything unusual going on, to spring upon a horse and bring him the intelligence without delay.

Meanwhile the knight summoned all his feudal vassals around him at Stramehl, and told them how his Grace had bestowed the Jena dues upon him, but the sturdy burghers of Stargard had dared to impugn his rights; therefore let each of them select two trusty followers, and meet all together on the morrow morn at Putzerlin, close to the Jena ferry. Then, if there came by any vessels laden with choice wines, let them be sure and drink a health to Stargard. So they all believed him, and came to the appointed place with twenty horsemen, and the knight himself brought twenty more. There they unsaddled and turned into the meadow, then set to work to throw a bridge over the river. As soon as the forest ranger spied them, he saddled his wild clipper, which he himself had caught in the Uckermund country, and flew like wind to the town (for the wild horses are much stouter and fleeter than the tame, but there are none to be found now in all Pomerania).

When the burgomaster heard this tale, he told him to go back the way he came, and keep perfectly still until he saw a rocket rise from St. Mary's Tower, then let him loose all his hounds upon the horses in the meadow, and he and the burghers would follow soon, and make a quick end of the robber knights and freebooters; but he would wait for three hours before giving the promised sign from St. Mary's Tower, that he might have time to get back to the wood. Still the knight and his followers continued working at the bridge right merrily. They took the ferryman's planks and poles, and cut down large oak trees, and everyone that went across the ferry must stop and help them; but their work was not quite completed, when three vessels appeared in sight, laden with all sorts of merchandise, and making direct for Stargard. As soon as Otto perceived them, he took half-a-dozen fellows with him, and jumped into a ferry-boat, crying, "Hold! until the dues are paid, you can go no farther. The river and the land alike belong to me now, and I must have my dues, as his Grace of Stettin has commanded."

The crew, however, strictly objected, saying that in the memory of man they had never paid dues upon their goods, and they would not pay them now; but Otto and his knights jumped on deck, followed by their squires, and having asked for the bill of lading, decimated all the goods, as a priest collecting his tithe of the sheaves. Then he took the best cask of wine, had it rolled on land, and called out to the crew, who were crying like children, "Now, good people, you may go your ways."

But the poor devils were in despair, and followed him on land, praying and beseeching him not to ruin them, but to restore their property, at which Otto laughed loudly, and bid the strongest of his followers chase the miserable varlets back to their vessel.

Meanwhile the cask of wine had been rolled up against a tree, and the knight and his followers set themselves round it upon the grass, and because they had no glasses, they drank out of kettles, and pots, and bowls, and dishes, or whatever the ferryman could give them. Yea, some of them drew off their boots and filled them with the wine, others drank it out of their caps, and so there they lay on the grass, swilling the wine, and the different wares they had seized lay all scattered round them, and they laughed and drank, and roared, "Thus we drink a health to Stargard!" Hereupon the crew, seeing that nothing could be got from the robbers, went their way with curses and imprecations, to which the knight and his party responded only with peals of laughter.

But the vessel had scarcely set sail, when a woman's voice was heard crying out loudly from the deck — "Father! father! I am here. Listen, Otto von Bork, your daughter Sidonia is here!"

When the knight heard this, he felt as if stunned by a blow, but immediately comforted himself by thinking that no doubt Prince Ernest was with her, particularly as he could observe in the twilight the figure of a man seated beside her on a bundle of goods. "This surely must be the Prince," he said to himself, and so called out with a joyful voice,

"Ah, my dearest daughter, Sidonia! how comest thou in the merchant vessel?"

Then he screamed to the sailors to stop and cast anchor; but they heeded neither his cries nor commands, and in place of stopping, began to crowd all sail. Otto now tried entreaties, and promised to restore all their goods, and even pay for the wine drunk, if they would only stop the vessel. This made them listen to him, but they demanded, beside, a compensation money of one hundred florins, for all the anxiety and delay they had suffered. This he promised also, only let them stop instantly. However, they would not trust his word, and not until he had pledged his knightly faith would they consent to stop. Some, indeed, were not even content with this, and required that he should stand bareheaded on the bank, and take a solemn oath, with his hand extended to heaven, that he would deal with them as he had promised.

To this also the knight consented, since they would not believe he held his knightly word higher than any oath; though, in my opinion, he would have done anything they demanded, such was his anxiety to behold the Prince and Princess of Pomerania, for he could imagine nothing else, but that his daughter and her husband had been turned out of Wolgast by the harsh Duchess and the old Grand Chamberlain, and were now on their way to his castle at Stramehl.

Here my gracious Prince will no doubt say, "But, Theodore, why did she not call on her father sooner, when, as you told me, he was on board this very vessel plundering the wares?"

I answer — "Serene Prince! your Grace must know that she and her paramour were at that time crouching in the cabin, through fear of Otto, for the sailors did not know her, or who she was. They had taken her and Appelmann in at Damm, and believed this story: that he was secretary to the Duke at Stettin, and Sidonia was his wife; they were on their way to Stargard, but preferred journeying by water, on account of the robbers who infested the high-roads, and who, they heard, had murdered three travelers only a few days before."

But when Sidonia had found what her father had done, and heard the crew cursing and vowing vengeance on him, she feared it would be worse for her even to fall into the hands of the Stargardians than into her father's, and therefore rushed up on deck and called out to him, though her paramour conjured her by heaven and earth to keep quiet, and not bring him under her father's sword.

Summa, as the vessel once more stood still, the knight sprang quick as thought into the ferry-boat along with some of his followers, and rowed off to the vessel, where his daughter sat upon a bundle of merchandise and wept, but Appelmann crept down again into the cabin.

When the knight stepped on board, he kissed and embraced her — but where was the young Prince whom he had seen standing beside her?

Illa. — "Alas! it was not the Prince; the young lord had shamefully deceived her!" (weeping.)

Hic. — "He would make him suffer for it, then; let her tell him the whole business. If he had trifled with her, she should be revenged. Was he not as powerful as any duke in Pomerania?"

Illa. — "He must send away all the bystanders first; did he not see how they all stood round, with their mouths open from wonder?" Hereupon the knight roared out, "Away, go all, all of ye, or I'll stick ye dead as calves. The devil take any of you who dare to listen!" His whole frame trembled meanwhile as an aspen leaf, and he could scarcely wait till the carls clambered over the bundles of goods — "What had happened? In the name of all the devils, let her speak, now that they were alone."

But here the cunning wanton began to weep so piteously, that not a word could she utter; however, as old Otto grew impatient, and began to curse and swear, and shake her by the arm, she at last commenced (while Appelmann was listening from the cabin): —

"Her dearest father knew how the young lord had bribed a priest in Crummyn to wed them privately; but this was all a trick which his wicked mother had suggested to him, in order to bring her to utter ruin; for on the very wedding night, while she was waiting for the Prince in her little room, according to promise, to flee with him to Crummyn, the perfidious Duchess, who was aware of the whole arrangement, sent a groom to her chamber at the appointed hour, and she being in the dark, embraced him, thinking he was the Prince. In the self-same instant the door was burst open, and the old revengeful hag, with Ulrich von Schwerin, rushed in, along with the young Prince and Marcus Bork, her cousin, amid a great crowd of people with lanterns. And no one would listen to her or heed her; so she was thrust that same night out of the castle, like a common swine-maid, though the young lord, when he saw the full extent of his wicked mother's treachery, fell down in a dead faint at her feet."

And here she wept and groaned, as if her heart would break.

"Who, then, was the gay youth who sat beside her there on the bundle?" screamed Otto.

Illa. — "That was the very groom that she had embraced, for they had sent him away with her, to make their wicked story seem true."

Hic. — "But what was his name? May the devil take her, to have gone off with a base-born groom. What was his name?"

Illa (weeping). — "What did he think of her, that she should love a common groom? truly, he had the title of equerry, but then he was nothing better than a common burgher carl. What could she do, when they turned her by night and cloud out of the castle? She must thank God for having had even this groom to protect her, but that he was her lover — fie! — no; that was, indeed, to think little of her."

Hic. — "He would strike her dead if she did not answer. Who was the knave? Where did he come from?"

Illa. — "He was called Johann Appelmann, and was son to the burgomaster of Stargard."

Here the knight raved and chafed like a wild beast, and drew his sword to kill Sidonia, but she fled away down to her paramour in the cabin. However, he had heard the whole conversation, and flew at her to beat her, crying, "Am I then a base-born groom? Ha! thou proud wanton, didst thou not run after me like a common street-girl? I will teach thee to call me a groom!"

And as the knight listened to all this, the sword dropped from his hands and fell into the hold, so that he could not get it up again. Then he was beside himself for rage, and seized a stone of the ballast, to rush down with it to the cabin.

But, behold! a rocket shot up from St. Mary's Tower, and poured its clear light upon the deepening twilight, like a starry meteor, and, at the same instant, the deep bay of ten or twelve blood-hounds resounded fearfully across the meadow where the horses were grazing, and the dogs flew on them, and tore some of them to the ground, and bit others, so that they dashed nearly to their masters, who were lying round the wine-cask, and others fled into the wood bleeding and groaning with pain and agony, as if they had been human creatures.

Then all the fellows jumped up from their wine-cask, and screamed as if the last day had come, and Otto let the stone fall from his hand with horror; but still called out boldly to his men to know what had happened. "Was the devil himself among them that accursed evening?"

Then they shouted in return, that he must hasten to land, for the Stargardians were upon them, and had killed all their horses.

"Strike them dead, then; kill all, and himself the last, but he would go over and help them."

So he jumped into the boat with his companions, but had not time to set foot on shore, when the Stargardians, horse and foot, with the burgomaster at their head, dashed forth from the wood, shouting, "So fall the Stargardians upon Stramehl!"

At this sight the knight could no longer restrain his impatience, but jumped out of the boat; and although the water reached up under his arms, strode forward, crying —

"Courage, my brave fellows; down with the churls. Kill, slay, give no quarter. He who brings me the head of the burgomaster shall be my heir! His vile son hath brought my daughter to shame. Kill all — all! I will never outlive this day. Ye shall all be my heritors — only kill! kill! kill!"

Then he jumps on land and goes to draw his sword, but he has none — only the scabbard is hanging there; and as the Stargard men are already pressing thick upon them, he shouts —

"A sword, a sword! give me a sword! My good castle of Stramehl for a sword, that I may slay this base-born churl of a burgomaster!"

But a blood-hound jumped at his throat, and tore him to the ground, and as he felt the horrible muzzle closer to his face, he screamed out —

"Save me! save me! Oh, woe is me!"

And at the same moment, Sidonia's voice was heard from the vessel, shrieking —

"Father, father, save me! this groom is beating me to death — he is killing me!" while a loud roar of laughter from the crew accompanied her cries.

No one, however, came to save the knight; for the Stargardians were slaying right and left, and Otto's followers were utterly discomfited. So the knight tried to draw his dagger, and having got hold of it, plunged it with great force into the heart of the ferocious animal, who fell back dead, and Otto sprang to his feet. Just then, however, a tanner recognized him, and seizing hold of him by the arms, carried him off to the other prisoners.

Now, indeed, might he call on the mountains to fall on him, and the hills to cover him (Hosea x.); and now he might feel, too, what a terrible thing it is to fall into the hands of the living God (Hebrews x.); for the Jesu wounds, I'm thinking, burned then like hell-fire in his heart.

Summa, as the wretched man was brought before the burgomaster, who sat down upon a bank and wiped his sword in the grass, the latter cried out —

"Well, sir knight, you would not heed me; you have worked your will. Now, do you understand what retaliation means — 'An eye for an eye, a tooth for a tooth'?"

And as the other stood quite silent, he continued —

"Where is your charter for the Jena dues? Perchance it is contained in this letter, which I have received today from her Grace of Wolgast, addressed to you. Hand a lantern here, that the knight may read it! If the charter is not therein, then he shall be flung into prison this night with his followers, until my lord, Duke Barnim, pronounces judgment upon him."

The ferryman advanced and held a light; but Otto had scarcely looked over the letter when he began to tremble as if he would fall to the ground, and then sighed forth, like the rich man in hell —

"Have mercy on me, and give me a drink of water!"

They brought him the water, and then he added —

"Jacob, hast thou, too, had any tidings of our children?"

"Alas!" the other answered; "Ulrich has written all to me."

"Then have mercy on me. Listen how your godless son there in the vessel is beating my daughter to death, and how she is shrieking for help."

As the burgomaster heard these unexpected tidings, he sent messengers to the vessel, with orders to bring the pair immediately before him.

Meanwhile the other prisoners besought the burgomaster to let them go, for they were feudal vassals of Otto Bork, and must do as he commanded them. Besides, he told them that Duke Barnim had given him the dues, and therefore they held it their duty to assist him in collecting them.

And as Otto confirmed their words, saying that he had indeed deceived them, the burgomaster turned to his party, and cried —

"How say you then, worthy burghers and dear friends, shall we let the vassals run, and keep the lord? for, if the master lies, are the servants to be punished if they believe him? Speak, worthy friends."

Then all the burghers cried —

"Let them go, let them go; but keep the knight a prisoner."

Upon which all the retainers took to their heels, not forgetting, though, to hoist the cask of wine upon their shoulders, and so they fled away into the wood.

Now comes a great crowd from all the vessels, accompanying the infamous pair, mocking, and gibing, and laughing at them, so that no one can hear a word for the tumult. But the burgomaster bids them hold their peace, and let the guilty pair be placed before him.

He remained a long while silent, gazing at them both, then sighing deeply, addressed his son —

"Oh, thou lost son, hast thou not yet given up thy dissolute courses? What is this I hear of thee in Wolgast? Now thou must needs humble this noble maiden, and bring dishonor on her house — flinging all thy father's admonitions to the wind —"

Here the son interrupted —

"True; but this noble maiden had thrown herself in his way, like a common girl, and he was only flesh and blood like other men. Why did she follow him so?"

Whereupon the father replied —

"Oh, thou shameless child, who, like the prodigal in Scripture, hast destroyed thy substance with harlots and riotous living, in place of humbleness and repentance, dost thou impudently tell of this poor young maiden's shame before all the world? Oh, son! oh, son! even the blind heathen said, *'Ego illum periisse puto, cui quidem periit pudor'** — which means, 'I esteem him dead in whom shame is dead.' Therefore is thy sin doubled, being a Christian, for thou hast boasted of thy shame before the people here, and held up the young maiden to their contempt, besides having beaten her so on board the vessel that many heard her screams, as if she were only a common wench, and not a castle and land dowered maiden."

To which Appelmann answered, that she had called him a common groom and a base-born burgher churl. But his father commanded him to be silent, and bid his men first bind the knight's hands behind his back, and then those of his son, and so carry them both to prison; but to let the maiden go free.

When the knight heard that he was to be bound, his pride revolted, and he offered any ransom, or to give any compensation that could be demanded for the injury he had done them. Everyone knew his wealth, and that he had power to keep his word to the uttermost. But the burgomaster made answer, "Eye for eye, and tooth for tooth; how say you, sir knight — speak the truth, if you had taken me prisoner, as I have taken you, would you have bound my hands or not?" To which the knight replied, "Well, Jacob, I will not speak a falsehood, for I feel that my end is near; — I would have bound your hands."

Hereupon the brave burgomaster answered, "I know it well; however, as you have answered me honestly, I will spare you. Burghers, do not bind his hands, neither those of my son. Ye have enough to suffer yet before ye, and God give you both grace to repent. And now to the town! The crew shall declare tomorrow morn, before the honorable council, what they have lost by the knight's means; and he shall make it all good again to them."

So all the people returned with great uproar and rejoicing back to the town, and the bell from St. Mary's and St. John's rung forth merry peals, and all the people of the town ran forth to meet them; but when they saw the knight a prisoner, and his empty scabbard hanging by his side,

---

* Plautus in Bacchid.

they clapped their hands and huzzaed, shouting, "So fell the Stargardians upon Stramehl." Thus with merry laughter, and jests, and mockings, they carried him up the street to the tower called the Red Sea, and there locked him up, well guarded.

Here again he prayed the burgomaster to accept a ransom, but in vain. Whereupon he at last solicited pen, paper, and ink, and a light, that he might indite a letter to his Grace, Duke Barnim; and this was granted to him.

As for his unworthy son, the burgomaster had him carried to his own house, and there placed him in a room, with three stout burghers as a guard over him. And Sidonia was placed by herself in another little chamber.

Chapter III

*Of Otto Bark's dreadful suicide — Item, how Sidonia and Johann
Appelmann were brought before the burgomaster*

*D*uring that night there was a strong suspicion upon everyone's mind that something terrible was going to happen; for a great storm arose at midnight, and raged fearfully round the Red Sea tower, so that it seemed to rock, and when the night-watch went round to examine it, behold three toads crept out, and set themselves upright upon the parapet like little manikins, as the hares sometimes make themselves into manikins.

What all this denoted was discovered next morning, for when the jailer entered Otto's cell in the tower, he saw him lying on the floor in a pool of blood, with his own dagger sticking in his heart. On the table stood the lamp which he had asked for, still burning feebly, and near it a great many written papers.

The man instantly ran for the burgomaster, who followed him with all speed to the tower. They felt the corpse, but it was already quite cold.

So then a messenger was dispatched for the chirurgeon, to hold a *visum repertum* over him.

Meantime they examined the papers, and found first my gracious Lady of Wolgast's letter to the unfortunate father — the same which had made him tremble so the day before — and therein was related all the shameful circumstances concerning Sidonia, just as Ulrich had stated them in the letter to the burgomaster. Then they came upon his last will and testament; but where the seal ought to have been, there lay a large drop of blood, with this memorandum beneath it: "This is my heart's first blood which I have affixed here, in place of a seal, and may he who slights it be accursed forevermore, even as my daughter Sidonia."

In this testament he had completely disinherited his daughter Sidonia, and made his son Otto sole inheritor of all his property, castles, and lands (for his daughter Clara was already dead, and had left no children). Nothing should his daughter Sidonia have but two farmhouses in Zachow,* just to keep her from beggary, and to save the ancient, illustrious name of their house from falling into further contempt. Yet should his son think proper to give her further *alimentum,* he was at liberty so to do. Lastly, for the second and third time, he cursed his daughter, to whom he owed all his misery, from the affair with the apprentice to that concerning the Jena dues, up to this his most miserable and wretched death. *Item,* the burgomaster picked up another letter, which was addressed to himself, and wherein the knight prayed, first, that his body might not be drawn by the executioner to burial, as was the custom with suicides, but conveyed honorably to Stramehl, and there deposited in the vault of his family; secondly, that his daughter Sidonia might be sent to Zachow, there to learn how to live humbly as a peasant maid — for that she might look to being a Duchess of Pomerania, only when she could keep her evil desires still for even a couple of days.

Then he cursed her so that it was pitiable to read; and proved that, if he had been a more God-fearing father, she might have been a different daughter; for as St. Paul says (Galatians vi.), "What a man soweth, that shall he also reap." The letter further said, that, for the good deed done to his corpse, the burgomaster should take all the gold found upon his person, consisting of eighty good rose-nobles, and indemnify himself therewith for the loss of his spices that day in Stramehl when they were scattered before the Jews. He lastly desired his last will and testament to be conveyed to his son, along with his corpse; and further, his son was to send compensation to the crew for the cask of wine and whatever

---

* A small town near Stramehl, a mile and a half from Regenwalde.

other losses they had sustained, according to his knightly word which he had pledged to them.

Summa, when the chirurgeon arrived and the body was examined, there was found upon the unfortunate knight a purse, embroidered with pearls and diamonds, containing eighty rose-nobles, which the burgomaster in no wise disdained to receive, and then laid the whole matter before the honorable council, with the petition of Otto concerning the corpse. The honorable council fully justified the burgomaster for all he had done, and gave their opinion, that as the good town had no jurisdiction over the knight, so they could have none over his body, and therefore let it be removed with all honor to Stramehl, particularly as he had in all things made amends for the wrong he had done them. As regarded Sidonia, two porters should be sent to convey her to Zachow.

Meantime Sidonia had heard of her father's horrible death, and lay on the ground nearly insensible from grief. Just then the burgomaster returned from the council-hall, and commanded that she and his profligate son should be brought before him. When they arrived, he asked how it happened that they were both found in the vessel, for Ulrich, the Grand Chamberlain, had written to inform him that Sidonia had been sent away in a coach to Stettin, with the executioner on the box.

Here Sidonia sobbed so violently that no word could she utter; therefore the son replied that such had been done, but that he had been given a horse from the ducal stables, and had followed the coach; and when they stopped at Uckermund for the night, he had secretly got speech with Sidonia, and advised her to try and remove the planks from the bottom of the carriage and escape to him, for that he would be quite close at hand. And he did what he could that night to loosen the boards himself. So in the morning Sidonia got them up easily, and first dropped her baggage out through the hole, which he picked up; and then, as they came to a soft, sandy tract where the coach had to go very slowly, she let herself also down through it, and sinking in the deep sand, let the coach go over her without any hurt. Then he came to her, and they fled to the next town, where he bought a wagon from some peasants, for her and her luggage to proceed into Stargard, for she was ashamed to appear before Duke Barnim, and wished to get on from Stargard to Stramehl; but when they reached Damm, they heard such wild tales of the robbers and partisans who infested the roads, that Sidonia grew alarmed, and made him go by water for safety. So he left the horse and wagon at the inn, and took ship with the merchants who were going to Stargard. These were their adventures. The rest his father knew as well as himself.

The burgomaster then asked Sidonia had he spoken truth. So she dried her eyes, and nodded her head for "Yes."

Then he admonished her gravely, for that she, a noble maiden, could have dishonored herself with a mere burgher's son, like his Johann, in whom even he, his own father, must say, there was nothing to tempt any girl. And now she knew the truth of those words of St. James: "Lust, when it hath conceived, bringeth forth sin; and sin, when it is finished, bringeth forth death."

Her sin had, indeed, brought forth her father's death; — would that he could say only his *temporal* death. This her father had himself asserted in his testament, which he held now in his hands, and for this cause had left all his goods, lands, and castles to her brother Otto — only giving her two farmhouses in Zachow to save her from the beggar's staff, and their noble name from falling into yet greater contempt — and, in addition, he had cursed her with terrible curses; but these might be yet turned away, if she would incline her heart to God, and lead a pious, honest life for the rest of her days. And much more the worthy man preached to her; but she interrupted him, having found her tongue at last, and exclaimed in wrath, "What! has the good-for-nothing old churl written this? Let me see it; it cannot be true."

So the burgomaster reached her the paper, and, as she read, her color changed, and at last she shrieked aloud and fell down before the burgomaster, clasping his knees, and praying by the Jesu cross not to send such a testament to her brother, for that he was still harder than her father, because he was by nature avaricious, and would grudge her even salt with her bread. Let him remember that his son had promised her marriage, and would he destroy his own children?

Then Jacob Appelmann turned to his profligate son, and asked, "Does she speak the truth? Have you promised her marriage?"

But the shameless knave answered, "True, I so promised her, when we were at Uckermund; but now that she has no money, I wash my hands of her."

Such villainy made the old man flame with indignation. "He would make him know that he must stand by his word — he would force him to it, if he could only think it would be for the advantage of this wretched girl. But he would admonish her to give him up; did she not see that he was shameless, cruel, and selfish? and how could she ever hope to turn to God and lead a new life with such an infamous partner? *Item,* his son should be made to work, and to feel poverty, so that his evil desires might be stifled; and as for her, let her go in God's name to Zachow, and there in solitude repent her sins, and strive to win the favor of God."

But that was no water for her mill; so she continued to lament, and weep, and pray the burgomaster not to send the will to her harsh brother; upon which he answered mildly, "Wert thou to lie at my feet till morning, it would not help thee: the testament goes this day to Stramehl; but I will do this for thee. Thy father left me some rose-nobles, in a purse which he carried about with him, as a compensation for my spices, which he strewed before the Jews in Stramehl, of which deed thou, too, wert also guilty, as I know; therefore I was not ashamed to take the money. But of the purse thy father said naught; so I had it in my mind to keep it – for, in truth, it is of more worth than the nobles it contained. If I mistake not, these are true pearls and diamonds with which it is broidered. Look, here it is. What sayest thou?"

Here she sobbed, and answered, "She knew it well; she had broidered the purse herself. They were her mother's pearls and diamonds, and part of her bridal gear; truly they were worth three thousand florins."

"Then," said the brave old man, "I will give thee this purse, since it was not named either for me or for thy brother at Stramehl. Take it to Zachow; thou wilt make a good penny of it. Be pious, and God-fearing, and industrious, remembering what the Holy Scripture says (Prov. xxxi.): 'A virtuous woman takes wool and flax, and labors diligently with her hands. She stretches out her hands to the wheel, and her fingers grasp the spindle.' Hadst thou learned this, in place of thy costly broidery, methinks it would have been better with thee this day."

As he thus spoke, he put the purse in her hands, and she instantly hid it in her pocket. But the profligate Johann now suddenly became repentant, for he thought, if I can obtain nothing good from my father, I may at least get the purse. So he began to weep and lament, and fell down, too, at his father's feet, saying, if he would only pardon him this once, he would indeed take this poor maiden to wife, as he had promised her, for he alone was guilty of her sin; only would his heart's dearest father forgive him? And so the hypocrite went on with his lies.

Whereupon his father made answer honorably and mildly – "Such promises thou hast often made, but never kept. However, I will try thee yet again. If thou wilt spend each day diligently writing in the council-office, and return each night to sleep in my chamber, and continue this good conduct for a few years, to testify thy repentance, as a brave and upright son, and Sidonia meanwhile continues to lead a godly and humble life at Zachow, then, in God's name, ye shall both marry, and make amends for your sin; but not before that."

As he said this, and bid his son stand up, the hypocrite answered, yes, he would do the will of his dear father; but then he must keep back this testament; so would his children be happy. Otherwise, wherefore should they marry? — what could they live on? A couple of cabins in Zachow would not be enough.

"Truly," replied the old man, "if I were as great a knave as thou art, I would do as thou hast said; yet, though the loss of the spices, which her father wickedly destroyed, did me such injury that I had to sell my house, to get the means of living and keeping thee at the University of Grypswald, I will keep my hands pure from the property of another, even if this property belonged to my greatest enemy, and the enemy of this good town also. *Summa,* this day thou shalt go to the council-office, the testament to Stramehl, and Sidonia to Zachow."

So the knave was silent: but Sidonia still resisted; she would not go to Zachow — never; but if he would send her to Stettin, she was certain the good Duke Barnim would be kind to an unfortunate maiden, who had done nothing more than what thousands do in secret. And whatever the gracious Prince resolved concerning her, she would abide by.

When the burgomaster heard this speech, he saw that no amendment was to be expected from her; and as he had no authority to compel her to Zachow, he promised, at last, to send her to Stettin on the following day, for there were two market wagons going, and she could travel in one, and thereby be more secure against all danger. And so it was done.

Chapter IV

How Sidonia meets Claude Uckermann again, and solicits him to wed her — Item, what he answered, and how my gracious Lord of Stettin received her

Sidonia, next morning, got a good soft seat in the wagon, upon the sack of a cloth merchant; he was cousin to the burgomaster, and promised to take her with him, out of friendship for him. All the men in the wagon were armed with spears and muskets, for fear of the robbers, who were growing more daring every day.

So they proceeded; but had not got far from the town when a horseman galloped furiously after them, and called out that he would accompany them; and this was Claude Uckermann, of whom I have spoken so much in my former book. He, too, was going to Stettin. Now when Sidonia saw him, her eyes glistened like a cat's when she sees a mouse, and she rejoiced at the prospect of such good company, for since the wedding of her sister, never had this handsome youth come across her, though she was constantly looking out for him. So as he rode up by the wagon, she greeted him, and prayed him to alight and come and sit by her upon the sack, that they might talk together of dear old times.

She imagined, no doubt, that he knew nothing of all that had happened; but her disgrace was as public at Stargard as if it had been pealed from the great bell of St. Mary's. He therefore knew her whole story, and answered, that sitting by her was disagreeable to him now; and he rode on. This was plain enough, one would think; but Sidonia still held by her delusion; for as they reached the first inn, and stopped to feed the horses, she saw him stepping aside to avoid her, and seating himself at some distance on a bank. So she put on her flattering face, and advanced to him, saying, "Would not the dear young knight make up with her? — what ailed him? — it was impossible he could resent her silly fun at her sister's wedding. Oh! if he had come again and asked her seriously to be his wife, in place of there in the middle of the dancing, as if he had been only jesting, she would never have had another husband, for from that till now, never had so handsome a knight met her eyes; but she was still free."

Hereupon the young man (as he told me himself) made answer — "Yes, she had rightly judged, he was only jesting, and taking his pastime with her, as they sat there upon the carpet, for he held in unspeakable aversion and disgust a cup from which everyone sipped."

Still Sidonia would not comprehend him, and began to talk about Wolgast. But he looked down straight before him in the grass, and never spake a word, but turned on his heel, and entered the inn, to see after his horse. So he got rid of her at last.

As the wagon set off again, she began to sing so merrily and loudly, that all the wood rang with it. And the young knight was not so stupid but that he truly discerned her meaning, which was to show him that she cared little for his words, since she could go away in such high spirits.

Summa, when they reached the inn at Stettin, Sidonia got all her baggage carried in from the wagon, and there dressed herself with all her finery: silken robes, golden hairnet, and golden chains, rings, and jewels, that all the people saluted her when she came forth, and went to the castle to ask for his Highness the Duke. He was in his workshop, and had just finished turning a spinning-wheel; he laughed aloud when she entered, ran to her, embraced her, and cried, "What! my treasure! — where hast thou been so long, my sugar-morsel? How I laughed when Master Hansen, whom my old, silly, sour cousin of Wolgast sent with thee, came in lately into my workshop, and told me he had brought thee hither in a ducal coach! I ran directly to the courtyard; but when the knave opened the door, my little thrush had flown. Where hast thou been so long, my sugar-morsel?"

As his Grace put all these questions, he continued kissing her, so that his long white beard got entangled in her golden chains; and as she pushed him away, a bunch of hair remained sticking to her brooch, so that he screamed for pain, and put his hand to his chin. At this, in rushed the court marshal and the treasurer (who were writing in the next chamber) as white as corpses, and asked, "Who is murdering his Grace?" but his Grace held up his hand over his bleeding mouth, and winked to them to go away. So when they saw that it was only a maiden combat, they went their way laughing.

Hereupon speaks his Grace — "See now, treasure, what thou hast done! Thou canst be so kind to a groom, yet thy own gracious Prince will treat so harshly!"

But Sidonia began to weep bitterly. "What did he think of her? The whole story was an invention by his old sour cousin of Wolgast to ruin her because she would not learn her catechism (and then she told the same tale as to her father); but would not his Grace take pity on a poor forsaken maiden, seeing that Prince Ernest could not deny he had promised to make her his bride, and wed her privately at Crummyn, on the very next night to that on which her Grace had so shamefully outraged her?"

"My sweet treasure!" answered the Duke, "the young Prince was only making a fool of you; therefore be content that things are no worse. For even if he had wedded you privately, it would have been all in vain, seeing that neither the princely widow nor the Elector of Brandenburg, his godfather, nor any of the princes of the holy Roman Empire, nor lastly, the Pomeranian States, would ever have permitted so unequal a marriage. Therefore, what the priest joined in Crummyn would have been put asunder next day by the tribunals. My poor nephew is a silly enthusiast not to have perceived this all along, before he put such absurdities in your head. That he talked gallantry to you was very natural, and I wished him all success; but that he should ever have talked of marriage shows him to be even sillier than I expected from his years."

Here Sidonia's tears burst forth anew. "Who would care for her now that her father was dead, and had left her penniless? All because he believed that old hypocrite of Wolgast more than his own daughter. Alas! alas! she was a poor orphan now! and all her possessions would be torn from her by her hard-hearted, avaricious brother. Yet surely his Grace might at least take pity on her innocence."

His Grace wondered much when he heard of Otto's death, for the letters brought by the market wagon from the honorable council, acquainting him with the matter, had not yet arrived, and he scratched behind his ear, and said, "It was an evil deed of that proud devil her father, to claim the Jena dues. He had got his answer at Wolgast, and ought to have left the dues alone. What right had he to break the peace of the land, to gratify his lust and greed? It was well that he was dead; but as concerning his testament, that must not be interfered with, he had no power over the property of individuals. Each one might leave his goods as best pleased him; yet he would make his treasurer write a letter in her favor to her brother Otto: that was all that he could do."

This threw Sidonia into despair; she fell at his feet, and told him, that let what would become of her, she would never go a step to Zachow, and her harsh brother would never give her one groschen, unless he were forced to it. His Grace ought to remember that it was by his advice she had gone to Wolgast, where all her misery had commenced; for by the traitorous conduct of the widow, there she had been robbed, not only of her good name, but also of her fortune. So his Grace comforted her, and said that as long as he lived she would want for nothing. He had a pretty house behind St. Mary's, and six young maidens lived there, who had nothing to do but spin and embroider, or comb out the beautiful herons' feathers as the birds molted; for he had a large stock of herons close to the house; and there was a darling little chamber there, which she could have immediately for herself. As to clothes, they might all get the handsomest they pleased, and their meals were supplied from the ducal kitchen.

As his Grace ended, and lifted up Sidonia and kissed her, she wept and sighed more than ever. "Could he think this of her? No; she would never enter the house which was the talk of all Pomerania. If she consented, then, indeed, would the world believe all the falsehoods that were told of her — of her, who was as innocent as a child!" Hereupon his Grace answered stiff and stern (yet this was not his wont, for he was a right tender master), "Then go your ways. Into that house or nowhere else." (Alas! let every maiden take warning, by this example, to guard against the first false step. Amen, chaste Jesus! Amen.)

That evening Sidonia took up her abode in the house. But that same evening there was a great *scandalum,* and tearing of each other's hair among the girls. For one of them, named Trina Wehlers, was a baker's daughter from Stramehl, and on the occasion of Clara's wedding she had headed a procession of young peasants to join the bridal party, but Sidonia had haughtily pushed her back, and forbid them to approach. This Trina was a fine rosy wench, and my Lord Duke took a fancy to her then, so that she looked with great jealousy on anyone that threatened to rob her of his favor. Now when Sidonia entered the house and saw the baker's daughter, she commenced again to play the part of the great lady, but the other only laughed, and mockingly asked her, "Where was the princely spouse, Duke Ernest of Wolgast? Would his Highness come to meet her there?"

Then Sidonia raged from shame and despair, that this peasant girl should dare to insult her, and she ran weeping to her chamber; but when supper was served, the *scandalum* broke out in earnest. For Sidonia had now grown a little comforted, and as there were many dainty dishes from the Duke's table sent to them, she began to enjoy herself somewhat, when all of a sudden the baker's daughter gave her a smart blow over the fingers with a fork. Sidonia instantly seized her by the hair; and now there was such an uproar of blows, screams, and tongues, that my gracious lord, the Duke, was sent for. Whereupon he scolded the baker's daughter right seriously for her insolence, and told her that as Sidonia was the only noble maiden amongst them, she was to bear rule. And if the others did not obey her humbly, as befitted her rank, they should all be whipped. His Grace wore a patch of black plaister on his chin, and attempted to kiss Sidonia again, but she pushed him away, saying that he must have told all that happened at Wolgast to these girls, otherwise how could the baker's daughter have mocked her about it.

Whereupon my gracious lord consoled her, and said that if she were quiet and well-behaved, he would take her with him to the Diet at Wollin, for all the young dukes of Pomerania were to attend it, and Prince Ernest amongst the number, seeing that he had summoned them all there, in order to give up the government of the land into their hands, as he was too old now himself to be tormented with state affairs.

When Sidonia heard this, hope sprang up within her heart, and she resolved to bear her destiny calmly.

Chapter V

How they went on meantime at Wolgast — Item, of the Diet at Wollin, and what happened there

With regard to their Serene Highnesses of Wolgast, I have already related, *libro primo,* that the young lord, Ernest Ludovicus, was carried out of Sidonia's chamber like one dead, when he beheld her abominable wickedness with his own eyes and all can easily believe that he lay for a long while sick unto death. In vain Dr. Pomius offered his celebrated specific; he would take nothing, did nothing day or night but sigh and groan —

"Ah, Sidonia; ah, my beloved heart's bride, Sidonia, can it be possible? Adored Sidonia, my heart is breaking. Sidonia, Sidonia, can it be possible?"

At last the idea struck Dr. Pomius that there must be magic and devil's work in it. So he searched through all his learned books, and finally came upon a recipe which was infallible in such cases. This was to burn the tooth of a dead man to powder, and let the sick bewitched person smoke the ashes. Such was solemnly recommended by Petrus Hispanus Ulyxbonensis, who, under the name of John XXII, ascended the papal throne. See his *Thesaurus Pauperum,* cap. ult.

But the Prince would neither take anything nor smoke anything, and the *delirium amatorium* grew more violent and alarming day by day, so that the whole ducal house was plunged into the deepest grief and despair.

Now there was a prisoner in the bastion tower at Wolgast, a carl from Katzow, who had been arrested and condemned for practicing horrible sorceries and magic — namely, having changed the calves of his neighbors into young hares, which instinctively started off to the woods, and were never seen more, as the whole town testified; and other devil's doings he had practiced, which I now forget; but they were fully proved against him, and so he was sentenced to be burned.

This man now sent a message to the authorities, that if they pardoned him and allowed him free passage from the town, he would tell of something to cure the young lord. This was agreed to; and when he was brought to the chamber of the Prince, he laid his ear down upon his breast, to listen if it were witchcraft that ailed him. Then he spake —

"Yes; the heart beats quite unnaturally, the sound was like the whimpering of a fly caught in a spider's web; their lordships might listen for themselves."

Whereupon all present, one after the other, laid their ear upon the breast of the young Prince, and heard really as he had described.

The earl now said that he would give his Highness a potion which would make him, from that hour, hate the woman who had bewitched him as much as he had adored her. *Item,* the young lord must sleep for three days, and when he woke, his strength would have returned to him; to procure this sleep, he must anoint his temples with goat's milk, which they must instantly bring him, and during his sleep the Lady Duchess must, every two hours, lay fresh ox-flesh upon his stomach.

When her Grace heard this, she rejoiced that her dear son would so soon hold the harlot in abhorrence who had bewitched him. And the earl gave him a red syrup, which he had no sooner swallowed than all care for Sidonia seemed to have vanished from his mind. Even before the goat's milk came, he exclaimed —

"Now that I think over it, what a great blessing that we have got rid of Sidonia."

And no sooner were his temples bathed with the milk than he fell into a deep sleep, which lasted for three days, and when he opened his eyes, his first words were —

"Where is that Sidonia? Is the wanton still here? Bring her before me, that I may tell her how I hate her. Oh, fool that I was, to peril my princely honor for a harlot. Where is she? I must have my revenge upon the light wanton."

Her Grace could hardly speak for joy when she heard these words; and she gave the earl, who had watched all the time by the bedside of the young Prince, so much ham and sausages from the ducal kitchen, that he finally could not walk, but was obliged to be drawn out of the town in a car. Then she asked Dr. Pomius how such a miracle could have been effected. At which he laid his finger on his nose, after his manner, and replied, such was accomplished through the introduction of the natural Life Balsam, which the learned called *confermentationem Mumie,* and so the fool went on prating, and her Grace devouring his words as if they were gospel.

Summa. — After a few days the young lord was able to leave his bed, and as they kept fresh ox-flesh continually applied to his stomach, he soon regained his strength, so that, in a couple of weeks, he could ride, fish, and hunt, and his cheeks were as fresh and rosy as ever. One day he mentioned "the groom's mistress," as he called her, and wished he could give her a lesson in lute-playing, it would be one to make her tremble. But when the letter arrived from Duke Barnim, declaring that, from his great age, he proposed resigning the government of Pomerania into the hands of her Grace's sons, there was no end to the rejoicings at Wolgast, and her Grace declared that she would herself accompany them to the Diet at Wollin.

We shall now see what a treat was waiting her at the old castle there. It was built wholly of wood, and has long since fallen; but at the time I write of, it was standing in all its glory.

Monday, the 15th May 1569, at eleven in the forenoon, his Grace of Stettin came with seven coaches and two hundred and fourteen horsemen into the courtyard. And there, on the steps of the castle, stood my gracious Lady of Wolgast, holding the little Casimir by the hand, in waiting to receive his Highness, and all her other sons stood round her — namely, the illustrious Bishop of Camyn, Johann Frederick, in his bishop's robes, with the staff and miter. *Item,* Duke Bogislaus, who had presented her Grace with a tame sea-gull. *Item,* Ernest Ludovicus, in a Spanish mantle of black velvet, embossed in gold, and upon his head a black velvet Spanish hat, looped up with diamonds, from which long white plumes descended to his shoulder. *Item,* Barnim the younger, who wore a dress similar to his brother's. *Item,* the Grand Chamberlain, Ulrich von Schwerin, and with him a great crowd of the counselors and state officers of Wolgast, besides all the nobles, prelates, knights, and chief burghers of the duchy. Among the nobles stood Otto von Bork, brother to Sidonia; and the burgomaster, Jacob Appelmann, held his place among the citizens.

As Duke Barnim drove up to the castle, the guards fired a salute, and the bells rang, and the cannon roared, and all the vessels in the harbor hoisted their flags, while the streets, houses, and courtyards were decorated with flowers, and all the people of the little town trotted round the carriage, shouting, "Vivat! vivat! vivat!" so that the like was never seen before in Wollin.

Now, when the coach stopped, her Grace the Duchess advanced to meet his Highness; and as old Duke Barnim's head appeared at the window, with his long white beard and yellow leather cap, her Grace stepped forward, and said — "Welcome, dearest Un —"

But she could get no farther, and stood as stiff as Lot's wife when she was turned into a pillar of salt, for there was Sidonia seated in the carriage beside the Duke! Old Ulrich, who followed, soon spied the cause of her Grace's dismay, and exclaimed —

"Three thousand devils, what does your Highness mean by bringing the accursed harlot a third time amongst us?"

But his Highness only laughed, and drew forth his last puppet, it was a Satan as he tempted Eve, saying —

"Hold this for me, good Ulrich, till I am out of the coach, and then I shall hear all about it."

To which the other answered —

"If you let me catch hold of this other Satan, whom ye bring with you, I think it were wiser done!"

Prince Ernest now sprang down the steps, his eye flaming with rage, and drawing his sword, cried —

"Hold me, or I will stab the serpent to the heart, who so disgraced me and my family honor. I will murder her there in the coach before your eyes."

Whereupon old Ulrich flung the little wooden Satan to the ground, and seized the young man by the arm, while Sidonia screamed violently. But the old Duke stepped deliberately out of the coach. Seeing, however, his wooden Satan lying broken on the ground, he became very wroth, and called loudly for a turner with his glue-pot. Then he ascended the steps, and when all had greeted him deferentially, he began —

"Dear niece, worthy cousins, and friends, ye have no doubt heard of the misfortune which hath befallen Sidonia von Bork, who sits there in the carriage. Her father has died; and, further, she has been disinherited. Thereupon she fled to me to seek a refuge. Now ye all know well that the Von Borks are an ancient, honorable, and illustrious race — none more so; therefore I had compassion upon the orphan, and brought her hither to effect a reconciliation between her and Otto Bork, her brother. Step forward, Otto Bork, where are you hiding? Step forth, and hand your sister from the carriage; I saw you amongst the nobles here today. Step forth!"

But Otto had disappeared; and as the Duke found he would not answer to his summons, he bid Sidonia come forth herself. Whereupon the young Prince swore fiercely that, if she but put a foot upon the step he would murder her. "What the devil! young man," said the Duke, laughing; "first you must needs wed her, and now you will slay her dead at our feet! This is somewhat inconsistent. Come forth, Sidonia; he will not be so cruel."

But she sat in the coach, and wept like a child who has lost its nurse. So my gracious lady stepped forward, and commanded the coachman to drive instantly with the maiden to the town inn; and so it was done.

Now the old Duke never ceased for the whole forenoon soliciting Otto Bork to take the poor orphan home with him, and there to treat her as a faithful and kind brother, in compensation for her father's harsh and unnatural will; but it was all in vain, as she indeed had prophesied. "Not the weight of a feather more should she get than the two farmhouses in Zachow; and never let her call him brother, for ancient as his race was, never had one of them borne the brand of infamy till now."

In the afternoon, all the prelates, nobles, and burghers assembled in the grand hall; then entered the ducal family, Barnim the elder at their head. He was dressed in a long black robe, such as the priests wear now, with white ruffles and Spanish frill, and was bareheaded. He took his seat at the top of the table, and thus spake —

"Illustrious Princess, dear cousins, nobles, and faithful burghers, ye all know that I have ruled this Pomeranian land for fifty years, upholding the pure doctrine of Doctor Martin Luther, and casting down papacy in all places and at all times. But as I am now old, and find it hard sometimes to keep my unruly vassals in order, whereof we have had a proof lately, it is my will and purpose to resign the government into the hands of my dear cousins, the illustrious Princes von Pommern-Wolgast, and retire to Oderburg in Old Stettin, there to rest in peace for the remainder of my days; but there are four princes (for the fifth, Casimir, tomorrow or next day shall get a church endowment) and but two duchies. For ye know that, by the Act passed in 1541, the Duchy of Pomerania can only be divided into two portions, the other princes of the family being entitled but to life-annuities. Therefore I have resolved to let it be decided by lot amongst the four Pomeranian princes (according to the example set us by the holy apostles), which of them shall succeed me in Stettin, which is to rule in Wolgast in the room of my loved brother, Philippus Primus of blessed memory; and, finally, which is to be content only with the life-annuity. And this shall now be ascertained in your presence."

Having ended, he commanded the Grand Marshal, Von Flemming, to bring the golden lottery-box with the tickets, and beckoned the young princes to the table. Then, while they drew the lots, he commanded all the nobles, knights, and burghers present to lift up their hands and repeat the Lord's Prayer aloud. So every hand was elevated, even the Duke and my gracious lady uplifting theirs, and the three young princes drew the lots, but not the fourth, and this was Bogislaff. So Duke Barnim wondered, and asked the reason. Whereupon he answered, "That he would not tempt God in aught. To govern a land was a serious thing; and he who had little to rule had little to be responsible for before God. He would therefore freely withdraw his claims, and be content with the annuity; then he could remain with his dear mother, and console her in her widowhood. He did not fear that he would ever repent his choice, for he had more pleasure in study than in the pomp of the world; and if he took the government, then must his beloved library be given up for food to the moths and spiders."

All arguments were vain to turn him from his resolve: so the lots were drawn, and it was found that Johann Frederick had come by the Dukedom of Stettin, and Ernest Ludovicus by that of Wolgast.

But as Barnim the younger went away empty, he was filled with envy and mortification, showing quite a different spirit from his meek, humble-minded brother, Bogislaff. He swore, and cursed his ill luck. "Why did not that fool of a bookworm give over his chance to him, if he would not profit by it himself? Why the devil should he descend to play the commoner, when he was born to play the prince?" and suchlike unamiable and ill-tempered speeches. However, he was now silenced by the drums and trumpets, which struck up the *Te Deum*, in which all present joined. Then Doctor Dannenbaum offered up a prayer, and so that grand ceremony concluded. But the feasting and drinking was carried on with such spirit all through the evening, and far into the night, that all the young lords, except Bogislaff, had well nigh drowned their senses in the wine-cup; and Ernest started up about midnight, declaring that he would go to the inn and murder Sidonia. Barnim was busy quarreling with Johann Frederick about his annuity. So Ernest would certainly have gone to Sidonia, if one of the nobles, by name Dinnies Kleist, a man of huge strength, had not detained him in a singular manner. For he laid a wager that, just with his little finger in the girdle of the young Prince, he would hold him fast; and if he (the Prince) moved but one inch from the spot where he stood, he was content to lose his wager.

And, in truth, Prince Ernest found that he could not stir one step from the spot where Dinnies Kleist held him; so he called a noble to assist him, who seized his hand and tried to draw him away, but in vain; then he called a second, a third, a fourth, up to a dozen, and they all held each other by the hand, and pulled and pulled away till their heads nearly touched the floor, but in vain; not one inch could they make the Prince to move. So Dinnies Kleist won his wager; and the Duke, Johann Frederick, was so delighted with this proof of his giant strength, that he took him into his service from that hour. So the whole night Dinnies amused the guests by performing equally wonderful feats even until day dawned.

Now, there was an enormous golden becker which Duke Ratibor I had taken away from the rich town of Konghalla, in Norway land, when he fell upon it and plundered it. This becker stood on the table filled with wine, and as the Duke handed it to him to pledge him, Dinnies said, "Shall I crush this in my hand, like fresh bread, for your Grace?" "You may try," said the Duke, laughing; and instantly he crushed it together with such force, that the wine dashed down all over the table-cover. *Item,* the Duke threw down some gold and silver medals — "Could he break them?"

"Aye, truly, if they were given to him; not else."

"Take, then, as many as you can break," said the Duke. So he broke them all as easily as altar wafers, and thrust them, laughing, into his pocket.

Item, there had been large quantities of preserved cherries at supper, and the lackeys had piled up the stones on a dish like a high mountain. From this mountain Dinnies took handful after handful, and squeezed them together, so that not a single stone remained whole in his hand. We shall hear a great deal more of this Dinnies Kleist, and his strength, as we proceed; therefore shall let him rest for the present.

Chapter VI

How Sidonia is again discovered with the groom, Johann Appelmann

It was a good day for Johann Appelmann, when his father went to the Diet at Wollin. For as the old burgomaster held strictly by his word, and sent him each day to the writing-office, and locked him up each night in his little room, the poor young man had found life growing very dull. Now he was his mother's pet, and all his sins and wickedness were owing to her as much as Sidonia's to her father. She had petted and spoiled him from his youth up, and stiffened his back against his father. For whenever worthy Jacob laid the stick upon the boy's shoulders, she cried and roared, and called him nothing but an old tyrant. Then how she was always stuffing him up with tit-bits and dainties, whenever his father's back was turned; and if there were a glass of wine left in the bottle, the boy must have it. Then she let him and his brother beat and abuse all the street-boys and send them away bleeding like dogs; and some were afraid to complain of them, as they were sons of the burgomaster; and if others came to the house to do so, she took good care to send them away with a stout blow or bloody nose.

And as the lads grew up, how she praised their beauty, and curled their hair and beards herself, telling them they were not to think of citizen wives, but to look after the richest and highest, for the proudest in the land might be glad to get them as husbands. So she prated away during her husband's absence, for he was in his office all day and most part of the evening. And God knows, bad fruit she brought forth with such rearing — not alone in Johann, but also in his brother Wittich, who, as I afterwards heard, got on no better in Pudgla, where he held the office of magistrate. So true it is what the Scripture says, "A wise woman buildeth her house, but the foolish plucketh it down with her hands" (Prov. xiv.) Then, another Scripture, "As moths from a garment, so from a woman wickedness" (Sirach xlii.)

For what did this fool do now? As soon as her upright and worthy husband had left the house, forgetting and despising all his admonitions respecting this son Johann, she called together all her acquaintance, and kept up a gormandizing and drinking day after day, all to comfort her heart's dear pet Johann, who had been used so harshly by his cross father. Think of her fine, handsome son being stuck down all day to a clerk's desk. Ah! was there ever such a tyrant as her husband to anyone, but especially to his own born children?

And so she went on complaining how she had thrown herself away upon such a hard-hearted monster, and had refused so many fine young carls, all to wed Satan himself at least. She could not make out why God had sent such a curse upon her.

When the brave Johann heard all this, he begged money from his mother, that he might seek another situation. Now that there was a new duke in Stettin, he would assuredly get employment there, but then he must treat all the young fellows and pages about the court, otherwise they would not put in a good word for him. Therefore he would give them a great carouse at the White Horse in the Monk's Close, and then assuredly he would be appointed chief equerry. So she believed every word he uttered; but as old Jacob had carried away all the money that was in the house with him, she sold the spices that had just come in, for a miserable sum, also her own pearl earrings and fur mantle, that her dear heart's son might have a gay carouse, to console him for all his father's hard treatment.

Summa. — When the rogue had got all he could from her, he took his father's best mare from the stable, and rode up to Stettin, where he put up at the White Horse Inn, and soon scraped acquaintance with all the idle young fellows about the court. So they drank and caroused until Johann's last penny was spent, but he had got no situation except in good promises. Truly the young pages had mentioned him to the Duke, and asked the place of equerry for their jovial companion, but his Highness, Duke Johann, had heard too much of his doings at Wolgast, and would by no means countenance him.

Then Johann bethought himself of Sidonia, for he had heard from his boon companions that she was in the Duke's house behind St. Mary's. And he remembered that purse embroidered with pearls and diamonds which his father had given her, so he went many days spying about the house, hoping to get a glimpse of Sidonia; but as she never appeared, he resolved to gain admission by playing the tailor. Wherefore, he tied on an apron, took a tailor's measure and shears, and went straight up to the house, asking boldly, if a young maiden named Sidonia did not live there? for he had got orders to make her a garment. Now the baker's daughter, Trim Wehlers, suspected all was not right, for she had seen my gay youth spying about the house before, and staring up at all the windows. However, she showed the tailor Sidonia's room, and then set herself down to watch. But the wonders of Providence are great. Although she could not hear a word they said, yet all that passed in Sidonia's room was made evident — it was in this wise. Just before the house rose up the church of St. Mary's, with all its stately pillars, and as if God's house wished in wrath to expose the wickedness of the pair, everything that passed in the room was shadowed on these pillars; so when Trina observed this, she ran for the other girls, crying, "Come here, come here, and see how the two shadows are kissing each other. They can be no other than Sidonia and her tailor. This would be fine news for our gracious lord!" They would tell him the whole story when his Highness came that evening, and so get rid of this proud, haughty dragon who played the great lady amongst them, and ruled everything her own way. Therefore they all set themselves to watch for the tailor when he left Sidonia's room; but the whole day passed, and he had not done with his measurement. Whereupon they concluded she must have secreted him in her chamber.

Now the Duke had a private key of the house, and was in the habit of walking over from Oderburg after dusk almost every evening; but as there was no sign of him now, they dispatched a messenger, bidding him come quick to his house, and his Grace would hear and see marvels. How the young girls gathered round him when he entered, all telling him together about Sidonia. And when at last he made out the story, his Grace fell into an unwonted rage (for he was generally mild and good-tempered) that a poacher should get into his preserves. So he runs to Sidonia's door and tries to open it, but the bolts are drawn. Then he threatened to send for Master Hansen if she did not instantly admit him, at which all the girls laughed and clapped their hands with joy. Whereupon Sidonia at last came to the door with looks of great astonishment, and demanded what his Grace could want. It was bed-time, and so, of course, she had locked her door to lie down in safety.

Ille. — "Where is that tailor churl who had come to her in the morning?"

Illa. — "She knew nothing about him, except that he had gone away long ago."

So the girls all screamed "No, no, that is not true! She and the tailor had been kissing each other, as they saw by the shadows on the wall, and making love."

Here Sidonia appeared truly horrified at such an accusation, for she was a cunning hypocrite; and taking up the coif-block* with an air of offended dignity, said, turning to his Grace, "It was this coif-block, methinks, I had at the window with me, and may those be accursed who blackened me to your face." So the Duke half believed her, and stood silent at the window; but Trina Wehlers cried out, "It is false! it is false! a coif-block could not give kisses!" Whereupon Sidonia in great wrath snatched up a robe that lay near her on a couch, to hit the baker's daughter with it across the face. But woe! woe! under the robe lay the tailor's cap, upon which all the girls screamed out, "There is the cap! there is the cap! now we'll soon find the tailor," pushing Sidonia aside, and beginning to search in every nook and corner of the room. Heyday, what an uproar there was now, when they caught sight of the tailor himself in the chimney and dragged him down; but he dashed them aside with his hands, right and left, so that many got bleeding noses, hit his Grace, too, a blow as he tried to seize him, and rushed out of the house.

Still the Duke had time to recognize the knave of Wolgast, and was so angry at his having escaped him, that he almost beat Sidonia. "She

---

* A block for headgears.

was at her old villainy. No good would ever come of her. He saw that now with his own eyes. Therefore this very night she and her baggage should pack off, to the devil if she chose, but he had done with her forever."

When Sidonia found that the affair was taking a bad turn, she tried soft words, but in vain. His Highness ordered up her two serving wenches to remove her and her luggage. And so, to the great joy of the other girls, who laughed and screamed, and clapped their hands, she was turned out, and having nowhere to go to, put up once more at the White Horse Inn.

Now Johann knew nothing of this until next morning, when, as he was toying with one of the maids, he heard a voice from the window, "Johann! Johann! I will give thee the diamond." And looking up, there was Sidonia. So the knave ran to her, and swore he was only jesting with the maid in the court, for that he would marry no one but her, as he had promised yesterday, only he must first wait till he was made equerry, then he would obtain letters of nobility, which could easily be done, as he was the son of a *patricius*; but gold, gold was wanting for all this, and to keep up with his friends at the court. Perhaps this very day he might get the place, if he had only some good claret to entertain them with; therefore she had better give him a couple of diamonds from the purse. And so he went on with his lies and humbug, until at last he got what he wanted.

Sidonia now felt so ashamed of her degradation, that she resolved to leave the White Horse, and take a little lodging in the Monk's Close until Johann obtained the post of equerry. But in vain she hoped and waited. Every day the rogue came, he begged for another pearl or diamond, and if she hesitated, then he swore it would be the last, for this very day he was certain of the situation. At last but two diamonds were left, and beg as he might, these he should not have. Then he beat her, and ran off to the White Horse, but came back again in less than an hour. Would she forgive him? Now they would be happy at last; he had received his appointment as chief equerry. His friends had behaved nobly and kept their word, therefore he must give them a right merry carouse out of gratitude; she might as well hand him those two little diamonds. Now they would want for nothing at last, but live like princes at the table of his Highness the Duke. Would she not be ready to marry him immediately?

Thereupon the unfortunate Sidonia handed over her two last jewels, but never laid eyes on the knave for two days after, when he came to tell her it was all up with him now, the traitors had deceived him, he had got no situation, and unless she gave him more money or jewels he never could marry her. She had still golden armlets and a gold chain, let her go for them, he must see them, and try what he could get for them. But he begged in vain. Then he stormed, swore, threatened, beat her, and finally rushed out of the house declaring that she might go to the devil, for as to him he would never give himself any further trouble about her.

Chapter VII

Of the distress in Pomeranian land — Item, how Sidonia and Johann Appelmann determine to join the robbers in the vicinity of Stargard

*W*hen my gracious lord, Duke Johann Frederick, succeeded to the government, he had no idea of hoarding up his money in old pots, but lavished it freely upon all kinds of buildings, hounds, horses – in short, upon everything that could make his court and castle luxurious and magnificent.

Indeed, he was often as prodigal, just to gratify a whim, as when he flung the gold coins to Dinnies Kleist, merely to see if he could break them. For instance, he was not content with the old ducal residence at Stettin, but must pull it down and build another in the forest, not far from Stargard, with churches, towers, stables, and all kinds of buildings; and this new residence he called after his own name, Friedrichswald.

Item, my gracious lord had many princely visitors, who would come with a train of six hundred horses or more; and his princely spouse, the Duchess Erdmuth, was a lady of munificent spirit, and flung away gold by handfuls; so that in a short time his Highness had run through all his forefathers' savings, and his incoming revenue was greatly diminished by the large annuity which he had to pay to old Duke Barnim.

Therefore he summoned the states, and requested them to assist him with more money; but they gave answer that his Highness wanted prudence; he ought to tie his purse tighter. Why did he build that new

castle of Friedrichswald? Was it ever heard in Pomerania that a prince
needed two state residences? But his Highness never entered the treasury
to look after the expenditure of the duchy — he did nothing but banquet,
hunt, fish, and build. The states, therefore, had no gold for such
extravagances.

When his Highness had received this same answer two or three times
from the states, he waxed wroth, and threatened to pronounce the
interdictum seculars over his poor land, and finally close the royal treasury
and all the courts of justice, until the states would give him money.

Now the old treasurer, Jacob Zitsewitz, who had quitted Wolgast to
enter the service of his Grace, was so shocked at these proceedings, that
he killed himself out of pure grief and shame. He was an upright,
excellent man, this old Zitsewitz, though perchance, like old Duke
Barnim, he loved the maidens and a lusty Pomeranian draft rather too
well. And he foretold all the evil that would result from this same
interdict; but his Highness resisted his entreaties; and when the old man
found his warnings unheeded and despised, he stabbed himself, as I
have said, there in the treasury, before his master's eyes, out of grief and
shame.

The misery which he prophesied soon fell upon the land; for it was
just at that time that the great house of Loitz failed in Stettin, leaving
debts to the amount of twenty tons of gold, it was said; by reason of
which many thousand men, widows, and orphans, were utterly beggared,
and great distress brought upon all ranks of the people. Such universal
grief and lamentation never had been known in all Pomerania, as I have
heard my father tell, of blessed memory; and as the princely treasury
was closed, as also all the courts of justice, and no redress could be
obtained, many misguided and ruined men resolved to revenge themselves; and this was now a welcome hearing to Johann Appelmann.

For having given up all hope of the post of equerry, he made
acquaintance with these disaffected persons, amongst whom was a
miller, one Philip Konneman by name, a notorious knave. With this
Konneman he sits down one evening in the inn to drink Rostock beer,
begins to curse and abuse the reigning family, who had ruined and
beggared the people even more than Hans Loitz. They ought to combine
together and right themselves. Where was the crime? Their cause was
good; and where there were no judges in the land, complaints would do
little good. He would be their captain. Let him speak to the others about
it, and see would they consent. He knew of many churches where there
were jewels and other valuables still remaining. Also in Stargard, where
his dear father played the burgomaster, there was much gold.

So they fixed a night when they should all meet at Lastadie,* near the ducal fish-house; and Johann then goes to Sidonia to wheedle her out of the gold chain, for handsel for the robbers.

"Now," he said, "the good old times were come back in Pomerania, when everyone trusted to his own good sword, and were not led like sheep at the beck of another; for the treasury and all the courts of justice were closed. So the glorious times of knight-errantry must come again, such as their forefathers had seen." His companions had promised to elect him captain; but then he must give them handsel for that, and the gold chain would just sell for the sum he wanted. What use was it to her? If she gave it, then he would take her with him, and the first rich prize they got he would marry her certainly, and settle down in Poland afterwards, or wherever else she wished. That would be a glorious life, and she would never regret the young Duke. And had not all the nobles in old time led the same life, and so gained their castles and lands?

But Sidonia began to weep. "Let him do what he would, she would never give the chain; and if he beat her, she would scream for help through the streets, and betray all his plans to the authorities. Now she saw plainly how she had been deceived. He had talked her out of all her gold, and now wanted to bring her to the gallows at last. No, never should he get the chain – it was all she had left; and she had determined at last to go and live quietly at her farm in Zachow, as soon as she could obtain a vehicle from Regenswald to Labes."

When Johann heard this, he was terribly alarmed, and kissed her little hands, and coaxed and flattered her – "Why did she weep? There were plenty of herons' feathers now in the garden behind St. Mary's, for the birds were molting. She could easily get some of them, and they were worth three times as much as the gold chain. Did she think it a crime to take a few feathers from that old sinner, Duke Barnim, or his girls? And if she really wished to leave him, she could sell the feathers even better in Dresden than here."

It was all in vain. Sidonia continued weeping – "Let him talk as he liked, she would never give the chain. He was a knave through and through. Woe to her that she had ever listened to him! He was the cause of all her misery!" and so she went on.

But the cunning fox would not give up his prey so easily. He now tried the same trick which he had played so successfully at Wolgast upon old Ulrich, and at Stargard upon his father; in short, he played the penitent, and began to weep and lament over his errors, and all the misery he had caused her. "It was, indeed, true that he was to blame for

---

* A suburb of Stettin.

all; but if she would only forgive him, and say she pardoned him, he would devote his life to her, and revenge her upon all her enemies. The moment for doing so was nigh at hand; for the young lord, Prince Ernest, who had so shamefully abandoned her, was coming here to Stettin with his young bride, the Princess Hedwig of Brunswick, to spend the honeymoon, and would he not take good care to waylay them on their journey to Wolgast, and give them something to think of for the rest of their lives?"

When Sidonia heard these tidings, her eyes flashed like a cat's in the dark. "Who told him that? She would not believe it, unless someone else confirmed the story."

So he answered — "That anyone could confirm it, for the whole castle was filled with workmen making preparations for their reception; the bridal chamber had been hung with new tapestry, and painters and carvers were busy all day long painting and carving the united arms of Pomerania and Brunswick upon all the furniture and glass."

Illa. — "Well, she would go into the town to inquire, and if his tale were true, and that he swore to marry her, he should have the chain."

Ille. — "There was a carver going by with his basket and tools — let her call him in, and hear what he said on the matter."

So my cunning fellow called out to the workman, who stepped in presently with his basket, and assured the lady politely, that in fourteen days the young Duke of Wolgast and his princely bride were to arrive at the castle, for the Court Marshal had told him this himself, and given him orders to have a large number of glasses cut with their united arms ready with all diligence.

When Sidonia heard this, and saw the glasses in his basket, she handed the golden chain to Johann, and the carver went his way. Then the aforesaid rogue fell down on his knees, swearing to marry her, and never to leave her more, for she had now given him all; and if this, too, were lost, she must beg her way to Zachow.

So the gallows-bird went off with the chain, turned it into money, drank and caroused, and with the remainder set off for Lastadie, to meet the ringleaders, near the ducal fishhouse, as agreed upon.

But Master Konneman had only been able to gather ten fellows together; the others held back, though they had talked so boldly at first, thinking, no doubt, that when the courts of justice were reopened, they would all be brought to the gallows.

So Johann thought the number too small for his purposes, and agreed with the others to send an envoy to the robber-band of the Stargard Wood, proposing a league between them, and offering himself (Johann Appelmann, a knight of excellent family and endowments) as their captain. Should they consent, the said Johann would give them right good handsel; and on the appointed day, meet them in the forest, with his illustrious and noble bride; and as a sign whereby they should know him, he would whistle three times loudly when he approached the wood.

Konneman undertook to be the bearer of the message, and returned in a few days, declaring that the robbers had received the proposal with joy. He found them encamped under a large nut tree in the forest, roasting a sheep upon a spear, at a large fire. So they made him sit down and eat with them, and told him it was a right jolly life, with no ruler but the great God above them. Better to live under the free heaven than die in their squalid cabins. The band was strong, besides many who had joined lately, since the bankruptcy of Hans Loitz, and there were some gypsies too, amongst whom was an old hag who told fortunes, and had lately prophesied to the band that a great prize was in store for them; they had just returned with some booty from the little town of Damm, where they had committed a robbery. One of their party, however, had been taken there.

When Johann heard the good result of his message, he summoned all his followers to another meeting at the ducal fish-house, gave them each money, and swore them to fidelity; then bid them disperse, and slip singly to the band, to avoid observation, and he would himself meet them in the forest next day.

Chapter VIII

How Johann and Sidonia meet an adventure, at Alten Damm — Item, of their reception by the robber-band

Now Johann Appelmann had a grudge against the newly appointed equerry to his Highness, for the man had swilled his claret, and been foremost in his promises, and yet now had stepped into the place himself, and left Johann in the lurch. The knave, therefore, determined on revenge; so invented a story, how that his father, old Appelmann, had sent for him to give him half of all he was worth, and as he must journey to Stargard directly, he prayed his friend the equerry to lend him a couple of horses and a wagon out of the ducal stables, with harness and all that would be necessary, swearing that when he brought them back he would give him and his other friends such a carouse at the inn, as they had never yet had in their lives.

And when the other asked, would not one horse be sufficient, Johann replied no, that he required the wagon for his luggage, and two horses would be necessary to draw it. *Summa,* the fool gives him two beautiful Andalusian stallions, with harness and saddles; *item,* a wagon, whereon my knave mounted next morning early, with Sidonia and her luggage, and took the miller, Konneman, with him as driver.

But as they passed through Alten Damm, a strange adventure happened, whereby the all-merciful God, no doubt, wished to turn them from their evil way; but they flung His warnings to the wind.

For the carl was going to be executed who belonged to the robberband, that had committed a burglary there, in the town, some days previously. However, the gallows having been blown down by a storm, the linen-weavers, according to old usage, came to erect another. This angered the millers, who also began to erect one of their own, declaring that the weavers had only a right to supply the ladder, but they were to erect the gallows. A great fight now arose between weavers and millers, while the poor thief stood by with his hands tied behind his back, and arrayed in his winding-sheet. But the sheriffs, and whatever other honorable citizens were by, having in vain endeavored to appease the quarrel, returned to the inn, to take the advice of the honorable council.

Just at this moment Johann and Sidonia drove into the middle of the crowd, and the former leaped off and laughed heartily, for a miller had thrown down a poor lean weaver close behind the criminal, and was belaboring him stoutly with his floured fists, whilst the poor wretch screamed loudly for succor or assistance to the criminal, who answered in his *Platt Deutsch,* "I cannot help thee, friend, for, see, my hands are bound." Upon this, Johann draws his knife from his girdle, and slipping behind the felon, cuts the ropes binding him.

He straightway, finding himself free, jumped upon the miller, and turned the flour all red upon his face with his heavy blows. Then he ran towards the wagon, but the guardsman caught hold of him by the shoulder, so the poor wretch left the winding-sheet in his hand, and jumping, naked as he was, on the back of one of the horses, set off, at top speed, to the forest, with Sidonia screaming and roaring fleeing with him.

Millers and weavers now left off their wrangling, and joined together in pursuit, but in vain; the fellow soon distanced them all, and was lost to sight in the wood.

When he had driven the wagon a good space, and still hearing the roaring of the people in pursuit, he stopped the horses, and jumped off, to take to his heels amongst the trees. Whereupon Konneman threw him a horse-cloth from the wagon, bidding him cover himself with it; so the carl snapped it up, and rolled it about his body with all alacrity. Now this horse-cloth was embroidered with the Pomeranian arms, and the poor Adam looked so absurd running away in such a garment, that Sidonia, notwithstanding all her fright, could not help bursting into a loud mocking laughter.

Whereupon the crowd came up, cursing, swearing, and cursing, that the thief had escaped them; Johann Appelmann, who was amongst them, and was just in the act of stepping up to the wagon, when Prince Johann Frederick and a company of carabineers galloped up along with the chief equerry and a large retinue, all on their way to Friedrichswald.

The Duke stopped to hear the cause of the tumult, and when they told him, he laughingly said, he would soon return with the gallows-knaves; then, turning to Appelmann, he asked who he was, and what brought him there?

When Johann gave his name, and said he was going to Stargard, his Grace exclaimed, with surprise —

"So thou art the knave of whom I have heard so much; and this woman here, I suppose, is Sidonia? Pity of her. She is a handsome wench, I see."

Then, as Sidonia blushed and looked down, he continued —

"And where did the fellow get these fine horses? Would he sell them?"

Now Appelmann had a great mind to tell the truth, and say he got them from the equerry, who was already turning white with pure fear; but recollecting that he might come in for some of the punishment himself, besides hoping to play a second trick upon his Highness, he answered, that his father at Stargard had made them a present to him.

The Duke, now turning to his equerry, asked him —

"Would not these horses match his Andalusian stallions perfectly?"

And as the other tremblingly answered, "Yes, perfectly," his Grace demanded if the knave would sell them.

Ille. — "Oh yes; to gratify his Serene Highness the Duke, he would sell the horses for 3000 florins."

"Let it be so," said the Duke; "but I must owe thee the money, fellow."

Ille. — "Then he would not make the bargain, for he wanted the money directly to take him to Stargard."

So the Duke frowned that he would not trust his own Prince; and as Appelmann attempted to move off with the wagon, his Highness took his plumed cap from his head, and cutting off the diamond agrafe with his dagger, flung it to him, exclaiming —

"Stay! take these jewels, they are worth 1300 florins, but leave me the horses."

Now the chief equerry nearly fell from his horse with shame as the knave picked up the agrafe, and shoved it into his pocket, then humbly addressing his Highness, prayed for permission just to leave the maiden and her luggage in Stargard, and then he would return instantly with both horses, and bring them himself to his gracious Highness at Friedrichswald.

The Duke having consented, the knave sprang up upon the wagon, and turning off to another road, drove away as hard as he could from the scene of this perilous adventure. After some time he whistled, but receiving no response, kept driving through the forest until evening, when a loud, shrill whistle at last replied to his, and on reaching a cross-road, he found the whole band dancing with great merriment round a large sign-board which had been stuck up there by the authorities, and on which was painted a gypsy lying under the gallows, while the executioner stood over him in the act of applying the torture, and beneath ran the inscription —

"Gypsy! from Pomerania flee,
  Or thus it shall be done to thee."

These words the robber crew had set to some sort of rude melody, and now sang it and danced to it round the sign, the fellow with the horse-cloth in the midst of them, the merriest of them all.

The moment they got a glimpse of their captain, men, women, and children ran off like mad to the wagon, clapping their hands and shouting, "Huzzah! huzzah! what a noble captain! Had he brought them anything to drink?" And when he said "Yes," and handed out three barrels of wine, there was no end to the jubilee of cheering. Then he must give them handsel, and after that they would make a large fire and swear fealty to him round it, as was the manner of the gypsies, for the band was mostly composed of gypsies, and numbered about fifty men altogether.

Summa. — A great fire was kindled, round which they all took the oath of obedience to their captain, and he swore fidelity to them in return. Then a couple of deer were roasted; and after they had eaten and drunk, the singing and dancing round the great sign-board was resumed, until the broad daylight glanced through the trees.

People may see from this to what a pitch of lawlessness and disorder the land came under the reign of Duke Johann. For, methinks, these robbers would never have dared to make such a mock of the authorities, only that my Lord Duke had shut up all the courts of justice in the kingdom.

During their jollity, our knave Appelmann cast his eyes upon a gypsy maiden, called the handsome Sioli; a tall, dark-eyed wench, but with scarcely a rag to cover her. Therefore he bade Sidonia run to her luggage, and take out one of her own best robes for the girl; but Sidonia turned away in great wrath, exclaiming —

"This was the way he kept his promise to her. She had given him all, and followed him even hither, and yet he cared more for a ragged gypsy girl than for her. But she would go away that very night, anywhere her steps might lead her, if only away from her present misery. Let him give her the Duke's diamonds, and she would leave him all the herons' feathers, and never come near him anymore."

But my knave only laughed, and bid her come take the diamonds if she wanted them, they were in his bosom. Then the gypsy girl and her mother, old Ussel, began to mock the fine lady. So Sidonia sat there weeping and wringing her hands, while Johann laughed, danced, drank, and kissed the gypsy wench, and finally threatened to go and take a robe himself out of the luggage, if Sidonia did not run for one instantly.

However, she would not stir; so Konnemann, the miller, took pity on her, and would have remonstrated, but Johann cut him short, saying —

"What the devil did he mean? Was he not the captain? and why should Konnemann dare to interfere with him?"

Then he strode over to the wagon to plunder Sidonia's baggage, which, when she observed, her heart seemed to break, and she kneeled down, lifted up her hands, and prayed thus: —

"Merciful Creator, I know Thee not, for my hard and unnatural father never brought me to Thee; therefore on his head be my sins. But if Thou hast pity on the young ravens, who likewise know Thee not, have pity upon me, and help me to leave this robber den with Thy gracious help."

Here such a shout of laughter resounded from all sides, that she sprang up, and seizing the best bundle in the wagon, plunged into the wood, with loud cries and lamentation; whilst Appelmann only said —

"Never heed her, let her do as she pleases; she will be back again soon enough, I warrant."

Accordingly, scarcely an hour had elapsed, when the unhappy maiden appeared again, to the great amusement of the whole band, who mocked her yet more than before. She came back crying and lamenting –

"She could go no further, for the wolves followed her, and howled round her on all sides. Ah! that she were a stone, and buried fathoms deep in the earth! That shameless knave, Appelmann, might indeed have pitied her, if he hoped for pity from God; but had he not taken her robe to put it on the gypsy beggar? She nearly died of shame at the sight. But she would never forgive the beggar's brat to the day of judgment for it. All she wanted now was some good Christian to guide her out of the wild forest. Would no one come with her? that was all she asked."

And so she went on crying, and lamenting in the deepest grief.

Summa. – When the knave heard all this, his heart seemed to relent; perhaps he dreaded the anger of her relations if she were treated too badly, or, mayhap, it was compassion, I cannot say; but he sprang up, kissed her, caressed her, and consoled her.

"Why should she leave them? He would remain faithful and constant to her, as he had sworn. Why should the gown for the beggar-girl anger her? When they get the herons' feathers on the morrow, he would buy her ten new gowns for the one he had taken." And so he continued in his old deceiving way, till she at last believed him, and was comforted.

Here the roll of a carriage was heard, and as many of the band as were not quite drunk seized their muskets and pikes, and rushed in the direction of the sound. But behold, the wagon and horses, with all Sidonia's luggage, was off! For, in truth, the equerry, seeing Johann's treachery, had secretly followed him, hiding himself in the bushes till it grew dark, but near enough to observe all that was going on; then, watching his opportunity, and knowing the robbers were all more or less drunk, he sprang upon the wagon, and galloped away as hard as he could. Johann gave chase for a little, but the equerry had got too good a start to be overtaken; and so Johann returned, cursing and raging, to the band. Then they all gathered round the fire again, and drank and caroused till morning dawned, when each sought out a good sleeping-place amongst the bushwood. There they lay till morn, when Johann summoned them to prepare for their excursion to the Duke's gardens at Zachan.

Chapter IX

How his Highness, Duke Barnim the elder, went a-hawking at Marienfliess — Item, of the shameful robbery at Zachan, and how burgomaster Appelmann remonstrates with his abandoned son

Lfter Duke Barnim the elder had resigned the government, he betook himself more than ever to field-sports; and amongst others, hawking became one of his most favorite pursuits. By this sport, he stocked his gardens at Zachan with an enormous number of herons, and made a considerable sum annually by the sale of the feathers. These gardens at Zachan covered an immense space, and were walled round. Within were many thousand herons' nests; and all the birds taken by the falcons were brought here, and their wings clipped. Then the keepers fed them with fish, frogs, and lizards, so that they became quite tame, and when their wings grew again, never attempted to leave the gardens, but diligently built their nests and reared their young. Now, though it cost a great sum to keep these gardens in order, and support all the people necessary to look after the birds, yet the Duke thought little of the expense, considering the vast sum which the feathers brought him at the molting season.

Accordingly, during the molting time, he generally took up his abode at a castle adjoining the gardens, called "The Stone Rampart," to inspect the gathering in of the feathers himself; and he was just on his journey thither with his falconers, hunters, and other retainers, when the robber-band caught sight of him from the wood. His Highness was seated in an open carriage, with Trina Wehlers, the baker's daughter, by his side; and Sidonia, who recognized her enemy, instantly entreated Johann to revenge her on the girl if possible; but, as he hesitated, the old gypsy mother stepped forward and whispered Sidonia, "that she would help her to a revenge, if she but gave her that little golden smelling-bottle which she wore suspended by a gold chain on her neck." Sidonia agreed, and the revenge soon followed; for the Duke left the carriage, and mounted a horse to follow the chase, the falconer having unloosed a couple of hawks and let them fly at a heron. Trina remained in the coach;

but the coachman, wishing to see the sport, tied his horses to a tree, and ran off, too, after the others into the wood. The hawk soared high above the heron, watching its opportunity to pounce upon the quarry; but the heron, just as it swooped down upon it, drove its sharp bill through the body of the hawk, and down they both came together covered with blood, right between the two carriage horses.

No doubt this was all done through the magic of the gypsy mother; for the horses took fright instantly, plunged and reared, and dashed off with the carriage, which was overturned some yards from the spot, and the baker's daughter had her leg broken. Hearing her screams, the Duke and the whole party ran to the spot; and his Highness first scolded the coachman for leaving his horses, then the falconer for having let fly his best falcon, which now lay there quite dead. The heron, however, was alive, and his Grace ordered it to be bound and carried off to Zachan. The baker's daughter prayed, but in vain, that the coachman might be hung upon the next tree. Then they all set off homeward, but Trina screamed so loudly, that his Grace stopped, and ordered a couple of stout huntsmen to carry her to the neighboring convent of Marienfliess, where, as I am credibly informed, in a short time she gave up the ghost.

Now, the robber-band were watching all these proceedings from the wood, but kept as still as mice. Not until his Grace had driven off a good space, and the baker's daughter had been carried away, did they venture to speak or move; then Sidonia jumped up, clapping her hands in ecstasy, and mimicking the groans and contortions of the poor girl, to the great amusement of the band, who laughed loudly; but Johann recalled them to business, and proposed that they should secretly follow his Highness, and hide themselves at Elsbruck, near the water-mill of Zachan, until the evening closed in. In order also to be quite certain of the place where his Grace had laid up all the herons' feathers of that season, Johann proposed that the miller, Konnemann, should visit his Grace at Zachan, giving out that he was a feather merchant from Berlin. Accordingly, when they reached Elsbruck, the miller put on my knave's best doublet (for he was almost naked before), and proceeded to the Stone Rampart, Sidonia bidding him, over and over again, to inquire at the castle when the young Lord of Wolgast and his bride were expected at Stettin. The Duke received Konnemann very graciously, when he found that he was a wealthy feather merchant from Berlin, who, having heard of the number and extent of his Grace's gardens at Zachan, had come to purchase all the last year's gathering of feathers. Would his Highness allow him to see the feathers?

Summa. — He had his wish; for his Grace brought him into a little room on the ground-floor, where lay two sacks full of the most perfect and beautiful feathers; and when the Duke demanded a thousand florins for them, the knave replied, "That he would willingly have the feathers, but must take the night to think over the price." Then he took good note of the room, and the garden, and all the passages of the castle, and so came back in the twilight to the band with great joy, assuring them that nothing would be easier than to rob the old turner's apprentice of his feathers.

Such, indeed, was the truth; for at midnight my knave Johann, with Konnemann and a few chosen accomplices, carried away those two sacks of feathers; and no one knew a word about the robbery until the next morning, when the band were far off in the forest, no one knew where. But a quarrel had arisen between my knave and Sidonia over the feathers: she wanted them for herself, that she might turn them into money, and so be enabled to get back to her own people; but Johann had no idea of employing his booty in this way. "What was she thinking of? If those fine stallions, indeed, had not been stolen from him, he might have given her the feathers; but now there was nothing else left wherewith to pay the band — she must wait for another good prize. Meantime they must settle accounts with the young Lord of Wolgast, who, as Konnemann had found out, was expected at Stettin in seven days."

Now, the daring robbery at Zachan was the talk of the whole country, and as the old burgomaster, Appelmann, had heard at Friedrichswald about the horses and wagon, and his son's shameful knavery, he could think of nothing else but that the same rascal had stolen the Duke's feathers at So he took some faithful burghers with him, and set off for the forest, to try and find his lost son. At last, after many wanderings, a peasant, who was cutting wood, told them that he had seen the robber-band encamped in a thick wood near Rehewinkel;* and when the miserable father and his burghers arrived at the place, there indeed was the robber-band stretched upon the long grass, and Sidonia seated upon the stump of a tree — for she must play the lute, while Johann, his godless son, was plaiting the long black hair of the handsome Sioli.

Methinks the knave must have felt somewhat startled when his father sprang from behind an oak, a dagger in his hand, exclaiming loudly, "Johann, Johann, thou lost, abandoned son! is it thus I find thee?"

The knave turned as white as a corpse upon the gallows, and his hands seemed to freeze upon the fair Sioli's hair; but the band jumped up and seized their arms, shouting, "Seize him! seize him!" The old man, however, cared little for their shouts; and still gazing on his son, cried out, "Dost thou not answer me, thou God-forgetting knave? Thou hast

---

* Two miles and a half from Stargard, and the present dwelling-place of the editor.

deceived and robbed thy own Prince. Answer me — who amongst all these is fitter for the gallows than thou art?"

So my knave at last came to his senses, and answered sullenly, "What did he want here? He had done nothing for him. He must earn his own bread."

Ille. — "God forgive thee thy sins; did I not take thee back as my son, and strive to correct thee as a true and loving father? Why didst thou run away from my house and the writing-office?"

Hic. — "He was born for something else than to lead the life of a dog."

Ille. — "He had never made him live any such life; and even if he had, better live like a dog than as a robber wolf."

Hic. — "He was no robber. Who had belied him so? He and his friends were on their way to Poland to join the army."

Ille. — "Wherefore, then, had he tricked his Highness of Stettin out of the horses?"

Hic. — "That was only a revenge upon the equerry, to pay him back in his own coin, for he was his enemy, and had broken faith with him."

Ille. — "But he had robbed his Grace Duke Barnim, likewise, of the herons' feathers. No one else had done it."

Hic. — "Who dared to say so? He was insulted and belied by everyone." Then he cursed and swore that he knew nothing whatever of these herons' feathers which he was making such a fuss about.

Meanwhile the band stood round with cocked muskets, and as the burghers now pressed forward, to save their leader, if any violence were offered, Konnemann called out, "Give the word, master — shall I shoot down the churl?"

Here Johann's conscience was moved a little, and he shouted, "Back! back! — he is my father!"

But the old gypsy mother sprang forward with a knife, crying, "Thy father, fool? — what care we for thy father? Let me at him, and I'll soon settle thy father with my knife."

When the unfortunate son heard and saw this, he seized a heavy stick that lay near him, and gave the gypsy such a blow on the crown, that she rolled, screaming, on the ground. Whereupon the whole band raised a wild yell, and rushed upon the burgomaster.

Then Johann cried, almost with anguish, "Back! back! he is my father! Do ye not remember your oaths to me? Spare my father! Wait, at least; he has something of importance to tell me."

And at last, though with difficulty, he succeeded in calming these children of Belial. Then drawing his father aside, under the shade of a great oak, he began — "Dearest father mine, it was fear of you, and despair of the future, that drove me to this work; but if you will now give me three hundred florins, I will go forth into the wide world, and take honorable service, wherever it is to be had, during the wars."

Ille. — "Had he yet married that unfortunate Sidonia, who he observed, to his surprise, was still with him?"

Hic. — "No; he could never marry the harlot now, for she had run away from old Duke Barnim, and followed him here to the forest."

Ille. — "What would become of her, then, when he joined the army?"

Hic. — "That was her look-out. Let her go to her farm at Zachow."

Hereupon the old man held his peace, and rested his arm against the oak, and his grey head upon his arm, and looked down long upon the grass without uttering a word; then he sighed deeply, and looking up, thus addressed Johann: —

"My son, I will trust thee yet again; but it shall be the last time; therefore take heed to what I say. Between Stargard and Pegelow there stands an old thorn upon the highway; there, tomorrow evening, by seven of the clock, my servant Caspar, whom thou knowest, shall bring thee three hundred florins; but on this one condition, that thou dost now swear solemnly to abandon this villainous robber-band, and seek an honorable living far away, in some other country, where thou must pray daily to God the Lord, to turn thee from thy evil ways, and help thee by His grace."

So the knave knelt down before his father, wept, and prayed for his father's forgiveness; then swore solemnly to abandon his sinful life, and with God's help to perform all that his father had enjoined. "And would he not give his last farewell to his dear, darling mother?" "Thy mother! — ah, thy mother!" sighed the old man; "but rise, now, and let me and mine homewards. God grant that my eyes have beheld thee for the last time. Come, I will take this Sidonia back with me."

So they forthwith joined the robber crew again, who were still making a great uproar, which, however, Johann appeased, and after some time obtained a free passage for his father and the burghers; but Sidonia would not accompany them. The upright old burgomaster admonished first, then he promised to drive her with his own horses to her farm at Zachow; but his words were all in vain, for the knave privately gave her a look, and whispered something in her ear, but no one knew what it was.

Nor did the old man omit to admonish the whole band likewise, telling them that if they did not now look up to the high God, they would one day look down from the high gallows, for all thieves and robbers came to dance in the wind at last: ten hung in Stargard, and he had seen twenty at Stettin, and not even the smallest town had its gallows empty. Hereat Konnemann cried out, "Ho! ho! who will hang us now? We know well the courts of justice are closed in all places." And as the old man sighed, and prepared to answer him, the whole band set up such a shout of laughter that he stood silent a space; then turning round, trod slowly out of the thick wood with all his burghers, and was soon lost to view.

The next evening Johann received the three hundred florins at the thorn-bush, along with a letter from his father, admonishing him yet again, and conjuring him to fulfill his promise speedily of abandoning his wicked life. Upon which, my knave gave some of the money to a peasant that he met on the highway, and bid him go into the town, purchase some wine and all sorts of eatables, and fetch them to the band in the wood, that they might have a merry carouse that same night. This very peasant had been one of their accomplices, and great was his joy when he beheld them all again, and, in particular, the gypsy mother. He told her that all her prophecy had come out true, for his daughter had been deserted, and her lover had taken Stina Krugers to wife; could she not, therefore, give him something that would make Stina childless, and cause her husband to hate her?

"Aye, if he crossed her hand with silver."

This the peasant did. Whereupon she gave him a padlock, and whispered some words in his ear.

When Sidonia heard that the man could be brought to hate his wife by some means, her eyes flashed wildly, and she called the horrible old gypsy mother aside, and asked her to tell her the charm.

Illa. — "Yes; but what would she give her? She had two pretty golden rings on her finger; let her give them, and she should have the secret."

Hæc. — "She would give one ring now, and the other if the charm succeeded. The peasant had only given her a few groschen."

Illa. — "Yes; but she had only given him half the charm."

Hæc. — "Was it anything to eat or drink?"

Illa. — "No; there was no eating or drinking: the charm did it all."

Hæc. — "Then let her teach it to her, and if it succeeded by the young Lord of Wolgast, she would have both rings; if not, but one."

Illa. — "It would succeed without doubt; if his young wife had no promise of offspring as yet, she would remain childless forever."

Summa. — The old gypsy taught her the charm, the same with which she afterward bewitched the whole princely Pomeranian race, so that they perished childless from off the face of the earth;* and this charm

---

* Marginal note of Duke Bogislaff XIV — "O ter quaterque detestabilem! Et ego testis adfui tametsi in actis de industria hand notatis. (Oh, thrice accursed! And I, too, was present at this confession, although I am not mentioned in the protocol.)"

Sidonia confessed upon the rack afterwards, in the Great Hall of Oderburg, July 28, A.D. 1620.

Chapter X

How the robbers attack Prince Ernest and his bride in the Uckermann
forest, and Marcus Bork and Dinnies Kleist come to their rescue

The young Lord of Wolgast and his young bride, the Princess Sophia
Hedwig, arrived in due time at the court of Stettin, on a visit to their
illustrious brother, Duke Johann Frederick. During the ten days of their
stay, there was no end to the banquetings, huntings, fishings, and
revelings of all kinds, to do honor to their presence.

The young lord has quite recovered from his long and strange illness.
But the young bride complains a little. Whereupon my Lord of Stettin
jests with her, and the courtiers make merry, so that the young bride
blushes and entreats her husband to take her away from this impudent
court of Stettin, and take her home to his illustrious mother at Wolgast.

Prince Ernest consents, but as the wind is contrary, he arranges to
make the journey with a couple of carriages through the Uckermann
forest, not waiting for the grand escort of cavaliers and citizens which
his lady mother had promised to send to Stettin, to convey the bride
with all becoming honor to her own future residence at Wolgast.

His brother reminded him of the great danger from the robber-band
in the wood, now that the courts of justice were closed, and that Sidonia
and Johann were hovering in the vicinity, ready for any iniquity. Indeed,
he trusted the states would soon be brought to reason by the dreadful
condition of the country, and give him the gold he wanted. These
robbers would do more for him than he could do for himself. And this
was not the only band that was to be feared; for, since the fatal
bankruptcy of the Loitz family, robbers, and partisans, and freebooters
had sprung up in every corner of the land. Then he related the trick

concerning his two Andalusian stallions. And Duke Barnim the elder told him of his loss at Zachan, and that no one else but the knave Appelmann had been at the bottom of it. So, at last, Prince Ernest half resolved to await the escort from Wolgast. However, the old Duke continued jesting with the bride, after his manner, so that the young Princess was blushing with shame every moment, and finally entreated her husband to set off at once.

When his Grace of Stettin found he could prevail nothing, he bade them a kind farewell, promising in eight days to visit them at Wolgast, for the wedding festivities; and he sent stout Dinnies Kleist, with six companions, to escort them through the most dangerous part of the forest, which was a tract extending for about seven miles.

Now, when they were halfway through the forest, a terrible storm came on of hail, rain, thunder, and lightning; and though the Prince and his bride were safe enough in the carriage, yet their escort were drenched to the skin, and dripped like rivulets. The princely pair therefore entreated them to return to Falkenwald, and dry their clothes, for there was no danger to be apprehended now, since they were more than half through the wood, and close to the village of Mutzelburg.

So Dinnies and his companions took their leave, and rode off. Shortly after the galloping of a horse was heard, and this was Marcus Bork; for he was on his way to purchase the lands of Crienke, previous to his marriage with Clara von Dewitz, and had a heavy sack of gold upon his shoulder, and a servant along with him. Having heard at Stettin that the Prince and his young bride were on the road, he had followed them, as fast as he could, to keep them company.

By this time they had reached Barnim's Cross, and the Prince halted to point it out to his bride, and tell her the legend concerning it; for the sun now shone forth from the clouds, and the storm was over. But he first addressed his faithful Marcus, and asked, had he heard tidings lately of his cousin Sidonia? But he had heard nothing. He would hear soon enough, I'm thinking.

Then seeing that his good vassal Marcus was thoroughly wet, his Grace advised him to put on dry clothes; but he had none with him. Whereupon his Grace handed him his own portmanteau out of the coach window, and bid him take what he wanted.

Marcus then lifted the money-bag from his shoulder, which his Grace drew into the coach through the window — and sprang into the wood with the portmanteau, to change his clothes. While the Prince tarried for him, he related the story of Barnim's Cross to his young wife, thus: —

"You must know, dearest, that my ancestor, Barnim, the second of the name, was murdered, out of revenge, in this very spot by one of his vassals, named Vidante von Muckerwitze. For this aforesaid ancestor had sent him into Poland under some pretence, in order the better to accomplish his designs upon the beautiful Mirostava of Warborg, Vidante's young wife. But the warder of Vogelsang, a village about two miles from here, pleasantly situated on the river Haff, and close to which lay the said Vidante's castle, discovered the amour, and informed the knight how he was dishonored. His wrath was terrible when the news was brought to him, but he spoke no word of the matter until St. John's day in the year —"

But here his Grace paused in his story, for he had forgotten the year; so he drove on the carriage close up to the cross, where he could read the date — "St John's day, A.D. MCCXCII" — and there stopped, with the blessed cross of our Lord covering and filling up the whole of the coach window.

Ah, well it is said — Prov. xx. 24 — "Each man's going is of the Lord, what man is there who understandeth his way?"

Now when the Princess had read the date for herself, she asked, what had happened to the Duke, his ancestor? To which the Prince replied —

"Here, in these very bushes, the jealous knight lay concealed, while the Duke was hunting. And here, in this spot, the Duke threw himself down upon the grass to rest, for he was weary. And he whistled for his retinue, who had been separated from him, when the knight sprang from his hiding place and murdered him where he lay. His false wife he reserved for a still more cruel death.

"For he brought a coppersmith from Stettin, and had him make a copper coffin for the wretched woman, who was obliged to help him in the work. Then he bade her put on her bridal dress, and forced her to enter the coffin, where he had her soldered up alive, and buried. And the story goes, that when anyone walks over the spot, the coffin clangs in the earth like a mass-bell, to this very day." Meanwhile Marcus had retreated behind a large oak, to dress himself in the young Duke's clothes; but the wicked robber crew were watching him all the time from the wood, and just as he drew the dry shirt over his head, before he had time to put on a single other garment, they sprang upon him with loud shouts, Sidonia the foremost of all, screaming, "Seize the knave! seize the base spy! he is my greatest enemy!" So Marcus rushed back to the coach, just as he was, and placing the cross as a shield between him and the robbers, cried out loudly to his Highness for a sword.

The Prince would have alighted to assist him, but his young bride wound her arms so fast around him, shrieking till the whole wood re-echoed, that he was forced to remain inside. Up came the robber-band now, and attacked the coach furiously; musket after musket was fired at it and the horses, but luckily the rain had spoiled the powder, so they threw away their muskets, while Sidonia screamed, "Seize the false-hearted liar, who broke his marriage promise to me! seize his screaming harlot! drag her from the coach! Where is she? — let me see her! — we will cram her into the old oak tree; there she can hold her marriage festival with the wildcats. Give her to me! — give her to me! I will teach her what marriage is!" And she sprang wildly forward, while the others flung their spears at Marcus. But the blessed cross protected him, and the spears stuck in the wood or in the body of the carriage, while he hewed away right and left, striking down all that approached him, till he stood in a pool of blood, and the white shirt on him was turned to red.

As Sidonia rushed to the coach, he wounded her in the hand, upon which, with loud curses and imprecations, she ran round to the other coach window, calling out, "Come hither, come hither, Johann! here is booty, here is the false cat! Come hither, and drag her out of the coach window for me!" And now Marcus Bork was in despair, for the coach-man had run away from fear, and though his sword did good service, yet their enemies were gathering thick round them. So he bade the Princess, in a low voice, to tear open his bag of money, for the love of heaven, with all speed, and scatter the gold out of the windows with both hands; for help was near, he heard the galloping of a horse; could they gain but a few moments, they were saved. Thereupon the Princess rained the gold pieces from the window, and the stupid mob instantly left all else to fling themselves on the ground for the bright coins, fighting with each other as to who should have them. In vain Johann roared, "Leave the gold, fools, and seize the birds here in this cage; ye can have the gold after." But they never heeded him, though he cursed and swore, and struck them right and left with his sword.

But Marcus, meanwhile, had nearly come to a sad end; for the old gypsy hag swore she would stab him with her knife, and while the poor Marcus was defending himself from a robber who had rushed at him with a dagger, she crept along upon the ground, and lifted her great knife to plunge into his side.

Just then, like a messenger from God, comes the stout Dinnies Kleist, galloping up to the rescue; for after he had ridden a good piece upon the homeward road, he stopped his horse to empty the water out of his large jack-boots, for there it was plumping up and down, and he was still far from Falkenwald. While one of his men emptied the boots, another wandered through the wood picking the wild strawberries, that blushed there as red as scarlet along the ground.

While he was so bent down close to the earth, the shrieks of my gracious lady reached his ear, upon which he ran to tell his master, who listened likewise; and finding they proceeded from the very direction where he had left the bridal pair, he suspected that some evil had befallen them. So springing into his saddle, he bade his fellows mount with ail speed, and dashed back to the spot where they had left the carriage.

Marcus was just now fainting from loss of blood, and his weary hand could scarcely hold the sword, while his frame swayed back and forward, as if he were near falling to the ground. The gypsy hag was close beside him, with her arm extended, ready to plunge the knife into his side, when the heavy stroke of a sword came down on it, and arm and knife fell together to the ground, and Dinnies shouting, "Jodute! Jodute!" swung round his sword a second time, and the head of the robber carl fell upon the arm of the hag. Then he dashed round on his good horse to the other side of the carriage, hewed right and left among the stupid fools who were scraping up the gold, while his fellows chased them into the wood, so that the alarmed band left all this booty, and ran in every direction to hide themselves in the forest. In vain Johann roared, and shouted, and swore, and opposed himself single-handed to the knight's followers. He received a blow that sent him flying, too, after his band, and Sidonia along with him, so that none but the dead remained around the carriage.

Thus did the brave Dinnies Kleist and Marcus Bork save the Prince and his bride, like true knights as they were; but Marcus is faint, and leans for support against the carriage, while before him lie three robber carls whom he had slain with his own hand, although he fought there only in his shirt; but the blessed cross had been his shield. And there, too, lay the gypsy's arm with the knife still clutched in the hand, but the hag herself had fled away; and round the brave Dinnies was a circle of dead men, seven in number, whom he and his followers had killed; and the earth all round looked like a ripe strawberry field, it was so red with blood.

One can imagine what joy filled the hearts of the princely pair, when they found that all their peril was past. They alighted from the coach, and when the Princess saw Marcus lying there in a dead faint, with his garment all covered with blood, she lamented loudly, and tore off her own veil to bind up his wounds, and brought wine from the carriage, which she poured herself through his lips, like a merciful Samaritan; and when he at last opened his eyes, and kissed the little hands of the Princess out of gratitude, she rejoiced greatly. And the Prince himself ran to the wood for the portmanteau, which they found behind the oak, and helped to dress the poor knight, who was so weak that he could not raise a finger.

Then they lifted him into the coach, while the Prince comforted him, saying, he trusted that he would soon be well again, for he would pray daily to the Lord Jesus for him, whose blessed cross had been their protection, and that he should have all his gold again, and the lands of Crienke in addition. So faithful a vassal must never be parted from his Prince, for inasmuch as he hated Sidonia, so he loved and praised him. They were like the two Judases in Scripture, of whom someone had said, "What one gave to the devil, the other brought back to God."

And now he saw the wonderful hand of God in all; for if it had not rained, the powder of the robber-band would have been dry, and then they were all lost. *Item,* the knight would not have stopped to empty his boots, and they never would have heard the screams of his dear wife. *Item,* if he had himself not forgotten the date, he would never have driven up close to the cross, which cross had saved them all, but, in particular, saved their dear Marcus, after a miraculous manner. "Look how the blessed wood is everywhere pierced with spears, and yet we are all living! Therefore let us hope in the Lord, for He is our helper and defender!"

Then the Duke turned to the stout Dinnies, and prayed him to enter his service, but in vain, for he was sworn vassal to his Highness of Stettin. So his Grace took off his golden collar, and put it on his neck, and the Princess drew off her diamond ring to give him, whereupon her spouse laughed heartily, and asked, Did she think the good knight had a finger for her little ring? To which she replied, But the brave knight may have a dear wife who could wear it for her sake, for he must not go without some token of her gratitude.

However, the knight put back the ring himself, saying that he had no spouse, and would never have one; therefore the ring was useless. So the Princess wonders, and asks why he will have no spouse; to which he replied, that he feared the fate of Samson, for had not love robbed him of his strength? He, too, might meet a Delilah, who would cut off his long hair. Then riding up close to the carriage, he removed his plumed hat from his head, and down fell his long black hair, that was gathered up under it, over his shoulders like a veil, even till it swept the flanks of his horse. Would not her Grace think it a grief and sorrow if a woman sheared those locks? In such pleasant discourse they reached Mutzelburg, where, as the good Marcus was so weak, they resolved to put up for the night, and send for a chirurgeon instantly to Uckermund. And so it was done.

Chapter XI

Of the ambassadors in the tavern of Mutzelburg — Item, how the miller, Konnemann, is discovered, and made by Dinnies Kleist to act as guide to the robber cave, where they find all the womenfolk lying apparently dead, through some devil's magic of the gypsy mother

*W*hen their Highnesses entered the inn at Mutzelburg, they found it filled with burghers and peasants out of Uckermund, Pasewalk, and other adjacent places, on their way to Stettin, to petition his Grace the Duke to open the courts of justice, for thieves and robbers had so multiplied throughout the land, that no road was safe; and all kinds of witchcraft, and imposture, and devil's work were so rife, that the poor people were plagued out of their lives, and no redress was to be had, seeing his Grace had closed all the courts of justice. Forty burghers had been selected to present the petition, and great was the joy to meet now with his Grace Prince Ernest, for assuredly he would give them a letter to his illustrious brother, and strengthen the prayer of their petition. The Prince readily promised to do this, particularly as his own life and that of his bride had just been in such sore peril, all owing to the obstinacy of his Grace of Stettin in not opening the courts.

Meanwhile the leech had visited good Marcus Bork, who was much easier after his wounds were dressed, and promised to do well, to the great joy of their Graces; and Dinnies Kleist went to the stable to see after his horse, there being so many there, in consequence of this gathering of envoys, that he feared they might fight. Now, as he passed through the kitchen, the knight observed a man bargaining with the innkeeper; and he had a kettle before him, into which he was cramming sausages, bread, ham, and all sorts of eatables. But he would have taken no further heed, only that the carl had but one tail to his coat, which made the knight at once recognize him as the very fellow whose coat-tail he had hewed off in the forest. He sprang on him, therefore; and as the man drew his knife, Dinnies seized hold of him and plumped him down, head foremost, into a hogshead of water, holding him straight up by the feet till he had drunk his fill. So the poor wretch began to quiver at last in his death agonies; whereupon the knight called out, "Wilt thou confess? or hast thou not drunk enough yet?"

"He would confess, if the knight promised him life. His name was Konnemann; he had lost his mill and all he was worth, by the Loitz bankruptcy, therefore had joined the robber-band, who held their meeting in an old cave in the forest, where also they kept their booty." On further question, he said it was an old, ruined place, with the walls all tumbling down. A man named Muckerwitze had lived there once, who buried his wife alive in this cave, therefore it had been deserted ever since.

Then the knight asked the innkeeper if he knew of such a place in the forest; who said, "Yes." Then he asked if he knew this fellow, Konnemann; but the host denied all knowledge of him (though he knew him well enough, I think). Upon which Konnemann said, "That he merely came to buy provisions for the band, who were hungry, and had dispatched him to see what he could get, while they remained hiding in the cave." The knight having laid these facts before their Graces and the envoys, it was agreed that they should steal a march upon the robbers next morning, and meanwhile keep Konnemann safe under lock and key.

Next morning they set off by break of day, taking Konnemann as guide, and surrounded the old ruin, which lay upon a hill buried in oak trees; but not a sound was heard inside. They approached nearer — listened at the cave — nothing was to be heard. This angered Dinnies Kleist, for he thought the miller had played a trick on them, who, however, swore he was innocent; and as the knight threatened to give him something fresh to drink in the castle well, he offered to light a pine torch and descend into the cave. Hardly was he down, however, when they heard him screaming — "The robbers have murdered the women — they are all lying here stone dead, but not a man is to be seen."

The knight then went down with his good sword drawn. True enough, there lay the old hag, her daughter, and Sidonia, all stained with blood, and stiff and cold, upon the damp ground. And when the knight asked, "Which is Sidonia?" the fellow put the pine torch close to her face, which was blue and cold. Then the knight took up her little hand, and dropped it again, and shook his head, for the said little hand was stiff and cold as that of a corpse.

Summa. — As there was nothing further to be done here, the knight left the corpses to molder away in the old cellar, and returned with the burghers to Mutzelburg, when his Highness wondered much over the strange event; but Marcus rejoiced that his wicked cousin was now dead, and could bring no further disgrace upon his ancient name.

But was the wicked cousin dead? She had heard every word that had been said in the cave; for they had all drunk some broth made by the gypsy mother, which can make men seem dead, though they hear and see everything around them. Such devil's work is used by robbers sometimes in extremity, as some toads have the power of seeming dead when people attempt to seize them. It will soon be seen what a horrible use Sidonia made of this devil's potion.

Wherefore she tried its effect upon herself now, I know not — I have my own thoughts upon the subject — but it is certain that the innkeeper, who was a secret friend of the robbers (as most innkeepers were in those evil times), had sent a messenger by night to warn them of their danger. So, while the band saved themselves by hiding in the forest, perhaps the old hag recommended this plan for the women, as they had got enough of cold steel the day before; or perhaps the robbers wished to have a proof of the power of this draft, in case they might want to save themselves, some time or other, by appearing dead. Still I cannot, with any certainty, assert why they should all three choose to simulate death.

Further, just to show the daring of these robber-bands, now that his Highness had closed the courts, I shall end this chapter by relating what happened at Monkbude, a town through which their Highnesses passed that same day, and which, although close to the Stettin border, belongs to Wolgast.

It was Sunday, and after the priest had said Amen from the pulpit, the sexton rung the kale-bell. This bell was a sign throughout all Pomerania land, to the womenfolk who were left at home in the houses, to prepare dinner; for then, in all the churches, the closing hymn began — "Give us, Lord, our daily bread." So the maid, at the first stroke of the bell, lifted off the kale-pot from the fire, and had the kale dished, with the sausages, and whatever else was wanting, by the time that the hymn was over, and father and mother had come out of church. Then, whatever poor wretch had fasted all the week, and never tasted a morsel of blessed bread, if he passed on a Sunday through the town, might get his fill; for when the hymn is sung, "Give us, Lord, our daily bread," the doors lie open, and no stranger or wayfarer is turned away empty.

Just before their Highnesses had entered the town, this kale-bell had been rung, and each maid in the houses had laid the kale and meat upon the table, ready for the family, when, behold! in rush a troop of robbers from the forest, Appelmann at their head — seize every dish with the kale and meat that had been laid on the tables, stick the loaves into their pockets, and gallop away as hard as they can across into the Stettin border.

How the maids screamed and lamented I leave unsaid; but if anyone of them followed and seized a robber by the hair, he drew his knife, so she was glad enough to run back again, while the impudent troop laughed and jeered. Thus was it then in dear Pomerania land! It seemed as if God had forsaken them; for the nobles began their feuds, as of old, and the Jews were tormented even to the death — yea, even the pastors were chased away, as if, indeed, they had all learned of Otto Bork, these nobles saying, "What need of these idle, prating swaddlers, with their prosy sermons and whining psalms, teaching, forsooth, that all men are equal, and that God makes no difference between lord and peasant? Away with them! If the people learn such doctrine, no wonder if they grow proud and disobedient — better no priests in the land." And suchlike ungodly talk was heard everywhere.

Chapter XII

How the peasants in Marienfliess want to burn a witch, but are hindered by Johann Appelmann and Sidonia, who discover an old acquaintance in the witch, the girl Wolde Albrechts

At this time, one David Grosskopf was pastor of Marienfliess. He was a learned and pious man, and like other pious priests, was in the habit of gathering all the womenfolk of the parish in his study of a winter's evening, particularly the young maidens, with their spinning-wheels. And there they all sat spinning round the comfortable fire, while he read out to them from God's Word, and questioned them on it, and exhorted them to their duties. Thus was it done every evening during the winter, the maidens spinning diligently till midnight without even growing weary; or if one of them nodded, she was given a cup of cold water to drink, to make her fresh again. So there was plenty of fine linen by each New Year's day, and their masters were well pleased. No peasant kept his daughter at home, but sent her to the priest, where she learned her duties, and was kept safe from the young men. Even old mothers went there, among whom Trina Bergen always gave the best answers, and was much commended by the priest in consequence. This pleased her mightily, so that she boasted everywhere of it; but withal she was an excellent old woman, only the neighbors looked rather jealously on her.

This same priest, with all his goodness and learning, was yet a bad logician; for by his careless speaking in one of his sermons, much commotion was raised in the village. In this sermon he asserted that anything out of the usual course of nature must be devil's work, and ought to be held in abhorrence by all good Christians: he suffered for this after-wards, as we shall see. On the Monday after this discourse, he journeyed into Poland, to visit a brother who dwelt in some town there, I know not which.

Then arose a great talking amongst the villagers concerning the said Trina Bergen; for the cocks began to sit upon the eggs in place of the hens, in her poultry-yard, and all the people came together to see the miracle, and as it was against the course of nature, it must be devil's work, and Trina Bergen was a witch.

In vain the old mother protested she knew nothing of it, then runs to the priest's house, but he is away; from that to the mayor of the village, but he is going out to shoot, and bid her and the villagers pack off with their silly stories.

So the poor old mother gets no help, and meanwhile the peasants storm her house, and search and ransack every corner for proofs of her witchcraft, but nothing can be found. Stay! there in the cellar sits a woman, who will not tell her name.

They drag her out, bring her up to the parlor, while the old mother sits wringing her hands. Who was this woman? and how did she come into the cellar?

Illa. — "She had hired her to spin, because her daughter was out at service till autumn, and she could not do all the work herself."

"Why then did she sit in the cellar, as if she shunned the light?"

Illa. — "The girl had prayed for leave to sit there, because the screaming of the young geese in the yard disturbed her; besides, she had been only two days with her."

"But who in the devil's name was the girl? It was easy to see she had bewitched the hens, for everything against the course of nature must be devil's work."

Illa. — "Ah, yes! this must be the truth. Let them chase the devil away. Now she saw why the girl would not sit in the light, and had refused to enter the blessed church with her the day before."

"What was her name? They should both be sent to the devil, if she did not tell the girl's name."

Illa. — "Alas! she had forgotten it, but ask herself. Her story was, that she had been married to a peasant in Usdom, who died lately, and his relations then turned her out, that she was now going to Daber, where she had a brother, a fisher in the service of the Dewitz family, and wanted to earn a traveling penny by spinning, to convey her there."

Now as the rumor of witchcraft spread through the village, all the people ran together, from every part, to Trina's house. And a pale young man pressed forward from amongst the crowd, to look at the supposed witch. When he stood before her, the girl cast down her eyes gloomily, and he cried out, "It is she! it is the very accursed witch who robbed me of my strength by her sorceries, and barely escaped from the fagot — seize her — that is Anna Wolde. Now he knew what the elder sticks meant, which he found set up as a gallows before his door this morning — the witch wanted to steal away his manhood from him again — burn her! burn her! Come and see the elder sticks, if they did not believe him!"

So the whole village ran to his cottage, where he had just brought home a widow, whom he was going to marry, and there indeed stood the elder sticks right before his door in the form of a gallows, upon which the sheriff was wroth, and commanded the girl to be brought before him with her hands bound.

But as she denied everything, Zabel Bucher, the sheriff, ordered the hangman to be sent for, to see what the rack might do in eliciting the truth. Further, he bade the people make a fire in the street, and burn the elder sticks therein.

So the fire is lit, but no one will touch the sticks. Then the sheriff called his hound and bade him fetch them; but Fixlein, who was acute enough at other times, pretended not to know what his master wanted. In vain the sheriff bent down on the ground, pointing with his finger, and crying, "Here, Fixlein! fetch, Fixlein!" No, Fixlein runs round and round the elder sticks till the dust rises up in a cloud, and yelps, and barks, and jumps, and stares at his master, but never touches the sticks, only at last seizes a stone in his mouth, and runs with it to the sheriff.

Now, indeed, there was a commotion amongst the people. Not even the dog would touch the accursed thing. So at last the sheriff called for a pair of tongs, to seize the sticks himself and fling them into the fire. Whereupon his wife screamed to prevent him; but the brave sheriff, strengthening his heart, advanced and touched them; whereupon Fixlein, as if he had never known until now what his master wanted, made a grab at them, but the sheriff gave him a blow on the nose with the tongs which sent him away howling, and then, with desperate courage and a stout heart, seizing the elder twigs in the tongs, flung them boldly into the fire.

Meanwhile Peter Bollerjahn, the hangman, has arrived, and when he hears of the devilry he shakes his head, but thinks he could make the girl speak, if they only let him try his way a little. But they must first get authority from the mayor. Now the mayor had not gone to the hunt, for some friends arrived to visit him, whom he was obliged to stay at home and entertain, so the whole crowd, with the sheriff, Zabel Bucher, at the head, set off to the mayoralty, bringing the witch with them, and prayed his lordship to make a terrible example of her, for that witchcraft was spreading fearfully in the land, and they would have no peace else.

Whereupon he came out with his guests to look at the miserable criminal, who, conscious of her guilt, stood there silent and glowering; but he could do nothing for them – did they not know that his Highness had closed all the courts of justice, therefore he could not help them, nor be troubled about their affairs? Upon which the sheriff cried out, "Then we shall help ourselves; let us burn the witch who bewitches our hens, and sticks up elder sticks before people's doors. Come, let us right ourselves!" So the mayor said they might do as they pleased, he had no power to hinder them, only let them remember that when the courts reopened, they would be called to a strict account for all this. And he went into his house, but the people shouted and dragged away the witch, with loud yells, to the hangman, bidding him stretch her on the rack before all their eyes.

When the girl saw and heard all this, and remembered how the old Lord Chamberlain at Wolgast had stretched her till her hip was broken, she cried out, "I will confess all, only spare me the torture, for I dread it more than death."

Upon this, the sheriff said, "He would ask her three questions, and pronounce judgment accordingly." (Oh! what evil times for dear Pomerania land, when the people could thus take the law into their own hands, and pronounce judgment, though no judges were there. Had the bailiff given her a little twist of the rack, just to get at the truth, it would at least have been more in accordance with the usages, although I say not he would have been justified in so doing; but without using the rack at all, to believe what this devil's wretch uttered, and judge her thereupon, was grossly improper and absurd.) *Summa*, here are the three questions: –

"First, whether she had bewitched the hens; and for what?"

Respond. — "Simply to amuse herself; for the time hung heavy in the cellar, and she could see them through the chinks in the wall." (Let her wait; Master Peter will soon give her something to amuse her.)

"Second, why and wherefore had she stuck up the elder twigs?"

Respond. — "Because she had been told that Albert was going to marry a widow; for he had promised her marriage, as all the world knew, and even called her by his name, Wolde Albrechts, and therefore she had put a spell upon him of elder twigs, that he might turn away the widow and marry her." (Let her wait; Master Peter will soon stick up elder twigs for her.)

"Third, whether she had a devil; and how was he named?"

Here she remained silent, then began to deny it, but was reminded of the rack, and Master Peter got ready his instruments as if for instant use; so she sighed heavily, and answered, "Yes, she had a familiar called Jurge, and he appeared always in the form of a man."

Upon this confession the sheriff roared, "Burn the witch!" and all the people shouted after him, "Burn the witch! the accursed witch!" and she was delivered over to Master Peter.

But he made answer that he had never burned a witch; he would, however, go over to Massow in the morning, to his brother-in-law, who had burned many, and learn the mode from him. Meanwhile the peasants might collect ten or twelve clumps of wood upon the Koppenberg, and so would they frighten all women from practicing this devil's magic. Would they not burn Trina Bergen likewise — the old hag who had the witch in her cellar? It would be a right pleasant spectacle to the whole town.

This, however, the peasants did not wish. Upon which the carl asked what he was to be paid for his trouble? Formerly the state paid for the criminal, but the courts now would have nothing to do with the business. What was he to get? So the peasants consulted together, and at last offered him a sack of oats at Michaelmas, just that they might have peace in the village. Whereupon he consented to burn her; only in addition they must give him a free journey to Massow on the morrow.

Summa. — When the third morning dawned, all the village came together to accompany the witch up the Koppenberg: the schoolmaster, with all his school going before, singing, "Now pray we to the Holy Ghost;" then came Master Peter with the witch, he bearing a pan of lighted coal in his hand. But, lo! when they reached the pile on the Koppenberg, behold it was wet wood which the stupid peasants had gathered.

Now the hangman fell into a great rage. Who the devil could burn a witch with wet wood? She must have bewitched it. This was as bad as the hen business.

Some of the people then offered to run for some dry wood and hay; but my knave saw that he might turn the matter to profit, so he proposed to sack the witch in place of burning her; "for," said he, "it will be a far more edifying spectacle and example to your children, this sacking in place of burning. There was a lake quite close to the town, and, indeed, he had forgotten yesterday to propose it to them. The plan was this. They were to tie her up in a leathern sack, with a dog, a cock, and a cat. (Ah, what a pity he had killed the wildcat which he had caught some weeks before in the fox-trap.) Then they would throw all into the lake, where the cat and dog, and cock and witch, would scream and fight, and bite and scratch, until they sank; but after a little while up would come the sack again, and the screaming, biting, and fighting would be renewed until they all sank down again and forever. Sometimes, indeed, they would tear a hole in the sack, which filled with water, and so they were all drowned. In any case it was a fine improving lesson to their children; let them ask the schoolmaster if the sacking was not a far better spectacle for the dear children than the burning."

"Aye, 'tis true," cried the schoolmaster; "sacking is better."

Upon which all the people shouted after him, "Aye, sack her! sack her!"

When the knave heard this, he continued —

"Now, they heard what the schoolmaster said, but he could not do all this for a sack of oats, for, indeed, leather sacks were very dear just now; but if each one added a sack of meal and a goose at Michaelmas, why, he would try and manage the sacking. The lake was broad and deep, and it lay right beneath them, so that all the dear children could see the sight from the hill."

However, the peasants would by no means agree to the sack of meal, whereupon a great dispute arose around the pile, and a bargaining about the price with great tumult and uproar.

Now the robber-band were in the vicinity, and Sidonia, hearing the noise, peeped out through the bushes and recognized Anna Wolde; then, guessing from the pile what they were going to do to her, she begged of Johann to save the poor girl, if possible; for Sidonia and the knave were now on the best of terms, since he had chased away the gypsy hag and her daughter for robbing him.

So Johann gives the word, and the band, which now numbered one hundred strong, burst forth from the wood with wild shouts and cries. Ho! how the people fled on all sides, like chaff before the wind! The executioner is the first off, throws away his pan of coals, and takes to his heels. *Item,* the schoolmaster, with all his school, take to their heels; the sheriff, the women, peasants, spectators-all, with one accord, take to their heels, screaming and roaring.

The witch alone remains, for she is lame and cannot run; but she screams, too, and wrings her hands, crying —

"Take me with you; oh, take me with you; for the love of God take me with you; I am lame and cannot run!"

Summa. — One can easily imagine how it all ended. The witch-girl was saved, and, as she now owed her life a second time to Sidonia, she swore eternal fidelity and gratitude to the lady, promising to give her something in recompense for all the benefits she had conferred on her. Alas, that I should have to say to Christian men what this was!*

And when Sidonia asked how things went on in Daber, great was her joy to hear that the whole castle and town were full of company, for the nuptials of Clara von Dewitz and Marcus Bork were celebrated there. And the old Duchess from Wolgast had arrived, along with Duke Johann Frederick, and the Dukes Barnim, Casimir, and Bogislaff. *Item,* a grand cavalcade of nobles had ridden to the wedding upon four hundred horses, and lords and ladies from all the country round thronged the castle.

Now Johann Appelmann would not credit the witch-girl, for he had seen none of all this company upon the roads; but she said her brother the fisherman told her that their Graces traveled by water as far as Wollin, for fear of the robbers, and from thence by land to Daber.

When Sidonia heard this she fell upon Johann's neck, exclaiming —

"Revenge me now, Johann! revenge me! Now is the time; they are all there. Revenge me in their blood!"

This seemed rather a difficult matter to Johann, but he promised to call together the whole band, and see what could be done. So he went his way to the band, and then the evil-minded witch-girl began again, and told Sidonia, that if she chose to burn the castle at Daber, and make an end of all her enemies at once, there was someone hard by in the bush who would help her, for he was stronger than all the band put together.

Illa. — "Who was her friend? Let her go and bring him."

Hæc. — "She must first cross her hand with gold, and give a piece of money for him;† then he would come and revenge her."

---

* Namely, the evil spirit Chim. See Sidonia's confession upon the rack, vol. iv. Dahnert's Pomeranian Library, p. 244.

† According to the witches, every evil spirit must be purchased, no matter how small the price, but something must be given-a ball of worsted, a kerchief, &c.

Sidonia's eyes now sparkled wildly, and she put some money in the woman's hand, who murmured, "For the evil one;" then stepped behind a tree, and returned in a short time with a black cat wrapped up in her apron.

"This," she said, "was the strong spirit Chim.* Let her give him plenty to eat, but show him to no one. When she wanted his assistance, strike him three times on the head, and he would assume the form of a man. Strike him six times to restore him again to this form."

Now Sidonia would scarcely credit this; so, looking round to see if they were quite alone, she struck the animal three times on the head, who instantly started up in the form of a gay young man, with red stockings, a black doublet, and cap with stately heron's plumes.

"Yes, yes," he exclaimed, "I know thy enemies, and will revenge thee, beautiful child. I will burn the castle of Daber for thee, if thou wilt only do my bidding; but now, quick! strike me again on the head, that I may reassume my original form, for someone may see us; and put me in a basket, so can I travel with thee wheresoever thou goest."

And thus did Sidonia with the evil spirit Chim, as she afterwards confessed upon the rack, when she was a horrible old hag of eighty-four years of age.

And he went with her everywhere, and suggested all the evil to her which she did, whereof we shall hear more in another place.†

---

* Joachim.

† Dahnert. – This belief in the power of evil spirits to assume the form of animals, comes to us from remotest antiquity – example, the serpent in Paradise. In all religions, and amongst all nations, this belief seems firmly rooted; but even if we do not see a visible devil, do we not, alas! know and feel that there is one ever with us, ever pre-sent, ever suggesting all wickedness to us, as this devil to Sidonia?-even our own evil nature. For what else is the Christian life, but a warfare between the divine within us and this ever-present Satan? – and through God's grace alone can we resist this devil.

Chapter XIII

Of the adventure with the boundary lads, and how one of them promises to admit Johann Appelmann into the castle of Daber that same night–Item, of what befell amongst the guests at the castle

W hen Johann and Sidonia proposed to the band that they should pillage the castle of Daber, they all shouted with delight, and swore that life and limb might be periled, but the castle should be theirs that night. Nevertheless my knave Johann thought it a dangerous undertaking, for they knew no one inside the walls, and Anna Wolde, the witch, could not come with them, seeing that she was lame. So at last he thought of sending Konnemann disguised as a beggar, to examine the courtyard and all the out offices — perchance he might spy out some unguarded door by which they could effect an entrance.

Then Sidonia said she would go too, and although Johann tried hard to persuade her, yet she begged so earnestly for leave that finally he consented. Yes, she must see the very spot where the viper was hatched which had stung her to death. Ah, she would brew something for her in return; pity only that the wedding was over, otherwise the little bride should never have touched a wedding-ring, if she could help it; but it was too late now.

So the three Satan's children slipped out upon the highway from the wood, and traveled on so near to the castle that the noise, and talking, and laughing, and barking of dogs, and neighing of horses, were all quite audible to their ears.

Now the castle of Daber is built upon a hill which is entirely surrounded by water, so that the castle can be approached only by two bridges — one southwards, leading from the town; the other eastwards, leading direct through the castle gardens. The castle itself was a noble, lofty pile, with strong towers and spires — almost as stately a building as my gracious lord's castle at Saatzig.

When Johann observed all this, his heart failed him, and as he and his two companions peeped out at it from behind a thorn-bush, they agreed that it would be hard work to take such a castle, garrisoned, as it was now, by four hundred men or more, with their mere handful of partisans.

But Satan knows how to help his own, for what happened while they were crouching there and arguing? Behold, the old Dewitz, as an offering to the church at Daber upon his daughter's marriage, had promised twenty good acres of land to be added to the glebe. And he comes now up the hill, with a great crowd of men to dig the boundary. So the Satan's children behind the thorn-bush feared they would be discovered; but it was not so, and the crowd passed on unheeding them.

Old Dewitz now called the witnesses, and bid them take note of the position of the boundary. There where the hill, the wild apple tree, and the town tower were all in one line, was the limit; let them keep this well in their minds. Then calling over six lads, he bid them take note likewise of the boundary, that when the old people were dead they might stand up as witnesses; but as such things were easily forgotten, he, the priest, and the churchwarden would write it down for them, so that it never, by any chance, could escape their memory.

Upon which the good knight, being lord and patron, took a stout stick the first, and cudgeled the young lads well, asking them between terms —

"Where is the boundary?"

To which they answered, screaming and roaring —

"Where the hill, the apple tree, and the town tower are all in one line."

Then the knight, laughing, handed over the stick to the priest, saying —

"It was still possible they might forget; they better, therefore, have another little memorandum from his reverence."

"No! no!" screamed the boys, "we will remember it to eternity."

However, his reverence just gave them a little touch of the stick in fun, till they roared out the boundary marks a second time.

But now stepped forth the churchwarden, to take his turn with the stick on the boys' backs. This man had been a forester of the old Baron Dewitz, and had often taken note of one of the young fellows present, how he had poached and stolen the buck-wheat, so he gladly seized this opportunity to punish him for all his misdeeds, and laying the cudgel on his shoulders, thrashed and belabored him so unmercifully, that the lad ran, shrieking, cursing, howling, and roaring, far away in amongst the bushes to hide himself, while the churchwarden cried out —

"Well! if all the other lads forget the boundary, I think my fine fellow here will bear the memorandum to the day of judgment."

And so they went away laughing from the place, and returned to the castle.

But the devil drew his profit from all this, for where should the lad run to, but close to the very spot where the robbers were hiding, and there he threw himself down upon the grass, writhing and howling, and swearing he would be revenged upon the churchwarden. This is a fine hearing for my knave in the bush, so he steps forward, and asks —

"What vile Josel had dared to ill-treat so brave a youth? He would help him to a revenge upon the base knave, for injustice was a thing he never could suffer. The tears really were in his eyes to think that such wickedness should be in the world;" and here he pretended to wipe his eyes. So the lad, being quite overcome by such compassionate sympathy, howled and cried ten times more —

"It was the forester Kell, the shameless hound; but he would play him a trick for it."

Ille. — "Right. He owed the fellow a drubbing already himself, and now he would have a double one, if he could only get hold of him."

Hic. — "He would run and tell him that a great lord wanted to speak to him here in the forest."

Ille. — "No, no; that would scarcely answer; but where did the fellow live?"

Hic. — "In the castle, where his father lived likewise."

Ille. — "Who was his father?"

Hic. — "His father was the steward."

Ille. — "Ah, then, he kept the keys of the castle?"

Hic. — "Oh yes, and the key of the back entrance also, which led through the gardens. His father kept one key, and the gardener the other."

Ille. — "Well, he would tell him a secret. This very Kell had deceived him once, like a knave as he was, and he was watching to punish him, but he daren't go up to the castle in the broad daylight, particularly now while the wedding was going on. How long would it last?"

Hic. — "For three days more; it had lasted three days already, and the castle was full of company, and great lords from all the country round, a great deal grander even than old Dewitz, were there."

Ille. — "Well, then, it would be quite impossible to go up to the castle and flog the churchwarden before all the company — he could see that himself. But supposing he let him in at night through the garden door, couldn't they get the knave out on some pretence, and then drub him to their heart's content?"

So the lad was delighted with the plan, particularly on hearing that he was to help in the drubbing; but then if the forester recognized him, what was to be done? he would be ruined. To which Johann answered —

"Just put on an old cloak, and speak no word; then, neither by dress nor voice will he know thee; besides, the night will be quite dark, so fear nothing. We'll teach him, I engage, how to beat a fine young fellow again, or to rob me of my gold, as he did, the base, unworthy knave."

Here the lad laughed outright with joy. "Yes, yes, that would just do; and he could put on his father's old mantle, and bring a stout crab-stick along with him."

Hic. — "All right, young friend; but how was he to get into the castle garden? Was there not a drawbridge which was lifted every night?"

Hic. — "Oh yes; but his father very often sent him to draw it up, and he could leave it down for tonight; then he would get the forester, by some means, into the shrubbery, where it was dark as pitch, and they could thrash the dog there without anyone knowing a word about it."

Ille. — "*Good! Then when the tower-clock struck nine, let him come himself and admit him into the garden — time enough after to run for the forester, while he was hiding himself in the shrubbery, for no one must know a word about his being there.*" Then he gave the lad a knife, and told him if all turned out well he should have a piece of gold in addition. "*Ah! they would give him a warm greeting, this dog of a forester! But after he had called him out, the lad must pretend as if he had nothing to do with the matter, and go back to the house, or slip down some by-path.*"

So the lad jumped with joy when he got hold of the knife, and skipped off to the castle, promising to be at the drawbridge when nine o'clock struck from the tower, to admit his good friend into the garden.

Meanwhile my gracious Lady of Wolgast was making preparations for her departure on the morrow from the castle, for she had been attending the wedding festivities with her four sons, and Ulrich, the Grand Chamberlain; but previous to taking leave of her dear son, Duke Johann Frederick, she wished to make one more attempt to induce him to take off the interdict from the country, and allow the courts of justice to be reopened, for thus would the land be freed from these wild hordes who haunted every road, and filled all hearts with fear.

For this purpose she went up to his own private chamber in the castle, bringing old Ulrich along with her; and when they entered, old Ulrich, having closed the door, began — "Now, gracious lady, speak to your son as befits a mother and your princely Grace to do."

Upon which he took his seat at the table, looking around him as sour as a vinegar-cruet.

So the Duchess lifted up her voice with many tears, and prayed his Highness of Stettin to stem all this violence that raged in the land, as a loving Prince and father towards his subjects. He had resisted all her entreaties until now, with those of his dear brothers and old Ulrich; and had not even his host and the whole nobility tried to soften his heart towards his people, who were suffering by his hard resolve? But surely he would not refuse her now, for she had come to take her leave of him, and had brought his old guardian and his brothers to plead along with her; besides, who knew what might happen next? For she heard, to her astonishment, that Sidonia was not dead at all, as they supposed, but roaming through the country with her accursed paramour. Had she known this, never would she have permitted this long journey, dear even as the bride was to her heart, but would have stayed at Wolgast to watch over her heart's dear son, Ernest, and his young spouse, who rightly feared to put themselves in danger again, after the sore peril they had encountered in the Stettin forest; and who knew what might happen to her on the journey homeward? for if she encountered Sidonia, what could she expect from her but the bitterest death? (weeping.) Ah, this all came upon them because the young Duke had despised the admonitions of his blessed father upon his deathbed, and thought not of that Scripture which saith, "The father's blessing buildeth the children's houses, but the curse of the mother pulleth them down."* She had never cursed him yet, but that day might come.

Then Duke Johann answered, "He was sad to see his darling mother chafe and fret about these same courts of justice, but his princely honor was pledged, and he could not retract one word until the states came back to their duty, and gave him the gold he demanded. For how could he stand before the world as a fool? He had begun this castle of Friedrichswald, and had ordered all kinds of statues, paintings, &c., from Italy, for which gold must be paid. How, then, if he had none?"

"But those were idle follies," his mother answered, "and showed how true were the words of Solomon — 'When a prince wanteth understanding, there is great oppression.'"†

Here the Duke grew angry. "It was false; he did not want understanding. Well it was that no one had dared to say this to him but his mother."

But my gracious lady could not hear him plainly; for his Serene Highness, Barnim the younger, who had drunk rather freely at dinner, began to snore so loudly, that he snored away a paper which lay before

---

*   Sirach iii. II.
†   Prov. xxviii. 16.

old Ulrich, upon which he had been sketching a list of *propositions* for the reconciliation of the Duke and the estates of the kingdom.

Hereupon the old chamberlain cursed and swore — "May the seven thousand devils take them! One snarls at his mother, and the other snores away his paper! Did the Prince think that Pomerania was like Saxony, when he began these fine buildings at Friedrichswald? His Grace had a house at Stettin; what did he want with a second? Was his Grace better than his forefathers? And would not his Grace have Oderburg when old Duke Barnim died? and castles and towns all round the land?"

But the Duke answered proudly, "That Ulrich should remember his guardianship had ended. He knew himself what to do and what to leave undone."

Herewith the young Lord Bogislaff broke in — "Yet, dearest brother, be advised by us. Bethink you how I resigned my chance of the duchy at the Diet of Wollin, and now I am ready to give you up the annuity which I then received, if it will help your necessities, and that you promise thereupon to release the land from the interdict, that all this fearful villainy and lawlessness which is devastating the country may have an end."

Ille. — "Matters were not so bad as he thought; besides, why cannot the people defend themselves, and take care of their own skin?"

Hic. — "So they do; but this only increased injustice and lawlessness." Then he related many examples of how the despairing people of the different towns had executed justice, after their own manner, upon the robbers who fell into their hands. In Stolpschen, for instance, three fellows had been caught plundering the corn, and the peasants nailed them up to a tree, and whipped them till they dropped down dead. Well might Satan laugh over the sin and wickedness that reigned now in poor Pomerania.

Item, he related how the peasants in Marienfliess were going to burn a witch, without trial or sentence. *Item,* how many peasants and villagers had hung up their own bailiffs, or strangled them. *Item,* how the priests had been chased away from many places, so that they now had to beg their bread upon the highway; and in such towns God's service was no more heard, but each one lived as it pleased him, and the peasants did as they chose. And now he would ask his heart's dear brother, which would be more upright and honorable in the sight of the great God — to build up this castle of Friedrichswald, or to let it fall, and build up the virtue and happiness of his people? He could not build the castle without money, and he had none; but he could restore his land to peace and happiness by a word. Let him, then, open these long-closed courts of justice, for this was his duty as a Prince; and let him remember that every prince was ordained of God, and must answer to Him for his government.

Hereupon the Stettin Duke made answer — "Pity, good Bogislaff, thou wert not a village priest! Hast thou finished thy sermon? Truly thou wert never meant for a prince, as we heard from thy own lips, the day of the Diet at Wollin. Thou hast no sense of princely honor, I see, but I stand by mine; and now, by my princely honor, I pledge my princely word, that, until the states give me the money, the land shall remain in all things as it is."

Here old Ulrich sprang to his feet (while my gracious lady sobbed aloud), clapped the table, and roared — "Seven thousand devils, my lord! are we to be robbed and murdered by those vile cutthroats that infest the land, and your Grace will fold your hands and do nothing, till they drive your Grace yourself out of the land, or run a spear through your body, as they would have done to your princely brother of Wolgast, only he had faithful vassals to defend him? If it is so to be, then must the nobles make their petition to the Emperor, and we shall see if his Imperial Majesty cannot bring your Grace to reason, though your mother and we all have failed to move you."

Here the little Casimir, who was playing with the paper which his brother had snored away, ran up to his mother, and pulling her by the gown, said, "Gracious lady mamma, what ails my brother, the Stettin Duke? Is he drunk, too?"

At which they all laughed, except Duke Johann, who gave a kick to his little brother, and then strode out of the room, exclaiming, "Sooner my life than my honor; I shall stay here no longer to be tutored and lectured, but will take my journey homewards this very night." And so he departed, but by a small side-door, for old Ulrich had locked the chief door on entering.

Now, indeed, her Grace wept bitterly: ah! she thought the evil had left her house, which the fatal business at her wedding had wrought on it, when Dr. Martinus dropped the ring; but, alas! it was only beginning now; and yet she could not curse him, for he was her son, and she had borne him in pain and sorrow.

Summa. — If many were displeased at these proceedings of his Grace, so also was the Lord God, as was seen clearly by many strange signs; for on that same night Duke Barnim the elder died at Oderburg, and all the crosses, knobs, and spires throughout the whole town turned quite black, though they had only been newly gilded a year before, and no rain, lightning, or thunder had been observed.[*]

---

[*] The Duke died 29th September 1573, aged 72 years. — *Micraelius.* 369.

But this was all clearly to show the anger of God over the sins of the young Duke, and by these signs He would admonish him to repentance, as a father might gently threaten a refractory child. As to what further happened his Grace when he went out by the little door, and the danger that befell him there, we shall hear more in another chapter.

Chapter XIV

How the knave Appelmann seizes his Serene Eminence Duke Johann by the throat, and how his Grace and the whole castle are saved by Marcus Bork and his young bride Clara; also, how Sidonia at last is taken prisoner

The castle was now almost quite still, for as the festival had already lasted three days, the guests were pretty well tired of dancing and drinking, and most of them, like young Prince Barnim, had lain down to snore. Yet still there were many drinking in the great hall, or dancing in the saloon, for the fiddles fiddled away merrily until far in the night.

And it was a beautiful night this one; not too dark, but starry, bright, and soft and still, so that Marcus and his young bride glided away from the dancing and drinking, to wander in the cool, fresh air of the shrubbery, before they retired to their chamber. So they passed down the broad path that led from the garden to the drawbridge by the water-mill, and seating themselves on a bank under the shade of the trees, began to kiss and caress, as may well become a young bridal pair to do.

Soon they heard nine o'clock strike from the town, and immediately after, stealthy footsteps coming along the shrubbery towards them. They held their breath, and remained quite still, thinking it was some half-drunken guest from the castle wandering this way; but then the draw-bridge was lowered, and three persons advanced to a youth, as they could see plainly. One said, "Now?" to which another answered, "No, when I whistle!" He who had so asked, then went back again, but Sidonia and my knave came on with the boundary lad over the bridge (for, of course, everyone will have guessed them) and entered the shrubbery where the young bridal pair were seated, but perfectly hidden, by reason of the darkness.

The boundary lad would now have drawn up the bridge, but the knave hindered him — "Let him leave it down; how would he escape else, if the carl roared, and all came running out of the castle to see what was the matter?" Then Sidonia asked the boy, if he thought the castle folk would hear him? To which he answered, no. They could thrash the hound securely, and he had brought a short cudgel with him for the purpose. Upon which my knave murmured to him, "Lead on, then; I must get out of this dark place to see what I am about. And when we get to the end of it, do you run and bring him out here. Then we shall both pay him off bravely."

So they crept on in the darkness towards the castle, but the young wedded pair had plenty of time to recognize both Sidonia and Appelmann by their voices. Therefore Marcus argued truly that the knave and his paramour could be about no good, for the whole land rang with their wickedness. And, no doubt, the band was in the vicinity, because Appelmann had answered, "No, when I whistle!"

So the good Marcus grew wroth over the villainy of this shameless pair, who had evidently resolved on nothing less than the destruction of the whole princely race, and even this castle of Daber was not to be spared, which belonged to his dear bride's father, so that their wicked purposes might be fulfilled. Then he whispered, did his dear wife know of any byway that led to the castle? as she was born here, perhaps some such little path might be known to her, so that she would escape meeting the villain. And as she whispered in return, "Yes, there was such a path," he bid her run along it quick as thought, have all the bells rung when she reached the castle, and even the cannon fired, which was ready loaded for the farewell salute to the Lady of Wolgast on the morrow; and to gather as many people together, of all stations and ages, as could be summoned on the instant, and let them shout "Murder! murder!" Meanwhile he would run and draw up the bridge, then track the fellow along the shrubbery, and seize him if possible.

How Clara trembled and hesitated, as a young girl might; but soon collecting herself, she said, although with much agitation, "I will trust in God: the Lord is my strength, of whom then should I be afraid?" and plunged alone into the darkest part of the shrubbery.

Marcus instantly ran down to the garden door, and began to draw up the bridge with as little noise as possible. "What are you doing?" called out a voice to him from the other side. "I hear steps," he answered,

"and perchance it is the castellan on his rounds; he would discover all."
So he draws up the bridge, and then glided along the shrubbery after
my knave.

Meanwhile Appelmann and Sidonia, with the boundary lad, had
reached the door of the castle, through which he was determined to
make good his entrance after the lad by any means.

But at that very instant it opened, and my gracious lord Duke Johann
Frederick stood before them. For it has been already mentioned, that
he left the chamber in which the family council was held, by a small
private door which led down to this portion of the castle. Here he was
looking about for his court-jester, Clas Hinze, to bid him order the
carriages to convey him and his suite that very night to Freienwald, and
by chance opened this very door which led out to the shrubbery.

Seeing no one from the darkness, the Duke called out, "Is Clas there?"
to which Appelmann answered, "Yes, my lord" (for he had recognized
the Duke by his voice), and at the same time he retreated a few steps
into the shrubbery, hoping the Duke would follow him.

But the Duke called out again, "Where art thou, Clas?" "Here!"
responded Appelmann, retreating still further. Whereupon the boundary lad whispered, "That is not him!" His Grace, however, heard the
whisper, and called out angrily, while he advanced from the door, "What
meanest thou, knave? It is I who call! Art thou drunk, fool? If so, thou
must have a bucket of water on thy head, for we ride away this night."

So speaking, his Highness went on still further into the shrubbery,
upon which my knave makes a spring at his throat and hurls him to
the ground, while he gives a loud, shrill whistle through the fingers of
his other hand. Now the boundary lad screamed in earnest; but Sidonia
threatened him, and bade him hold his tongue, and run for the other
fellows, and not mind them. But she screamed yet louder herself, when
a powerful arm seized her round the waist, and she found herself in the
grasp of Marcus Bork.

Appelmann, who had stuffed his kerchief into the Duke's mouth to
stifle his cries, and placed one knee upon his breast, now sprang up in
terror at her scream, while at the same instant the bells rang, the cannon
was fired, and all the court was filled with people shouting, "Murder!
murder!" So he let go his hold of the Duke, and without waiting to
release Sidonia, darted down the shrubbery, reached the bridge, and
finding it raised, plunged into the water, and swam to the other side.

And here we see the hand of the all-merciful God; for had the bridge
been down, the band would have rushed over at their captain's whistle,
and then, methinks, there would have been a sad end to the whole
princely race, for, as I have said, half the guests were drunk and half

were snoring, so that but for Marcus this evil and accursed woman would
have destroyed them all, as she had sworn. True, they were destroyed by
her at last, but not until God gave them over to destruction, in consequence of their sins, no doubt, and of the wickedness of the land.

Summa. — When my gracious lord felt himself free, he sprang up,
crying, "Help! help!" and ran as quick as he could back into the castle.
Marcus Bork followed with Sidonia, who drew a knife to stab him, but
he saw the glitter of the blade by the light of the lanterns (for one can
easily imagine that the bells and the cannon had brought all the snorers
to their legs), and giving her a blow upon the arm that made her drop
the knife, dragged her through the little door, after the Duke, as fast as
he was able.

So the whole princely party stood there, and great and small shouted
when the upright Marcus appeared, holding Sidonia firmly by the back,
while she writhed and twisted, and kicked him with her heels till the
sweat poured down his face.

But when old Ulrich beheld her, he exclaimed, "Seven thousand
devils! — do my eyes deceive me, or is this Sidonia again?" Her Grace,
too, turned pale, and all were horrified at seeing the evil one, for they
knew her wickedness.

Then Marcus must relate the whole story, and how he came to bring
to naught the counsel of the devil.

And when Duke Johann heard the whole extent of the danger from
which he had been saved, he fell upon the neck of the loyal Marcus,
and, pressing him to his heart, exclaimed, "Well-beloved Marcus, and
dear friend, thou hast saved my brother of Wolgast in the Stettin forest,
so hast thou saved me this night, therefore accept knighthood from my
hands; and I make thee governor of my fortress of Saatzig."

To which the other answered, "He thanked his Grace heartily for the
honors; but he had already promised to remain in the service of his
princely brother of Wolgast; and for that object had made purchase of
the lands of Crienke."

But his Highness would hear of no refusal. Only let him look at
Saatzig; it was the finest fortress in the land. What would he do in a
miserable fishing village? The castle was almost grander than his own
ducal house at Stettin; and the knights' hall, with its stone pillars and
carved capitals, was the most stately work of architecture in the kingdom. Where would he find such a dwelling in his village nest? Old
Kleist, the governor, had just died, and to whom could he give the castle
sooner than to his right worthy and loyal Marcus?

When old Dewitz heard this (he was a little, dry old man, with long
grey hair), he pressed forward to his son-in-law, and bade him by no

means refuse a Prince's offer; besides, Saatzig was but two miles off, and they could see each other every Sunday. Also, if they had a hunt, a standard erected on the tower of one castle could be seen plainly from the tower of the other, and so they could lead a right pleasant, neighborly life, almost as if they all lived together.

Still Marcus will not consent. Upon which his mother-in-law can no longer suppress her feelings, and comes forward to entreat him. (She was a good, pious matron, and as fat as her husband was thin.) So she stroked his cheeks — "And where in the land, as far as Usdom, could he find such fine muranes and maranes* — this fish he loved so much? — and where was such fine flax to be had, for his young wife to spin? — no flax in the land equaled that of Saatzig! — since ever she was a little girl, people talked of the fine Saatzig flax. Let her dear daughter Clara come over, and see could she prevail aught with her stern husband. Why, they could send pudding hot to each other, the castles were so near."

And now the mild young bride approached her husband, and taking his hand gently, looked up into his eyes with soft, beseeching glances, but spake no word; so that the princely widow of Wolgast was moved, and said, "Good Marcus, if you only fear to offend my son of Wolgast by taking service at Saatzig, be composed on that head, for I myself will make your peace. Great, indeed, would be my joy to have you and your young spouse settled at Crienke, which, you know, is but half a mile from Pudgla, my dower-castle, where I mean to reside; yet these beseeching glances of my little Clara fill my heart with compassion, for do I not read in her clear eyes that she would love to stay near her dear parents, as indeed is natural? Therefore, in God's name accept the offer of your Prince. I myself command you."

Hereupon Marcus inclined himself gracefully to the Duchess and Duke Johann, and pressed his little wife to his heart. "But what need, gracious Prince, of a governor at Saatzig, when all the courts are closed and no justice can be done? I shall eat my bread in idleness, like a worn-out hound. But, marry, if your Grace consents to open the courts, I will accept your offer with thanks, and do my duty as governor with all justice and fidelity." Then his Grace answered, "What! good Marcus, dost thou begin again on that old theme which roused my wrath so lately, and made me fall into that peril? But I bethink me of thy bravery, and will say no bitter word; only, thou mayest hold thy peace, for I have sworn by my princely honor, and from that there is no retreating.

---

* The great marana weighs from ten to twelve pounds, and is a species of salmon-trout. The murana is of the same race, but not larger than the herring. It must not be confounded with the *murana* of which the Romans were so fond, which was a species of eel.

However, thou hast leave to hold jurisdiction in thy own government, and execute justice according to thy own upright judgment."

So Marcus was silent; but the Duchess and the other princes took up the subject, and assailed his Highness with earnest petitions – "Had he not himself felt and seen the danger of permitting these freebooters to get such a head in the land? Had not the finger of God warned him this very night, in hopes of turning him back to the right path? Let him reflect, for the peace of his land was at stake." But all in vain. Even though old Ulrich tumbled into the argument with his seven thousand devils, yet could they obtain no other answer from his Highness but – "If the states give me gold, I shall open the courts; if they give no gold, the courts shall remain closed forever. Were he to be brought before the Emperor, or Pontius Pilate himself, it was all alike; they might tear him in pieces, but not one nail's breadth of his princely word would he retreat from, or break it like a woman, for their prayers."

Then he rose, and calling his fool Clas to him, bid him run to the old priest, and tell him he would sleep at his quarters that night, for he must have peace; but the merry Clas, as he was running out, got behind his Highness, and stuck his fool's cap upon the head of his Grace, crying out, "Here, keep my cap for me."

However, his Highness did not relish the joke, for everyone laughed; and he ran after the fool, trying to catch him, and threatening to have his head cut off; but Clas got behind the others, and clapping his hands, cried out, "You can't, for the courts are closed. Huzza! the courts are closed!" Whereupon he runs out at the door, and my gracious lord after him, with the fool's cap upon his head. Nor did he return again to the hall, but went to sleep at the priest's quarters, as he had said; and next morning, by the first dawn of day, set off on his journey homeward.

All this while no one had troubled himself about Sidonia. My gracious lady wept, the young lords laughed, old Ulrich swore, whilst the good Marcus murmured softly to his young wife, "Be happy, Clara; for thy sake I shall consent to go to Saatzig. I have decided."

This filled her with such joy that she danced, and smiled, and flung herself into her mother's arms; nothing was wanting now to her happiness! Just then her eyes rested upon Sidonia, who was leaning against the wall, as pale as a corpse. Clara grew quite calm in a moment, and asked, compassionately, "What aileth thee, poor Sidonia?"

"I am hungry!" was the answer. At this the gentle bride was so shocked, that the tears filled her eyes, and she exclaimed, "Wait, thou shalt partake of my wedding-feast;" and away went she.

The attention of the others was, by this time, also directed to Sidonia. And old Ulrich said, "Compose yourself, gracious lady; I trust your son, the Prince, will not be so hard and stern as he promises; now that the water has touched his own neck, methinks he will soon come to reason. But what shall we do now with Sidonia?"

Upon which my Lady of Wolgast turned to her, and asked if she were yet wedded to her gallows-bird? "Not yet," was the answer; "but she would soon be." Then my gracious lady spat out at her; and, addressing Ulrich, asked what he would advise.

So the stout old knight said, "If the matter were left to him, he would just send for the executioner, and have her ears and nose slit, as a warning and example, for no good could ever come of her now, and then pack her off next day to her farm at Zachow; for if they let her loose, she would run to her paramour again, and come at last to gallows and wheel; but if they just slit her nose, then he would hold her in abhorrence, as well as all other menfolk."

During this, Clara had entered, and set fish, and wild boar, and meat, and bread, before the girl; and as she heard Ulrich's last words, she bent down and whispered, "Fear nothing, Sidonia, I hope to be able to protect thee, as I did once before; only eat, Sidonia! Ah! hadst thou followed my advice! I always meant well by thee; and even now, if I thought thou wouldst repent truly, poor Sidonia, I would take thee with me to the castle of Saatzig, and never let thee want for aught through life."

When Sidonia heard this, she wept, and promised amendment. Only let Clara try her, for she could never go to Zachow and play the peasant-girl. Upon which Clara turned to her Highness, and prayed her Grace to give Sidonia up to her. See how she was weeping; misfortune truly had softened her, and she would soon be brought back to God. Only let her take her to Saatzig, and treat her as a sister. At this, however, old Ulrich shook his head — "Clara, Clara," he exclaimed, "knowest thou not that the Moor cannot change his skin, nor the leopard his spots? I cannot, then, let the serpent go. Think on our mother, girl; it is a bad work playing with serpents."

Her Grace, too, became thoughtful, and said at last —

"Could we not send her to the convent at Marienfliess, or somewhere else?"

"What the devil would she do in a convent?" exclaimed the old knight. "To infect the young maidens with her vices, or plague them with her pride? Now, there was nothing else for her but to be packed off to Zachow."

Now Clara looked up once again at her husband with her soft, tearful eyes, for he had said no word all this time, but remained quite mute; and he drew her to him, and said —

"I understand thy wish, dear Clara, but the old knight is right. It is a dangerous business, dear Clara! Let Sidonia go."

At this Sidonia crawled forth like a serpent from her corner, and howled —

"Clara had pity on her, but he would turn her out to starve — he, who bore her own name, and was of her own blood."

Alas! the good knight was ashamed to refuse any longer, and finally promised the evil one that she should go with them to Saatzig. So her Grace at last consented, but old Ulrich shook his grey head ten times more.

"He had lived many years in the world, but never had it come to his knowledge that a godless man was tamed by love. Fear was the only teacher for them. All their love would be thrown away on this harlot; for even if the stout Marcus kept her tight with bit and rein, and tried to bring her back by fear, yet the moment his back was turned, Clara would spoil all again by love and kindness."

However, nobody minded the good knight, though it all came to pass just as he had prophesied.

Chapter XV

How Sidonia demeans herself at the castle of Saatzig, and how Clara forgets the injunctions of her beloved husband, when he leaves her to attend the Diet at Wollin, on the subject of the courts — Item, how the Serene Prince Duke Johann Frederick beheads his court fool with a sausage

*S*umma. — Sidonia went to the castle of Saatzig, and her worthy cousin Marcus gave her a little chamber to herself, in the third story, close to the tower. It was the same room in which she afterwards sat as a witch, for some days ere she was taken to Oderburg. There was a right cheerful view from the windows down upon the lake, which was close to the castle, and over the little town of Jacobshagen, as far even as the meadows beyond. Here, too, was left a Bible for her, and the *Opera Lutheri* in addition, with plenty of materials for spinning and embroidery, for she had refused to weave. *Item,* a serving-wench was appointed to attend on her, and she had permission to walk where she pleased within the castle walls; but if ever seen beyond the domain, the keepers had orders to bring her back by force, if she would not return willingly.

In fine, the careful knight took every precaution possible to render her presence as little baneful as could be, for, truth to say, he had no faith whatever in her tears and seeming repentance.

First, he strictly forbade all his secretaries to interchange a word with her, or even look at her. They need not know his reason, but anyone who transgressed his slightest command in this particular, should be chased away instantly from the castle.

Secondly, he prayed his dear wife to let Sidonia eat her meals alone, in her own little room, and never to see her but in the presence of a third person.

Also, never to accept the slightest gift from her hand — fruit, flower, or any kind of food whatsoever. These injunctions were the more necessary, as the young bride had already given hopes of an heir. Sidonia's rage and jealousy at this prospect of complete happiness for Clara may be divined from her words to her maid, Lene Penkun, a short time after she reached the castle —

"Ha! they are talking of the baptism already, forsooth; but it might have been otherwise if I had come across her a little sooner!"

This same maid also she sent to Daber for the spirit Chim, which had been left behind at the last resting-place of the robbers, never telling her it was a spirit, however, only a tame cat, that was a great pet of hers. "It must be half dead with hunger now, for it was four days since she had left it in the hollow of an old oak in the forest, the poor creature! So let the maid take a flask of sweet milk and a little saucer to feed it. She could not miss her way, for, when she stepped out of the high-road at Daber into the forest, there was a thorn-bush to her left hand, and just beyond it a large oak where the ravens had their nests; in a hollow of this oak, to the north side, lay her dear little cat. But she must not tell anyone about the matter, or they would laugh at her for sending her maid two miles and more to look for a cat. Men had no compassion or tenderheartedness nowadays to each other, much less to a poor dumb animal. No; just let her say that she went to fetch a robe which her mistress had left in the oak. Here was an old gown; take this with her, and it would do to wrap up the poor little pussy in it after she had fed it and warmed it, so that no one might see it, for what a mock would all these pitiless men make of her, if they heard the object of her message; but she was not cruel like them."

Now, after some time, it happened that the states of the duchy assembled at Wollin, to come to some arrangement with his Highness respecting the opening of the courts of justice; and Marcus Bork, along with all the other nobles, was summoned to attend the Diet. So, with great grief, he had to leave his dear wife, but promised, if possible, to return before she was taken with her illness. Then he bid her be of good courage, and, above all things, to guard herself, against Sidonia, and mind strictly all his injunctions concerning her.

Alas! she too soon flung them all to the winds! For, behold, scarcely had the good knight arrived at Wollin, when Clara was delivered of a little son, at which great joy filled the whole castle. And one messenger was dispatched to Marcus, and another to old Dewitz and his wife, with the tidings; but woe, alas! the good old mother was going to stand sponsor for a nobleman's child in the neighborhood, and could not hasten then to save her dear daughter from a terrible and cruel death. She cooked some broth, however, for the young mother, and pouring it into a silver flask, bid the messenger ride back with all speed to Saatzig, that it might not be too cold. She herself would be over in the morning early with her husband, and let her dear little daughter keep herself warm and quiet.

Meanwhile Sidonia had heard of the birth, and sent her maid to wish the young mother joy, and ask her permission just to give one little kiss to her new cousin, for they told her he was a beautiful infant.

Alas, alas! that Clara's joy should make her forget the judicious cautions of her husband! Permission was given to the murderess, and down she comes directly to offer her congratulations; even affecting to weep for joy as she kissed the infant, and praying to be allowed to act as nurse until her mother came from Daber.

"Why, she had no one about her but common serving-women! How could she leave her dearest friend to the care of these old hags, when she was in the castle, who owed everything to her dear Clara?"

And so she went on till poor Clara, even if she did not quite believe her, felt ashamed to doubt so much apparent affection and tenderness.

Summa. — She permitted her to remain, and we shall soon see what murderous deeds Sidonia was planning against the poor young mother. But first I must relate what happened at the Diet of Wollin, to which Marcus Bork had been summoned.

His Highness Duke Johann had become somewhat more gracious to the states since they had come to the Diet at their own cost, which was out of the usage; and further, because, as old Ulrich prophesied, he himself had felt the inconveniences resulting from the present lawless state of the country.

Still he was ill-tempered enough, particularly as he had a fever on him; and when the states promised at last that they would let him have the money, he said, "So far good; but, till he saw the gold, the courts should not be opened. Not that he misdoubted them, but then he knew that they were sometimes as tedious in handing out money as a peasant in paying his rent. The courts, therefore, should not be opened until he had the gold in his pot, so it would be to their own profit to use as much diligence as possible." At this same Diet his Grace related how he first met Clas, his fool, which story I shall set down here for the reader's pastime.

This same fool had been nothing but a poor goose-herd; and one day as he was on the road to Friedrichswald with his flock, my gracious lord rode up, and growing impatient at the geese running hither and thither in his path, bid the boy collect them together, or he would strike them all dead.

Upon which the knave took up goose after goose by the throat, and stuck them by their long necks into his girdle, till a circle of geese hung entirely round his body, all dangling by the head from his waist.

This merry device pleased my lord so much, that he made the lad court-jester from that day, and many a droll trick he had played from that to this, particularly when his Highness was gloomy, so as to make him laugh again. Once, for instance, when the Duke was sore pressed for money, by reason of the opposition of the states, he became very sad, and all the doctors were consulted, but could do nothing. For unless his Grace could be brought to laugh (they said to the Lady Erdmuth), it was all over with him. Then my gracious lady had the fool whipped for a stupid jester, who could not drive his trade; for if he did not make the Duke laugh, why should he stay at all in the castle?

What did my fool? He collected all the princely soldatesca, and got leave from their Graces to review them; and surely never were seen such strange evolutions as he put them through, for they must do everything he bid them. And when his Highness came forth to look, he laughed so loud as never had fool made him laugh before; and calling the Duchess, bid him repeat his *experimentum* many times for her. In fine, the fool got the good town of Butterdorf for his fee, which changed its name in honor of him, and is called Hinzendorf to this day (for his name was Hinze).

But Clas Hinze had not been able to cure my Lord Duke of his fever, which attacked him at the Diet at Wollin, nor all the doctors from Stettin, nor even Doctor Pomius, who had been sent from Wolgast by the old Duchess, to attend her dear son; and as the doctor (as I have said) was a formal, priggish little man, he and the fool were always bickering and snarling.

Now, one day at Wollin, the weather being beautiful, his Grace, with several of the chief prelates, and many of the nobility, went forth to walk by the river's side, and the fool ran along with them; *item,* Doctor Pomius, who, if he could not run, at least tried to walk majestically; and he munched a piece of sugar all the time, for he never could keep his mouth still a moment. Seeing his Grace now about to cross the bridge, the doctor started forward with as much haste as was consistent with his dignity, and seizing his Highness by the tail of the coat, drew him back, declaring, "That he must not pass the water; all water would give strength to the fever-devil." But his Highness, who was talking Latin to the Deacon of Colberg, turned on the doctor with — "Apage te asine!" and strode forward, whilst one of the nobles gave a free translation aloud for the benefit of the others, saying, "And that means: Begone, thou ass!"

When the fool heard this, he clapped the little man on the back, shouting, "Well done, ass! and there is thy fee for curing our gracious Prince of his fever."

This so nettled the doctor that he spat out the lump of sugar for rage, and tried to seize the fool; but the crowd laughed still louder when Clas jumped on the back of an old woman, giving her the spur with his yellow boots in the side, and shaking his head with the cap and bells at the little doctor in mockery, who could not get near him for the crowd. So the woman screamed and roared, and the people laughed, till at last the Duke stopped in the middle of the bridge to see what was the matter. When the fool observed this, he sprang off the old woman's back, and calling out to the doctor — "See how I cure our gracious lord's fever," ran upon the bridge like wind, and, seizing the Duke with all his force, jumped with him into the water.

Now the people screamed from horror, as much as before from mirth, and thirty or forty burghers, along with Marcus Bork, plunged in to rescue his Highness, whilst others tried to seize the fool, threatening to tear him in pieces. This was a joyful hearing to Doctor Pomius. He drew forth his knife — "Would they not finish the knave at once? Here was a knife just ready."

But the fool, who was strong and supple, swung himself up to the bridge, and crouched in between the arches, catching hold of the beams, so that no one dared to touch him there, and his Highness was soon carried to land. He was in a flaming rage as he shook off the water.

"Where is that accursed fool? He had only threatened to cut off his head at Daber, but now it should be done in earnest."

So the fool shouted from under the bridge — "Ho! ho! the courts are all closed! the courts are all closed!" At which the crowd laughed so heartily, that my Lord Duke grew still more angry, and commanded them to bring the fool to him dead or alive.

Hearing this, the fool crept forward of himself, and whimpered in his Low Dutch, "My good Lord Duke, praise be to God that we've made the doctor fly. I'll give him a little piece of drink-money for his journey, and then I'll be your doctor myself. For if the fright has not cured you, marry, let the deacon be your fool, and I will be your deacon as long as I live."

However, my gracious lord was in no humor for fun, but bid them carry off the fool to prison, and lock him up there; for though, indeed, the fever had really quite gone, as his Highness perceived to his joy, yet he was resolved to give the fool a right good fright in return.

Therefore, on the third day from that, he commanded him to be brought out and beheaded on the scaffold at Wollin. He wore a white shroud, bordered with black gauze, over his motley jacket, and a priest and melancholy music accompanied him all the way; but Master Hansen had directions that, when the fool was seated in the chair with his eyes bound, he should strike the said fool on the neck with a sausage in place of the sword.

However, no one suspected this, and a great crowd followed the poor fool up to the scaffold; even Doctor Pomius was there, and kept close up to the condemned. As the fool passed the ducal house, there was my lord seated at a window looking out, and the fool looked up, saying, "My gracious master, is this a fool's jest you are playing me, or is it earnest?"

To which the Duke answered, "You see it is earnest."

Then answered the fool, "Well, if I must, I must; yet I crave one boon!"

When the promise was granted, the knave, who could not give up his jesting even on the death-road, said, "Then make Doctor Pomius herewith to be fool in my place, for look how he is learning all my tricks from me — sticking himself close up to my side."

Hereat a great shout of laughter pealed from the crowd, and the Duke motioned with the hand to proceed to the scaffold.

Still the poor fool kept looking round every moment, thinking his Grace would send a message after them to stop the execution, but no one appeared. Then his teeth chattered, and he trembled like an aspen leaf; for Master Hansen seized hold of him now, and put him down upon the chair, and bound his eyes. Still he asked, with his eyes bound, "Master, is anyone coming?"

"No!" replied the executioner; and throwing back his red cloak, drew forth a large sausage in place of a sword, to the great amusement of the people. With this he strikes my fool on the neck, who thereupon tumbles down from the stool, as stone dead from the mere fright as if his head and body had parted company — yea, more dead, for never a finger or a muscle did the poor fool move more.

This sad ending moved his Grace even to tears; and he fell into a yet greater melancholy than before, crying, "Woe! alas! He gave me my life through fright, and through fright I have taken away his poor life! Ah, never shall I meet with so good and merry a fool again!"

Then he gave command to all the physicians to try and restore him, and he himself stood by while they bled him and felt his pulse, but all was in vain; even Doctor Pomius tried his skill, but nothing would help, so that my lord cried out angrily —

"Marry, the fool was right. The fools should be doctors, for the doctors are all fools. Away with ye all, and your gibberish, to the devil!"

After this he had the said fool placed in a handsome black coffin, and conveyed to his own town of Hinzendorf, there to be buried; and over his grave my lord erected a stately monument, on which was represented the poor fool, as large as life, with his cap and bells, and staff in his hand; and round his waist was a girdle, from which many geese dangled, all cut like life, while at his side lay his shepherd's bag, and at his feet a beer-can. The figure is five feet two inches long, and bears a Latin inscription above it, which I forget; but the initials G. H. are carved upon each cheek.*

Shortly after the death of the fool a messenger arrived from Saatzig to Marcus Bork, bringing him the joyful tidings that the Lord God had granted him the blessing of a little son. So he is away to my Lord Duke, to solicit permission to leave the Diet and return to his castle. This the Duke readily granted, seeing that he himself was going away to attend the funeral of the poor fool at Hinzendorf. Then he wished Marcus joy with all his heart, which so emboldened the knight that he ventured to make one more effort about the opening of the courts, praying his Grace to put faith in the word of his faithful states, and open the courts and the treasury without further delay.

---

* His original name was Gürgen Hinze, not Clas. The Latin inscription is nearly effaced, but the beginning is still visible, and runs thus: "Caput ecce manus gestus que;" from which Oelrichs concludes that the whole was written in hexameters. (See his estimable work, "Memoirs of the Pomeranian Dukes," p. 41.)

But his Grace is wroth: "What should he be troubled for? The states could give the money when they chose, and then all would be right. Let the nobles do their duty. He never saw a penny come out of their pockets for their Prince."

"But his Highness knew the poor peasants were all beggared; and where could the nobles get the money?"

"Let them go to their saving-pots, then, where the money was turning green from age; better for them if they had less avarice. Why did not he himself bring him some gold, in place of dressing up his wife in silks and jewels, finer than the Princess Erdmuth herself, his own princely spouse? Then, indeed, the courts might be soon opened," &c. So the sorrowing knight took his leave, and each went his different way.

Chapter XVI

How Sidonia makes poor Clara appear quite dead, and of the great mourning at Saatzig over her burial, while Sidonia dances on her coffin and sings the 109th psalm — Item, of the sermon and the anathema pronounced upon a wicked sinner from the altar of the church

I must first state that this horrible wickedness of Sidonia, which no eye had seen nor ear heard, neither had it entered into the heart of man to conceive (for only in hell could such have been imagined), never would have come to light but that she herself made confession thereof to Dr. Cramero, thy well-beloved godfather, in her last trial. And he, to show how far Satan can lead a poor human creature who has once fallen from God, related the same to my worthy father-in-law, Master David Reutzio, some time superintendent at the criminal court, from whose own lips I received the story.

And this was her confession: — That when the messenger returned from Daber with the broth, he had ridden so fast that it was still, in truth, quite hot, but she (the horrible Sidonia), who was standing at the bed of the young mother, along with the other women, pretended that it was too cold for a woman in her state, and must just get one little heating on the fire.

The poor Clara, indeed, showed unwillingness to permit this, but she ran down with it, and secretly, without being seen by any of the other women, poured in a philtrum that had been given her by the gypsy hag, and then went back again for a moment. This philtrum was the one which produced all the appearance of death. It had no taste, except, perhaps, that it was a little saltish. Therefore Clara perceived nothing wrong, only when she tasted it, said, "My heart's dearest mother, in her joy, has put a little too much salt into her broth; still, what a heart's dearest mother sends, must always taste good!" However, in one hour after that, Clara lay as stiff and cold as a corpse, only her breath came a little; but even this ceased in a short time, and then a great cry and lamentation resounded through the whole castle. No one suspected Sidonia, for many said that young women died so often; but even the old mother, who arrived a few hours after, and hearing the cries from the castle while she was yet far off, began to weep likewise; for her mother's heart revealed the cause to her ere she had yet descended from the carriage.

But it was a sadder sight next evening, when the husband arrived at the castle from Wollin. He could not take his eyes from the corpse. One while he kissed the infant, then fixed his eyes again upon his dead wife, and sighed and groaned as if he lay upon the rack. He alone suspected Sidonia, but when she cried more than they all, and wrung her hands, exclaiming, who would have pity on her now, for her best friend lay there dead! and flung herself upon the seeming corpse, kissing it and bedewing it with her tears, and praying to have leave to watch all night beside it, for how could she sleep in her sore grief and sorrow? the knight was ashamed of his suspicions, and even tried to comfort her himself.

Then came the physicians out of Stargard and other places, who had been summoned in all haste, and they gabbled away, saying, "It could not have been the broth, but puerperal fever." This at least was Dr. Hamster's opinion, who knew all along it would be a bad case. Indeed, the last time he was at the castle visiting the mower's wife, he was frightened at the look of the poor lady. Still, if they had only sent for him in time, this great evil could not have happened, for his *pulvis antispasmodicus* was never known to fail; and so he went on chattering, by which one can see that doctors have always been the same from that time even till now.

Summa. – On the third day the poor Clara was laid in her coffin, and carried to her grave, with such weeping and lamentation of the mourners and bearers as never had been heard till then. And all the nobles of the vicinage, with the knights and gentlemen, came to attend her funeral at Saatzig Cathedral, for she was to be buried in this new church just finished by his Grace Duke Johann, and but one corpse had been laid in the vaults before her.*

But what does the devil's sorceress do now? She knew that the poor Clara would awake the next day (which was Sunday) about noon, and if any should hear her cries, her plans would be detected. Therefore, about ten of the clock she ran to Marcus, with her hair all flowing down her shoulders, saying, that he must let her away that very day to Zachow, for what would the world say if she, a young unmarried thing, should remain here all alone with him in his castle? No; sooner would she swallow the bitter cup her father had left her than peril her name. But first, would he allow her to go and pray alone in the church? Surely he would not deny her this.

Thereupon the simple knight gave her instant leave — "Let her go and pray, in God's name. He himself would soon be there to hear the Reverend Dr. Wudargensis preach the funeral sermon over his heart's dear wife. And after service he would desire a carriage to be in readiness to convey her to Zachow."

Then he called to the warder from the window, bidding him let Sidonia pass. So she went forth in deep mourning garments, glided through the castle gardens, and concealing herself by the trees, slipped into the church without anyone having perceived her; for the sexton had left the door open to admit fresh air, on account of the corpse. Then she stepped over to the little grated door near the altar, which led down into the vault, and softly lifting it, stepped down, drawing the door down again close over her head. Clara's coffin was lying beneath, and first she laid her ear on it and listened, but all was quite still within. Then removing the pall, she sat herself down upon the lid. Time passed, and still no sound. The sexton began to ring the bell, and the people were assembling in the church above. Soon the hymn commenced, "Now in peace the loved one sleepeth," and ere the first verse had ended, a knocking was heard in the coffin, then a cry — "Where am I? What brought me here? Let me out, for God's sake let me out! I am not dead. Where is my child? Where is my good Marcus? Ah! there is someone near me. Who is it? Let me out! let me out!" Then (oh! horror of horrors!) the devil's harlot on her coffin answered, "It is I, Sidonia! this pays thee for acting the spy at Wolgast. Lie there and writhe till thou art stifled in thy blood!" Now the voice came again from the coffin, praying and

---

* The beautifully painted escutcheon of Duke Johann and his wife, Erdmuth of Brandenburg, is still to be seen on the chancel windows of this stately staircase.

beseeching, so that many times it went through her stony heart like a sword. And just then the first verse of the hymn ended, and the voice of the priest was heard asking the lord governor whether they should go and sing the remainder over the vault of his dear spouse, for it was indeed sung in her honor, seeing she had been ever a mother to the orphan, and a holy, pious, and Christian wife; or, since the people all knew her worth, and mourned for her with bitter mourning, should they sing it here in the nave, that the whole congregation might join in chorus?*

To this the governor, in a loud yet mournful voice, gave answer —

"Alas, good friends, do what you will in this sad case; I am content."

But Sidonia, this devil's witch, was in a horrible fright, lest the priest would come up to the altar to sing the hymn, and so hear the knocking within the coffin. However, the devil protects his own, for, at that instant, many voices called out —

"Let the hymn be sung here, that we may all join to the honor of the blessed soul of the good lady."

And mournfully the second verse was heard pealing through the church, from the lips of the whole congregation, so that poor Clara's groans were quite smothered. For, when the voice of her dear husband reached her ear, she had knocked and cried out with all her strength —

"Marcus! Marcus! Alas, dear Lord, will you not come to me!" Then again — "Sidonia, by the Jesu cross, I pray thee have pity on me. Save me — save me — I am stifling. Oh, run for someone, if thou canst not lift the lid thyself!"

But the devil made answer to the poor living corpse —

"Dost thou take me for a silly fool like thyself, that I should now undo all I have done?"

And as the voice went on from the coffin, but feebler and fainter —

"Think on my husband — on my child, Sidonia!"

She answered —

"Didst thou think of that when, but for thee, I might have been a Duchess of Pomerania, and the proud mother of a prince, in place of being as I now am."

Then all became still within the coffin, and Sidonia sprang upon it and danced, chanting the 109th psalm;† and as she came to the words,

---

*   These interruptions were by no means unusual at that period.

†   Superstition has found many sinful usages for this psalm. The Jews, for example, took a new vessel, poured a mixture of mustard and water therein, and after repeating this psalm over it for three consecutive days, poured it out before the door of their enemy, as a certain means to ensure his destruction. In the middle ages monks and nuns were frequently obliged to repeat it in superstitious ceremonies, at the com-

"Let none show mercy to him; let none have pity on his orphans; let his posterity be cut off and his name be blotted out," there was a loud knocking again within the coffin, and a faint, stifled cry — "I am dying!" then followed a gurgling sound, and all became still. At that moment the congregation above raised the last verse of the hymn: —

"In the grave, with bitter weeping,
  Loving hands have laid her down;
There she resteth, calmly sleeping,
  Till an angel lifts the stone."

But the sermon which now followed she remembered her life long. It was on the tears, the soft tears of our Lord and Saviour Jesus Christ. And as her spirit became oppressed by the silence in the vault, now that all was still within the coffin, she lifted the lid after the exordium, to see if Clara were indeed quite dead.

It was an easy matter to remove the cover, for the screws were not fastened; but — O God! what has she beheld? A sight that will never more leave her brain! The poor corpse lay all torn and disfigured from the writhings in the coffin, and a blood-vessel must have burst at last to relieve her from her agony, for the blood lay yet warm on the hands as she lifted the cover. But more horrible than all were the fixed glassy eyes of the corpse, staring immovably upon her, from which clear tears were yet flowing, and blending with the blood upon the cheek; and, as if the priest above had known what was passing beneath, he exclaimed —

"Oh, let us moisten our couch with tears; let tears be our meat day and night. They are noble tears that do not fall to earth, but ascend up to God's throne. Yea, the Lord gathers them in His vials, like costly wine. They are noble tears, for if they fill the eyes of God's chosen in this life, yet, in that other world, the Lord Jesus will wipe away tears from off all faces, as the dew is dried by the morning sun. Oh, wondrous beauty of those eyes which are dried by the Lord Jesus! Oh, blessed eyes! Oh, sun-clear eyes! Oh, joyful and ever-smiling eyes!"

She heard no more, but felt the eyes of the corpse were upon her, and fell down like one dead beside the coffin; and Clara's eyes and the

---

mand of some powerful revengeful man. And that its efficacy was Considered as something miraculously powerful, even by the evangelical Church, is proved by this example of Sidonia, who made frequent use of this terrible psalm in her sorceries, as anyone may see by referring to the records of the trial in Dähnert. And other interesting examples are found in the treatise of Job. Andreas Schmidii, *Abusus Psalmi 109 imprecatorii*; vulgo, *The Death Prayer,* Helmstadt, 1708.

sermon never left her brain from that day, and often have they risen before her in dreams.

But the Holy Spirit had yet a greater torment in store for her, if that were possible.

For, after the sermon, a consistorium was held in the church upon a grievous sinner named Trina Wolken, who, it appeared, had many times done penance for her unchaste life, but had in no wise amended. And she heard the priest asking, "Who accuseth this woman?" To which, after a short silence, a deep, small voice responded —

"I accuse her; for I detected her in sin, and though I besought her with Christian words to turn from her evil ways, and that I would save her from public shame if she would so turn, yet she gave herself up wholly to the devil, and out of revenge bewitched my best sheep, so that it died the very day after it had brought forth a lamb. Alas! what will become of the poor lamb? And it was such a beautiful little lamb!"

When Marcus Bork heard this, he began to sob aloud; and each word seemed to run like a sharp dagger through Sidonia's heart, so that she bitterly repented her evil deeds. And all the congregation broke out into loud weeping, and even the priest continued, in a broken voice, to ask the sinner what she had to say to this terrible accusation.

Upon which a woman's voice was heard swearing that all was a malignant lie, for her accuser was a shameless liar and open sinner, who wished to ruin her because she had refused his son.

Then the priest commanded the witnesses to be called, not only to prove the unchastity, but also the witchcraft. And after this, she was asked if she could make good the loss of the sheep? No; she had no money. And the people testified also that the harlot had nothing but her shame. Thereupon the priest rose up, and said —

"That she had long been notorious in the Christian communion for her wicked life, and that all her penance and repentance having proved but falsehood and deceit, he was commissioned by the honorable consistorium to pronounce upon her the solemn curse and sentence of excommunication. For she had this day been convicted of strange and terrible crimes, on the testimony of competent witnesses. Therefore he called upon the whole Christian congregation to stand up and listen to the words of the anathema, by which he gave over Trina Wolken to the devil, in the name of the Almighty God."

And as he spoke the curse, it fell word by word upon the head of Sidonia, as if he were indeed pronouncing it over herself —

"Dear Christian Friends, — Because Trina Wolken hath broken her baptismal vows, and given herself over to the devil, to work all uncleanness with greediness; and though divers times admonished to repentance by the Church, yet hath stiffened her neck in corruption, and hardened her heart in unrighteousness, therefore we herewith place the said Trina Wolken under the ban of the excommunication. Henceforth she is a thing accursed – cast off from the communion of the Church, and participation in the holy sacraments. Henceforth she is given up to Satan for this life and the next, unless the blessed Saviour reach forth His hand to her as He did to the sinking Peter, for all things are possible with God. And this we do by the power of the keys granted by Christ to His Church, to bind and loose on earth as in heaven, in the name of the Father, of the Son, and of the Holy Ghost. Amen."

And now Sidonia heard distinctly the screams of the wretched sinner, as she was hunted out of the church, and all the congregation followed soon after, and then all was still above.

Now, indeed, terror took such hold of her that she trembled like an aspen leaf, and the lid fell many times from her hand with great clatter on the ground, as she tried to replace it on the coffin. For she had closed her eyes, for fear of meeting the ghastly stare of the corpse again. At last she got it up, and the corpse was covered; but she would not stay to replace the screws, only hastened out of the vault, closing the little grated door after her, reached the church door, which had no lock, but only a latch, and plunged into the castle gardens to hide herself amongst the trees.

Here she remained crouched for some hours, trying to recover her self-possession; and when she found that she could weep as well as ever when it pleased her, she set off for the castle, and met her cousin Marcus with loud weeping and lamentations, entreating him to let her go that instant to Zachow. Eat and drink could she not from grief, though she had eaten nothing the whole morning. So the mournful knight, who had himself risen from the table without eating, to hasten to his little motherless lamb, asked her where she had passed the morning, for he had not seen her in the church? To which she answered, that she had sunk down almost dead on the altar-steps; and, as he seemed to doubt her, she repeated part of the sermon, and spoke of the curse pronounced upon the girl, and told how she had remained behind in the church, to weep and pray alone. Upon which he exclaimed joyfully –

"Now, I thank God that my blessed spouse counseled me to take thee home with us. Ah! I see that thou hast indeed repented of thy sins. Go thy ways, then; and, with God's help, thou shalt never want a true and faithful friend while I live."

He bid her also take all his blessed wife's wardrobe with her, amongst which was a brocaded damask with citron flowers, which she had only got a year before; *item,* her shoes and kerchiefs: *summa,* all that she had worn, he wished never to see them again. And so she went away in haste from the castle, after having given a farewell kiss to the little motherless lamb. For though the evil spirit Chim, which she carried under her mantle, whispered to her to give the little bastard a squeeze that would make him follow his mother, or to let him do so, she would not consent, but pinched him for his advice till he squalled, though Marcus certainly could not have heard him, for he was attending Sidonia to the coach; but then the good knight was so absorbed in grief that he had neither ears nor eyes for anything.

Chapter XVII

How Sidonia is chased by the wolves to Rehewinkel, and finds Johann Appelmann again in the inn, with whom she goes away a second time by night

*W*hen Sidonia left Saatzig, the day was far advanced, so that the good knight recommended her to stop at Daber that night with his blessed wife's mourning parents, and, for this purpose, sent a letter by her to them. Also he gave a fine one-year-old foal in charge to the coachman, who tied it to the side of the carriage; and Marcus bid him deliver it up safely to the pastor of Rehewinkel, his good friend, for he had only been keeping the young thing at grass for him, and the pastor now wished it back — they must therefore go by Rehewinkel. So they drove away; but many strange things happened by reason of this same foal; for it was so restive and impatient at being tied, that many times they had to stop and quiet it, lest the poor beast might get hurt by the wheel.

This so delayed their journey, that evening came on before they were out of the forest; and as the sun went down, the wolves began to appear in every direction. Finally, a pack of ten or twelve pursued the carriage; and though the coach-man whipped his horses with might and main, still the wolves gained on them, and stared up in their faces, licking their jaws with their red tongues. Some even were daring enough to spring up behind the carriage, but finding nothing but trunks, had to tumble down again.

This so terrified Sidonia that she screamed and shrieked, and, drawing forth a knife, cut the cords that bound the foal, which instantly galloped away, and the wolves after it. How the carl drove now, thinking to get help in time to save the poor foal! but not so. The poor beast, in its terror, galloped into the town of Rehewinkel; and as the paddock is closed, it springs into the churchyard, the wolves after it, and runs into the belfry-tower, the door of which is lying open — the wolves rush in too, and there they tear the poor animal to pieces, before the pastor could collect peasants enough to try and save it.

Meanwhile Sidonia has reached the town likewise; and as there is a great uproar, some of the peasants crowding into the churchyard, others setting off full chase after the wolves, which had taken the road to Freienwald, Sidonia did not choose to move on (for she must have traveled that very road), but desired the coachman to drive up to the inn; and as she entered, lo! there sat my knave, with two companions, at a table, drinking. Up he jumps, and seizes Sidonia to kiss her, but she pushed him away. "Let him not attempt to come near her. She had done with such low fellows."

So the knave feigned great sorrow — "Alas! had she quite forgotten him — and he treasured her memory so in his heart! Where had she come from? He saw a great many trunks and bags on the carriage. What had she in them?"

Illa. — "Ah! he would, no doubt, like to get hold of them; but she would take care and inform the people what sort of robber carls they had now in the house. She came from Saatzig, and was going to Daber; for as old Dewitz had lost his daughter, he intended to adopt her in the place of one. Therefore let him not attempt to approach her, for she was now, more than ever, a castle and land dowered maiden, and from such a low burgher carl as he was, would cross and bless herself."

But my knave knew her well; so he answered — "Woe is me, Sidonia! do not grieve me by such words; for know that I have given up my old free courses of which you talk; and my father is so pleased with my present mode of life, that he has promised to give me my heritage, and even this very night I am to receive it at Bruchhausen, and am on my way there, as you see. Truly I meant to purchase some land in Poland with the money, and then search throughout all places for you, that we might be wedded like pious Christians. Alas! I thought to have sold your poor cabins at Zachow, and brought you home to my castle in Poland; but for all my love you only give me this proud answer!"

Now Sidonia scarcely believed the knave; so she called one of his comrades aside, and asked him was it true, and where they came from. Upon which he confirmed all that Johann had said — "The devil had dispersed the whole band, so that only two were left with the captain — himself and Konnemann; and they came from Nörenburg, where the master had been striking a bargain with Elias von Wedel, for a town in Poland. The town was called Lembrowo, and there was a stately castle there, as grand almost as the castle of old Dewitz at Daber. They were going this very night to Bruchhausen, to get gold from the old stiff-neck of Stargard, so that the bargain might be concluded next day."

This was a pleasant hearing for Sidonia. She became more friendly, and said, "He could not blame her for doubting him, as he had deceived her so often; still it was wonderful how her heart clung to him through all. Where had he been so long? and what had happened since they parted?"

Hereupon he answered, "That he could not speak while the people were all going to and fro in the inn; but if she came out with him (as the night was fine), they could walk down to the river-side, and he would tell her all."

Summa. — She went with him, and they sat down upon the green grass to discourse, never knowing that the pastor of Rehewinkel was hid behind the next tree; for he had gone forth to lament over the loss of his poor foal, and sat there weeping bitterly. He had got it home to sell, that he might buy a warm coat for the winter, which now he cannot do; therefore the old man had gone forth mournfully into the clear night, thrown himself down, and wept.

By this chance he heard the whole story from my knave, and related it afterwards to the old burgomaster in Stargard. It was as follows: —

Some time after his flight from Daber, a friend from Stettin told him that Dinnies von Kleist (the same who had spoiled their work in the Uckermund forest) had got a great sum of gold in his knapsack, and was off to his castle at Dame,* while the rest were feasting at Daber. This sum he had won by a wager from the Princes of Saxony, Brandenburg, and Mecklenburg. For he had bet, at table, that he would carry five casks of Italian wine at once, and without help, up from the cellar to the dining-hall, in the castle of Old Stettin. Duke Johann refused the bet, knowing his man well, but the others took it up; upon which, after grace, the whole noble company stood up and accompanied him to the cellar. Here Dinnies took up a cask under each arm, another in each hand by the plugs, and a fifth between his teeth by the plug also; thus

---

* A town near Polzin, in Lower Pomerania, and an ancient feudal hold of the Kleists.

laden, he carried the five casks up every step from the cellar to the dining-hall. So the money was paid to him, as the lackeys witnessed, and having put the same in his knapsack, he set off for his castle at Dame, to give it to his father. And the knave went on — "After I heard this news from my good friend, I resolved to set off for Dame and revenge myself on this strong ox, burn his castle, and take his gold. The band agreed; but woe, alas! there was one traitor amongst them. The fellow was called Kaff, and I might well have suspected him; for latterly I observed that when we were about any business, particularly church-robbing, he tried to be off, and asked to be left to keep the watch. Divers nights, too, as I passed him, there was the carl praying; and so I ought to have dismissed the coward knave at once, or he would have had half the band praying likewise before long.

"In short, this arrant villain slips off at night from his post, just as we had all set ourselves down before the castle, waiting for the darkest hour of midnight to attack the foxes in their den, and betrays the whole business to Kleist himself, telling him the strength of the band, and how and when we were to attack him, with all other particulars. Whereupon a great lamentation was heard in the castle, and old Kleist, a little white-headed man, wrung his hands, and seemed ready to go mad with fear; for half the retainers were at the annual fair, others far away at the coal-mines, and finally, they could scarcely muster in all ten fighting men. Besides this, the castle fosse was filled with rubbish, though the old man had been bidding his sons, for the last year, to get it cleared, but they never minded him, the idle knaves. All this troubled stout Dinnies mightily; and as he walked up and down the hall, his eyes often rested on a painting which represented the devil cutting off the head of a gambler, and flying with it out of the window.

"Again and again he looked at the picture, then called out for a hound, stuck him under his arm, and cut off his head, as if it had been only a dove; then he called for a calf from the stall, put it under his arm likewise, and cut off the head. Then he asked for the mask which represented the devil, and which he had got from Stettin to frighten his dissolute brothers, when they caroused too late over their cups. The young Johann, indeed, had sometimes dropped the wine-flask by reason of it, but Detloff still ran after the young maidens as much as ever, though even he had got such a fright that there was hope for his poor soul yet. So the mask was brought, and all the proper disguise to play the devil — namely, a yellow jerkin slashed with black, a red mantle, and a large wooden horse's foot.

"When Dinnies beheld all this, and the man who played the devil instructed him how to put them on, he rejoiced greatly, and declared that now he alone could save the castle. I knew nothing of all this at the time," said Johann, "nor of the treason, neither did the band. We were all seated under a shed in the wood, that had been built for the young deer in the winter time, and had stuck a lantern against the wall while we gamed and drank, and our provider poured us out large mugs of the best beer, when, just at midnight, we heard a report like a clap of thunder outside, so that the earth shook under us (it was no thunderclap, however, but an explosion of powder, which the traitor had laid down all round the shed, for we found the trace of it next day).

"And as we all sprang up, in strode the devil himself bodily, with his horse's foot and cocks' feathers, and a long calf's tail, making the most horrible grimaces, and shaking his long hair at us. Fire came out of his mouth and nostrils, and roaring like a wild boar, he seized the little dwarf (whom you may remember, Sidonia), tucked him under his arm like a cock – and just as he was uttering a curse over his good game being interrupted – and cut his head clean off; then, throwing the head at me, growled forth –

"Every day one,
  Only Sundays none"

and disappeared through the door like a flash of lightning, carrying the headless trunk along with him.

"When my comrades heard that the devil was to carry off one of them every day but Sunday, they all set up a screaming, like so many rooks when a shot is fired in amongst them, and rushed out in the night, seizing hold of horses or wagons, or whatever they could lay their hands on, and rode away east and west, and west and east, or north and south, as it may be.

"*Summa.* – When I came to my senses (for I had sunk down insensible from horror, when the head of the dwarf was thrown at me), I found that the said head had bit me by the arm, so that I had to drag it away by force; then I looked about me, and every knave had fled – even my wagon had been carried off, and not a soul was left in the place of all these fine fellows, who had sworn to be true to me till death.

"This base desertion nearly broke my heart, and I resolved to change my course of life and go to some pious priest for confession, telling him how the devil had first tempted me to sin, and then punished me in this terrible manner (as, indeed, I well deserved).

"So next morning I took my way to the town, after observing, to my great annoyance, that the castle could have been as easily taken as a bird's nest; and seeing a beer-glass painted on a sign-board, I guessed that here was the inn. Truth to say, my heart wanted strengthening sorely, and I entered. There was a pretty wench washing crabs in the kitchen, and as I made up to her, after my manner, to have a little pastime, she drew back and said, laughing, 'May the devil take you, as he took the others last night in the barn!' upon which she laughed again so loud and long, that I thought she would have fallen down, and could not utter a word more for laughing.

"This seemed a strange thing to me, for I had never heard a Christian man, much less a woman, laugh when the talk was of the bodily Satan himself. So I asked what there was so pleasant in the thought? whereupon she related what the young knight Dinnies Kleist had done to save his castle from the robbers. I would not believe her, but while I sat myself down on a bench to drink, the host comes in and confirmed her story. *Summa,* I let the conversion lie over for a time yet, and set about looking for my comrades, but not finding one, I fell into despair, and resolved to get into Poland, and take service in the army there — especially as all my money had vanished."

Here the old parson said that Sidonia cried out, "How now, sir knave, you are going to buy castle and lands forsooth, and have no money? Truly the base villain is deceiving me yet again."

But my knave answered, "Alas! woe that thou shouldst think so hardly of me! Have I not told thee that my father is going to give me my heritage? So listen further what I tell thee: — In Poland I met with Konnemann and Stephen Pruski, who had one of my wagons with them, in which all my gold was hid, and when I threatened to complain to the authorities, the cowards let me have my own property again, on condition that I would take them into my service, when I went to live at my own castle. This I promised; therefore they are here with me, as you see. And Konnemann went lately to my father at my request, and brought me back the joyful intelligence that he would assign me over my portion of his goods and property."

So far the Pastor Rehewinkelensis heard. What follows concerning the wicked knave was related by his own sorrowing father to my worthy father-in-law, along with other pious priests, and from him I had the story when I visited him at Marienfliess.

For what was my knave's next act? When he returned to the town, and heard from his comrades that the coachman of Saatzig was snoring away there in the stable with open mouth, he stuffed in some hay to prevent him screaming, and tied him hands and feet, then drew his horses out of the stall, yoked them to the carriage, and drove it himself a little piece out of the town down into the hollow, then went back for Sidonia, telling her that her stupid coachman had made some mistake and driven off without her, but he had put all her baggage on his own carriage, which was now quite ready, if she would walk with him a little way just outside the town. Hereupon she paid the reckoning, mine host troubling himself little about the affair of the wagon, and they set off on foot.

When they reached the carriage, Sidonia asked if all her baggage were really there, for she could not see in the darkness. And when she felt, and reckoned all her bundles and trunks, and found all right, my knave said, "Now, she saw herself that he meant truly by her. Here was even a nice place made in the straw sack for her, where he had sat down first himself, that she might have an easy seat. *Item,* she now saw his own carriage which he had fished up in Poland and kept till now, that he might travel in it to Bruchhausen to receive his heritage, and he was going there this very night. She saw that he had lied in nothing."

Whereupon Sidonia got into the carriage with him, never discovering his knavery on account of the darkness, and about midnight they reached the inn at Bruchhausen.

Chapter XVIII

How a new leaf is turned over at Bruchhausen in a very fearful manner — Old Appelmann takes his worthless son prisoner, and admonishes him to repentance — Of Johann's wonderful conversion, and execution next morning in the churchyard, Sidonia being present thereby

My knave halted a little way before they reached the inn, for he had his suspicions that all was not quite right, and sent on the forenamed Pruski to ascertain whether the money was really come for him. For there was a bright light in the tap-room, and the sound of many voices, which was strange, seeing that it was late enough for everyone to be in bed. Pruski was back again soon — yes, it was all right. There were men in there from Stargard, who said they had brought gold for the young burgomaster.

Marry! how my knave jumped down from the carriage, and brought Sidonia along with him, bidding Pruski to stay and watch the things. But, behold, as my knave entered, six men seized him, bound him firmly, and bid him sit down quietly on a bench by the table, till his father arrived. So he cursed and swore, but this was no help to him; and when Sidonia saw that she had been deceived again, she tried to slip out and get to the carriage, but the men stopped her, saying, unless she wished a pair of handcuffs on, she had better sit down quietly on another bench opposite Johann. And she asked in vain what all this meant. *Item,* my knave asked in vain, but no one answered them.

They had not long been waiting, when a carriage stopped before the door, more voices were heard, and, alas! who should enter but the old burgomaster himself, with Mag. Vito, Diaconus of St. John's. And after them came the executioner, with six assistants bearing a black coffin.

My knave now turned as white as a corpse, and trembled like an aspen leaf; no word could he utter, but fell with his back against the wall. Then a dead silence reigned throughout the chamber, and Sidonia looked as white as her paramour.

When the assistants had placed the coffin on the ground, the old father advanced to the table, and spake thus — "Oh, thou fallen and godless child! thou thrice lost son! how often have I sought to turn thee from evil, and trusted in thy promises; but in place of better, thou hast grown worse, and wickedness has increased in thee day by day, as poison in the young viper. On thy infamous hands lie so many robberies, murders, and seductions, that they cannot be reckoned. I speak not of past years, for then truly the night would not be long enough to count them; I speak only of thy last deeds in Poland, as old Elias von Wedel related them to me yesterday in Stargard. Deny, if thou darest, here in the face of thy death and thy coffin, how thou didst join thyself to the Lansquenets in Poland, and then along with two vile fellows got entrance into Lembrowo, telling the old castellan, Elias von Wedel, that thou wast a laborer, upon which he took thee into his service. But at night thou (O wicked son!) didst rise up and beat the old Elias almost unto death, demanding all his money, which, when he refused, thou and thy robber villains seized his cattle and his horses, and drove them away with thee. *Item,* canst thou deny that on meeting the same old Elias at Norenberg by the hunt in the forest, thou didst mock him, and ask, would he sell his castle of Lembrowo in Poland, for thou wouldst buy it of him, seeing thy father had promised thee plenty of gold?

"*Item,* canst thou deny having written me a threatening letter, declaring that if by this very night a hundred dollars were not sent to thee here at Bruchhausen, a red beacon should rise up from my sheepfolds and barns, which meant nothing else than that thou wouldst burn the whole good town of Stargard, for thou knowest well that all the sheepfolds and barns of the burghers adjoin one to the other? Canst thou deny this, O thou lost son? If so, deny it now."

Here Johann began again with his old knavery. He wept, and threw himself on the ground, crawling under the table to get to his father's feet, then howled forth, that he repented of his sins, and would lead a better life truly for the future, if his hard, stern father would only forgive him now.

But Sidonia screamed aloud, and as the burgomaster in his sorrow had not observed her before, he turned his eyes now on her, and exclaimed, "Woe, alas! thou godless son, hast thou this noble maiden with thee yet? I thought she was at Saatzig; or perchance thou hast made her thy wife?"

Ille. — "Alas, no; but he would marry her soon, to make amends for the wrong he had done her."

Hic. — "This thou hast ten times promised, but in vain, and thy sins have increased a hundredfold; because, like all profligates, thou hast shunned the holy estate of matrimony, and preferred to wallow in the mire of unchastity, with anyone who fell in the way of thy adulterous and licentious eyes."

Ille. — "Alas! his heart's dearest father was right; but he would amend his evil life; and, in proof of it, let the reverend deacon, M. Vitus, here present, wed him now instantly to Sidonia."

Hic. — "It is too late. I counsel thee rather to wed thy poor soul to the holy Saviour, like the repentant thief on the cross. See — here is a priest, and there is a coffin."

Here the executioner broke in upon the old, deeply afflicted father, telling him the coffin was too short, as, indeed, his worship had told him, but he would not believe the young man was so tall. Where could he put the head? It must be stuck between his feet, or under his arm, cried out another. So some proposed one thing and some another, till a great uproar arose.

Upon which the old mourning father cried out — "Do you want to break my heart? Is there not time enough to talk of this after?"

Then he turned again to his profligate son, and asked him —

"Would he not repent, and take the holy body and blood of our Lord and Saviour Jesus Christ, as a passport with him on this long journey?

If so, let him go into the little room and pray with the priest, and repent of his sins; there was yet time."

Ille. — "Alas, he had repented already. What had he ever done so wicked that his own bodily father should thirst after his blood? The courts were all closed, and law or justice could no man have in all Pomerania. What wonder then if club-law and the right of the strongest should obtain in all places, as in the olden time?"

Hic. — "That law and justice had ceased in the land was, alas! but too true. However, he was not to answer for this, but his princely Grace of Stettin. And because they had ceased in the land, was he, as an upright magistrate, called upon to do his duty yet more sternly, even though the criminal were his own born son. For the Lord, the just Judge, the Almighty and jealous God, called to him daily, from His holy Word — 'Ye shall not respect persons in judgment, nor be afraid of the face of man; for the judgment is God's.'* Woe to the land's Prince who had not considered this, but compelled him, the miserable judge, to steep his father's hands in the blood of his own son. But righteous Abraham conquered through faith, because he was obedient unto God, and bound his own innocent son upon the altar, and drew forth his knife to slay him. Therefore he, too, would conquer through faith, if he bound his *guilty* son, and drew out the sword against him, obedient to the words of the Lord. Therefore let him prepare himself for death, and follow the priest into the adjoining little chamber."

When Johann found that his father could in no wise be softened, he began horribly to curse him and the hour of his birth, so that the hair of all who heard him stood on end. And he called the devil to help him, and adjured him to come and carry away this fierce and unnatural father, who was more bloodthirsty than the wild beasts of the forest — for who had ever heard that they murdered their own blood?

"Come, devil," he screamed; "come, devil, and tear this bloodthirsty monster of a father to pieces before my eyes, so will I give myself to thee, body and soul! Hearest thou, Satan! Come and destroy my father, and all who have here come out to murder me, only leave me a little while longer in this life to do thy service, and then I am thine for eternity!"

Now all eyes were turned in fear and horror to the door, but no Satan entered, for the just God would not permit it, else, methinks, he would have run to catch such a morsel for his supper. However, the old man trembled, and seemed dwindling away into nothing before the eyes of the bystanders as his son uttered the curse. But he soon recovered, and

---

* Deut. i. 17.

laying his quivering hands upon the head of the imprecator, broke forth
into loud weeping, while he prayed thus —

"O Thou just and Almighty God, who bringest the devices of the
wicked to naught, close Thine ears against this horrible curse of my false
son; remember Thine own word — 'Into an evil soul wisdom cannot
enter, nor dwell in a body subject unto sin.'* Thou alone canst make
the sinful soul wise, and the body of sin a temple of the Holy Ghost.
O Lord Jesus Christ, hast Thou no drop of living water, no crumb of
strengthening manna for this sinful and foolish soul? Hast Thou no
glance of Thy holy eyes for this denying Peter, that he may go forth and
weep bitterly? Hast Thou no word to strike the heart of this dying thief
— of this lost son, who, here bound for death, has cursed his own father,
and given himself up, body and soul, to the enemy of mankind? O
blessed Spirit, who comest and goest as the wind, enter the heavenly
temple, which is yet the work of Thy hands, and make it, by Thy
presence, a temple of the Most High! O Lord God, dwell there but one
moment, that so in his death-anguish he may feel the sweetness of Thy
presence, and the heaven-high comfort of Thy promise! O Thou Holy
Trinity, who hast kept my steps from falling, through so much care and
trouble, through so much shame and disgrace, through so much watching and tears, and even now through these terrible curses of my son,
come and say Amen to this my last blessing, which I, poor father, give
him for his curse.

"Yes, Johann; the Lord bless thee and keep thee in the death hour.
The Lord shed his grace on thee, and give thee peace in thy last agonies!

"Yes, Johann; the Lord bless thee and keep thee, and give thee peace
upon earth, and peace above the earth! Amen, amen, amen!"

When the trembling old man had so prayed, many wept aloud, and
his son trembled likewise, and followed the priest, silently and humbly,
into the neighboring chamber.

Then the old man turned to Sidonia, and asked why she had left her
worthy cousin Marcus of Saatzig?

Upon which she told him, weeping, how his son had deceived her,
in order to get her once more into his power, in order that he might
rob her, and all she wanted now was to be let go her way in peace to her
farmhouses in Zachow.

But this the old man refused.

"No; this must not be yet. She was as evil-minded as his own son,
and needed an example to warn her from sin. Not a step should she
move till his head was off."

---

* Wisdom i. 4.

And, for this purpose, he bid two burghers seize hold of her by the hands, and carry her to the scaffold when the execution was going to take place. The grave must be nearly ready now, which he bade them dig in a corner of the churchyard close by, and he had ordered a car-load of sand likewise to be laid down there, for the execution should take place in the churchyard.

Meanwhile the poor criminal has come out of the inner chamber with M. Vitus, and going up to the bench where the poor father had sunk down exhausted by emotion, he flings himself at his feet, exclaiming, with the prodigal son in the parable —

"Father, I have sinned before heaven and in thy sight, and am no more worthy to be called thy son."

Then he kissed his feet, and bedewed them with his tears.

Now the father thought this was all pretence, as formerly, so he gave no answer. Upon which the poor sinner rose up, and reached his hand to each one in the chamber, praying their forgiveness for all the evil he had done, but which he was now going to expiate in his blood. *Item*, he advanced to Sidonia, sighing —

"Would not she too forgive him, for the love of God? Woe, alas! She had more to forgive than anyone; but would not she give him her pardon, for some comfort on this last journey; and so would he bear her remembrance before the throne of God?"

But Sidonia pushed away his hand.

"He should be ashamed of such old-womanish weakness. Did he not see that his father was only trying to frighten him? For were he in earnest, then were he more cruel even than her own unnatural father, who, though he had only left her two cabins in Zachow, out of all his great riches, yet had left her, at least, her poor life."

Hereupon the poor sinner made answer —

"Not so; I know my father; he is not cruel; what he does is right; therefore I willingly die, trusting in my blessed Saviour, whose body will sanctify my body in the grave. For had I committed no other sin, yet the curse I uttered just now is alone sufficient to make me worthy of death, as it is written — 'He that curseth father or mother shall surely be put to death.'"*

When the old man heard suchlike words, he resolved to put his son's sincerity to the test, for truly it seemed to him impossible that the Almighty God should so suddenly make the crooked straight, and the dead to live, and a child of heaven out of a child of hell. So he spake —

---

* Exodus xxi. 17.

"Thy repentance seemeth good unto me, my son, what sayest thou? will it last, think you, if I now bestow thy life on thee?"

Hereat Sidonia laughed aloud, exclaiming —

"Said I not right? It was all a jest of thy dear father's." But the poor sinner would not turn again to his wallowing in the mire. He sat down upon a bench, covering his face with his hands, and sobbed aloud. At last he answered —

"Alas! father, life is sweet and death is bitter; but since the Holy Spirit hath entered into me with the body of our Lord, I say, death is sweet and life is bitter. No; off with my head! 'I find a law in my members warring against the law of my spirit, and making me a prisoner under the law of sin;'* for if I see my neighbor rich and I am poor, then the demon of covetousness rises in me, and my fingers itch to seize my share. Or, if the foaming flask is before me, how can I resist to drain it, for the spirit of gluttony is within me? Or, if I see a maiden, the blood throbs in my veins, and the demon of lust has taken possession of me. 'Oh, wretched man that I am, who will deliver me from the body of this death?' You will, dearest father. You will release me from this life, as you once gave it to me, for it is now a life in death. Ah! show mercy! Come quickly, and release me from the body of this death!"

When he ceased, the old man sprung up like a youth, and pressing his lost son to his heart, sobbed forth like him of the Gospel —

"O friends, see! 'This my son was dead, but is alive again; he was lost, and is found.' Yea, yea, see all that nothing is impossible with God. O Thou Holy Trinity, Father, Son, and Holy Spirit, now I have nothing more to ask, but that I too may soon be released from the body of this death, and go forth to meet my new-found son amidst the bright circle of the Holy Angels."

Then the son answered —

"Let me go now, father. See, the morning dawn shines already through the window; so hath the loving mercy of my God come to me, who sat in darkness and the shadow of death. Farewell, father; let me go now. Away with this head in the clear early morning light, so that my feet be fixed forevermore upon the path to peace."

And so speaking, he seized M. Vitus by the hand, who was sobbing loudly, as well as most of the burghers, and the executioner with his assistants bearing the coffin were going to follow, when the old man, who had sunk down upon a bench, called back his son, though he had already gone out at the door, and prayed the executioner to let him stay one little while longer. For he remembered that his son had a welt upon

---

* Romans vii. 23.

his neck, and he must see whether it would interfere with the sword. Woe, woe! if he should have to strike twice or thrice before the head fell!

So the executioner removed the neck-cloth from the poor sinner (who, by the great mercy of God, was stronger than any of them), and having felt the welt, said —

"No; the welt was close up to the head, but he would take the neck in the middle, as indeed was his usual custom. His worship may make his mind quite easy; he would stake his life on it that the head would fall with the first blow. This was his one hundred and fiftieth, and he never yet had failed."

Then the unhappy criminal tied his cravat on again, took M. Vitus by the hand, and said —

"Farewell, my father; once more forgive me for all that I have done!"

After which he went out quickly, without waiting to hear a word more from his father, and the executioner followed him.

Meanwhile the afflicted father was sore troubled in mind. Three times he repeated the text — "Ye shall not respect persons in judgment, nor be afraid of the face of man, for the judgment is God's." Then he called upon God to forgive the Prince who, by taking away law and justice from the land, had obliged him to be the judge and condemner of his son. How the Lord dealt with the Prince we shall hear farther on. One while he sent mine host to look over the hedge, and tell him if the head were off yet. Then he would begin to pray that he might soon follow this poor son, who had never given him one moment of joy but through his death, and pass quickly after him through the vale of tears.

The son, however, is steadfast unto the end. For when they reached the churchyard, he stood still a while gazing on the heap of sand. Then he desired to be led to the spot where his grave was dug; and near this same grave there being a tombstone, on which was figured a man kneeling before a crucifix, he asked —

"Who was to share his grave bed here?"

Whereupon M. Vitus replied —

"He was a *rector scholæ* out of Stargard, a very learned man, who had retired from active life, and settled down here at Bruchhausen, where he died not long since."

Whereat the poor sinner stood still a while, and then repeated this beautiful distich, no doubt by the inspiration of the Holy Ghost, to warn all learned sinners against that demon of pride and vain-glory which too often takes possession of them.

"Quid juvat innumeros scire atque evolvere casus
  Si facieuda fugis et fugienda facis?"*

Then he looked calmly at his grave, and only prayed the executioner not to put his head between his feet; after which he returned to the sand-heap and exclaimed —

"Now to God!"

Upon which, M. Vitus blessed him yet again, and spake —

"O God, Father, who hast brought back this lost son, and filled this foolish soul with wisdom; ah! Jesus, Saviour, who, in truth, hast turned Thy holy eyes on him as on the denying Peter and on the dying thief. O Holy Spirit, who hast not scorned to make this poor vessel a temple for Thyself to dwell in, that in the death-anguish this sinner may find the sweetness of Thy presence and the heaven-high comfort of Thy promises! O Thou Holy Trinity — to Thee — to Thee — to Thee — to Thy grace, Thy power, Thy protection, we resign this dying mortal in his last agonies. Help him, Lord God! *Kyrie Eleison!* Give Thy holy angels command to bear this poor soul into Abraham's bosom. O come, Lord Jesus; help him, O Lord our God. *Kyrie Eleison!* Amen."

And hereupon he pronounced a last blessing over him. And when the executioner took off his upper garment and bound the kerchief over his eyes, M. Vitus again spake —

"Think on the holy martyrs, of whom Basilius Magnus testifies that they exclaimed, when undressing for their death — *Non vestes exuimus, sed veterem hommem deponimus.*"[*]

Upon which he answered from under the kerchief something in Latin, but the executioner had laid the cloth so thickly even over his mouth and chin, that no one could catch the words. Then he kneeled down, and while the executioner drew his sword, M. Vitus chanted —

"When my lips no more can speak,
    May Thy Spirit in me cry;
When my eyes are faint and weak,
    May my soul see Heaven nigh!

When my heart is sore dismayed,
    This dying frame has lost its strength,
May my spirit, with Thy aid,
    Cry — Jesu, take me home at length!"

---

‡ "What is the use of knowledge and all our infinite learning,
    If we fly what is right and do what we ought to fly?"

* "We lay not off our clothes, but the old man." — Basil the Great, Archbishop of Caesarea, A.D. 379.

And all who stood round saw, as it were, a wonderful sign from God; for as the executioner let the sword fall, head and sun appeared at the same moment — the head upon the earth, the sun above the earth; and there was a deep silence. Sidonia alone laughed out loud, and cried, "So ends the conversion!" And while the psalm was singing, "Now, pray we to the Holy Ghost," the executioner acting as clerk, she disappeared, and for thirty years, as we shall hear presently, no one could ascertain where she went to or how she lived; though sometimes, like a horrible ghost, she was seen occasionally here and there.

Summa. — The miserable criminal was laid in his coffin, and as, in truth, it was too short for the corpse, and the poor sinner had requested that his head might not be placed between his feet, so it was laid upon his chest, with his hands folded over it, and thus he was buried.

The old father rejoiced greatly that his son remained steadfast in the truth until the last, and thanked God for it. Then he returned to Stargard; and I may just mention, to conclude concerning him, that the merciful God heard the prayer of this His faithful servant, for he scarcely survived his son a year, but, after a short illness, fell asleep in Jesus.*

Chapter XIX

Of Sidonia's disappearance for thirty years — Item, how the young Princess Elizabeth Magdelene was possessed by a devil, and of the sudden death of her father, Ernest Ludovicus of Pomerania

I have said that Sidonia disappeared after the execution at Bruch-hausen, and that for thirty years no one knew where she lived or how she lived. At her farmhouse at Zachow she never appeared; but the *Acta Criminalia* set forth that during that period she wandered about the

---

* For further particulars concerning this truly worthy man, who may well be called the Pomeranian Manlius, see Friedeborn, "Description of Old Stettin," vol. ii. p. 113; and Barthold, "Pomeranian History," pp. 46, 419.

towns of Freienwald, Regenwald, Stargard, and other places, in company with Peter Konnemann and divers other knaves.

However, the ducal prosecutor, although he instituted the strictest inquiries at the period of her trial, could ascertain nothing beyond this, except that, in consequence of her evil habits and licentious tongue, she was held everywhere in fear and abhorrence, and was chased away from every place she entered after about six or eight o'clock. Further, that some misfortune always fell upon everyone who had dealings with her, particularly young married people. To the said Konnemann, she betrothed herself after the death of her first paramour, but afterwards gave him fifty florins to get rid of the contract, as she confessed at the seventeenth question upon the rack, according to the *Actis Lothmanni.* Meantime her brother and cousins were so completely turned against her, that her brother even took those two farmhouses to himself; and though Sidonia wrote to him, begging that an annuity might be settled on her, yet she never received a line in answer — and this was the manner in which the whole cousinhood treated her in her despair and poverty.

I myself made many inquiries as to her mode of life during those thirty years, but in vain. Some said that she went into Poland and there kept a little tavern for twenty years; some had seen her living at Riigen at the old wall, where in heathen times the goddess Hertha was honored. Some said she went to Riiden, a little uninhabited island between Riigen and Usdom, where the wild geese and other birds flock in the molting season and drop their feathers. Thence, they said, she gathered the eggs, and killed the birds with clubs. At least this was the story of the Usdom fishermen, but whether it were Sidonia or some other outcast woman, I cannot in strict verity declare. Only in Freienwald did I hear for certain that she lived there twelve years with some earl whom she called her shield-knight; but one day they quarreled, and beat each other till the blood flowed, after which they both ran out of the town, and went different ways.

Summa. — On the 1st of May 1592, when the witches gather in the Brocken to hold their Walpurgis night, and the princely castle of Wolgast was well guarded from the evil one by white and black crosses placed on every door, an old wrinkled hag was seen about eight o'clock of the morning (just the time she had returned from the Blocksberg, according to my thinking), walking slowly up and down the great corridor of the princely castle. And the providence of the great God so willed it that at that moment the young and beautiful Princess Elizabeth Magdalena (who had been betrothed to the Duke Frederick of Courland) opened her chamber-door and slipped forth to pay her morning greetings to her illustrious father, Duke Ernest, and his spouse, the Lady Sophia

Hedwig of Brunswick, who sat together drinking their warm beer,* and had sent for her.

So the hag advanced with much friendliness and cried out, "Hey, what a beautiful young damsel! But her lord papa was called 'the handsome' in his time, and wasn't she as like him as one egg to another. Might she take her ladyship's little hand and kiss it?" Now as the hag was bold in her bearing, and the young Princess was a timid thing, she feared to refuse; so she reached forth her hand, alas! to the witch, who first three times blew on it, murmuring some words before she kissed it; then as the young Princess asked her who she was and what she wanted, the evil hag answered, "I would speak with your gracious father, for I have known him well. Ask his princely Grace to come to me, for I have somewhat to say to him." Now the Princess, in her simplicity, omitted to ask the hag's name, whereby much evil came to pass, for had she told her gracious father that SIDONIA wished to speak to him, assuredly he never would have come forth, and that fatal and malignant glance of the witch would not have fallen upon him.

However, his Serene Grace, having a mild Christian nature, stepped out into the corridor at the request of his dear daughter, and asked the hag who she was and what she wanted. Upon this, she fixed her eyes on him in silence for a long while, so that he shuddered, and his blood seemed to turn to ice in his veins.† At last she spake: "It is a strange thing, truly, that your Grace should no longer remember the maiden to whom you once promised marriage." At this his Grace recoiled in horror, and exclaimed, "Ha, Sidonia! but how you are changed." "Ah!" she answered, with a scornful laugh, "you may well triumph, now that my cheek is hollow, and my beauty gone, and that I have come to you for justice against my own brother in Stramehl, who denies me even the means of subsistence – you, who brought me to this pass."

Upon which his Grace answered that her brother was a subject of the Duke of Stettin. Let her go then to Stettin, and demand justice there.

Illa. – "She had been there, but the Duke refused to see her, and to her request for a *proebenda* in the convent of Marienfliess had returned no answer. She prayed his Grace, therefore, out of old good friendship, to take up her cause, and use his influence with the Lord Duke of Stettin

---

* Before the introduction of coffee or chocolate, warm beer was in general use at breakfast.

† This belief in the witchcraft of a glance was very general during the witch period. And even the ancients notice it (Pliny, Hist. Nat. vii. 2), also Aul. Gell. Noct. Attic, ix. 4; and Virgil, Eclog. in. 103. The glance of a woman with double pupils was particularly feared.

to obtain the *proebenda* for her, also to send a good scolding to her brother at Stramehl under his own hand."

Now my gracious Prince was so anxious to get rid of her, that he promised everything she asked. Whereupon she would kiss his hand, but he drew it back shuddering, upon which she went down the great castle steps again, murmuring to herself.

But her wickedness soon came to light; for mark — scarcely a few days had passed over, when the beautiful young Princess was possessed by Satan; she rolls herself upon the ground, twists and writhes her hands and feet, speaks with a great coarse voice like a common carl, blasphemes God and her parents; and what was more wonderful than all, her throat swelled, and when they laid their hand on it, something living seemed creeping up and down in it. Then it went up to her mouth, and her tongue swelled so, that her eyes seemed starting from their sockets, and the gracious young lady became fearful to look at.

Item, then she began to speak Latin, though she had never learned this tongue, whereupon many, and in particular Mag. Michael Aspius, the court chaplain (for Dr. Gerschovius was long since dead) pronounced that Satan himself verily must be in the maiden.* This was

---

* The ancients name three distinguishing marks of demoniacal possession: —

    1st, When the patient blasphemes God and cannot repeat the leading articles of his Christian belief.

    2nd, When he foretells events which afterwards come to pass.

    3rd, When he speaks in a strange tongue, which it can be proved he never learned.

    Now the somnambulists of our day fulfill the second and third conditions without dispute; and some account for the divining power by saying it is the effect of the increased activity of the soul. They also assert that the patient speaks in a strange tongue only when the magnetizer with whom he is in *en rapport* understands the tongue himself, and the patient speaks it because all the thoughts, feelings, words, &c., of the operator become his — in short, their souls become one. This explanation, however, is very improbable, and has not been confirmed by facts; for the phenomenon of speaking in a strange tongue often appears before a perfect *rapport* has been obtained between the patient and the operator. Indeed, Psellus gives an instance to show that it is not even at all necessary. (Psellus lived about the eleventh century, and wrote *De Operatione Doemonum,* also *De Mysteriis Ægyptiorum,* his works are very remarkable, and well worth a perusal.) He states that a sick woman all at once began to speak in a strange and barbarous tongue no one had ever heard before. At last some of the women about her brought an Armenian magician to see her, who instantly found that she spoke Armenian, though she had never in her life beheld one of that nation. Psellus describes him as an old lean wrinkled man. He acted quite differently from our modern magnetizers, for he never sought to place himself in sympathetic relation with her by passes or touches; on the contrary, he drew his sword, and placing himself beside the bed, began tittering the most harsh and cruel words he could think of in the Armenian tongue *(acriter conviciatus est).* The woman retorted in the Armenian tongue likewise, and tried to get out of

fully proved on the following Sunday; for during divine service in the Church of St. Peter, the young Princess was carried in on a litter and laid down before the altar, whereupon she commenced uttering horrible blasphemies, and mocking the holy prayer in a coarse bass voice, while she foamed and raged so violently, that eight men could scarcely hold her in her bed. Whereat the whole Christian congregation were admonished to pray to the Lord for this poor maiden, that she might be freed from the devil within her; and during the week all priests throughout the land were commanded to offer up prayers day and night for her princely Grace. But on Sundays all the people were to unite in one common supplication to the throne of grace for the like object.

And it seemed, after some weeks, as if God had heard their prayers, and commanded Satan to leave the body of the young maiden, for she had now rest for fourteen days, and was able to pray again. Also her rosy cheeks began to bloom once more, so that her parents were filled with joy, and resolved to hold a thank-festival throughout the land, and receive the Holy Sacrament in St. Peter's Church with their beloved daughter.

But what happened? For as the godly discourse had ended, and their Graces stepped to the altar to make a rich offering on the plate which lay upon the little desk, free of approach from all sides, my knave Satan has again begun his work. Truly, he waited with cunning till her Grace had swallowed the Sacrament, that his blasphemies might seem more horrible. And this was the way he manifested himself.

After the court marshal and the castellan had laid down a black velvet carpet, embroidered in gold with the Pomeranian and Brandenburg arms, for their Graces to kneel upon, they took another black velvet cloth, on which the Holy Supper was represented embroidered in silver, to hold before their Graces like a serviette, while they received the blessed elements. Then advanced the priest with the Sacrament, but scarcely had the gracious young Princess swallowed the same, when she uttered a loud cry and fell backwards with her head upon the ground, while Satan raged so in her that it might have melted the heart of a stone.

So M. Aspius bade the organ cease, and then placed the young lady upon a seat, after which he called upon their Graces and the whole

---

bed to fight with him. Then the barbarian grew as if mad, and endeavored to stab her, upon which she shrunk back terrified and trembling, and soon fell into a deep sleep. Psellus seems to have witnessed this, for he says the woman was wife to his eldest brother. As further regards demoniacal possession, the New Testament is full of examples thereof; and though in the last century the reality of the fact was assailed, yet Franz Meyer has again defended it with arguments that cannot be overthrown. Remarkable examples of possession in modern times we find in the *Didiskalia*, No. 81, of the year 1833, and in Berner's "History of Satanic Possession," p. 20.

congregation to join him in offering up a prayer. Then he solemnly adjured the evil spirit to come out of her; it, however, had grown so daring that it only laughed at the priest; and when asked where it had been for so long, and in particular where it had lain while the Jesu bride was wedded to her Holy Saviour in the Blessed Sacrament, it impatiently answered that it had lain under her tongue; many knaves might lie under a bridge while an honorable seigneur passed overhead, and why should not it do the like? And here, to the unspeakable horror of the whole congregation, it seemed to move up and down in the chest and throat of the young Princess, like some animal.

But the long-suffering of God was now at an end, for while the Reverend Dr. Aspius was talking himself weary with adjurations, and gaining no good by it, for the evil spirit only mocked and jeered him, crying, "Look at the fat parson how he sweats, maybe it will help as much as his chattering over the wine," who should enter the church (sent no doubt by the all-merciful God) but the Reverend Dr. Joel, Professor at Grypswald, for he had heard how this lusty Satan had taken possession of the princely maiden. When the devil saw him, he began to tremble through all the limbs of the young Princess, and exclaimed in Latin, *"Consummatum est."** For this Dr. Joel was a powerful man, and learned in all the cunning shifts of the arch-enemy, having many times disputed de Magis.†

Now when he advanced to the young Princess, and saw how the evil spirit ran up and down her poor form, like a mouse in a net, he was filled with horror, and removing his hat, exclaimed, without taking much heed of his Latin, *"Deus misereatur peccatoris."* Upon which the devil, in a deep bass voice, corrected him, crying, *"Die peccatricls, die peccatricls."*‡

However, Satan himself felt that his hour had come; for when Doctor Joel laid his hand upon the maiden, and repeated a powerful adjuration from the *Clavilcula Salomonis,* Satan immediately promised to obey if he were allowed to take away the oblation-cloth which lay upon the desk.

Ille. — "What did he want with the oblation-cloth?"

Satanas. — "There was a coin in it which vexed him."

Ille. — "What coin could it be, and wherefore did it vex him?"

Satanas. — "He would not say."

Ille. — (Adjures him again.)

Satanas. — "Let him have it, or he would tear the young maiden to pieces." And here he began to foam and rage so horribly, that her eyes

---

*   "It is over."

†   Of Witchcraft; see Barthold, iv. 2, 412.

‡   Peccatoris is masculine, Peccatricis feminine.

turned in her head, and she gnashed with her teeth, so that father and
mother had to cover their eyes not to see her great agony. Whereupon
Doctor Joel bent down and wrote with his finger upon her breast the
Tetragrammaton, crying out − *

"Away, thou unclean spirit, and give place to the Holy Ghost!"

Upon which the young maiden sank down as quiet as a corpse, and
the oblation-cloth, which lay upon the desk, whirled round of itself in
the middle of the church with great noise and clatter, as if seized by a
storm-wind, and the money therein was all scattered about the church,
so that the old wives who sat upon the benches fell down upon the
floor, right and left, to try and catch it. Great horror and amazement
now filled the whole congregation; yet as some had expressed an opinion
that the young Princess was only afflicted by a sickness, and not
possessed at all, Doctor Joel thought it needful to admonish them in
the following words: −

"Those wise persons who, forsooth, would not credit such a thing as
Satanic possession, might see now of a truth, by the oblation-cloth, that
Satan bodily had been amongst them. He knew there were many such
wise knaves in the church; therefore let them hold their tongue forevermore, and remember that such signs had been permitted before of God,
to testify of the real bodily presence of the devil. Example (Matt. viii.),
where, on the command of Christ, a legion of devils went into the swine
of the Gergasenes; so that these animals, contrary to their nature, ran
down into the sea and were drowned. But the wise people of this day
little heed these divine signs; so he will add two from historical records
which he happened to remember.

"First, the Jew Josephus relates that, in presence of the world-re-
nowned Roman captain Vespasian, of his son Titus, also of all the
officers and troops of the army, an acquaintance of his, by name Eleazer,
adjured the devil out of one possessed by means of the ring of Solomon,
repeating at the same time the powerful spell which, no doubt, the great
king himself employed to control the demons, and which, probably,
was the very one he had just now exorcised the devil with, out of the
Clavicula Salomonis. And to show the bystanders that it was indeed a
devil which he had exorcised out of the nose of the patient, the said
Eleazer bid him, as he was passing, to overturn a vessel of water that lay
there, which indeed was done, to the great wonderment of all present.
Thus even the blind heathen were convinced, though the would-be wise
of the present day ignorantly doubted.

---

* The four letters which compose the name Jehovah. It was employed by the Theurgists
in all their most powerful conjurations.

"But people might say this happened in old times, and was only told by a stupid Jew; therefore he would give a modern example.

"There was a woman named Kronisha (she was still well remembered by the old people of Stralsund), who was sorely given to pomp and vanity, wherefore a devil was sent into her to punish her; and after the preacher at St. Nicholas had exorcised him to the best of his power, the wicked spirit said, mockingly, that he would go if they gave him a pane of glass out of the window over the tower door; and this being granted, one of the panes was instantly scattered with a loud clang, and the devil flew away through the opening.*

"So the Christian congregation might now see what silly fools these wise people were who presumed to doubt," &c. Then Doctor Joel admonished the Prince himself to keep a diligent eye over this Satan, who, day by day, was growing more impudent in the land — no doubt because the pure doctrine of Dr. Luther vexed him sorely.

And indeed his Highness, to show his gratitude for the recovery of his dear daughter, did not cease in his endeavors to banish witches from the land, knowing that Sidonia had brought all the evil upon the young Princess. Fifteen were seized and burned at this time, to the great joy of the country; but, alas! these truly princely and Christian measures little helped among the godless race, for evil seemed still to strengthen in the land, and many wonderful signs appeared, one of which I would not set down here, as it was only seen by the court-fool, but that events confirmed it.

I mean that strange thing, along with a three-legged hare, which appeared eighty years before at the death of Duke Bogislaus the Great, and since at the death of each Duke of his house. By a strange whim of Satan's, this apparition was only visible to fools; until indeed (as we shall hear anon) it appeared to the nuns at Marienfliess, who bore witness of it.

Summa. — On the very day wherein the devil's brides were burned at Wolgast, the fool was walking at evening time up and down the great corridor, when a little manikin, hardly three hands high, started out from behind a beer-barrel, riding on a three-legged hare. He was dressed all in black, except little red boots which he had on, and he rides up and down the corridor — hop! hop! hop! — stares at my fool and makes a face at him; then rides off again — hop! hop! hop! — till he vanished behind the barrel.

No one would believe the fool's story; but woe, alas! it soon became clear what the little manikin Puck denoted. For my gracious Prince, who

---

* See Sastrowen, his family, birth, and adventures. Edited by Mohnike, part i. 73.

had grown quite weak ever since this horrible witch-work, which had been raging for some weeks – so that Pomerania never had seen the like – became daily worse, and not even the fine Falernian wine from Italy, which used to cure him, helped him now. So he died on the 17th July 1591, aged forty-six years, seven months, and fifteen days, leaving his only son, Philippus Julius, a child of eight years old, to reign in his place. Whereupon the deeply afflicted widow placed the boy under the tutelage and guardianship of his uncle, the princely Lord of Stettin; but, woe! woe! the guardian must soon follow his dear brother! and all through the evil wickedness of Sidonia, as we shall hear in the following chapters.

Chapter XX

How Sidonia demeans herself at the Convent of Marienfliess — Item, how their Princely and Electoral Graces of Pomerania, Brandenburg, and Mecklenburg, went on sleighs to Wolgast, and of the divers pastimes of the journey

*A*fter this, Sidonia disappeared again for a couple of years, and no man knew whither she had flown or what she did, until one morning she appeared at the convent of Marienfliess, driving a little one-horse wagon herself, and dressed no better than a fish-wife. On driving into the court, she desired to speak with the abbess, Magdalena von Peters-dorf; and when she came, Sidonia ordered the cell of the deceased nun, Barbara Kleist, to be got ready for her reception, as his Highness of Stettin had presented her to a *præbenda* here.

So the pious old abbess believed the story, and forthwith conducted her to the cell, No. 11; but Sidonia spat out at it, said it was a pig-sty, and began to run clattering through all the cells till she reached the refectory, a large chamber where the nuns assembled for evening prayer. This, she said, was the only spot fit for her to put her nose in, and she would keep it for herself. Meanwhile, the whole sisterhood ran together to the refectory to see Sidonia; and as most of them were girls under twenty, they tittered and laughed, as young womenfolk will do when they behold a hag. This angered her.

"Ha!" she exclaimed, "the flesh and the devil have not been destroyed in them yet, but I will soon give them something else to think of than their lovers."

And here, as one of them laughed louder than the rest, Sidonia gave her a blow on the mouth.

"Let that teach the peasant-girl more respect for a castle and land dowered maiden."

When the good abbess saw and heard all this, she nearly fainted with shame, and had to hold by a stool, or she would have fallen to the ground. However she gained fresh courage, when, upon asking for Sidonia's documents, she found that there were none to show. Without more ado, therefore, she bade her leave the convent; and, amidst the jeers and laughter of all the sisterhood, Sidonia was obliged to mount her one-horse cart again, or the convent porter had orders to force her out.

By this all may perceive that, in place of repenting, Sidonia had fallen still further in the mire, wherein she wallowed yet for many years, as if it were, indeed, her true and natural element, like that beetle of which Albertus Magnus speaks, that died if one covered it with rose-leaves, but came to life again when laid in dung.

Hardly had she left the convent-gate when the old abbess bade a carl get ready a carriage, and flew in it to Stettin herself, to lay the whole case before my gracious Prince, and entreat him, even on her knees, not to send such a notorious creature amongst them; for what blessing could the convent hope to obtain if they harbored such an infamous sinner? So his Grace wonders much over the daring of the harlot; for he had given her no *proebenda*, though she was writing to him constantly requesting one. Nor would he ever think of giving her one; for why should he send such a hell-besom to sweep the pious convent of Marienfliess? The good abbess might rise up, for as long as he lived Sidonia should never enter the convent.

And his Grace held by his word, though it cost him his life, as I shall just now relate with bitter sighs.

It happened that, A.D. 1600, there was a terribly hard winter, so that the fresh Haff* was quite frozen over, and able to bear heavy beams. Now, as the ice was smooth and beautiful as a mirror, my Lord of Stettin

---

* The river Haff

proposed to his guests — Joachim Friedrich, Elector of Brandenburg, his brother-in-law, and old Duke Ulrich of Mecklenburg, his uncle, to go over the Haff in sleighs, and pay a visit to the princely widow and her little son.

Their Graces were well pleased at the idea. Whereupon his Highness of Stettin gave orders to have such a procession formed as never had been seen in Pomerania before for magnificence and beauty, and therefore I shall note down some particulars here.

There were a hundred sleighs, some drawn by reindeer caparisoned like horses, and all decorated gaily. The three ducal sleighs in particular were entirely girded and lined with sable skin; each was drawn by four Andalusian horses; and my Lady Erdmuth, who was a great lover of show and pomp, had hers hung with little tinkling bells and chains of gold, so that no one to look at them could imagine how very little of the dear gold her gracious lord and husband had in his purse, by reason of the hardness of the times.

The adornments of the other sleighs were less costly. Upon them came the ministers, the officials, and others pertaining to the retinue of the three princes: *item,* the ladies-in-waiting, and divers of the reverend clergy; last of all came the Duke's henchman, with a pack of wolf-dogs in leash: *item,* several live hares and foxes; a live bear, which they purposed to let slip, for the pleasure and pastime of their Graces. But the young men out of the town, fifty head strong, and many of the knights, ran along on skates, headed by Dinnies Kleist, that mighty man, who bore in one hand the blood-banner of Pomerania, and in the other that of Brandenburg. Barthold von Ramin ran by his side with the Mecklenburg standard. He was a strong knight too. But ah! my God! how my Ramin, with his ox-head, was distanced by the wild men of Pomerania, as they ran upon the ice over the Haff!* Two reserve sleighs, drawn by six Frisian horses, finished the procession; they were laden with axes, planks, ropes, and dry garments, both for men and women.

When their Graces mounted the sleighs amidst the ringing of bells and roaring of cannon, great was their astonishment to see their own initials stamped into the hard ice by Dinnies Kleist, as thus: F. U. J. E. J. F., which, however, afterwards caused much dismay to the honest burghers, for one of them — M. Faber, *a præceptor* — mistaking the J. for

---

* The blood-standard was granted by the Emperor Maximilian II to Duke Johann Friedrich of Pomerania because he carried the imperial banner during the Turkish war of 1566. It only differed from the old banner by having a red ground — from thence its name. Both Pomerania and Brandenburg had wild men in their escutcheon, while Mecklenburg bore an ox's head.

a G., read plainly upon the ice: "Fuge, J. F." — that is, "Fly, Johann Frederick!"

Ah! truly has the gracious Prince flown from thence; but it is to a bitter death.

During the journey, Duke Johann had much jesting with his brother-in-law, the Elector, who was filled with wonder at the strength of Dinnies Kleist, for he kept ahead even of the Andalusian stallions, and waved aloft the two banners of Pomerania and Brandenburg, while his long hair floated behind him; and sometimes he stopped, kissed the banners, and then inclined them to their Serene Princely Graces. Whereupon Duke Johann exclaimed, "Aye, brother, you might well give me a thousand of your wide-mouthed Berliners for this carl; though, methinks, if he had his will, he would make their wide mouths still wider." At this, his Electoral Grace looked rather vexed, and began to uphold the men of Cologne. Upon which his Highness cut him short, saying, "Marry, brother, you know the old proverb —

"'The men of Cologne
   Have no hues of their own,
   But the men of Stettin
   Are the true ever-green.'

For where truly could your fellows find the true green in their sandy dust-box? Marry, cousin, one Pomerania is worth ten Margravates; and I will show your Grace just now that my land in winter is more productive than yours even in autumn."

His Grace here alluded to the fisheries; for along the way, for twelve or fourteen miles, the fishermen had been ordered to set their nets by torchlight the night before, in holes dug through the ice, so that on the arrival of the princely party the nets might be drawn up, and the draft exhibited to their Graces.

Now, when they entered the fresh Haff, which lay before them like a large mirror, six miles long and four broad, his Grace of Pomerania called out —

"See here, brother, this is my first storeroom; let us try what it will give us to eat."

Upon which he signed to Dinnies Kleist to steer over to the first heap of nets, which lay like a black wood in the distance. These belonged to the Ziegenort fishermen, as the old schoolmaster, Peter Leisticow, himself told me; and as they had taken a great draft the day before, many people from the towns of Warp, Stepenitz, and Uckermund were assembled there to buy up the fish, and then retail it, as was their custom, throughout the country. They had made a fire upon a large sheet of iron laid upon the ice, while their horses were feeding close by upon hay, which they shook out before them. And having taken a merry carouse together, they all set to dancing upon the ice with the women to the bagpipe, so that the encampment looked right jovial as their Graces arrived.

Now when the grand train came up, the peasants roared out –

"Donnerwetter,* look at the plötz-eaters! See the cursed plötz-eaters! Donnerwetter, what plötz-eaters!"†

And now they observed, during their shouting, that the water had risen up to their knees; and when the ducal procession rushed up, the abyss re-echoed with a noise like thunder, so that the foreign princes were alarmed, but soon grew accustomed thereto. Then the pressure of such a crowd upon the ice caused the water to spout out of the holes to the height of a man. So that by the time they were two bowshots from the nets, all the folk, the women and children especially, were running, screaming, in every direction, trying to save themselves on the firm ice, to the great amusement of their Graces, while a peasant cried out to the sleigh drivers –

"Stop, stop! or ye'll go into the cellar!"

Hereupon his Grace of Pomerania beckoned over the Ziegenort schoolmaster, and asked him what they had taken, to which he answered –

"Gracious Prince, we have taken bley; the nets are all loaded; we've taken seventy schümers,‡ and your Grace ought to take one with you for supper."

Now his Highness the Elector wished to see the nets emptied, so they rested a space while the peasants shoveled out the fish, and pitched them into the aforesaid schümers. But ah! woe to the fish-thieves who had come over from Warp and other places; for the water having risen up and become all muddy with fish-slime, they never saw the great holes, and tumbled in, to the great amusement of the peasants and pastime of their Graces.

How their Highnesses laughed when the poor carls in the water tried to get hold of a net or a rope or a firm piece of ice, while they floundered

---

* A common oath.

† Plötz-eaters was a nickname given by the Pomeranians to the people of the Margravates. For the plötz (*Cyprinus Exythrophthalmus*) is a very poor tasteless fish, while the rivers of Pomerania are stocked with the very finest of all kinds. In return, the men of the Marks called the Pomeranians "Feather-heads," from the quantity of moor-palms (*Eriophorum vaginatum*) which grow in their numerous rich meadows.

‡ A schümer was a measure which contained twelve bushels.

about in the water, and the peasants fished them up with their long hooks, at the same time giving many of them a sharp prod on the shoulder, crying out —

"Ha! will ye steal again? Take that for your pains, you robbers!"

Now when their Graces were tired laughing and looking at the fish hauled, they prepared to depart; but the schoolmaster prayed his Highness of Stettin yet again to take a schümer of fish for their supper, as their Graces were going to stop for the night in Uckermund.

"But what could I do with all the fish?" quoth the Duke.

To which the carl answered in his jargon —

"Eh! gracious master, give them to the plötz-eaters; that will be something new for them. Never fear but they'll eat them all up!"

Hereupon his Highness the Elector grew nettled, and cried out —

"Ho! thou damned peasant, thinkest thou we have no bley?"

"Well, ye've none here," replied the man cunningly.

So their Graces laughed, and ordered a couple of bushels of the largest to be placed upon the safety sleigh.

Now when they had gone a little farther and found the ice as smooth as glass, the henchman let loose the bear and the wolf-dogs after it. My stout Bruin first growls and paws the ice, then sets himself in earnest for the race, and, on account of his sharp claws, ran on straight for Uckermund without ever slipping, while the hounds fell down on all sides, or tumbled on their backs, howling with rage and disappointment.

Yet more pleasant was the hare-hunt, for hounds and hares both tumbled down together, and the hares squeaked and the hounds yelped; some hares indeed were killed, but only after infinite trouble, while others ran away after the bear.

After the hunt they came to another fishery, and so on till they reached Uckermund, passing six fisheries in succession, whereof each draft was as large as the first, so that his Grace the Elector marveled much at the abundance, and seeing the nets full of zannats at the last halting-place, cried out —

"Marry, brother, your storeroom is well furnished. I might grow dainty here myself. Let us take a bushel of these along with us for supper, for zannat is the fish for me!"

This greatly rejoiced his Grace of Stettin, who ordered the fish to be laid on the sumpter sleigh, and in good time they reached the ducal house at Uckermund, Dinnies Kleist still keeping foremost, and waving his two banners over his head, while Barthold Barnim and the other skaters hung weary and tired upon the backs of the sleighs.

Chapter XXI

How Sidonia meets their Graces upon the ice — Item, how Dinnies Kleist beheads himself, and my gracious lord of Wolgast perishes miserably

*T*he next morning early the whole train set off from Uckermund in the highest spirits, passing net after net, till the Duke of Mecklenburg, as well as the Elector, lifted their hands in astonishment. From the Haff they entered the Pene, and from that the Achterwasser.* Here a great crowd of people stood upon the ice, for the town of Quilitz lay quite near; besides, more fish had been taken here than had yet been seen upon the journey, so that people from Wolgast, Usdom, Lassahn, and all the neighboring towns had run together to bid for it. But what happened?

Alas! that his Grace should have desired to halt, for scarcely had his sleigh stopped, when a little old woman, meanly clad, with fisher's boots, and a net filled with bley-fish in her hand, stepped up to it and said —

"My good Lord, I am Sidonia von Bork; wherefore have you not replied to my demand for the *proebenda* of Barbara von Kleist in Marienfliess?"

"How could he answer her? He knew nothing at all of her mode of living, or where she dwelt."

Illa. — "She had bid him lay the answer upon the altar of St. Jacob's in Stettin. Why had he not done so?"

"That was no place for such letters, only for the words of the Holy Spirit and the Blessed Sacrament of his Saviour; therefore, let her say now where she dwelt."

Illa. — "The richest maiden in Pomerania could ill say where the poorest now dwelt," weeping.

"The richest maiden had only herself to blame if she were now the poorest; better had she wept before. The *proebenda* she could never have; let her cease to think of it; but here was an alms, and she might now go her ways."

---

* A large bay formed by the Pene.

Illa. – (Refuses to take it, and murmurs.) "Your Grace will soon have bitter sorrow for this."

As she so menaced and spat out three times, the thing angered Dinnies Kleist (who held her in abhorrence ever since the adventure in the Uckermund forest), and as he had lost none of his early strength, he hit her a blow with the blood-standard over the shoulder, exclaiming, "Pack off to the devil, thou shameless hag! What does the witch mean by her spittings? The *proebenda* of my sister Barbara shalt thou never have!"

However, the hag stirred not from the spot, answered no word, but spat out again; and as the illustrious party drove off she still stood there, and spat out after them.

What this devil's sorcery denoted we shall soon see; for as they approached Ziemitze, and the ducal house of Wolgast appeared in sight, Dinnies Kleist started on before the safety sleigh; and as soon as the high towers of the castle rose above the trees, he waved the two banners above his head, and brought them together till they kissed. Having so held them for a space, he set forward again with giant strides, in order to be the first to arrive – although, indeed, the town was aware of the advance of the princely train, for the bells were ringing, and the blood-standard waved from St. Peter's and the three other towers.

But woe, alas! Dinnies, in his impatience, never observed a windwake direct in his path, and down he sank, while the sharp ice cut his head clean off, as if an executioner had done it; and the head, with the long hair, rolled hither and thither, while the body remained fast in the hole, only one arm stuck up above the ice – it was that which held the Brandenburg standard, but the blood-banner of Pomerania had sunk forever in the abyss.*

When his Grace of Stettin beheld this, he was filled with more sorrow than even at the death of his fool; and, weeping bitterly, commanded seven sleighs to return and seize the evil hag; then with all speed, and for a terrible example, to burn her upon the Quilitz mountain.

But when many present assured his Grace that suchlike accidents were very common, and many skaters had perished thus, whereof even Duke Ulrich named several instances, so that his Grace of Stettin need not impute such natural accidents to witchcraft or the power of the hag, he was somewhat calmed. Still he commanded the seven sleighs to return and bring the witch bound to Wolgast, that he might question her as to wherefore she had spat out.

---

* A windwake is a hole formed by the wind in the thawing season, and which afterwards becomes covered with a thin coating of ice by a subsequent frost.

So the sleighs returned, but the vile sorceress was no longer on the ice, neither did anyone know whither she had gone; whereupon the sleighs hastened back again after the others.

Now it was the Friday before Shrove Tuesday, about mid-day, when the princely party arrived at Wolgast; and Prince Bogislaff of Barth was there to receive them, with his five sons — namely, Philip, Franz, George, Ulrich, and Bogislaff.* And there was a great uproar in the castle — some of the young lords playing ball in the castle court with the young Prince, Philip Julius, others preparing for the carnival mummeries, which were to commence next evening by a great banquet and dance in the hall. Indeed, that same evening their Graces had a brave carouse, to try and make Duke Johann forget his grief about his well-beloved Dinnies Kleist: and his Grace thus began to discourse concerning him: —

"Truly, brothers, who knows what the devil may have in store for us? for it was a strange thing how my blood-standard sunk in the abyss, while that of my brother of Brandenburg floated above it. Think you that our male line will become extinct, and the heritage of fair Pomerania descend to Brandenburg? For, in truth, it is strange that, out of five brothers, two of us only have heirs — Bogislaff and Ernest Ludovicus, who has left indeed but one only son."

Then Duke Bogislaff (whom our Lord God had surely blessed for his humility in resigning the government, and also because of his dutiful conduct ever towards his mother, even in his youth having brought her a tame seagull) made answer, laughingly: "Dear brother, I think Herr Bacchus has done more to turn Frau Venus against our race than Sidonia or any of her spells, therefore ye need not wonder if ye have no heirs. However, if my five young Princes listen to my warnings and shun the wine-cup, trust me the blood-standard will be lifted up again, and our ancient name never want a fitting representative."

Meanwhile, as they so discoursed, and the gracious ladies looked down for shame upon the ground, young Lord Philip began a Latin argument with the Rev. Dr. Glambecken, court chaplain at Wolgast *de monetis;* and pulled out of his pocket a large bag of old coins, which had been presented to him by Doctor Chytraeus, professor of theology at Rostock, with whom his Grace interchanged Latin epistles.†

---

* Marginal note of Duke Bogislaff XIV — "This is not true; for I had a fever at the time, and remained at home."

† See the Latin letters of the talented young Prince in Oelrich's "Contributions to the Literary History of the Pomeranian Dukes," vol. i. p. 67. He fell a victim to intemperance, though his death was imputed likewise to Sidonia, and formed the subject of the sixth torture examination.

This gave the conversation a new turn, and the ladies particularly were much pleased examining the coins; but the devil himself surely must have anagrammatized one of them, for over the letters, Pomerania, figures were scratched 356412789 — thus — Pomerania — giving the terrible meaning, *rape omnia* (rob all); and many said that this must have been the very coin which the devil took that time he rent the oblation-table, at the exorcism of the young Princess.

This discovery filled the Pomeranian Duke with strong apprehensions, and young Prince Franz handed over the coin to the Elector of Brandenburg, saying bitterly, "Yes, rob all! Doctor Joel of Grypswald has long since told me that it would all end this way — even as Satan himself has scratched down here — but my lord father will not credit him, he is so proud of his five sons. Doctor Joel, however, is a right learned man, and no one knows the mysteries of the black art better; besides, who reads the stars more diligently each night than he?"

And behold, while he is speaking, the fool runs into the hall, pale, and trembling in every limb.

"Alas! Lord Franz," he exclaimed, "I have seen the manikin again on his three-legged hare, which appeared at the death of Duke Ernest Ludovicus."

But the young lord boxed him, crying, "Away, thou knave! must thy chatter help to make us more melancholy?"

However Duke Bogislaff bid the fool stay, and tell them when and where he had seen the imp.

My fool wiped his eyes, and began: "The young Lord Franz had bid him put on his best jacket (that which had been given him as a Christmas-box) for the carnival mummings on Shrove Tuesday; so he went up to the garret to get it himself out of the trunk, but, before he had quite reached the trunk, the black dwarf, with his little red boots, rode out from behind it on his three-legged hare — hop! hop! hop! — made a frightful face at him, and after a little while rode back again — hop! hop! hop! behind his old boots, which stood in a corner, and disappeared!"

What the malicious Puck denoted we shall soon see — Oh, woe! woe!

Next day all sorts of amusements were set on foot, to chase away gloomy thoughts out of the hearts of the illustrious guests — such as tilting with lances, dancing upon stilts, wrestling, rope-dancing. *Item,* pickleherring and harlequins. Amongst these last the fool showed off to great advantage, for who could twist his face into more laughable grimaces? *Item,* in the evening there was a mask of mummers, in which one fellow played the angel, and another dressed as Satan, with a large horse's foot and cock's plume, spat red fire from his mouth, and roared horribly when the angel overcame him (but withal I think the gloomy thoughts stayed there yet).

And mark what in truth soon happened! When the drums and trumpets struck up the last mask dance in the great Ritter Hall, which everyone joins in, old and young, his Grace, Duke Johann, went to the room of his dear cousin Hedwig, the princely widow, and prayed her to tread the dance with him; but she refuses, and sits by the fire and weeps.

"Let not my dear cousin fret," said the Duke, "about the chatter of the fool."

To which she replied, "Alas! wherefore not? For surely it betokens death to my darling little son, Philip Julius."

"No," exclaimed the Duke quickly, "it betokens mine!" and he fell flat upon the ground.

One can easily imagine how the gracious lady screamed, so that all ran in from the Knight's Hall in their masks and mumming-dresses, to see indeed the mumming of the true bodily Satan; and Doctor Pomius, who was at the mask likewise, ran in with a smelling-bottle, but all was in vain. His Grace lingered for three days, and then having received the Holy Sacrament from Doctor Glambecken, died in the same chamber in which he was born, having lived fifty-seven years, five months, twelve days, and fourteen hours. How can I describe the lamentations of the princely company — yea, indeed, of the whole town; for everyone saw now plainly that the anger of God rested upon this ancient and illustrious Pomeranian race, and that He had given it over helplessly to the power of the evil one.

Summa. — On the 9th February the princely corse was laid in the very sleigh which had brought it a living body, and, followed by a grand train of princes, nobles, and knights, along with a strong guard of the ducal soldatesca, was conveyed back to Stettin; and there, with all due and befitting ceremonies, was buried on Palm Sunday in the vault of the castle church.

Chapter XXII

How Barnim the Tenth succeeds to the government, and how Sidonia meets him as she is gathering bilberries. Item, of the unnatural witch-storm at his Grace's funeral, and how Duke Casimir refuses, in consequence, to succeed him

Now Barnim the Tenth succeeded to that very duchy about which he had been so wroth the day of the Diet at Wollin, but it brought him little good. He was, however, a pious Prince, and much beloved at his dower of Rügenwald, where he spent his time in making a little library of all the Lutheran hymn-books which he could collect, and these he carried with him in his carriage wherever he went; so that his subjects of Rügenwald shed many tears at losing so pious a ruler.

Item, the moment his Grace succeeded to the government, he caused all the courts to be reopened, along with the treasury and the chancery, which his deceased Grace had kept closed to the last; and for this goodness towards his people, the states of the kingdom promised to pay all his debts, which was done; and thus lawlessness and robbery were crushed in the land.

But woe, alas! — Sidonia can no man crush! She wrote immediately to his Grace, soliciting the *proebenda*, and even presented herself at the ducal house of Stettin; but his Grace positively refused to lay eyes on her, knowing how fatal a meeting with her had proved to each of his brothers, who no sooner met her evil glance than they sickened and died.

Therefore his Highness held all old women in abhorrence. Indeed, such was his fear of them, that not one was allowed to approach the castle; and when he rode or drove out, lackeys and squires went before with great horsewhips, to chase away all the old women out of his Grace's path, for truly Sidonia might be amongst them. From this, it came to pass that as soon as it was rumored in the town, "His Grace is coming," all the old mothers seized up their pattens, and scampered off, helter-skelter, to get out of reach of the horsewhips.

But who can provide against all the arts of the devil? for though it is true that Sidonia destroyed his two brothers, also his Grace himself, along with Philip II, by her breath and glance, yet she caused a great number of other unfortunate persons to perish, without using these means, as we shall hear further on; whereby many imagined that her familiar Chim could not have been so weak a spirit as she represented him, on the rack, in order to save her life, but a strong and terrible demon. These things, however, will come in their proper place.

Summa. – After Duke Barnim had reigned several years, with great blessing to his people, it happened that word came from Rügenwald how that his brother, Duke Casimir, was sick. This was the Prince whom, we may remember, Sidonia had whipped with her irreverent hands upon his princely *podex*, when he was a little boy.

Now Duke Barnim had quarreled with the estates because they refused funds for the Turkish war; however, he became somewhat merrier that evening with the Count Stephen of Naugard, when the evil tidings came to him of his beloved brother (yet more bitter sorrow is before him, I think). So the next morning the Duke set off with a train of six carriages to visit his sick brother, and by the third evening they reached the wood which lies close beside Rügenwald. Here there was a large oak, the stem of which had often served his Grace for a target, when he amused himself by practicing firing. So he stopped the carriage, and alighted to see if the twenty or thirty balls he had shot into it were still there.

But alas! as he reached the oak, that devil's specter (I mean Sidonia) stepped from behind it; she had an old pot in her hand filled with bilberries, and asked his Grace, would he not take some to refresh himself after his journey.

His Highness, however, recoiled horror-struck, and asked who she was.

She was Sidonia von Bork, and prayed his Grace yet once more for the *proebenda* in Marienfliess.

Hereat the Duke was still more horrified, and exclaimed, "Curse upon thy *proebenda*, but thou shalt get something else, I warrant thee! Thou art a vile witch, and hast in thy mind to destroy our whole noble race with thy detestable sorceries."

Illa. – "Alas! no one had called her a witch before; how could she bewitch them? It was a strange story to tell of her."

The Duke. – "How did it happen, then, that he had no children by his beloved Amrick?"*

---

* Anna Maria, second daughter of John George, Elector of Brandenburg.

Illa (laughing). — "He better ask his beloved Amrick herself. How could she know?"

But here she began to contort her face horribly, and to spit out, whereupon the Duke called out to his retinue — "Come here, and hang me this hag upon the oak tree; she is at her devil's sorceries again! And woe! woe! already I feel strange pains all through my body!"

Upon this, divers persons sprang forward to seize her, but the nimble night-bird darted behind a clump of fir trees, and disappeared. Unluckily they had no bloodhounds along with them, otherwise I think the devil would have been easily seized, and hung up like an acorn on the oak tree. But God did not so will it, for though they sent a pack of hounds from Rügenwald, the moment they arrived there, yet no trace of the hag could be found in the forest.

And now mark the result: the Duke became worse hour by hour, and as Duke Casimir had grown much better by the time he arrived, and was in a fair way of recovery, his Grace resolved to take leave of him and return with all speed to his own house at Stettin; but on the second day, while they were still a mile from Stettin, Duke Barnim grew so much worse, that they had to stop at Alt-Damm for the night. And scarcely had he laid himself down in bed when he expired. This was on the 1st of September 1603, when he was fifty-four years, six months, sixteen days, and sixteen hours old.

But the old, unclean night-bird would not let his blessed Highness go to his grave in peace (probably because he had called her an accursed witch). For the 18th of the same month, when all the nobles and estates were assembled to witness the ceremonial of interment, along with several members of the ducal house, and other illustrious personages, such a storm of hail, rain, and wind, came on just at a quarter to three, as they had reached the middle of the service, that the priest dropped the book from his hands, and the church became so suddenly dark, that the sexton had to light the candles to enable the preacher to read his text. Never, too, was heard such thunder, so that many thought St. Jacob's Tower had fallen in, and the princes and nobles rushed out of the church to shelter themselves in the houses, while the most terrific lightning flashed round them at every step.

Yet truly it must have been all witch-work, for when the funeral was over, the weather became as serene and beautiful as possible.

And a great gloom fell upon everyone in consequence, for that it was no natural storm, a child could have seen. Indeed, Dr. Joel, who was wise in these matters, declared to his Highness Duke Bogislaff XIII that without doubt it was a witch-storm, for the doctor was present at the funeral, as representative of the University of Grypswald. And respecting the clouds, he observed particularly that they were formed like dogs' tails, that is, when a dog carries his tail in the air so that it forms an arc of a circle. And this, indeed, was the truth.

Summa. — As by the death of Duke Barnim the government devolved upon Duke Casimir of Rügenwald, the estates proceeded thither to offer him their homage, but the Prince hesitated, said he was sickly, and who could tell whether it would not go as ill with him as with his brothers? But the estates, both temporal and spiritual, prayed him so earnestly to accept the rule, that he promised to meet them on the next morning by ten of the clock, in the great Rittersaal (knights' hall), and make them acquainted with his decision.

The faithful states considered this a favorable answer, and were in waiting next morning, at the appointed hour, in the Rittersaal. But what happened? Behold, as the great door was thrown open, in walked the Duke, not with any of the insignia of his princely station, but in the dress of a fisherman. He wore a linen jacket, a blue smock, a large hat, and great, high fisher's boots, reaching nearly to his waist. *Item,* on his back the Duke carried a fisherman's basket; six fishermen similarly dressed accompanied him, and others in a like garb followed.

All present wondered much at this, and a great murmur arose in the hall; but the Duke threw his basket down by his side, and leaned his elbow on it, while he thus went on to speak: "Ye see here, my good friends, what government I intend to hold in future with these honest fishers, who accompanied me up to my dear brother's funeral. I shall return this day to Rügenwald. The devil may rule in Pomerania, but I will not; if you kill an ox there is an end of it, but here there is no end. Satan treats us worse than the poor ox. Choose a duke wheresoever you will; but as for me, I think fishing and ruling the rudder is pleasanter work than to rule your land."

And when the unambitious Prince had so spoken, he drew forth a little flask containing branntwein* (a new drink which some esteemed more excellent than wine, which, however, I leave in its old pre-eminence; I tasted the other indeed but once, but it seemed to me to set my mouth on fire — such is not for my drinking), and drank to the fishers, crying, "What say you, children — shall we not go and flounder again upon the Rügenwald strand?" Upon which they all shouted, "Aye! aye!"

His Grace then drank to the states for a farewell, and leaving the hall, proceeded with his followers to the vessel, which he ascended, singing gaily, and sailed home directly to his new fishing-lodge at Neuhausen.

---

* Whisky

Such humility, however, availed his Grace nothing in preserving him from the claws of Satan; for scarcely a year and a half had elapsed when he was seized suddenly, even as his brothers, and died on the 10th May 1605, at the early age of forty-eight years, one month, twenty-one days, and seventeen hours.

But to return to the states. They were dumb with grief and despair when his Grace left the hall. The land marshal stood with the staff, the court marshal with the sword, and the chancellor with the seals, like stone statues there, till a noble at the window called out —

"Let us hasten quickly to Prince Bogislaff, before he journeys off, too, with his five sons, and we are left without any ruler. See, there are the horses just putting to his carriage!"

Upon this, they all ran out to the coach, and the chancellor asked, in a lamentable voice, "If his Grace were indeed going to leave them, like that other gracious Prince who owned the dukedom by right? The states would promise everything he desired — they would pay all his debts — only his Grace must not leave them and their poor fatherland in their sore need."

Hereat his Grace laughed, and told them, "He was not going to his castle of Franzburg, only as far as Oderkrug, with his dear sons, to look at the great sheep-pens there, and drink a bowl of ewe's milk with the shepherds under the apple tree. He hoped to arrive there before his brother Casimir in his boat, and then they might discuss the *casus* together; indeed, when he showed him the sheep-pens, it was not probable that he would refuse a duchy which had a fold of twenty thousand sheep, for his brother Casimir was a great lover of sheep as well as of fish."

Upon this, the states and privy council declared that they would follow him to Oderkrug to learn the result, but meanwhile begged of his Grace not to delay setting off, lest Duke Casimir might have left Oderkrug before he reached it.

Chapter XXIII

Duke Bogislaff XIII accepts the government of the duchy, and gives Sidonia at last the long-desired proebenda *— Item, of her arrival at the convent of Marienfliess*

Now my gracious Lord Bogislaff had scarcely alighted at Oderkrug from his carriage, and drunk a bowl of milk under the apple tree, when he spied the yellow sails of his brother's boat above the high reeds; upon which he ran down to the shore, and called out himself —

"Will you not land, brother, and drink a bowl of ewe's milk with us, or take a glance at the great sheep-pen? It is a rare wonder, and my lord brother was always a great lover of sheep!"

But Prince Casimir went on, and never slackened sail. Whereupon his Highness called out again, "The states and privy councilors are coming, brother, and want to have a few words with you."

Hereat Prince Casimir laughed in the boat, and returned for answer — "He knew well enough what they wanted; but no — he had no desire to be bewitched to death. Just give him the lands of Lauenburg and Butow as an addition to his dower, and then his dear Bogislaff might take all Pomerania to himself if he pleased."

After which, doffing his hat for an *addio,* he steered bravely through the *Pappenwasser.*

When young Prince Franz heard this, he laughed loud, and said, "Truly our uncle is the wisest — he will not be bewitched to death, as he says — but what will my lord father do now, for see, here come the states already in their carriages over the hill!"

Duke Bogislaff answered, "What else remains for me to do but to accept the government?"

Ille. — "Yes, and be struck dead by witchcraft, like my three uncles! Ah, my gracious lord father, before ever you accept the rule of the duchy, let the witch be seized and burned. Doctor Joel hath told me much about these witches; and believe me, there is no wiser man in all Pomerania than this magister. He can do something more than eat bread." Then he fell upon his father's neck, and caressed him – "Ah, dear father, do not jump at once into the government; burn the witch first: we cannot spare our dear lord father!"

And the two young Princes George and Ulrich prayed him in like manner; but young Philip Secundus spake – "I think, brothers, it were better if our dear father gave this long-talked-of *proebenda* to the witch at once; then, whether she bewitches or not, we are safe at all events."

Hereupon his Highness answered – "My Philip is right; for in truth no one can say whether your uncles died by Sidonia's sorceries or by those of the evil man Bacchus. Therefore I warn you, dear children, flee from this worst of all sorcerers; not starting at appearances, as a horse at a shadow, for appearance is the shadow of truth. Be admonished, therefore, by St. Peter, and 'gird up the loins of your spirit: be sober, and watch unto prayer.' Then ye may laugh all witches to scorn; for God will turn the devices of your enemy to folly."

Meanwhile the states have arrived; and having alighted from their coaches at the great sheep-pen, they advanced respectfully to the Duke, who was seated under the apple tree – the land marshal first, with the staff, then the court marshal with the sword, and lastly the chancellor with the seals.

The had seen from the hill how Duke Casimir sailed away without waiting to hear them, and prayed and hoped that his Highness would accept the insignia which they here respectfully tendered, and not abandon his poor fatherland in such dire need. The devil and wicked men could do much, but God could do more, as none knew better than his Highness.

Herewith his Grace sighed deeply, and taking the insignia, laid staff and sword beside him; then, taking up the sword hastily again, he held it in his hand while he thus spake: –

"My faithful, true, and honorable states, ye know how that I resigned the government, out of free will, at the Diet at Wollin, because I thought, and still think, that nothing weighs heavier than this sword which I hold in my hand. Therefore I went to my dower at Barth, and have founded the beautiful little town of Franzburg to keep the Stralsund knaves in submission, and also to teach our nobles that there is some nobler work for a man to do in life than eating, drinking, and hunting. *Item,* I have encouraged commerce, and especially given my protection to the woolen trade; but all my labors will now fall to the ground, and the Stralsund knaves be overjoyed;* however, I must obey God's will,

---

* The apprehension was justified by the event; for on the departure of Duke Bogislaff, Franzburg fell rapidly to a mere village, to the great joy of the Stralsunders, who looked with much envy on a new town springing up in their vicinity.

and not kick against the pricks. Therefore I take the sword of my father, hoping that it will not prove too heavy for me, an old man;* and that He who puts it into my hand (even the strong God) will help me to bear it. So let His holy will be done. Amen."

Then his Highness delivered back the insignia to the states, who reverently kissed his hand, and blessed God for having given so good and pious a Prince to reign over them. Then they approached the five young lords, and kissed their hands likewise, wishing at the same time that many fair olive-branches might yet stand around their table. This made the old Duke laugh heartily, and he prayed the states to remain a little and drink ewe's milk with them for a pleasant pastime; the shepherds would set out the bowls.

Duke Philip alone went away into the town to examine the library, and all the vases, pictures, statues, and other costly works of art, which his deceased uncle, Duke Johann Frederick, had collected; and these he delivered over to the marshal's care, with strict injunctions as to their preservation. But a strange thing happened next day; for as the Duke and his sons were sitting at breakfast, and the wine-can had just been locked up, because each young lord had drunk his allotted portion, namely, seven glasses (the Duke himself only drank six), a lackey entered with a note from Sidonia, in which she again demanded the *proebenda*, and hoped that his Highness would be more merciful that his dead brothers, now that he had succeeded to the duchy. Let him therefore send an order for her admission to the cloister of Marienfliess. The answer was to be laid upon St. Mary's altar.

Here young Lord Francis grew quite pale, and dropped the fork from his hands, then spake — "Now truly we see this hag learns of the devil, for how else could she have known that our gracious father had accepted the government, unless Satan had visited her in her den? But let his dearest father be careful. In his opinion, the Duke should promise her the *proebenda;* but as soon as the accursed hag showed herself at the cloister (for the devil now kept her concealed), let her be seized and burned publicly, for a terrible warning and example."

This advice did not please the old Duke. "Franz," he said, "thou art a fool, and God forbid that ever thou shouldst reign in the land; for know that the word of a Prince is sacred. Yes, Sidonia shall have the *proebenda;* but I will not entrap my enemy through deceit to death, but will try to win her over by gentleness. The chancellor shall answer her instantly, and write another letter to the abbess of Petersdorf; and

---

* The Duke was then sixty.

Sidonia's shall be laid upon the altar of St. Mary's this night, as she requested, by one of my lackeys."

Then Duke Philip kissed his pious father's hand, and the tears fell from the good youth's eyes as he exclaimed —

"Alas, if she should murder you too!"

And here are the two letters, according to the copies which are yet to be seen in the princely chancery. *Sub. Hit. Marienfliess K, No. 683.*

"WE, BOGISLAFF, BY THE GRACE OF GOD, DUKE OF STETTIN, POMERANIA, CASSUBEN, AND WENDEN; PRINCE OF RUGEN; COUNT OF CUTZKOW, OF THE LANDS OF LAUENBURG AND BUTOW; LORD, &C.

"In consequence of your repeated entreaties for a *proetenda* in the cloister of Marienfliess, We, of our great goodness, hereby grant the same unto you; hoping that, in future, you will lead an humble, quiet life, as beseems a cloistered maiden, and, in especial, that you will always show yourself an obedient and faithful servant of our princely house. So we commit you to God's keeping!

Signatum, Old Stettin, the 20th October 1603

"BOGISLAFF"

The other letter, to the abbess of Petersdorf, was sent by a salmon lad to the convent, as we shall hear further on, and ran thus: —

"WE, BOGISLAFF, &C.

"WORTHY ABBESS, TRUSTY AND WELL-BELOVED FRIEND!

"Hereby we send to you a noble damsel, named Sidonia von Bork, and desire a cell for her in your cloisters, even as the other nuns. We trust that misery may have softened her heart towards God; but if she do not demean herself with Christian sobriety, you have our commands to send her, along with the fish peasants and others, to our court for judgment.

"God keep you; pray for us! Signatum, &c.

"BOGISLAFF"

The letter to Sidonia was, in truth, laid that same night upon the altar of St. Mary's, by a lackey, who was further desired to hide himself in the church, and see what became of it. Now, the fellow had a horrible dread of staying alone in the church by night, so he took the cook, Jeremias Bild, along with him; and after they had laid the letter down upon the altar, they crept both of them into a high pew close by, belonging to the Aulick Counselor, Dieterick Stempel.

Now mark what happened. They had been there about an hour, and the moon was pouring down as clear as daylight from the high altar window; when, all at once, the letter upon the altar began to move about of itself, as if it were alive, then it hopped down upon the floor, from that danced down the altar steps, and so on all along the nave, though no human being laid hands on it the while, and not a breath or stir was heard in the church.*

Our two carls nearly died of the fright, and solemnly attested by oath to his Highness the truth of their relation. Thereby young Lord Franz was more strengthened in his belief concerning Sidonia's witchcraft, and had many arguments with his father in consequence.

"His lord father might easily know that a letter could not move of itself without devil's magic. Now, this letter had moved of itself; *ergo,*" &c.

Whereupon his Highness answered —

"When had he ever doubted the power of Satan? Ah, never; but in this instance who could tell what the carls in their fright had seen or not seen? For, perhaps, Sidonia, when she observed them hiding in the pew, had stuck a fish-hook into the letter, and so drawn it over to herself. He remembered in his youth a trick that had been played on the patron — for this patron always went to sleep during the sermon. So the sexton let down a fish-hook through the ceiling of the church, which, catching hold of the patron's wig, drew it up in the sight of the whole congregation, who afterwards swore that they had seen the said wig of their patron carried up to the roof of the church by witchcraft, and disappear through a hole in the ceiling, as if it had been a bird. Some time after, however, the sexton confessed his knavery, and the patron's flying wig had been a standing joke in the country ever since."

But the young lord still shook his head —

"Ah, they would yet see who was right. He was still of the same opinion."

But I shall leave these arguments at once, for the result will fully show which party was in the right.

Summa. — Sidonia, next day, drove in her one-horse cart again to the convent gate at Marienfliess, accompanied by another old hag as her servant. Now the peasants had just arrived with the salmon, which the Duke dispatched every fortnight as a present to the convent, and the letter of his Grace had arrived also. So, many of the nuns were assembled on the great steps looking at the fish, and waiting for the abbess to divide it amongst them, as was her custom. Others were gathered round

---

* Something similar is related in the *Seherin of Prevorst,* where a glass of water moved of its own accord to another place.

the abbess, weeping as she told them of the Duke's letter, and the good mother herself nearly fainted when she read it.

So Sidonia drove straight into the court, as the gates were lying open, and shouted —

"What the devil! Is this a nuns' cloister, where all the gates lie open, and the carls come in and out as if it were a dove-cot? Shame on ye, for light wantons! Wait; Sidonia will bring you into order. Ha! ye turned me out; but now ye must have me, whether ye will or no!"

At such blasphemies the nuns were struck dumb. However, the abbess seemed as though she heard them not, but advancing, bid Sidonia welcome, and said —

"It was not possible to receive her into the cloister, until she had command from his Grace so to do, which command she now held in her hand."

This softened Sidonia somewhat, and she asked —

"What are the nuns doing there with the fish?"

"Dividing the salmon," was the answer.

Whereupon she jumped out of the cart, and declared that she must get her portion also, for salmon was a right good thing for supper.

Whereupon the sub-prioress, Dorothea von Stettin, cut her off a fine large headpiece, which Sidonia, however, pushed away scornfully, crying —

"Fie! what did she mean by that? The devil might eat the headpiece, but give her the tail. She had never in her life eaten anything but the tail-piece; the tail was fatter."

So the abbess signed to them to give her the tail-end; after which, she asked to see her cell, and, on being shown it, cried out again —

"Fie on them! was that a cell for a lady of her degree? Why, it was a pig-sty. Let the abbess put her young litter of nuns there; they would be better in it than running up and down the convent court with the fish-carls. She must and will have the refectory."

And when the abbess answered —

"That was the prayer-room, where the sisters met night and morning for vespers and matins," she heeded not, but said —

"Let them pray in the chapel — the chapel is large enough."

And so saying, she commanded her maid, who was no other than Wolde Albrechts, though not a soul in the convent knew her, to carry all her luggage straight into the refectory.

What could the poor abbess do? She had to submit, and not only give her up the refectory, but, finding that she had no bed, order one in for her. *Item,* seeing that Sidonia was in rags, she desired black serge for a robe to be brought, and a white veil, such as the sisterhood wore, and bid the nuns stitch them up for her, thinking thus to win her over by kindness. Also she desired tables, stools, &c., to be arranged in the refectory, since she so ardently desired to possess this room. But what fruit all this kindness brought forth we shall see in *liber tertius*.

BOOK III

FROM THE RECEPTION OF SIDONIA INTO THE CONVENT AT MARIENFLIESS UP TILL HER EXECUTION, AUGUST 19TH, 1620

Chapter I

How the sub-prioress, Dorothea Stettin, visits Sidonia and extols her virtue — Item, of Sidonia's quarrel with the dairywoman, and how she beats the sheriff himself, Eggert Sparling, with a broom-stick

MOST EMINENT AND ILLUSTRIOUS PRINCE! —

Your Serene Highness will surely pardon me if I pass over, in *libra tertio*, many of the quarrels, bickerings, strifes, and evil deeds, with which Sidonia disturbed the peace of the convent, and brought many a goodly person therein to a cruel end; first, because these things are already much known and talked of; and secondly, because such dire and Satanic wickedness must not be so much as named to gentle ears by me.

I shall therefore only set down a few of the principal events of her convent life, by which your Grace and others may easily conjecture much of what still remains unsaid; for truly wickedness advanced and strengthened in her day by day, as decay in a rotting tree.

The morning after her arrival in the convent, while it was yet quite early, and Wolde Albrechts, her lame maid, was sweeping out the refectory, the sub-prioress, Dorothea Stettin, came to pay her a visit. She had a piece of salmon, and a fine haddock's liver, on a plate, to present to the lady, and was full of joy and gratitude that so pious and chaste a maiden should have entered this convent. "Ah, yes! it was indeed terrible to see how the convent gates lay open, and the menfolk walked in and out, as the lady herself had seen yesterday. And would sister Sidonia believe it, sometimes the carls came in bare-legged? Not alone old Matthias Winterfeld, the convent porter, but others — yea, even in their shirt-sleeves sometimes — oh, it was shocking even to think of! She had talked about it long enough, but no one heeded her, though truly she was sub-prioress, and ought to have authority. However, if sister Sidonia would make common cause with her from this time forth, modesty and sobriety might yet be brought back to their blessed clois-ter."

Sidonia desired nothing better than to make common cause with the good, simple Dorothea — but for her own purposes. Therefore she answered, "Aye, truly; this matter of the open gates was a grievous sin and shame. What else were these giddy wantons thinking of but lovers and matrimony? She really blushed to see them yesterday."

Illa. — "True, true; that was just it. All about love and marriage was the talk forever amongst them. It made her heart die within her to think what the young maidens were nowadays."

Hæc. — "Had she any instances to bring forward; what had they done?"

Illa. — "Alas! instances enough. Why, not long since, a nun had married with a clerk, and this last chaplain, David Grosskopf, had taken another nun to wife himself."

Hæc. — "Oh, she was ready to faint with horror."

Illa (sobbing, weeping, and falling upon Sidonia's neck). — "God be praised that she had found one righteous soul in this Sodom and Gomorrah. Now she would swear friendship to her for life and death! And had she a little drop of wine, just to pour on the haddock's liver? it tasted so much better stewed in wine! but she would go for some of her own. The liver must just get one turn on the fire, and then the butter and spices have to be added. She would teach her how to do it if she did not know, only let the old maid make up the fire."

Hæc. — "What was she talking about? Cooking was child's play to her; she had other things to cook than haddocks' livers."

Illa (weeping). — "Ah! let not her chaste sister be angry; she had meant it all in kindness."

Hæc. — "No doubt — but why did she call the convent a Sodom and Gomorrah? Did the nuns ever admit a lover into their cells?"

Illa (screaming with horror). — "No, no, fie! how could the chaste sister bring her lips to utter such words?"

Hæc. – "What did she mean, then, by the Sodom and Gomorrah?"

Illa. – "Alas! the whole world was a Sodom and Gomorrah, why, then, not the convent, since it lay in the world? For though we do not sin in words or works, yet we may sin in thought; and this was evidently the case with some of these young things, for if the talk in their hearing was of marriage, they laughed and tittered, so that it was a scandal and abomination!"

Hæc. – "But had she anything else to tell her – what had she come for?"

Illa. – "Ah! she had forgotten. The abbess sent to say, that she must begin to knit the gloves directly for the canons of Camyn. Here was the thread."

Hæc. – "Thousand devils! what did she mean?" *Illa* (crossing herself). – "Ah! the pious sister might let the devils alone, though (God be good to us) the world was indeed full of them!"

Hæc. – "What did she mean, then, by this knitting – to talk to her so – the lady of castles and lands?"

Illa. – "Why, the matter was thus. The reverend canons of Camyn, who were twelve in number, purchased their beer always from the convent – for such had been the usage from the old Catholic times – and sent a wagon regularly every half-year to fetch it home. In return for this goodness, the nuns knit a pair of thread gloves for each canon in spring, and a pair of woolen ones in winter."

Hæc. – "Then the devil may knit them if he chooses, but she never will. What! a lady of her rank to knit gloves for these old fat paunches! No, no; the abbess must come to her! Send a message to bid her come."

And truly, in a little time, the abbess, Magdalena von Petersdorf, came as she was bid; for she had resolved to try and conquer Sidonia's pride and insolence by softness and humility.

But what a storm of words fell upon the worthy matron!

"Was this treatment, forsooth, for a noble lady? To be told to knit gloves for a set of lazy canons. Marry, she had better send the men at once to her room, to have them tried on. No wonder that levity and wantonness should reign throughout the convent!"

Here the good mother interposed –

"But could not sister Sidonia moderate her language a little? Such violence ill became a spiritual maiden. If she would not hold by the old usage, let her say so quietly, and then she herself, the abbess, would undertake to knit the gloves, since the work so displeased her."

Then she turned to leave the room, but, on opening the door, tumbled right against sister Anna Apenborg, who was stuck up close to it, with her ear against the crevice, listening to what was passing inside. Anna screamed at first, for the good mother's head had given her a stout blow, but recovering quickly, as the two prioresses passed out, curtsied to Sidonia —

"Her name was Anna Apenborg. Her father, Elias, dwelt in Nadrensee, near Old Stettin, and her great-great-grandfather, Caspar, had been with Bogislaff X in the Holy Land. She had come to pay her respects to the new sister, for she was cooking in the kitchen yesterday when the lady arrived, and never got a sight of her, but she heard that this dear new sister was a great lady, with castles and lands. Her father's cabin was only a poor thing thatched with straw," &c.

All this pleased the proud Sidonia mightily, so she beckoned her into the room, where the aforesaid Anna immediately began to stare about her, and devour everything with her eyes; but seeing such scanty furniture, remarked inquiringly —

"The dear sister's goods are, of course, on the road?"

This spoiled all Sidonia's good-humor in a moment, and she snappishly asked —

"What brought her there?"

Hereupon the other excused herself —

"The maid had told her that the dear sister was going to eat her salmon for her lunch, with bread and butter, but it was much better with kale, and if she had none, her maid might come down now and cut some in the garden. This was what she had to say. She heard, indeed, that the sub-prioress and Agnes Kleist ate their salmon stewed in butter, but that was too rich; for one should be very particular about salmon, it was so apt to disagree. However, if sister Sidonia would just mind her, she would teach her all the different ways of dressing it, and no one was ever the worse for eating salmon, if they followed her plan."

But before Sidonia had time to answer, the chatterbox had run to the door and lifted the latch —

"There was a strange woman in the courtyard, with something under her apron. She must go and see what it was, but would be back again instantly with the news."

In a short time she returned, bringing along with her Sheriff Sparling's dairy-woman, who carried a large bundle of flax under her apron. This she set down before Sidonia —

"And his worship bid her say that she must spin all this for him without delay, for he wanted a new set of shirts, and the thread must be with the weaver by Christmas."

When Sidonia heard this, she fell into a right rage in earnest —

"May the devil wring his ears, the peasant carl! To send such a message to a lady of her degree!"

Then she pitched the flax out of the door, and wanted to shove the dairy-woman out after it, but she stopped, and said —

"His worship gave all the nuns a bushel of seed for their trouble, and sowed it for them; so she had better do as the others did."

Sidonia, however, was not to be appeased —

"May the devil take her and her flax, if she did not trot out of that instantly."

So she pushed the poor woman out, and then panting and blowing with rage, asked Anna Apenborg to tell her what this boor of a sheriff was like?

Illa. — "He was a strange man. Ate fish every day, and always cooked the one way, namely, in beer. How this was possible she could not understand. Today she heard he was to have pike for his dinner."

Hæc. — "Was she asking the fool what he ate? What did she care about his dinners? But what sort of man was he, and did all the nuns, in truth, spin for him?"

Illa. — "Aye, truly, except Barbara Schetzkow; she was dead now. But once when he went storming to her cell, she just turned him out, and so she had peace ever after. For he roared like a bear, but, in truth, was a cowardly rabbit, this same sheriff. And she heard, that one time, when he was challenged by a noble, he shrank away, and never stood up to his quarrel."

But just then in walked the sheriff himself, with a horse-whip in his hand. He was a thickset, grey-headed fellow, and roared at Sidonia —

"What! thou old, lean hag — so thou wilt spin no flax? May the devil take thee, but thou shalt obey my commands!"

While he thus scolded, Sidonia quietly caught hold of the broom, and grasping it with both hands, gave such a blow with the handle on the grey pate of the sheriff, that he tumbled against the door, while she screamed out —

"Ha! thou peasant boor, take that for calling me a hag — the lady of castle and lands!"

Then she struck him again and again, till the sheriff at last got the door open and bolted out, running down the stairs as hard as he could, and into the courtyard, where, when he was safely landed, he shook the horsewhip up at Sidonia's windows, crying out —

"I will make you pay dear for this. Anna Apenborg was witness of the assault. I will swear information this very day before his Highness, how the hag assaulted me, the sheriff, and superintendent of the convent, in the performance of my duty, and pray him to deliver an honorable cloister from the presence of such a vagabond."

Then he went to the abbess, and begged her and the nuns to sustain him in his accusation —

"Such wickedness and arrogance had never yet been seen under the sun. Let the good abbess only feel his head; there was a lump as big as an egg on it. Truly, he had had a mind to horsewhip her black and blue; but that would have been illegal; so he thanked God that he had restrained himself."

Then he made the abbess feel his head again; also Anna Apenborg, who happened to come in that moment. But the worthy mother knew not what to do. She told the sheriff of Sidonia's behavior as she drove into the convent; also how she had possessed herself of the refectory by force, refused to knit or spin, and had sent for her, the abbess, bidding her come to her, as if she were no better than a serving-wench.

At last the sheriff desired all the nuns to be sent for, and in their presence drew up a petition to his Highness, praying that the honorable convent might be delivered from the presence of this dragon, for that no peace could be expected within the walls until this vagabond and evil-minded old hag were turned out on the road again, or wherever else his Highness pleased. Everyone present signed this, with the exception of Anna Apenborg and the sub-prioress, Dorothea Stettin. And many think that in consideration of this gentleness, Sidonia afterwards spared their lives, and did not bring them to a premature grave, like as she did the worthy abbess and others.

For the next time that she caught Anna at her old habit of listening, Sidonia said, while boxing her —

"You should get something worse than a box on the ear, only for your refusal to sign that lying petition to his Highness."

Summa. — After a few days, an answer arrived from his Grace the Duke of Stettin, and the abbess, with the sheriff, proceeded with it to Sidonia's apartment.

They found her brewing beer, an art in which she excelled; and the letter which they handed to her ran thus, according to the copy received likewise by the convent: —

"WE, BOGISLAFF, BY THE GRACE OF GOD, DUKE OF STETTIN, &C.

"Having heard from our sheriff and the pious sisterhood of Marienfliess, of thy unseemly behavior, in causing uproars and tumults in the convent; further, of thy having struck our worthy sheriff on the head with a broom-stick — We hereby declare, desire, and command, that, unless thou givest due obedience to the authorities, lay and spiritual, doing this well, with humility and meekness, even as the other sisters, the said authorities shall have full power to turn thee out of the convent, by means of their bailiffs or otherwise, as they please, giving thee back again to that perdition from which thou wast rescued. Further, thou art herewith to deliver up the refectory to the abbess, of which We hear thou hast shamefully possessed thyself.

"Old Stettin, 10th November, 1603.
"BOGISLAFF"

Sidonia scarcely looked at the letter, but thrust it under the pot on the fire, where it soon blazed away to help the brewing, and exclaimed —

"They had forged it between them; the Prince never wrote a line of it. Nor would he have sent it to her by the hands of her enemies. Let it burn there. Little trouble would she take to read their villainy. But never fear, they should have something in return for their pains."

Hereupon she blew on them both, and they had scarcely reached the court, after leaving her apartment, when both were seized with excruciating pains in their limbs; both the sheriff and the abbess were affected in precisely the same way — a violent pain first in the little finger, then on through the hand, up the arm, finally, throughout the whole frame, as if the members were tearing asunder, till they both screamed aloud for very agony. Doctor Schwalenberg is sent for from Stargard, but his salve does no good; they grow worse rather, and their cries are dreadful to listen to, for the pain has become intolerable.

So my brave sheriff turns from a roaring ox into a poor cowardly hare, and sends off the dairy-woman with a fine haunch of venison and a sweetbread to Sidonia: "His worship's compliments to the illustrious lady with these, and begged to know if she could send him anything good for the rheumatism, which had attacked him quite suddenly. The Stargard doctor was not worth the air he breathed, and his salve had only made him worse in place of better. He would send the illustrious lady also some pounds of wax-lights; she might like them through the winter, but they were not made yet."

When Sidonia heard this she laughed loudly, danced about, and repeated the verse which was then heard for the first time from her lips; but afterwards she made use of it, when about any evil deed: —

"Also kleien und also kratzen,
Meine Hunde und meine Katzen."*

---

* "So claw and so scratch,
My dogs and my cats."

The dairy-woman stood by in silent wonder, first looking at Sidonia, then at Wolde, who began to dance likewise, and chanted: —

"Also kleien und also kratzen,
  Unsre Hunde und unsre Katzen."*

At last Sidonia answered, "This time I will help him; but if he ever bring the roaring ox out of the stall again, assuredly he will repent it."

Hereon the dairy-mother turned to depart, but suddenly stood quite still, staring at Anne Wolde; at length said, "Did I not see thee years ago spinning flax in my mother's cellar, when the folk wanted to bring thee to an ill end?"

But the hag denied it all — "The devil may have been in her mother's cellar, but she had never seen Marienfliess in her life before, till she came hither with this illustrious lady."

So the other seemed to believe her, and went out; and by the time she reached her master's door, his pains had all vanished, so that he rode that same day at noon to the hunt.

The poor abbess heard of all this through Anna Apenborg, and thereupon bethought herself of a little embassy likewise.

So she bid Anna take all sorts of good pastry, and a new kettle, and greet the Lady Sidonia from her — "Could the dear sister give her anything for the rheumatism?" She heard the sheriff was quite cured, and all the doctor's salves and plasters were only making her worse. She sent the dear sister a few dainties — *item,* a new kettle, as her own kettle had not yet arrived. *Item,* she begged her acceptance of all the furniture, &c., which she had lent her for her apartment.

At this second message, the horrible witch laughed and danced as before, repeating the same couplet; and the old hag, Wolde, danced behind her like her shadow.

Now Anna Apenborg's curiosity was excited in the highest degree at all this, and her feet began to beat up and down on the floor as if she were dying to dance likewise; at last she exclaimed, "Ah, dear lady! what is the meaning of that? Could you not teach it to me, if it cures the rheumatism? that is, if there be no devil's work in it (from which God keep us). I have twelve pounds of wool lying by me; will you take it, dear lady, for teaching me the secret?"

But Sidonia answered, "Keep your wool, good Anna, and I will keep my secret, seeing that it is impossible for me to teach it to you; for know, that a woman can only learn it of a man, and a man of a woman; and

---

* "So claw and so scratch,
  Our dogs and our cats."

this we call the doctrine of sympathies. However, go your ways now, and tell the abbess that, if she does my will, I will visit her and see what I can do to help her; but, remember, my will she must do."

Hereupon sister Anna was all eagerness to know what her will was, but Sidonia bade her hold her tongue, and then locked up the viands in the press, while Wolde went into the kitchen with the kettle, where Anna Apenborg followed her slowly, to try and pick something out of the old hag, but without any success, as one may easily imagine.

Chapter II

How Sidonia visits the abbess, Magdalena von Petersdorf, and explains her wishes, but is diverted to other objects by a sight of David Ludeck, the chaplain to the convent

*W*hen Sidonia went to visit the abbess, as she had promised, she found her lying in bed and moaning, so that it might have melted the heart of a stone; but the old witch seemed quite surprised – "What could be the matter with the dear, good mother? but by God's help she would try and cure her. Only, concerning this little matter of the refectory, it might as well be settled first, for Anna Apenborg told her the room was to be taken from her; but would not the good mother permit her to keep it?"

And when the tortured matron answered, "Oh yes; keep it, keep it," Sidonia went on –

"There was just another little favor she expected for curing her dear mother (for, by God's help, she expected to cure her). This was, to make her sub-prioress in place of Dorothea Stettin; for, in the first place, the situation was due to her rank, she being the most illustrious lady in the convent, dowered with castles and lands; secondly, because her illustrious forefathers had helped to found this convent; and thirdly, it was due to her age, for she was the natural mother of all these young doves, and much more fitted to keep them in order and strict behavior than Dorothea Stettin."

Here the abbess answered, "How could she make her sub-prioress while the other lived? This was not to be done? Truly sister Dorothea was somewhat prudish and whining, this she could not deny, for she had suffered many crosses in her path; but, withal, she was an upright, honest creature, with the best and simplest heart in the world; and so little selfishness, that verily she would lay down her life for the sister-hood, if it were necessary."

Illa. — "A good heart was all very well, but what could it do without respect? and how could a poor fool be respected who fell into fits if she saw a bride, particularly here, where the young sisters thought of nothing but marriage from morning till night."

Hæc. — "Yet she was held in great respect and honor by all the sisterhood, as she herself could testify."

Illa. — "Stuff! she must be sub-prioress, and there was an end of it, or the abbess might lie groaning there till she was as stiff as a pole."

"Alas! Sidonia," answered the abbess, "I would rather lie here as stiff as a pole — or, in other words, lie here a corpse, for I understand thy meaning — than do aught that was unjust."

Illa. — "What was unjust? The old goose need not be turned out of her office by force, but persuaded out of it — that would be an easy matter, if she were so humble and excellent a creature."

Hæc. — "But then deceit must be practiced, and that she could never bring herself to."

Illa. — "Yet you could all practice deceit against me, and send off that complaint to his Highness the Prince."

Hæc. — "There was no falsehood there nor deceit, but the openly expressed wish of the whole convent, and of his worship the sheriff."

Illa. — "Then let the whole convent and his worship the sheriff make her well again; she would not trouble herself about the matter."

Whereupon she rose to depart, but the suffering abbess stretched out her hands, and begged, for the sake of Jesus, that she would release her from this torture! "Take everything — everything thou wishest, Sidonia — only leave me my good conscience. Thy dying hour must one day come too; oh! think on that."

Illa. — "The dying hour is a long way off yet" (and she moved to the door).

Hæc (murmuring): —

"Why should health from God estrange thee?
  Morning cometh and may change thee;

Life, today, its hues may borrow
Where the grave-worm feeds tomorrow."

Illa. – "Look to yourself then. Speak! Make me sub-prioress, and be
Cured on the instant."

Hæc (turning herself back upon the pillow). – "No, no, temptress;
begone: –

"'Softest pillow for the dying,
  Is a conscience void of dread.'

Go, leave me; my life is in the hand of God. 'For if we live, we live unto
the Lord; and if we die, we die unto the Lord. Living, therefore, or dying,
we are the Lord's.'"

So saying, the pious mother turned her face to the wall, and Sidonia
went out of the chamber.

In a little while, however, she returned – "Would the good mother
promise, at least, to offer no opposition, if Dorothea Stettin proposed,
of her own free will, to resign the office of sub-prioress? If so, let her
reach forth her hand; she would soon find the pains leave her."

The poor abbess assented to this, and oh, wonder! as it came, so it
went; first out of the little finger, and then by degrees out of the whole
body, so that the old mother wept for joy, and thanked her murderess.

Just then the door opened, and David Ludeck, the chaplain, whom
the abbess had sent for, entered in his surplice. He was a fine tall man,
of about thirty-five years, with bright red lips and jet-black beard.

He wondered much on hearing how the abbess had been cured by
what Sidonia called "sympathies," and smelled devil's work in it, but
said nothing – for he was afraid; spoke kindly to the witch-hag even,
and extolled her learning and the nobility of her race; declaring that he
knew well that the Von Borks had helped mainly to found this cloister.

This mightily pleased the sorceress, and she grew quite friendly, asking
him at last, "What news he had of his wife and children?" And when
he answered, "He had no wife nor children," her eyes lit up again like
old cinders, and she began to jest with him about his going about so
freely in a cloister, as she observed he did. But when she saw that the
priest looked grave at the jestings, she changed her tone, and demurely
asked him, "If he would be ready after sermon on Sunday to assist at
her assuming the nun's dress; for though many had given up this old
usage, yet she would hold by it, for love of Jesu." This pleased the priest,
and he promised to be prepared. Then Sidonia took her leave; but
scarcely had she reached her own apartment when she sent for Anna

Apenborg. "What sort of man was this chaplain? she saw that he went about the convent at his pleasure. This was strange when he was unmarried."

Illa. — "He was a right friendly and well-behaved gentleman. Nothing unseemly in word or deed had ever been heard of him."

Hæc. — "Then he must have some private love-affair."

Illa. — "Some said he was paying court to Bamberg's sister there in Jacobshagen."

Hæc. — "Ha! very probable. But was it true? for otherwise he should never go about amongst the nuns the way he did. It was quite abominable: an unmarried man; Dorothea Stettin was right. But how could they ascertain the fact?"

Illa. — "That was easily done. She was going next morning to Jacobshagen, and would make out the whole story for her. Indeed, she herself, too, was curious about it."

Hæc. — "All right. This must be done for the honor of the cloister. For according to the rules of 1569, the court chaplain was to be an old man, who should teach the sisters to read and write. Whereas, here was a fine carl with red lips and a black beard — unmarried too. Did he perchance ever teach any of them to read or write?"

Illa. — "No; for they all knew how already."

Hæc. — "Still there was something wrong in it. No, no, in such matters youth has no truth; Dorothea Stettin was quite right. Ah, what a wonderful creature, that excellent Dorothea! Such modesty and purity she had never met with before. Would that all young maidens were like her, and then this wicked world would be something better."

Illa (sighing). — "Ah, yes; but then sister Dorothea went rather far in her notions."

Hæc. — "How so? In these matters one could never go too far."

Illa. — "Why, when a couple were called in church, or a woman was churched, Dorothea nearly fainted. Then, there was a niche in the chancel for which old Duke Barnim had given them an Adam and Eve, which he turned and carved himself. But Dorothea was quite shocked at the Adam, and made a little apron to hang before him, though the abbess and the whole convent said that it was not necessary. But she told them, that unless Adam wore his apron, never would she set foot in the chapel. Now, truly this was going rather far. *Item,* she has been heard to wonder how the Lord God could send all the animals naked into the world; as cats, dogs, horses, and the like. Indeed, she one day disputed sharply on the matter with the chaplain; but he only laughed at her, whereupon Dorothea went away in a sulk."

Here Sidonia laughed outright too; but soon said with grave decorum, "Quite right. The excellent Dorothea was a treasure above all treasures for the convent. Ah, such chastity and virtue were rarely to be met with in this wicked world."

Now Anna Apenborg had hardly turned her back, to go and chatter all this back again to the sub-prioress, when Sidonia proceeded to tap some of her beer, and called the convent porter to her, Matthias Winterfeld, bidding him carry it with her greetings to the chaplain, David Ludeck. (For her own maid, Wolde, was lame, ever since the racking she got at Wolgast. So Sidonia was in the habit of sending the porter all her messages, much to his annoyance.) When he came now he was in his shirt-sleeves, at which Sidonia was wroth — "What did he mean by going about the convent in shirt-sleeves? Never let him appear before her eyes in such unseemly trim. And was this a time even for shirt-sleeves, when they were in the month of November? But winter or summer, he must never appear so,"

Hereupon the fellow excused himself. He was killing geese for some of the nuns, and had just put off his coat, not to have it spoiled by the down; but she is nothing mollified — scolds him still, so the fellow makes off without another word, fearing he might get a touch of the rheumatism, like the abbess and his worship the sheriff, and carries the beer-can to the reverend chaplain; from whom he soon brings back "his grateful acknowledgments to the Lady Sidonia."

Two days now passed over, but on the third morning Anna Apenborg trotted into the refectory full of news. She was quite tired from her journey yesterday; for the snow was deep on the roads, but to pleasure sister Sidonia (and besides, as it was a matter that concerned the honor of the convent) she had set off to Jacobshagen, though indeed the snow lay ankle-deep. However, she was well repaid, and had heard all she wanted; oh, there was great news!

Illa. — "Quick! what? how? why? Remember it is for the honor and reputation of the entire convent."

Hæc. — "She had first gone to one person, who pretended not to know anything at all of the matter; but then another person had told her the whole story — under the seal of the strictest secrecy, however."

Illa. — "What is it? what is it? How she went on chattering of nothing."

Hæc. — "But will the dear sister promise not to breathe it to mortal? She would be ruined with her best friend otherwise."

Illa. — "Nonsense, girl; who could I repeat it to? Come, out with it!"

So Anna began, in a very long-winded manner, to explain how the burgomaster's wife in Jacobshagen said that her maid said that Provost Bamberg's maid said, that while she was sweeping his study the other morning, she heard the provost's sister say to her brother in the adjoining room, that she could not bear the chaplain, David Ludeck, for he had been visiting there off and on forever so long, and yet never had asked her the question. He was a faint-hearted coward evidently, and she hated faint-hearted men.

Sidonia grew as red as a lire-beacon when she heard this, and walked up and down the apartment as if much perturbed, so that Anna asked if the dear sister were ill? "No," was the answer. "She was only thinking how best to get rid of this priest, and prevent him running in and out of the convent whenever he pleased. She must try and have an order issued, that he was only to visit the nuns when they were sick. This very day she would see about it. Could the good Anna tell her what the sheriff had for lunch today?"

Illa. — "Aye, truly, could she; for the milk-girl, who had brought her some fresh milk, told her that he had got plenty of wild fowl, which the keeper had snared in the net; and there was to be a sweetbread besides. But what was the dear sister herself to eat?"

Hæc. — "No matter — but did she not hear a great ringing of bells? What could the ringing be for?"

Illa. — "That was a strange thing, truly. And there was no one dead, nor any child to be christened, that she had heard of. She would just run out and see, and bring the dear sister word."

Illa. — "Well then, wait till evening, for it is near noon now, and I expect a guest to lunch."

Hæc. — "Eh? a guest! — and who could it be?"

Illa. — "Why, the chaplain himself. I want to arrange about his dismissal."

So, hardly had she got rid of the chatterbox, when Sidonia called the porter, Matthias, and bid him greet the reverend chaplain from her, and say, that as she had somewhat to ask him concerning the investiture on Sunday, would he be her guest that day at dinner? She hoped to have some game with a sweetbread, and excellent beer to set before him.

When the porter returned with the answer from his reverence, accepting the invitation, she sent him straight to the sheriff with a couple of covered dishes, and a message, begging his worship to send her half-a-dozen brace or so of game, for she heard that a great many had been taken in his nets; and a sweetbread, if he had it, for she had a guest today at dinner.

So the dishes came back full — everything just ready to be served; for the cunning hag knew well that he dare not refuse her; and immediately afterwards the priest arrived to dinner. He was very friendly, but Sidonia caught him looking very suspiciously at a couple of brooms which she had laid crosswise under the table. So she observed, "I lay these brooms there, to preserve our dear mother and the sheriff from falling again into this sickness. It is part of the doctrine of sympathies, and I learned it out of my Herbal, as I can show you." Upon which she went to her trunk and got the book for the priest, whose fears diminished when he saw that it was *printed*; but he could not prevail on her to lend it to him.

Summa. — The priest grew still more friendly over the good eating and drinking; and she, the old hypocrite, discoursed him the while about her heavenly bridegroom, and threw up her eyes and sighed, at the same time pressing his hand fervently. But the priest never minded it, for she was old enough to be his mother, and besides, he remembered the Scripture — "No man can call Jesus Lord, except through the Holy Ghost." So as her every third word was "Jesus," he looked upon her as a most discreet and pious Christian, and went away much satisfied by her and the good dinner.

Chapter III

Sidonia tries another way to catch the priest, but fails through a mistake — Item, of her horrible spell, whereby she bewitched the whole princely race of Pomerania, so that, to the grievous sorrow of their fatherland, they remain barren even unto this day*

*A*s soon as the pious abbess was able to leave her bed, she sent for the priest, for she had strange suspicions about Sidonia, and asked the reverend clerk, if indeed her cure could have been effected by sympathy? and were it not rather some work of the bodily Satan himself? But my priest assured her concerning Sidonia's Christian faith; *item*, told, to the great wonderment of the abbess, that she no longer cared for the sub-prioret (we know why — she would sooner have the priest than the

---

*   Note of Duke Bogislaff XIV — "Aye, and will to the last day, *vaeh mihi.*"

prioret), but was content to let Dorothea Stettin keep it or resign it, just as she pleased.

After this, the investiture of Sidonia took place, and the priest blessed her at the altar, and admonished her to take as her model the wise virgins mentioned Matt. xxv. (but God knows, she had followed the foolish virgins up to that period, and never ceased doing so to the end of her days).

Even on that very night, we shall see her conduct; for she bid her maid, Wolde, run and call up the convent porter, and dispatch him instantly for the priest, saying that she was very ill, and he must come and pray with her. This excited no suspicion, since she herself had forbade the priest entering the convent, unless any of the sisters were sick. But Anna Apenborg slipped out of bed when she heard the noise, and watched from the windows for the porter's return. Then she tossed up the window, though the snow blew in all over her bed, and called out, "Well, what says he? will he come? will he come?"

And when the fellow grunted in answer, "Yes, he's coming," she wrapped a garment round her, and set herself to watch, though her teeth were chattering from cold all the time. In due time the priest came, whereupon the curious virgin crept out of her garret, and down the stairs to a little window in the passage which looked in upon the refectory, and through which, in former times, provisions were sometimes handed in. There she could hear everything that passed.

When the priest entered, Sidonia stretched out her meager arms towards him, and thanked him for coming; would he sit down here on the bed, for there was no other seat in the room? she had much to tell him that was truly wonderful. But the priest remained standing: let her speak on.

Illa. — "Ah! it concerned himself. She had dreamt a strange dream (God be thanked that it was not a reality), but it left her no peace. Three times she awoke, and three fell asleep and dreamt it again. At last she sent for him, for there might be danger in store for him, and she would turn it away if possible."

Hic. — "It was strange, truly. What, then, had she dreamed?"

Illa. — "It seemed to her that murderers had got up into his room through the window, and just as they were on the point of strangling him, she had appeared and put them to flight, whereupon —" (here she paused and sighed).

Hic (in great agitation). — "Go on, for God's sake go on — what further?"

Illa. — "Whereupon — ah! she must tell him now, since he forced her to do it. Whereupon, out of gratitude, he took her to be his wife, and they were married" (sighing, and holding both hands before her eyes).

Hic (clasping his hands). — "Merciful Heaven! how strange! I dreamt all that precisely myself."*

Upon which Sidonia cried out, "How can it be possible? Oh, it is the will of God, David — it is the will of God" (and she seized him by both hands).

But the priest remained as cold as the snow outside, drew back his head, and said, "Ah! no doubt these absurdities about marriage came into my head because I had been thinking so much over our young Lord Philip of Wolgast, who was wedded today at Berlin."

Sidonia started up at this, and screamed in rage and anger — "What! Duke Philip married today in Berlin? The accursed prioress told me the wedding was not to be for eight days after the next new moon."

The priest now was more astonished at her manner than even at the coincidence of the dreams, and he started back from the bed. Whereupon, perceiving the mistake she had made, the horrible witch threw herself down again, and letting her head fall upon the pillow, murmured, "Oh! my head! my head! She must have locked up the moon in the cellar. How will the poor people see now by night? — why did the prioress lock up the moon? Oh! my head! my head!" Then she thanked the priest for coming — it was so good of him; but she was worse — much worse. "Ah! her head! her head! Better go now — but let him come again in the morning to see her." So the good priest believed in truth that the detestable hag was very ill, and evidently suffering from fever; so he went his way pitying her much, and without the least suspicion of her wicked purposes.

Scarcely, however, had he closed the door, when Sidonia sprang like a cat from her bed, and called out, "Wolde, Wolde!" And as the old witch hobbled in with her lame leg, Sidonia raged and stamped, crying out,

---

* The power of producing particular dreams by volition, was recognized by the ancients and philosophers of the Middle Ages. *Ex.* Albertus Magnus relates (*De Mirabilibus Mundi* 205) that horrible dreams can be produced by placing an ape's skin under the pillow. He also gives a receipt for making women tell their secrets in sleep (but this I shall keep to myself). Such phenomena are neither physiologically nor psychologically impossible, but our modern physiologists are content to take the mere poor form of nature, dissect it, anatomize it, and then bury it beneath the sand of their hypotheses. Thus, indeed, "the dead bury their dead," while all the strange, mysterious, inner powers of nature, which the philosophers of the Middle Ages, as Psellus, Albertus Magnus, Trithemius, Cardanus, Theophastus, &c., did so much to elucidate, are at once flippantly and ignorantly placed in the category of "Superstitions," "Absurdities," and "Artful Deceptions."

"The accursed abbess has lied to me. Ernest Ludovicus' brat was married today at Berlin. Oh! if I am too late now, as on his father's marriage, I shall hang myself in the laundry. Where is Chim — the good-for-nothing spirit? — he should have seen to this." And she dragged him out and beat him, while he quaked like a hare.

Whereupon Wolde called out, "Bring the padlock from the trunk." The other answered, "What use now? — the bridal pair are long since wedded and asleep." To which the old witch replied, "No; it is twelve o'clock here, but in Berlin it wants a quarter to it yet. There is time. The Berlin brides never retire to their apartment till the clock strikes twelve. There is time still."

"Then," exclaimed Sidonia, "since the devil cannot tell me on what day they hold bridal, I will make an end now of the whole accursed griffin brood, in all its relationships, branch and root, now and forevermore, in Wolgast as in Stettin; be they destroyed and rooted out forever and forever." Then she took the padlock, and murmured some words over it, of which Anna Apenborg could only catch the names, Philip, Francis, George, Ulrich, Bogislaff, who were all sons to Duke Bogislaff XIII, and, in truth, died each one without leaving an heir. And, during the incantation, the light trembled and burned dim upon the table, and the thing which she had beaten seemed to speak with a human voice, and the bells on the turret swung in the wind with a low sound, so that Anna fell on her knees from horror, and scarcely dared to breathe. Then the accursed sorceress gave the padlock and key to Wolde, bidding her go forth by night and fling it into the sea, repeating the words: —

"Hid deep in the sea
 Let my dark spell be,
 Forever, forever!
 To rise up never!"

Then Wolde asked, "Had she forgotten Duke Casimir?" Whereat Sidonia laughed and said, "The spell had long been on him." And immediately after, Anna Apenborg beheld *three* shadows, in place of two, thrown upon the white wall opposite the little window. So she strengthened her heart to look in, and truly there was *another* form present now. And the three danced together, and chanted strange rhymes, while the shadows on the wall danced up and down likewise. Then a deep bass voice called out, "Ha! there is Christian flesh here! Ha! there is Christian flesh!" Whereupon Anna, though nearly dead with fright, crept up to her garret on her knees, while loud laughter resounded behind her; and it seemed as if old pots were flung up the stairs after her. *

For the rest of that night she could not close her eyes.

Next morning, one can easily imagine with what eagerness she hurried to the abbess, to relate the past night's horrible tale. Sidonia likewise is astir early, for by daybreak she dispatched her old lame Wolde to the chaplain (the porter was not up yet) with a can of beer for his great trouble the night before, and trusted it would strengthen his heart. In this beer she had poured her detestable love-philtrum, to awaken a passion for herself in the breast of the reverend David, but it turned out quite otherwise, and ended after the most ludicrous fashion, no doubt all owing to the malice of the spirit Chim, in revenge for the blows she had given him the night previous; for, behold, as soon as the priest had swallowed a right good draft of beer, he began to stare at the old hag and murmur; then he passed his hand over his eyes, and motioned her to remain. Again he looked at her — twice, thrice — put some silver into her hand, and at last spake — "Ah! Wolde, what a beautiful creature you are! Where have my eyes been, that I never discovered this before?"

The cunning hag saw now plainly what the drink had done, and which way the wind blew. So she sat herself down simpering, by the stove, and my priest crept up close beside her; he took her hand — "Ah! how fat and plump it was — such a beautiful hand."

But the old hag drew it back, saying, "Let me go, Mr. David!" To which he answered, "Yes, go, my treasure! I love to see you walk! What an exquisite limp! How stupid are men nowadays not to see all the beauty of a limp! Ah! Venus knew it well, and therefore chose Vulcan, for he, too, limped like my Wolde. Give me a kiss then, loveliest of women! Ah! what enchanting snow-white hair, like the purest silver, has my treasure on her head."

No wonder the old lame hag was tickled with the commendations, for, in all the sixty years of her life, she never had heard the like before. But she played the prude, and pushed away the priest with her hand, just as, by good fortune, a messenger from the abbess knocked at the

---

¶ Note of Duke Bogislaff XIV — Incredibile sane, et tamen verum. Cur, mi Deus? — (It seems impossible, and yet how true. Wherefore, my God?)

The spell by knotting the girdle is noticed by Virgil, 8th eclogue:

"Necte tribus nodis ternos Amarylli colores; Necte Amarylli modo, et Veneris die vincula necto."

{That is, "In three knots Amaryllis weaves three different colors; Amaryllis knots and says: I knot the girdle of Venus."}

The use of the padlock is not mentioned until the Middle Ages, when it seems to have been so much employed that severe ordinances were directed against its use.

door, with a request that the chaplain would come to the good mother without delay. So the old hag went away with the maid of the abbess, and the priest stopped to dress himself more decently.

But in some time the abbess, who was on the watch, saw him striding past her door; so she opened the window and called out to know "Where was he going? Had he forgotten that she lived there?" To which he answered, "He must first visit Sidonia." At this the worthy matron stared at him in horror; but my priest went on; and as he cared more for the maid than the mistress now, ran at once into the kitchen, without waiting to see Sidonia in the refectory; and seizing hold of Wolde, whispered, "That she must give him the kiss now — she need not be such a prude, for he had no wife. And what beautiful hair! Never in his life had he seen such beautiful white hair!" But the old hag still resisted; and in the struggle a stool, on which lay a pot, was thrown down.

Sidonia rushed in at the noise; and behold! there was my priest holding Wolde by the hand. She nearly fainted at the sight. What was he doing with her maid? Then seizing a heavy log of wood, she began to lay it on Wolde's shoulders, who screamed and roared, while my priest slunk away ashamed, without a word; and as he ran down the steps, heard the blows and the screams still resounding from the kitchen.

As he passed the door of the abbess's room, again she called him in; but as he entered, she exclaimed in terror, "My God, what ails your reverence? You look as black and red in the face as if you had had a fit, and had grown ten years older in one night!"

"Nothing ails me," he answered; then sighed, and walked up and down the room, murmuring, "What is the world to me? Why should I care what the world thinks?" Then falls flat on the ground as if he were dead, while the good abbess screams and calls for help. In runs Anna Apenborg — *item,* several other sisters with their maids, and they stretch the priest out upon a bench near the stove, where he soon begins to foam at the mouth, and throw up all the beer, with the love-philtrum therein, which he had drunk (Sidonia's power effected this, no doubt, since she saw how matters stood).

Then he heaved a deep sigh, opened his eyes, and asked, "Where am I?" Whereupon, finding that his reason and clear understanding had been restored to him, he requested the sisterhood to depart (for they had all rushed in to hear what was going on) and leave him alone with the abbess, as he had matter of grave import to discuss with her. Whereupon they all went out, except Anna Apenborg, who said that she, too, had matter of grave import to relate. So finding she would not stir, the priest took her by the hand, and put her out at the door along with the others.

Now when they were both left alone, we can easily imagine the subject of their conversation. The poor priest made his confession, concealing nothing, only lamenting bitterly how he had disgraced his holy calling; but he had felt like one in a dream, or under some influence which he could not shake off. In return, the abbess told him of the horrible scene witnessed by Anna Apenborg the night before; upon which they both agreed that no more accursed witch and sorceress was in the world than their poor cloister held at that moment. Finally, putting all the circumstances together, the reverend David began to perceive what designs Sidonia had upon him, particularly when he heard of Anna Apenborg's visit to Jacobshagen, and the news which she had brought back from thence. So to destroy all hope at once in the accursed sorceress, and save himself from further importunity and persecution on her part, he resolved to offer his hand the very next day to Barbara Bamberg, for, in truth, he had long had an eye of Christian love upon the maiden, who was pious and discreet, and just suited to be a pastor's wife.

Then they agreed to send for the sheriff, and impart the whole matter to him, he being cloister superintendent; but his answer was, "Let them go to him, if they wanted to speak to him; for, as to him, he would never enter the convent again — his poor body had suffered too much there the last time."

Whereupon they went to him; but he could give no counsel, only to leave the matter in the hands of God the Lord; for if they appealed to the Prince, the sorceress would surely bewitch them again, and they would be screaming day and night, or maybe die at once, and then what help for them, &c.

Sidonia meanwhile was not idle; for she sent messages throughout the whole convent that she lay in her bed sick unto death, and they must needs come and pray with her, along with the priest, before they assembled in the chapel for service. At this open blasphemy and hypocrisy, a great fear and horror fell upon the abbess, likewise upon the priest, since the witch had specially named him, and desired that he would come *before* service to pray with her. For a long while he hesitated, at last promised to visit her *after* service; but again bethought himself that it would be more advisable to visit her before, for he might possibly succeed in unveiling all her iniquities, or if not, he could pray afterwards in the church, "that if indeed Sidonia were really sick, and a child of God, the just and merciful Father would raise her up and strengthen her in her weakness; but if she were practicing deceit, and were no child of God, but an accursed limb of Satan, then he would give her up into the hands of God for punishment, for had He not said, 'Vengeance is Mine, I will repay, saith the Lord'? (Romans xii. 19.)"

This pleased the abbess, and forthwith the reverend David proceeded to the refectory.

Now Sidonia had not expected him so early, and she was up and dressed, busily brewing another hellish drink to have ready for him by the time he arrived; but when his step sounded in the passage, she whipped into bed and covered herself up with the clothes, not so entirely, however, but that a long tail of her black robe fell outside from under the white sheet — this, unluckily for herself, she knew nothing of. The priest, however, saw it plainly, and had, moreover, heard the jump she gave into bed just as he opened the door; but he made no remark, only greeted her as usual, and asked what she wanted with him.

Illa. — "Ah! she was sick, sick unto death — would he not pray for her? for the night before she was too ill to pray, and no doubt the Lord was angry with her, by reason of the omission. This morning, indeed, she had crept out of bed, just to scold her awkward maid for breaking all the pots and pans, as he himself saw, but had to go to bed again, and was growing weaker and weaker every quarter of an hour. But the good priest must taste her beer; let him drink a can of it first to strengthen his heart. It was the best beer she had made yet, and her maid had just tapped a fresh barrel."

Here the reverend David made answer — "He thanked her for her beer, but would drink none. He could not believe, either, that she was as ill as she said, and had been lying in bed all the morning."

But she persisted so vehemently in her falsehoods that the very boards under her must have felt ashamed, if they had possessed any consciousness. Whereupon the priest shuddered in horror and disgust, bent down silently, and lifted up the piece of her robe which lay outside.

"What did this mean? did she wear her nun's dress in bed? or was she not rather making a mock of him, and the whole convent, by her pretended sickness?"

Here Sidonia grew red with shame and wrath; but, ere she could utter a word, the priest continued with a holy and righteous anger —

"Woe to thee, Sidonia! for thou art a byword amongst the people. Woe to thee, Sidonia! for thou hast passed thy youth in wantonness and thy old age in sin. Woe to thee, Sidonia! for thy hellish arts brought thy mother the abbess, and thy father the superintendent, nearly to their graves. Woe to thee, Sidonia! for this past night thou hast taken a horrible revenge upon the whole princely race, and cursed them by the power which the devil gives thee. Woe to thee, Sidonia! for by thy hellish drink thou didst seek to destroy me, the servant of the living God, to thy horrible maid still more horribly attracting me. Woe to thee, Sidonia! accursed witch and sorceress, blasphemer of God and man!

Behold, thy God liveth, and thy Prince liveth, and they will rain fire and brimstone upon thy infamous head. Woe to thee! woe to thee! woe to thee! thou false serpent — thou accursed above all the generations of vipers — how wilt thou escape eternal damnation?"

When the righteous priest of God had ended his fearful malediction, he started at himself, for he knew not how the words had come into his mouth; then turned from the bed and went out, while a peal of laughter followed him from the room. But no evil happened to him at that time, as he had fully expected, from Sidonia (probably she feared to exasperate the convent and the Prince against her too much); but she treasured up her vengeance to another opportunity, as we shall hear further on.

END OF VOLUME I